Journey into Antiquity

Novel

Denis Brault

ISBN 978-989352-17-5

Published by FlowerPublish

Flowerpublish
www.flowerpublish.com
Montreal, Canada

For my grandchildren: Aiden Cruz, Everly Rose, Mandy Rose and Melody

May their journey through life be filled with wonder!

Chapter One: My Grandson

After forty years of teaching Latin at university, I am now Professor Emeritus Holden Hainsworth. My career, by most standards, would be deemed successful. I recall the very first day - meeting the Classics Department secretary, that middle-aged *maenad* bent on becoming a bare-breasted seductive siren. Although Dionysos – really Denys – was also my name, she would quickly realize that ecstasy was not my game! In order to save face – the only part of her anatomy that I was actually looking at – she indicated that she would like to show me the Department's collection of ancient gems. [*] And, contrary to my years as a graduate student, I never again had to deftly dodge the advances of deluded damsels.

Nor did I "imprison" myself in the ivory tower of academia. I did not "perish" by failing to publish. I did have my books on Seneca and on Roman religion published, as well as several scholarly articles on those subjects and on the Latin language. However, my focus always remained teaching – both graduate seminars and, to my credit, undergraduate courses. I must admit that the modular course on university teaching that I enrolled in as a graduate student paid dividends. Here I am not boasting, but rather merely pointing out that in this latter respect, I was a bit of a renegade with regards to the norm.

*Publisher's Note: See Epilogue in *The Latin Student*.

The "Latin Student" became the "Latin Teacher". To me it seemed a natural progression. My one regret is not having published any novels. The elusive evocation of a priest who survived life-threatening encounters on several occasions – "The Nine Lives of Father Marcus" – remains a notion, not a novel. But I may yet bring to fruition projects that I have harbored since my student days.

It is a matter of personal pride that I never missed a class nor canceled office hours. I was fortunate in never being seriously ill (*mens sana in corpore sano* and all that!). When I accepted invitations as a Visiting Professor, the students in my Department benefitted, in turn, from courses given by visiting scholars. The conferences I attended – and there were many – and the local talks I gave, including presentations in several French and English high schools and a few elementary schools, always took place on "days off" in my university schedule or during my vacation! I can humbly claim that my networking inspired enthusiastic teachers who had a knowledge of the Greeks and Romans – and in some cases, even knew Latin and some Greek – to start up classics clubs for their students. Some of these clubs had original names, like the 4-C Club (Chambly County Classics Club) – the name, I assume, modelled after the popular 4-H clubs. Another was the YNCA – the Young Neophytes Classics Association. I can almost imagine them opening their meetings by dancing to a certain song! Kudos to the club moderator for "neophyte"! Since I was not an archaeologist, I did not have to miss semesters to do field work – and it is fine work indeed! My *in situ* work was done in libraries! I continued to teach Ancient Greek courses most summers, and I taught Latin, Greek and Greco-Roman culture in the Outreach progam for five years beyond my retirement. Briefly then, despite the misinformed and mistaken myth that the study of Classics and those who teach it are elitist, I believe I successfully portrayed myself as a genuine and popular populist (of positive persuasion!), and not as an egotistical elitist. I would argue that this is the true portrait of Classical Studies (Latin and Ancient Greek included). My mission – not an "impossible" one - to make Latin (and Greek) available to all was not – with apologies to Jonathan Swift - an "immodest proposal", as some narrow-minded educators maintained. Considering that I taught university courses for five years as a graduate student, my "world" of teaching lasted fifty years. I've always been a fan of longevity, and as my long-time friend Jeremy used to say: "It's quite easy to reach a ripe old age – you just have to live a long time"! He was a friend, not a philosopher!

My professional focus was indeed on teaching, but my inspiration and meaning in life centered on my family. Manon and I married after my first year of teaching, and we raised two daughters. Well, if truth be told, Manon did the lion's share of parenting. I liked to tease my wife by often referring to our daughters as "BB", knowing that Manon could still be irritated by what she presumed - falsely - was my infatuation with Brigitte Bardot! In fact, the reference was to our "beautiful and bilingual" girls. During my latter years of teaching, as I approached retirement, quoting from a Beatles song, I once asked Manon – "Will you still need me when I'm sixty-four?". To my surprise, she answered with clever lyrics – "Yes, years for sure, and for many more!" Who knew I was married to a Joni Mitchell wannabe! Truth be told – I have a good life because I have a good wife! I never became rich and famous. Being known as the "Lord of Latin" (which is what my daughters teasingly called me) didn't exactly make me a household name. Of course, if I had been the "Lord of the Flies" or the "Lord of the Rings", I might have known some modicum of fame. I should take some solace in the fact that my name will live forever (perhaps!) on the cover of the books I have written. But in the financial sphere, we were conveniently comfortable. We did take a few family trips to Paris, re-enacting for the girls my marriage proposal at the Eiffel Tower, and to Greece and Italy. Naturally, we occasionally drove down to my hometown of Cincinnati to visit my mother – my father passed away – and my sister Phoebe and her family. Walking through Burnet Woods brought back some great memories. I'm also a fan of nostalgia! I, of course, became a Canadian citizen.

Nowadays I spend much of my summers playing golf. I hit the ball just as straight as during my younger days - which is fortunate, since I now have to hit the ball more often! I no longer play hockey, having likewise retired from the university league of faculty and students. I played all forty years I was a professor. In my later years I often got the impression that students thought their marks would improve if they constantly fed me passes on the ice. But, in my book, that would have been tantamount to an "academic" interference penalty! I still hold two league records – no, not goals and points. Total years and games played! Again, not to boast, but in my last few years, I set a record every time I skated onto the ice! Not that I was particularly thrilled by players who would blurt out "You played with my father", or – even more diabolically – "You taught my dad"!

I must say that I seem to have been blessed with some "mild" form of "Socratic wisdom" in never having been discouraged or deterred from actively pursuing my interests. But enough about me! My "beautiful and bilingual" daughters have made Manon and me proud and doting grandparents. The eldest – my grandson Cruz – is the only boy.

Cruz has become my deepest source of joy. I sometimes call him "Marcus" Cruz after the character in the Latin book I have used for so many years. Full disclosure – I haven't completely retired from teaching, since my twelve-year-old grandson has been my "Latin Student" for three years. During the past year, I have also been teaching him Ancient Greek. He is about to become an altar boy – as I was at his age. However, unlike the young me, he will understand the Latin responses, and will be able to recite the "Our Father" – *Pater noster*. He will even recognize the Greek in *Kyrie eleison* - "Lord have mercy". I am glad his parish celebrates the Latin mass once a month. It's so rare these days, but people enjoy this "beautiful ceremony", even though most of them don't understand the words! I imagine this "not knowing or understanding" leads to a new – and quite genuine - meaning of the word "faith"! I cannot truthfully claim that Cruz is "the spitting image" of me when I was his age, since he is quite a handsome young boy! I do intend to teach the classical languages to my grand-daughters - one of whom is his sister – but they are still too young to sit at the feet of the master! They will most likely want to persevere in Greek in order to read those melodic verses composed by Sappho on the island of Lesbos. For now, I like to tease Everly Rose with songs by the Everly Brothers! Whenever I start warbling "All I have to do is dream", Cruz jumps in with a cute little reflection – "don't we all"? I try to entertain their cousin Mandy Rose with, of course, Barry Manilow's signature song - "Mandy"! Mandy's sister Melody instantly makes me think of the songs "Unchained Melody", "Broken-Hearted Melody", and of course the Ames Brothers song "Melodie d'Amour" – our little "melody of love"!

My grandson is bright – even, in his own way, brilliant. He is generous, sensitive and caring – in this respect, quite mature for his age. My sister Phoebe, who has met him on the couple of road trips the family has made to Cincinnati, is adamant in claiming that Cruz shares many traits of character that his grandfather displayed growing up. Even my mother – his great-grandnanny – has seen similarities on so many levels! Manon and my daughters have likewise remarked on an "amazing likeness". No wonder the lad is the object of my exalted but not exaggerated epithets!

Not all of the time – and the occasions are frequent – that I spend with Cruz involves Latin and Greek. We share activities – kicking the soccer ball, hitting a baseball, skating and playing hockey on the nearby rink, playing tennis, throwing a football (he is impressed with the MVP trophy I won as a high school quarterback, and which now sits on his dresser). I especially enjoy playing golf with Cruz - the only physical activity in which I can keep up with him (don't ask me to bring up our jogging and cycling excursions!). As I did at his age, he caddies at the local golf course, where he has just become a junior member. I occasionally rent a golf-cart, and let Cruz drive when he promises not to laugh when I miss a shot – which requires a great deal of self-discipline on his part! Nevertheless, I will always have my claim to fame – a hole-in-one. Again, the plaque for this exploit has a place of honor on his dresser.

Cruz is my master in many other endeavours. He constantly thrashes me in soccer-table games, and always wins the variety of board-games we play. I'd like to say that I sometimes let him win – I'd really like to, but alas... He has a certain dexterity, but the luck he enjoys would have allowed him to best many a soldier while rolling knucklebones in ancient Rome. And as for our chess games, well let's say he is always kind, but convincing in victory. A gallant gladiator! Speaking of which, he is quite adept at karate. At exhibitions, I have a front-row seat to watch my very own "Karate Kid". He once told me of an overweight friend of his who was teased with the name "Piggy" – has everybody read *Lord of the Flies*? "Piggy" became rather adept at karate, and I asked Cruz if he was then called Pork Chop? I went on to mention the war film *Pork Chop Hill*, which starred Gregory Peck. My daughter said it was before their time. I sometimes had the feeling that old Professor Hainsworth was before everybody's time!

I always look forward to outings together with Cruz, and we are often accompanied by his whole family. Movies and bowling are always fun. We've even gone to museums.The train museum is his favorite. From a very early age Cruz has been fascinated by trains, building and re-building train-track sets for his model trains. Someday I'd like to embark on an extended train trip with Cruz and criss-cross (no pun intended on his name, which is Spanish for ""Cross") Canada and the United States. Perhaps, like Phileas Fogg, we could complete our trip in 80 days. We've been to professional football games. Not just the Montreal Alouettes, but we had the occasion to attend a Bengals game, and a Reds baseball game on one of our trips to Cincinnati. He always has a good time when we attend a CF Montreal soccer game or Canadiens hockey game at the Bell Center. His favorite Habs player is Cole Caufield – he's just a little taller than Cruz, who is tall for his age. Just think – that name is so close to "Caulfield", as in the "Holden" character in J.D.Salinger's *The Catcher in the Rye*, for whom I was named. Hopefully, we'll get to see the new Montreal basketball team – the Montreal Alliance - in action. Cruz is sure to notice the difference with the Harlem Globetrotters that we saw once. I admit to following even now the Cincinnati sports teams, including the University of Cincinnati Bearcats and the Eastern Coast Hockey League Cincinnati Cyclones – a good name for them since Cincinnati is located in a tornado zone!

To Cruz, I am part-time mentor and teacher, as well as his number one fan, but I am especially his "Papi", taking the name from the French side of his genes. He is very much in tune with the current fads. He is an indefatigable builder of Lego models – he has already advanced to models for "sixteen-year-olds"! His passions are Pokemon cards and Nintendo games. So he is (almost sadly, in my view) very normal! But we do share a love of reading. I have passed on to Cruz my books featuring the adventures of Tintin, Alix the heroic Gallo-Roman, Asterix and Company, Harry Potter (including the Latin and Greek versions), as well as my Latin copies of *Alice in Wonderland*, *The Little Prince*, *Ferdinand the Bull*, *Winnie the Pooh* and many others. Some day Cruz will inherit his grandfather's mini Classics library of almost a thousand books and over two hundred and fifty films and documentaries.

We get to spend time on Mount Royal, at St. Joseph's Oratory, and in Quebec City, where Papi studied, and where Papi and Manie (which is what Cruz calls Manon) met. Visits to the Château Frontenac recall happy moments for Manon and me. Again, nostalgia! Who says nostalgia is a place you can't go back to? Nor is it a time in the past that is forever lost – our memories bring us back there! I do enjoy attending Sunday Mass with Cruz, and I often treat him to a restaurant breakfast afterwards. We share ideas, and I do my best to give him sound advice, such as avoiding temptations (avoid The Temptations, his mother would say, referring to one of the Motown groups I still listen to!), and not being discouraged by an initial failure to succeed. Cruz, like his mother, is not into Papi's music from the '50's, '60's and'70's. I guess it's an acquired taste! I like to tell my grandson stories, which I hope he believes –

because most of them are true! Like the time when, as a student, I was with Manon in Paris, and I was mistaken for Jim Morrison. Interestingly enough, the singer of The Doors had an infatuation with Dionysos, and my second name – Denys – is derived from that Greco-Roman god! In any event, Cruz has now in his room my sculptured "mask of Dionysos", along with my bust of Alexander the Great, and a few statuettes of Greeks and Romans.

Some of my favourite moments – "magic moments forever to remember" – are the walks we take near the wooded area behind his house. The promenades I cherish most are in autumn and during a winter snowfall. As we admire the kaleidoscope of leaves changing color, the delightful piano notes of Roger Williams playing "Autumn Leaves" dance in my head. We are always in awe of the geese flying south overhead. In winter we often walk on snowshoes. I am always titillated by freshly falling snowflakes melting into my face. On those occasions, the eloquent words of Robert Frost always appear in my thoughts –

"The woods are lonely, dark and deep

But I have promises to keep

And miles to go before I sleep

And miles to go before I sleep."

And just like the Walrus in Lewis Carroll's poem, it's our "time to talk of many things". Sometimes seriously, sometimes less so. Cruz seems to have developed a sense of humour – marked with puns – that is akin to my own attempts at mirthful interplay (which his father says is not necessarily a good thing!). Here's a sample: Papi, did you know that a meteorologist's career depends on the weather? On good or bad weather, Cruz? Neither, but on **whether** his predictions are accurate or not! I have to admit – he shows promise. At his age, I never even tried to tell jokes. Perhaps because he is my grandson – but really more despite the fact he is my grandson – I can't help portraying Cruz as a virtuous young boy. He hasn't yet reached his teenage years, and can rightly be said to still be in an "age of innocence". Nonetheless, I recognize in him what the Greeks called *arete* and the Romans knew as *virtus*. No, not in the original Roman sense of those words, that is "manliness and courage", but in the later meaning of "moral goodness". Basically, Cruz is a really nice boy - in the context of modern society. However, his character probably won't really be admired until he is a bit older.

"Oh Cruz, of whom I am so deeply fond

Such joy you bring in our unique bond"!

That's just me waxing poetic, as I am sometimes wont to do.

You will probably have guessed that I am subtly encouraging Cruz towards a knowledge and an appreciation of the classical world of the ancient Greeks and Romans. To this end, as a treat for Easter, which is just around the corner, we are both heading off tomorrow to the Science Museum in the Old Port to experience "time travel" in a simulated time machine. We will be able to imagine that we are "travelling" back to ancient Greece and Rome. Both of us are super excited!

Chapter Two: The Journey Begins

As a student and a professor, as a husband, father and grandfather, I've always managed to eventually push the irrational world of dreams into the rational world of reality. Yet I have often wondered if fantasy doesn't sometimes, somewhere, somehow triumph over that reality.

- We're here, Papi. The Science Museum is a cool building!

- Just look at those time machines. Even though they are not real, they are still state of the art as far as 3-D technology goes. I'm glad we came early. We're at the front of the line, and I have a feeling our voyage in time will take all day. There are neat visual and sound effects to help us imagine that we are in a distant place in a distant time in the past. Remember now, that we will be pushing red buttons to "transport" us first to ancient Greece, and then to ancient Rome.

- What are the green buttons for, Papi?

- Those are "category" buttons, Cruz. We will be "visiting" the worlds of the ancient Greeks and Romans in two phases. First we will be projected into the realm of Greek mythology, and then we move on to meet historical characters and witness actual events from Greek history. The final two phases will allow us to likewise "participate" in Roman myths, and then make our way through major events in Roman history. First of all, let me explain the difference between mythology and history. The Greek word *muthos* meant simply a "story", whereas the word *historia* referred to an "inquiry" or "investigation". It was coined by the Greek historian Herodotus, the "Father of History", whom I'm sure we'll get to "meet".

-        But Papi, the word "history" has the word "story" in it.

-        Nice observation, Cruz, True, the early Greeks believed that their myths were true stories, and some Greek and Roman historians included "stories" in their accounts that were not true – including Herodotus himself! We'll just have to judge for ourselves what seemed possible and what must have been completely invented. So let's begin this journey, which might end up seeming "real" to our fertile imaginations. The fact that period costumes are supplied will help "authenticate" our trip. So, let's put on our tunics! I thought it might help us to pretend we are in ancient Greece if we adopted Greek names. You can be Stavros, which is also the Greek word for "cross", since that is what your name Cruz means. I'll choose Dionysios, the name which Denys comes from. When in Rome – do as the Romans, so when we move on to Ancient Rome you will be Lucius Crux – the "cross that brings light" – kind of Christian-sounding, isn't it! "Light" in Latin is *lux*, which is kind of ironic, since I'm the one with the good "looks"! For the Romans I can be Dionysius. They'll think I'm a Romanized Greek from Sicily or southern Italy. You remember when I talked to you about *Magna Graecia*. I hope the Greeks and Romans will not confuse my name with "Dionysos" or "Dionysus", and mistake me for a Greek/Roman god.

\-   No chance, Papi – I mean Dionysios! But I guess the "crux" of the matter is my name – you know, Papi Dionysios - "the heart of the matter"!

\-   Or perhaps, "a matter of the heart"! Reminds me of a novel by Graham Greene – *The Heart of the Matter*. Your Greco-Roman hairstyle will help you blend right in, and this walking-stick and my balding grayish hair should give me that serious look of a Greek philosopher. You keep laughing, Stavros, and you won't be the only one here who is "cross"! I'll let you push the first red and green buttons... And we're off to Mt. Olympus to meet the Greek gods and goddesses!

***

\-   Papi, I feel like I'm on top of the world!

\-   We're on Mount Olympus in Ancient Greece – you **are** on top of the world! And call me Dionysios! This god in the winged boots and carrying a caduceus wand will surely bring us into the realm of the gods.

\-   Father Zeus, I've brought you two mortals from down below, who claim to come in peace. One of them is wearing a strange bracelet with small moving arms and twelve notches that I can't make out. Is Timex a wood nymph I haven't heard about?

\-   How many times have I told you, Hermes, that if they come claiming peace, they can't be Greeks. The inhabitants of those Greek city-states - we'll ask them if they know the word *polis* – are always fighting among themselves. I'm afraid they are going to set a bad example for the future of mankind. The problem is

19

some of those mortals are so dangerously – I should say deviously – clever that they will end up making weapons that will massively destroy much of what we have created for them. Where's the gratitude? And if they are Greeks, and that bracelet is some kind of gift, they can't be trusted. I read that in a poem written by a Roman. If you were bilingual like me, my little *psychopompos*, you could read that poem by Vergil. How about you, good-looking young man, do you know the poem? Say, you could replace my cup-bearer Ganymede on his day off.

-        My name is Stavros, and do you mean the poem that starts off with *Arma virumque cano Troiae qui primus ab oris*, where the poet sings about a man and his weapons – so a hero who will have to fight, even as he has just arrived from the shores of Troy? And you shouldn't shoot the messenger-god. He was just doing his job!

-        Thanks for having my back, little guy. Father Zeus referred to my role as leader of souls. Do either of you know about the soul?

-        Sorry, Stavros. I forgot to remove my watch. If I do give it to Zeus, my Timex will become my "ex-time"! I don't see them laughing. I better do my soul thing. "I'm a soul man…soul man".

-        Your voice sounds familiar. Were you ever here before? Did you have a habit of drinking wine, pretending to worship my dancing son Dionysos? You say your name is Dionysios. That's suspiciously similar!

- I think he's making reference to that poem about the Greek gods that you said you wrote in high school, Papi Dionysios.

- Well, Father of gods and men, Stavros and I will be happy to attest back on earth that you all do indeed exist.

- Of course we do. And to imagine that some misguided soul – you all end up just being souls – wrote a short story saying we were statues that came back to life. How preposterous! We never died – we're immortal, for gods' sake! Notice how important the position of the apostrophe is!

- You're blushing, Papi. That writer was you, wasn't it?

- I think I'll try singing again. "Love is in the air…it's everywhere I go …Love is in the air…it's everywhere I look around …Love is in the air…in every sight and every sound….oh, oh, oh… Love is in the air…Love is in the air"!

- I love that song!

- You're all about love, Aphrodite! You can't even utter a sentence without the word "love". And singing bard, I think we get your point!

- I love when you're angry, Hades. I'd love to argue with you, but you have to return to your katachthonian kingdom – meaning your underground hang-out, baby! Don't you just love my alliteration? Old man with the stick, sing a song that the Dark One will love.

-       Yes, O goddess of Love and Beauty! You command my desire – I mean your desire is my command! "The heat was on, rising to the top…I heard somebody say…Disco Inferno"!

-       Great song – I'll sing it to Persephone so she won't give me hades for getting home late! And the kid with you has great dance moves! Here comes her mother, who is none too happy. Does anyone ever get along with a mother-in-law? Have to taxi out of here because Demeter's running!

-       Gosh, Dionysios, I didn't know the gods were into puns. Now I know why the weather has been bad lately.

-       Yes, Stavros, a bad joke - some gods are immortal and immoral! So no crops growing while Demeter is deprived of her daughter. I guess singing a song by The Four Seasons would not go down well. Which is okay, since I would never be able to hit Frankie Valli's high notes. Do you really think he got that voice from wearing his underwear too tight? Demeter's cold winter needs a "fire" song. "Baby, you know we couldn't get much higher…you know my life would be a funeral pyre…come on, baby, light my fire"!

-       Are you singing that song for my sister Hestia? True, she takes care of all our domestic fires, and being on Mt. Olympus, she couldn't get much higher. But she's hardly a "baby"! Say, isn't that the song that made a certain Ed Sullivan angry when it was sung on his show? You wouldn't know him since he was long after your time. But some clever mortal invented television, and we used to watch "The Ed Sullivan Show" all the time. He was able to prove to us that mortals could demonstrate a certain talent with his guests who would sing and dance. But come to think of it, you Greeks invented those forms of entertainment. Dionysios, would you have any songs about water in your repertoire? My brother Poseidon, the god of the sea, is sulking over there chewing on his trident. That would be a good name for a chewing gum, wouldn't it!

-       I hope he likes this one, Zeus. "Somewhere beyond the sea…somewhere waiting for me…happy we'll be beyond the sea…and never again I'll go sailing."

-       Great job, but gotta go. Mrs. Zeus is on the prowl!

-       Greetings, gentlemen. I've been admiring your singing and dancing. I see Zeus is trying to make himself scarce. He's forever claiming that he has to teach you Greeks religious fervour by periodically going on retreats. But I know him – I suspect that Demeter is not the only one sowing wild oats down on earth!

-       O great Hera. My grandson and I bow before your majesty. But there's heavy thunder right now. Seems like there's a major storm brewing.

-       Bowing is fine – but I prefer a Homeric Hymn! No, that's not thunder – it's Zeus breaking wind! That always happens when he eats too much ambrosia and drinks too much nectar. When I want him to show his face, I get Apollo to sing his favorite song – "Lightning

Strikes". It's by a singer named Lou Christie, whom you'll never get to meet, since he's much after your time. Apparently, he buys his underwear at the same store as does Frankie Valli.

- We noticed Apollo playing his lyre and doing back-up vocals while my grandfather was singing. We hope to visit his oracle at Delphi. I love his maxims – "Know yourself" and "Nothing in excess". They are very "pithy-an"!

- Forgive my grandson, Hera. He can be a bit of a "snake" when it comes to puns.

- As can you, it seems. But I know the mythology about the Pythian snake. After all, I'm **part** of Greek mythology! Now listen to the original Greek chorus singing. You might not like all the voices – Hephaistos can't hold a tune, and one time I got so mad at his off-key singing that I tossed him down to earth and the poor lummox twisted his ankle and, as you can tell by looking at him, he also suffered some facial damage. What future athletes will call upper-body injuries are, in his case, all "above the neck" and specifically "between the ears". He once tried to protest, claiming that if Asklepios, our god of medicine, were to examine that spot, he would find nothing there. Alas, I rest my case! Appreciating the efforts of our singing group is an "a- CHOIR- ed" taste! Right now they're teasing Ares with a song that a future group called the Beatles will record called "Fool on the Hill". The song is inspired by the "hill of Ares" – the Areopagus – where the Athenians hold their court trials. He is really going to brood now…listen!

-       "War, what is it good for?" "All we are saying is give peace a chance".

-       Do you think you could cheer him up, dear Dionysios, with a song, and young Stavros, using your staff, could do a delightful disco dance? Stavros and "staffros". One day there will come along a Latin student with my knack for humourous alliteration. Say, Dionysios, you look a bit like him, just not so handsome! And you too, young Stavros, bear a resemblance to him, much like the features you have similar to those of Dionysios.

-       Hey Ares – "Everybody was kung-fu fighting…fast as lightning"!

-       Thanks, you two. That finally put a smile on his face. I bet he wished he had been "fast as lightning" when Hephaistos found him in bed with Aphrodite – who, believe it or not, was married to Hephaistos! Go figure – I guess opposites really do attract! Maybe you could have a few words with our "maker of weapons".

-       We are not into Heavy Metal like you, Hephaistos, but here's a song for you."If I had a hammer, I'd hammer in the morning…I'd hammer in the evening… all over this land"! Did you know that blacksmiths in westerns will forever be inspired by you – always big and brawny, walking with a limp?

-       Westerns – you mean Western Civilization? Wow!

-       No, Hephaistos, westerns as in cowboy shows like "Gunsmoke"! Say, Stavros, here comes a girl with

25

a bow and arrows – but she doesn't look like she belongs in a cowboys and Indians movie.

-	Greetings, mortals! I am Artemis, Huntress and Protectress of animals.

-	Isn't that a bit contradictory – I mean saving animals, but also killing them?

-	Not at all, young man. You are very handsome, and like my faithful follower Hippolytus, you could join my band of worshippers. Just don't get on the wrong side of parents – especially if there is a step-mother in the picture. And avoid Aphrodite – and her followers singing "Love Potion Number Nine"! Actually, by hunting and killing some wild beasts, I practice what you mortals will eventually call "natural selection", but with a divine twist. Besides, I know some veterinarians who enjoy hunting!

-	It makes sense, O goddess. Perhaps, if Hippolytus had seen the movie *The Graduate*, he might have known about the problems caused by a "conflict of interest" with Phaedra! And I myself know about sticky situations that graduate students can find themselves in - I could write a book about it! But why did you have Actaeon killed by his own hounds?

-	Well, he saw me naked, and I wasn't about to let him post my picture wearing only a quiver and a G-string – that is a "goddess-string" - on all the trees and temple columns in Greece! You do know that some hunters will do anything for a buck?

-	She's talking about an ancient form of social media, Stavros. Lady Artemis, I caught your "buck" joke - it's priceless! I imagine that before his untimely death, Actaeon would have been popular at stag parties! I guess like your twin Apollo you appreciate music and song. I'm betting your favorite group is the Animals.

-        Right you are! Especially since they have a couple of songs that explain my lifestyle – "It's My Life… and I'll do what I want" and "Please Don't Let Me Be Misunderstood". Oh, here comes the tipsy god of wine, Dionysos. When you get a chance, check out my temple at Ephesus.

-        Hi you two! I see four figures, so I am assuming there are only two of you! Are you here for the wine-tasting? Have you seen the mean ads for my wine companies? "Very sweet and fresh from the vine – just what you need to make you feel fine"! Are you fellas Greeks? You must be real proud of your most famous warrior, Alexander the Grape?

-        He means Alexander the Great, Cruz. And did you catch his pun on the wine-drinking "*maenads*"? This is my grandson Stavros, and I am Dionysios. We've heard that you appreciate song and dance.

-        Dionysios? I sometimes say my name that way. You have to be completely sober to pronounce my name correctly – the Greeks say "-sos" as in "sauce" (no mystery there!), not "sios" as in "does he see us" (which I most certainly do!). And you have to be initiated – are you in..i..shits?

-        No, but we love your group, The BGs – The Bacchus Guys! Your song "Tragedy" has become very popular with Greek theater-goers.

-      Thanks and don't you just love the girls who back us up – The *Bacchae*?

-      Gee, Papi, he can make up puns even when he's drunk. And he just said he carries a stick, his *thyrsos*, because he's always "thyrsty"!

-      If you "stick around" - you know, dance with a *thyrsos* – you can attend one of my parties. How do I organize a party in the heavens? I just "plan it"! And if you are wondering why Hermes doesn't usually attend my parties, he spends a lot of time flying around in the heavens. Apparently, he often needs some space. Besides, when he does show up, he always asks me if I have Occasionally wine. When I answer in the negative, he says "What a shame – I only drink Occasionally"! But remember not to drink and drive, guys, like Phaethon and the chariot of the Sun.

-      He wasn't drunk, Dionysos!

-      Oh, yes, he was drunk with the thrill of driving across the sky. So, he was high – literally and emotionally.

-      I guess you're right, Dionysos. You must have enjoyed the song "Summer Wine"by Nancy Sinatra and Lee Hazlewood.

-      So much so that I gave Miss Sinatra a pair of boots…that were made for walking of course. I gave her father hunting boots. Unfortunately, he was another male who didn't hit it off with Artemis, when he tried hunting after dark. Talk about your strangers in the night! And I like movies…well, not all movies. For instance, I was a little sour on the film *The Grapes of Wrath*.

-      Another pun, Papi? You know – "sour grapes"!

-      Possibly, Cruz, but we better not mention the novel of the same name, on which the film was based. You must have liked the movie *Days of Wine and Roses*, Dionysos, since it involved drinking and alcoholics?

-      As a matter of fact, I did. I'm an AA, you know. An "**A**ccomplished **A**rtist". As a matter of fact, in my younger days – funny how, unlike the other Olympians, I'm sometimes represented as being young, sometimes old by you Greeks – well, I used to romp through the fields and woods of Boiotia, with young women fawning over me, and enjoying the company of wild animals. Naturally, I especially appreciated the company of the fawns! My buddies used to feed me with clever jokes that I would later use to entertain the other divinities on Mt. Olympus. I called those guys the "cunning hams". One of them was quite wealthy, and we called him "**Rich**ie". Those were such happy days! Alas, a king of Thebes declared me *persona non grata* – that's an expression you won't understand since it's in a language called Latin. That king, though, eventually got his comeuppance! He didn't have the class of the founding king of Thebes in Boiotia, Cadmus, who married Harmonia. I think they named a potent drink after her, that once made me very sick.

-      I think he probably drank ammonia, Cruz! By the way, the marriage of Harmonia with the foreigner

29

Cadmus was a myth invented to explain the influence of Eastern culture on Greek, or "Western" culture. Dionysos himself is a symbol of the "harmony" of Eastern and Western culture. A certain Alexander the Great will eventually attempt to make that "harmony" a reality. Hard to believe that the mysteries of this Dionysos, along with those of Demeter, involve bread and wine, just like those of the Christians, sometimes suggesting the association of the Dionysos-figure with Christ – probably because of his persecution in the story told in *The Bacchae.*

-        It's been great jammin' and jivin' with you guys, but here comes some serious stuff. The figure in the helmet – and we're not talking Tom Brady – is not to be messed with. That is a potent spear she is carrying – so I'm not just "talking about Shaft"! So many Greeks owe her their lives, and if, like Odysseus, you were to think she no longer gives a hoot about you, just take a look at the owl on her shield!

-        Papi, should we tell Dionysos we know Latin?

-        No, Cruz, that will just make him more confused than he already is. Strange, though, all the while he was describing his good old days I kept thinking of a television show I used to watch. Let's greet the goddess who is approaching.

-        I was informed of your presence, and am here to offer you my protection as you travel through Greece. Years - nay centuries - from now, mortals will refer to this protection as travel insurance. Let me express myself in song. If you find yourself in a tight spot, "I'll Be There"! If you're ever lost and need directions, "I'll Be Around"! The Spinners sing that song – a real group, not the Fates spinning the web of your destiny! Always remember that no matter what your problem, no matter how great the danger, "I Can Help"! That song was sung by a real singer as well, but his name – Billy Swan – gives Hera the creeps. Something about her husband Zeus and Leda. Almost turned out to be his "swan song"!

- We are so lucky, Stavros, that aegis-bearing Athena is here declaring to be "besties" with us!

- Your temple on the Acropolis, the Parthenon, is my favorite.

- I taught my grandson that the word means "maiden".

- And that the later iron-clad bombs that would eventually destroy part of your temple would therefore make you an "Iron Maiden"!

- Stifle, Stavros! And "Hallowed Be Thy Name", O Pallas Athena!

- So much for hallows and hellos, "I Never Can Say Good-By". So I'll just vanish into thin air, like I usually do! But not to worry. In Greece, I have many contacts. I am really quite the influencer!

- Gosh, it must be cool to have the same name as a great city!

- Well, Cruz, she earned that right when the Athenians chose her gift of the olive tree over Poseidon's offer of a horse. For them it would remain "A Horse with No Name"! Maybe that's why Odysseus would later tell Poseidon's favourite Cyclops that he "had no name"! But you can be proud that there is a city in California called Santa Cruz. Citizens wanted it to be known as "Surf City", but two singers named Jan and Dean went all out.

-        Were they beach boys, Papi?

-        No, they weren't Beach Boys, but they sounded a lot like them! You might say "Everybody was surfing" in that part of the U.S.A. Of course, not surfing the Internet like everybody today! But you can be especially proud that Santa Cruz with its own campus of the University of California is basically a college town! Now I've probably got you "California Dreaming"! This name thing reminds me of my nephew Aiden who grew up spending so much time in the beautiful garden his mother had made that she called it her "Garden of Aiden". It was full of flowers and trees, and I once remarked that Aiden seemed to be blossoming like the flowers. Interesting, though, my sister never planted any apple trees in that garden.

-        Who would have thought the gods and goddesses of Olympus were so much into music, Papi?

-        Well, Cruz, they are Greeks, after all! I think Zeus is approaching to tell us our "Passport to Paradise" has now expired.

-        It is amazing, O Zeus, that the gods of Olympus know everything about the future including song lyrics!

-        Our knowledge, Dionysios, is timeless. Speaking of which, that Timex watch you were wearing did not escape my notice. No mortals planning tricks will reach Mount Olympus on my watch! Yes, pun intended! As was the dig against Hermes, known as the "trickster"! You humans do not have a monopoly on humour! However, I realize that your hearts are in the right place – if they were in another part of your body, you'd just be more strangely-shaped monsters that we've created! Just more humor for the road! You don't sing all that well, Dionysios, but anybody who knows all those songs is okay in my book – my song-book, that is! I know that in future, "Olympians" will refer to accomplished athletes, but never forget the "real Olympians", for "We are the Champions…we are the champions…of the world!"

-       It's back to the land of mortals, Cruz, even though I no longer feel like "A Stranger in Paradise"! And Athena – visible or invisible – will have our backs!

-       It's raining, Papi!

-       No, Cruz, "Zeus is raining", as they say. He "reigns" on Olympus, and he "rains" on earth! Like Gene Kelly, I feel like "Dancing in the Rain"!

-       I hear you, Papi. "Raindrops Keep Falling On My Head"…

Chapter Three: From the Heights to the Depths

-       Judging by these clay tablets, Cruzie, I'd say we are now on the island of Crete back in Minoan times. I can't make out those Linear A tablets – nobody can nowadays. But I can read the Linear B script, thanks to Michael Ventris, who deciphered it with the help of John Chadwick, a specialist on early Greek, and after consulting a grid developed by Alice Kober. His real inspiration, though, was the "father of Minoan archaeology", Sir Arthur Evans, who led a school trip to Crete that a young Ventris participated in. Talk about fate!

-       Welcome to Knossos, strangers. I am Daedalus. I'm an engineer, specializing in underground tunnels, wooden cows, and artificial wings.

-       I am Dionysios, and this is my grandson Stavros. We are here as objective observers with the expedition of Theseus of Athens, who has the mission of slaying the Minotaur, the monster kept in the Labyrinth by King Minos.

-       You mean King "Minus"! He's not all there, you know. The "Minotaur" is his big, ugly, deformed son. The "head of a bull" part is actually "bull" - if you get my drift. Your friend Theseus has already killed our Cretan Bull, and has come as part of a circus act, where he and his young friends leap over charging bulls – they get the bulls to charge by waving red capes at them, and when the bulls get close, somebody sticks swords in them to make them slow down. Maybe you've seen the posters with the double-edged horns that represent the bulls. It's no secret that Ariadne, the King's daughter, and half-sister to the "Minotaur", finds her brother a real pain, and hopes Theseus can get rid of him for her. I deliberately avoided putting an elevator in the Labyrinth in order to make it a real challenge to get out! I'd like to show you around, but I'm in a bit of a hurry, since my son Icarus and I have a "flight" to catch – if you know what I mean! I could give you a mini tour, though.

-        Thanks just the same, Daedalus, but Theseus is about to descend into the Labyrinth and we are obliged to accompany him. Look out for your son, since I suspect he hasn't earned his frequent-flier points!

-        "Mini tour" to see the Minotaur? Is there no end to these puns, Papi?

-        Fortunately, I've immunized you against them, Cruz, with my perennial personal puns! Let's follow Theseus into the depths of the Palace of Knossos. I thought Daedalus was stringing us along, but I see that Theseus is carrying some kind of rope, and he's not hanging around!

-        Look, Papi – Theseus has slain the Minotaur, and he has run off with the string.

-        Fortunately, your skill in Lego construction will enable you to figure out all the passages that will lead to the exit.

- That was an a…mazing experience, Papi!

- *Et tu*, Cruz? *Et tu*?

- Look, Papi – Theseus is sailing off with Ariadne. He has forgotten us!

- Full disclosure, Cruz, Theseus is a very forgetful guy. I wouldn't be surprised if he forgets Ariadne after the scheduled stop at Naxos, and that he even forgets to change the black sails back to white. Well, at least we will be able to sail the "Aegean" sea later on!

- There's something I have to ask you. Why did Ariadne say she wished I was older?

- I'll tell you someday, Cruz – when you're older!

- Papi, there is a huge man approaching, and he's carrying a club and wearing a lion's skin.

- Surely you recognize Herakles, Cruz. Do you remember that I told you his name means "glory" of Hera. It came about when, after a messy birth involving a married mortal woman – Alcmena – Hera refused to acknowledge this child born of Zeus. She actually sent snakes to the infant's crib. The baby thought they were rattles, and shook them to death. Now that I think about it, they could have been rattlesnakes! But Hera eventually accepted him, and even made a place for him on Mt. Olympus, going from "Oh god, no" at his birth to "O god" at his death! Consequently, the Greek word for glory - *kleos* - which actually signifies some sort of glorified acceptance, became part of the hero's name to reflect his ultimate acceptance by Hera.

-        Greetings, strangers! Have you come for my autograph, or as eyewitnesses to my last couple of labors? Are you aware that I wear the Nemean Lion's flayed skin because I get the lion's share of glory among all Greek heroes?

-        Papi, isn't there a song about Herakles dragging the lion?

-        No Cruz, the Tommy James and The Shondells song you are referring to is "Draggin' the Line"! I am Dionysios and this is Stavros. No, we would like to be up front with you, Herakles. I am Holden Hainsworth, and this is my grandson Cruz. We have come from the future via time travel.

-        Cheers! Here everybody knows my name! I hope you are smarter than those three guys who previously came to see me in a time machine. What a bunch of stooges!

-        I think you are talking about the film called *The Three Stooges Meet Hercules*. I hope you never get to see *Hercules in New York*. It was the actor's first film, and he could hardly speak English, let alone Greek! But he did get better. He once said "I'll be back". We didn't realize at the time that it would be as the Governor of California. Another actor became Governor of California, and then President of the United States. At first, the people went ape over him – I don't know if that had to do with a movie he once made.

-        You see, my grandfather is super smart. He taught me Greek and Latin. The Romans are going to call you Hercules, and ages from now you are going to be the star of many movies ! You are my favorite hero!

- This lad obviously has good taste! You two care to join me on my trip to the underworld? I have to see a man about a dog.

- We can wait while you go to the bathroom. I realize that cleaning out the Augean Stables might have given you cramps.

- No, old man, I really do have to see about a dog! A three-headed hound, to be exact. Are you in or out?

- You don't mind going down into the depths, Cruz? I mean, the underground Labyrinth will seem like a skyscraper compared to Hades.

- Not at all. Maybe Hades will still remember my disco moves!

- Well there's Charon, waiting for us with his boat, ready to transport us across the Styx.

- Didn't think he'd be there to "Ferry… us… Across the Mersey"!

- Say what? I've been down here before, so I have a pass. Came down with Theseus. You said something about having met him already. So, free for me, but you pay, pal!

- No problem, Cruz. I still have a few *drachmai* from my last visit to Greece with your grandmother. Charon will flip, because that's a lot of *obols*! Herakles, did Orpheus have to pay, or play, his way in?

- Poor Orpheus. He and his wife had day passes, but he blew it! For Eurydice, it definitely was "The Last Train to Clarksville"! Now, how do we get that fierce guardian of the gate, Cerberus, out of here.

- Herakles, there are three of us. We can each talk gently to one of the three heads while feeding him dog biscuits. He is sure to come eagerly – wagging his one tail!

- Doggone – that was a brilliant idea, young man! And you expressed it without being dogmatic - unlike some other mortals who think they are gods' gift. Which they are, but you know what I mean! I'm going to drop Cerberus off temporarily at the pound, while I fetch the apples of the Hesperides. Apparently, they're out by the Pillars of Hercules – so no biggie!

- Cruz has become attached to Cerberus, and wants to spend a bit more time with him. Besides, I think he's still too young to hear all that talk about love and sex connected with "throwing and catching apples". I told him the story of the banquet where the uninvited Eris – whose name, surprise, surprise, means "conflict" – threw a golden apple among the goddesses Hera, Athena, and Aphrodite with the inscription "for the fairest". Paris was chosen to judge the contest, and was bribed by all three goddesses. However, when asked for the apple by Aphrodite, Paris was offered the chance to receive for himself the most beautiful woman on earth. "I'll bite" – well that's what he said – "who is she"? A recent survey among Greek princes had declared that this was Helen. The apple then became sacred to Aphrodite, and the story continued with one of the greatest moments in Greek history – or mythology – take your pick! That's why, during a race, Atalanta was seduced by the apples thrown at her by Milanion.

-        You mean Hippomenes!

-        Whatever! Meleager also had the hots for Atalanta – literally – as he ended up burning to death. So, at the risk of mixing apples with oranges, I prefer to spare young Cruz the lurid tales of sex involving gods, heroes, nymphs, satyrs, and yes, young boys, that are ubiquitous in Greek mythology.

-        Fair enough! I'll be off. I need to get some directions from Atlas – don't worry, I can read him like a book! Now, if I had GPS - the **G**ods' **P**rivate **S**ystem – I could have bypassed the big lout, since I'll have to put up with his complaints about how life in the world is such a burden.

-        *Bon voyage*, Herakles!

-        Thanks! And could you do me a favor? If you run into a young hero named Jason, could you tell him I'll catch up to him on the Argo. Better still, would you and your grandson board that ship with the Argonauts to temporarily replace me. They are headed for a place called Colchis. Jason will explain why.

-        Sounds like fun!

Chapter Four: I Embark on a Cruise with Cruz

-        It may seem odd to you, Cruz, to be accompanying forty Argonauts on a mission to get hold of the Golden Fleece, after watching forty or so Argonauts from Toronto on Montreal's football field playing a game in their quest to win the Grey Cup. It's always about the ultimate goal. Which is why Jason and his heroic companions are ready to face and overcome all obstacles in order to attain their objective. And dangers there are indeed. We will soon come face to face with the Symplegades, those clashing rocks that can slash a boat in two. Cruz, I can tell you've noticed something, and you're anxious to share your observation with Jason.

-        Jason, just a moment ago a bird flew between the rocks, and had its tail snapped off. But then the rocks parted. If you sent a bundle wrapped up with blankets floating towards the clashing rocks, they would certainly lash out and crush the bundle. They would immediately separate, and the Argo could speedily slip through before the rocks had a chance to come together again to crush it.

-        Your plan worked perfectly, er... Stavros, you said your name was. Still, more dangers are lurking. Before us to the left lies Charybdis, the swirling creature that swallows ships whole. On the right, we would face Scylla, the six-headed dog-monster who snatches terrified sailors standing helpless aboard their ships - a victim for the piercing jowls of each thrusting head.

-        If I may make a suggestion, Jason. I don't think there is any defense against the whirlpool you call Charybdis, but if you send all your men – and I include myself along with my grandfather Dionysios – down below, leaving only your *kubernetes* – your steersman – at the rudder, you can deceive Scylla by standing six bundles on the deck where sailors would normally be taking position, and sail straight towards the cave where the monster awaits her victims. After each head has grabbed a bundle in her voracious jaws, your *gubernator* – that would be his Latin name, and my grandfather has taught me English derivatives such as "governor" and "gubernatorial" – could sail the ship past the satiated monster.

-        Splendid suggestion! Young Stavros, you are indeed a "bundle" of ideas! You can be truly proud of your grandson, Dionysios.

-        I am indeed, especially of his vocabulary, which has evidently been enriched by this excursion. I must admit to having been quite nervous as we sailed past Scylla. I couldn't utter a word – not even a "Scylla-ble"! Moreover, songs by Three Dog Night were running through my head. I know these words and notions are foreign to you, Jason, but they might help to prepare your foray into that foreign land near the Black Sea. I suspect that Stavros was inspired by the many episodes of Ninjago Warriors defeating monsters that he watches on television and the Ninjago Legos he is constantly building. But you needn't dwell on my mysterious mutterings, no more than you should if I were to tell you that your story - in more than one version - will be shown in movie theaters many generations from now.

-       Your fantastic stories will not deter me from seeking the Golden Fleece, but your puns may do my head in!

-       Jason, there is an enormous rock lying towards the west. Can we explore it?

-       Stavros, that rock is where Prometheus is chained as punishment by Zeus. I don't think you can stomach seeing him.

-       The Titan Prometheus? My grandfather has told me his story. Please let us visit him!

-       Since you were largely responsible for our escape from sea monsters, Stavros, I guess I should grant your request. But we will only sail close enough for you and Dionysios to swim towards the rock.

-       No problem, Jason. We are both excellent swimmers.

-       Well, Cruz, who does that creature with his feet chained together to the rock and his arms spread out and bound to the rock remind you of?

-       He looks like Jesus on the cross!

-       True. That is why some scholars have compared him to Christ. As a Titan, Prometheus was not of the human race, but joined it to save mankind by bringing fire as a sign of hope to comfort them in their suffering. You know that Jesus Christ offers hope through the water of baptism, and that he suffered like

Prometheus for the sake of the human race. So there is a "fire and water" connection.

-        It's a bit like that song you try to sing, Papi – "I've seen fire and I've seen rain". James Taylor you're not! I can't understand, though, how his liver keeps growing back after the eagle eats it.

-        Today, liver transplants are possible, and the Greeks apparently knew about hepatic regeneration from observing warriors wounded in battle recover from liver wounds. The word hepatitis comes from the Greek word for liver, and may you never suffer from that inflammation! So just like Jesus Christ, Prometheus never dies.

-        I get it, Papi. We continue to remember Christ's suffering every year, but it will be Easter in a few days, and we will celebrate His triumph over death. Do you think Prometheus can be redeemed?

-        Don't know, Cruz, but while we're here let's talk to him, and try to cheer him up. Anything we can do for you, Prometheus, since we know you will be here for a stretch.

-        Please – it hurts when I laugh!

-        Sorry, but if it's any consolation, your name and the name Titan will exist long into the future. I've enjoyed watching movies called Clash of the Titans and Wrath of the Titans, as well as a film called Prometheus. On a spaceship of that name, the crew must save the human race from extinction. Does that story ring a bell? Oh, and my grandson here gets a kick out of watching the cartoon show "Teenage Titans

Go". I must admit that the satire on that show keeps me interested as well. And I've watched football games on TV involving the Tennessee Titans!

- Since you're talking about the future, could you do me a couple of favors?

- My grandfather and I would be glad to. We've met Zeus, and I know he won't be angry with us as he obviously is with you.

- Well then, could you get word to my son Deucalion that Zeus is planning to destroy the world with a great flood.

- Noah way!

- Please, Papi – he already told you it hurts when he laughs!

- This is what my son has to do. He must cut down trees from the forest, build a huge boat and board it with his wife Pyrrha. It should - knock on wood – stay afloat. When the rain stops, and the water starts to recede, he and his wife are to take the stones I had given them to save for a rainy day, and toss them behind themselves. And believe me – this will be one heck of a rainy day! From those stones will arise the new race of men and women. That's why I didn't tell mankind how to make glass, so Deucalion wouldn't furnish his boat with glass windows, since he was going to be throwing stones.

- Sounds like a plan. But shouldn't they also bring the different species of animals aboard, and thus preserve them as well?

- I didn't think of that – you're a clever young lad! Tell Deucalion to check out the forests, jungles and zoos. No, I didn't say "Zeus". Geez but it hurts when I laugh! And by the way, Deucalion's son Hellen has to accompany him.

- His son is named Helen, like Helen of Troy?

- No, Cruz, it's Hellen with two l's. He will be the founder of the Hellenes – the Greeks. Today, they still call themselves Hellenes – very "Hellenistic" of them, don't you think? Their country is *Hellas*. It was the Romans who named the country *Graecia* and her people *Graecoi* - maybe from a Greek tribe they had encountered. Be that as it may, all non-Hellenes have followed the Romans – and who didn't in those days – in calling the country Greece, and the people Greeks. But the Greeks got back at the rest of the world by calling the Romans and everybody else who didn't speak Greek "barbarians" because all non-Greek languages sounded like gibberish – "*bar bar*"! True, the Beach Boys did okay with "Bar Bar Barbara Ann"! But I digress. Besides, today the word of choice to describe uncouth behaviour is "Ostrogoth"!

- I can see where the boy gets his great learning. One more favor, please. My sister-in-law Pandora has received a gift-jar from Zeus –you see where I'm going with this – and it is filled with evils, except for one gift, which could go either way. I'm talking about hope, which can be "false" or "encouraging". I have faith that humans will accept hope and be inspired to practice charity! Since Pandora's name means "all the gifts", she's liable to think the jar contains only gifts that she is supposed - in an "all-giving" way – to release for mankind. I tried to warn her husband, my brother Epimetheus, but "He Ain't Heavy, He's My Brother" notwithstanding, his dullness in serious matters does add to the weight on my shoulders. Let's just say, if he ever got hit with a spear, he wouldn't get the point! Someone has to get to Pandora before she releases hope as an evil thing. Hope must remain in the jar for all time as a saving grace to keep mankind optimistic about the future.

- My grandfather and I are on it, Prometheus. And guess what? Herakles will be joining us soon on the Argo. I'll get him to come and rescue you. He is bound to do it - he owes us!

- Okay! Until then I'll remain "bound" here – ouch, that hurt! But "Prometheus Unbound" has a nice ring to it! Farewell and happy sailing!

- Papi, imagine if your niece Joanie had been around to board that big boat with Deucalion and Pyrrha. She could have gotten her name in the history books as Joan of the Ark!

- Hark! You two are finally back. I was beginning to worry that the eagle of Zeus would attack you, and you'd become chopped liver…what – too soon? So are you going to save the world?

- Actually, Jason,.. say, what is that sweet soul music I hear?

- Pay no attention, Dionysios. Those are the Sirens. They'll entice you towards their island with the honeyed sounds of R&B, pop rock, country and disco, and when you reach their lavish music studio, you will be trapped into listening to heavy metal, punk and rap, and be condemned for all eternity into singing karaoke!

- Say, Jason, I have an idea. Why don't we strap my grandfather to the mast, and the rest of us will put wax in our ears, as we sail out of reach of the Sirens' concert. He won't be able to dive in and swim towards what he imagines as some kind of "Hitsville", but will get to listen to golden oldies to his heart's content.

- Aren't you the clever little DJ – "**d**evilish **j**ester"!

- I guess you're right, Jason. While the Greek bards spin their tales, I'm spinning records! Hey, my grandfather is no longer rolling his arms like The Temptations, so I guess he is no longer being "tempted" by the Sirens. Maybe we are out of earshot. But what is that little island yonder with a small hill protruding from its base.

- Your grandfather is right, Stavros. Your vocabulary is quite impressive. I would have simply said "sticking out"! That island is known for its big rock – nothing to write home about – wherever your home is.

- Rest assured that it's not "wherever I lay my hat" – or *pilos*, to use the Greek word. But after our meeting with Prometheus, I'm feeling bolder and would like to investigate that boulder.

- With a play on words like that, I'd describe you not as bold, but rather brash!

- So can we go have a look?

-       All right, you and your grandfather swim ashore and explore. I hope you appreciate my interruption from a schedule that is so tight and busy, such that it might make me dizzy!

-       I'm grateful for the permission, not so much for your attempt at poetry.

-       What do you expect? I'm a hero, not a singer of heroic tales! See you in a bit.

***

-       Papi, look over there. I see a man rolling a huge rock up the hill.

-       What are you two staring at? Anybody would think you were at a Rolling Stones concert! And for your information, I am not getting any satisfaction spending my time just like a rolling stone.

-       I don't think I should tease him, Cruz, by singing "Papa was a Rolling Stone" or "Proud Mary ... rolling... rolling..." or "Stoned Love" or "I Am a Rock". My grandson and I were wondering why all this effort. We noticed that when you get to the top, the rock rolls back to the bottom of the hill.

-       I am Sisyphus. Zeus was always calling me "Sissy puss". I couldn't take it any longer and to show him up, I cheated death – not once, but twice! For this crime of *hubris* I was condemned to roll a rock up this hill for all eternity.

-       Cruz, *hubris* is the Greek sin of pride that makes you think you can outsmart Zeus. The myth of

Sisyphus illustrates the plight of suffering mankind. At least that's what Albert Camus said in his famous book.

-       I have an idea, Sisyphus. Why don't you chip big chunks out of the rock, and when you get to the top, it will rest there, since it will no longer be smooth enough to roll down.

-       That just might work, since Zeus no longer checks up on me. He now feels free to pursue girls. He isn't afraid anymore that I might snitch on him to Hera.

-       Yes, if his wife were to hear about his romantic romps, he would never Hera the end of it!

-       Nice play on words, old man!

-       Thanks, Sisyphus! I'm on a roll! Oops – sorry – my bad!

***

-       So how did it go, Stavros? Did you learn anything?

-       We learned that life can have its ups and downs, but we must continue to fight the plight because might is not always right!

-       O..o..kay! You obviously didn't learn any poetry! That island over there – don't even think about it, Stavros! It's the home of Circe, the witch who transforms humans into animals.

-       Holy *moly*!

50

-       Wish we had some, boy.

-       You probably didn't understand, Cruz, that *moly* was the antidote against Circe's witchcraft . I don't think there is any point in explaining to Jason that we humans are also of the animal species. However, Jason has to continue on his quest. It's not the Holy Grail...but still.

-       Do you have a quest, son?

-       Would you have the answer, Jason?

-       I said **quest**, **son** - not **question**!

-       Sorry, Jason.

-       Maybe, Cruz, like Kenny Vance and the Planotones, your quest could be looking for an echo – an answer to your prayer!

-       So you two know the story of Echo and Narcissus?

-       Yes, Jason, therefore you don't have to repeat it.

-       I know there's an "echo" joke there somewhere.

-       Yes, Jason, I'm rather "echo friendly"! What about that big island over there? Is it inhabited?

-       Why yes. The Lotophagi live there.

-       Could we go chew the fat with them?

-       Cruz, their Greek name means "Lotus-eaters". It won't be "fat" that they will be chewing on! You know how you are constantly being warned at home and at school not to do drugs. If you go to that island, those dregs will drag you into drugs! You won't be grooving, you will be grovelling!

- Amen to that – although all that alliteration made Dionysios sound like a real DG. So the voice of authority! But not quite **D**ionysios the **G**reat!

- Cruz, not to steal the thunder from Christopher Columbus – nor from Zeus! – but you are exploring a whole New World, albeit an ancient one!

- I didn't understand what your grandfather just said, but yeah, he's right! Before we reach Colchis, I want to point out one final landmark rock that we will be sailing by. Shades of Prometheus, you may say, but a young princess named Andromeda had been chained to it as a sacrifice to a sea monster. Yes, you can see monsters everywhere. Sea monsters! She was rescued by Perseus.

- I give you a C for your word play, Jason. But you are quite right to bring up the greatest Greek hero and slayer of monsters after Herakles. And like Herakles, his father was Zeus! I can see the connection between your ship, the Argo, and Argos, the home of his mother Danae. But Perseus was the legendary founder of Mycenae. We will probably be meeting the king of Mycenae in our travels, Stavros. One of the sons of Perseus, Persis, was the ancestor of the Persians. What's in a name, right? Well, the name Perseus might mean "destroyer". He certainly destroyed that mortal Gorgon Medusa! He had magic weapons – the helmet of darkness that made him invisible, the adamantine sword that made him invincible, and the winged sandals that made him invigorated – all making him very "in" to be sure – a regular "James Bond" with those groovy gadgets. Superman and Batman had nothing on him. I know, Stavros, you are thinking he would be no match for the Ninjago Warriors, nor for that matter would he be a worthy foe for Cat Noir and Ladybug! Be that as it may, Perseus sneaked up – "snuck up" is not proper English - on the sleeping Medusa, using his shield as a mirror in order to avoid her petrifying stare, and smote her head – "cut off" sounds so pedestrian. Like Herakles, Perseus also had to deal with snakes - those that had formed Medusa's dreadlocks! No more would the world have to listen to "Turn to Stone" – except on retro radio stations!

-         Papi, er, Dionysios – Snakes! Talk about your bad hair day! Perseus sounds a lot like the hero in those books you gave me. You know - Percy Jackson! Oh, and I really liked the two DVDs about his adventures.

-         Well, if truth be told, "Percy" most likely gets his name from "Perseus". And as you know, Percy Jackson's adventures involve the Titans, the Olympians, and sea monsters like those Perseus had to face. Of course, Percy's stories take place in the United States. But then, America today is a bit like Greece in ancient times – a dominating economic and cultural force. Like the U.S. today, Greece was a political and military power – just ask the Persians! Besides, Percy – like all great Greek heroes - has to prevail in Hades, and the entrance to the underworld was always believed to be in the west.

\-   I get it, Papi, today America is the West! In some ways, maybe even still the "wild, wild West"!

\-   Great guns, Cruz, a pretty perspicacious perception! Jason, I think we've just reached Colchis.

\-   I have to fetch the Golden Fleece without the help of my companions, but for some reason, I feel compelled to bring you and Stavros along. And what's with all the "p's"? Are you a **Pi-** ed piper?

\-   You'll appreciate the Greek letter for "p" when you study higher math, Cruz!

***

\-   Greetings, O King. I'll cut straight to the chase – I've come for the wool of a ram that is entirely made of gold. The same ram that dropped Helle into the Hellespont – I've skipped some details, but that's how it played out.

\-   I don't follow.

\-   He means the Golden Fleece, O King.

\-   Why didn't you say so? No problem.

\-   Papi, this sounds too easy.

\-   I suspect there will be a "by the way" – there usually is.

\-   By the way, Jason – you didn't tell me your name, but I heard you were coming. As I was saying, by the way, a fire-breathing dragon is guarding the

Golden Fleece. You will have to slay it, and then sow the dragon's teeth in the ground.

-        I knew there would be a catch, Papi.

-        Well, one thing I've learned is never to sell yourself short in the Dragon's Den. I don't recall where I learned it though. No matter – help is on the way. There's the King's daughter, and if Jason plays his cards right – by that I mean, if he waves his blonde locks and flashes his blue eyes at her, she will do everything in her power to protect him.

-        Gosh, Papi she looks like a Circe with heavy make-up! And she does seem to have power – maybe even magical.

-        I've learned that her name is Medea. Her father is King Aeëtes. She's rubbing some kind of oil on Jason's body. Either that is meant to protect him against the flames of the fire-breathing dragon, or she just wanted an excuse to rub his body. But let's give her the benefit of the doubt.

-        Look. Papi – Jason has slain the dragon, and the King's men are draggin' the dragon away. In a puff, the magic dragon is gone! But Jason is not dragging his heels – he is planting its teeth in the ground. What's this – armed soldiers are marching out of the ground! I'm sure Jason didn't bank on this development.

-        Medea has left. I wonder if she thinks it's game over for Jason. Unless she was so confident of the hero's triumph that she went to pack her bags. I suspect that her ultimate goal is to leave Colchis with Jason – and without her father finding out.

-        I've just had a flash, Papi. Gather those stones on the ground, and since we are only a stone's throw away from them, we'll throw the stones into the group of soldiers.

-        Dionysios, Stavros – those soldiers are killing each other. They must all have thought that the stones were being thrown by others in their group. I've won! I mean we've won – thanks for your help, guys!

-        Jason, soon to be King Jason, we have indeed won! I am returning with you to Iolcos, where I shall be your Queen. Let us make our escape, while my father's soldiers are looking for my brother. I hid him in the wine-cellar.

-        Gee, Papi, she isn't so cruel after all. But the Golden Fleece is torn in a few places. I thought it was supposed to be sacred.

-        "Holey" – "sacred" – same thing, Cruz!

-        Gee, Papi, you tear me up! Holy smokes - now I think the dragon's fire was sacred!

-        I'm not wholly convinced, Cruz! Nor am I so sure I buy Medea's story about the wine-cellar. From what I learned about her brother, that's the first place the soldiers would have looked. I think there's more than meets the eye to "MADea", and I don't trust her. And as far as living happily ever after with Jason – I just don't see that happening. But ours is not to wonder who, what or how - ours is to continue our journey right now!

-      We'll be returning to mainland Greece, and we'll let you two off on the coast of Boiotia, if that's all right. And after your crude rhyme, the sooner the better!

-      That would be great, Jason. We've lived an adventure that my grandson will share with his own grandchildren – who will be my great-great grandchildren!

-      Well, Cruz, Jason has his ram's fleece, but I hope he realizes he also has a witch in sheep's clothing!

Chapter Five: Cruz Helps Solve a Riddle

- We'll head for Thebes, Cruz. But you remember that Dionysos caused some grief there, so pronounce my name very carefully – Dion-ys-i-os!

- Papi, why are Boiotians called pigs? I'm thinking of that expression you taught me - *Boiotia hus*.

- The expression – like a "Boiotian pig" – was meant as an insult, referring to a country bumpkin, since most of the population lived in the countryside. Ironically, the pig is a relatively intelligent animal. Unless it's because the Boiotians had a really good sense of humor, and they were always trying to "ham" it up!

- They could certainly count on you to "egg" them on, Papi! Say, let's help that man over there. He seems to have trouble walking.

- I'm headed for Thebes. Are you two "going my way"?

- Just a coincidence, Cruz, he couldn't have seen the movie. And Theban priests don't sing like Bing Crosby! Are you travelling alone?

- Yes I've become a travelling man. I'm a wanderer, you might say.

- Again, Cruz, pure coincidence. He couldn't possibly know those songs by Ricky Nelson and Dion. Would you like the use of my walking stick? And my grandson here can attach leather supports to your feet to strengthen them. He needed those supports when he was very young because his feet were turning inwards.

-        Much obliged. I was hitch-hiking, when a cart sped by, knocking me down. The men in the cart got angry, and attacked me. While protecting myself, I killed one of the men. The others must have thought highly of him, because they called him "King". I guess they'll be lonesome tonight without the "King".

-        Don't even suggest it, Cruz! You could always plead involuntary homicide, Stranger.

-        What does that even mean?

-        No matter. Why are you limping? Would you like to share our food? We have some barley cakes.

-        Thank you. If you must know, I have a birth defect.

-        Crushed nuts?

-        Why no – swollen ankles!

-        No, no – I was asking if you would like some nuts with your barley cakes.

-        Sorry! Since the incident, it's no wonder I'm feeling uptight, and should probably remain out of sight.

-        Let it go, Cruz! Stevie Wonder does not even enter the equation! We are entering Thebes, but everybody has this funny look – like they've been gassed. Hey you there, what's happening?

-      It's the Sphinx - she's looking for her next victim. If you can't solve her riddle, she chucks you over a cliff. Nobody knows how this scourge will end.

-      I see – a real cliffhanger!

-      Papi!

-      Thebes… a sphinx. I can see an Egyptian parallel. Did you know, Cruz, that some scholars maintain that Greek culture originated with Egyptian and Sumerian civilization?

-      Say, Mister – I don't know your name, so, "Mister-y"! Now you've got me making lame puns, Dion-ys-i-os! Oh, Sir, so sorry! I didn't mean to offend.

-      No offense taken. My name is Oedipus.

-      Sh! Papi, there's a play about an Oedipus who ruins his life and his family – "Oedipus Wrecks".

-      That's *Oedipus Rex*, Cruz – "Oedipus the King".

-      I wonder what the riddle is, Papi.

-      One of the citizens - still aghast - told me. It goes like this: What is it that at dawn walks on four legs, at noon on two legs, and at twilight on three legs?

-      That's a tough one, although it does look a little like one of the acts we saw when you took me to the circus.

-      Let's all gather around this water trough, and pretend we are at a think tank!

-    Okay, Papi, you stand there with your walking stick. You stand over here, Oedipus. I'll squeeze in here, but I'll have to get on all fours to actually look into the trough. Thinking caps on, everybody?

-    The Sphinx is standing by the cliff, Cruz. Now would be a good time to come up with an answer.

-    One would think we could arrive at the answer. Here we are – a young boy, not long ago an infant crawling at his mother's feet, myself – a man in the prime of life, and an elderly man leaning on his trusty walking stick.

-    Papi, don't you see what Oedipus has just described? Four-two-three!

-    Unless you expect me to hike a football, no I can't say that I do see it.

-    How about you, Oedipus? What have you been describing? Gentlemen, what are we?

-    Men!

-    Louder!

-    Men!

-    I can't hear you!

-    MEN!

-    What is the singular form of men?

-    MAN!

-    Look, Cruz, the citizens are all cheering.

-       Naturally – the Sphinx has just jumped off the cliff!

-       Cruz, since their king was recently killed, and we solved the riddle, the citizens want one of us to be King of Thebes.

-       Well, it's a no-brainer. Oedipus was the one who gave the description of man and so he is the logical choice for King. Three cheers for King Oedipus!

-       You two have been so helpful. I know you want to be off, but please attend the banquet tonight in honor of my bride-to-be, Queen Jocasta. True, her snooty brother Creon will be there. I am told he's quite the "by the book kind of guy". Doesn't he know that having a name that simply means "ruler" leaves him without any special identity of his own. A very respected seer will be there tonight, and I would like for both of you to meet him.

-       On behalf of my grandson and myself, invitation accepted! After all, we must celebrate the feat you accomplished by counting feet. You finally got to taste the thrill of victory after your agony of the feet! Cruz, we'll get to seER, even though it's a HIM!

-       Papi, Oedipus isn't the only one around here who is lame!

***

-       Papi, it's the seer Teiresias. Even though he is blind, he keeps singing that song "I can see clearly now"!

- But his favorite song, Cruz, is "I've looked at love from both sides now". That's because he spent part of his life as a woman. It had something to do with watching snakes coupling, and nothing to do with transgender operations. I realize you don't understand anything of what I'm saying, Cruz, and at your age, that's a good thing!

- Greetings. I understand you have been privy to the exploits of some of our greatest heroes. Tomorrow, "the truth is plain to see… a virgin… ships …will be leaving from the coast". You will be heading off to Troy. In spite of the darkness of my blind condition, I can catch a glimmer of "A Whiter Shade of Pale"!

- But Teiresias, we had told nobody about our plans and destination. How did you know?

- I am a seer – that's what I do! You will witness some of the tragedy of the Trojan War, and get to spend some time with Odysseus on his journey back home. You won't be going down to the underworld with him, since you've already been there and done that – you may even have the T-shirt! Besides, you can read all about it in Book Eleven of Homer's *Odyssey* – the *Nekuia*. A woman will be the cause of that war at Troy. I am a seer, so I see her.

- I see. Oh, I don't mean to step on your toes by carrying on the word play, Teiresias, but as we arrived tonight, we noticed many people in the streets bent over with a serious illness. What's happening?

- Several severely serious series of crimes have been committed, and this curse will only be lifted when the truth is revealed. It will be the fatal end for a woman who loves her son as a wife, and her husband as a mother. I can tell you that King Oedipus and I will not see eye to eye on the cause of the curse, and the poor King will be blindsided by the Fates. And I don't mean to step on his toes, given his problems with swollen ankles! But with his false accusation against me, he is putting his foot in his mouth!

- Wow! You had me with your all-star alliteration when you uttered the first four words of your answer. And I'm impressed that even a seer can utter prophecies with a play on words.

- You and your grandson are fortunate to be leaving Thebes before all the coming tragic events – an uncle declaring death for his niece, a lover and a mother taking their own lives, brothers slaying one another. I could go on, but let me send you off with the tragi-comic account of murders I resolved. When I arrived in Thebes, a number of deaths were being reported. After I had determined that all the deaths occurred in the morning, I was able to discern that the victims had all died of poisoning while consuming breakfast. Before long the culprit was apprehended, and condemned as both a serial and a cereal killer!

- Farewell, Teiresias! Farewell, Thebes!

Chapter Six: Cruz and I "Play Statue" on Our Way to Troy

- Here we are at Aulis, Cruz.

- Wow! Look at all those ships!

- A certain Helen won't be satisfied unless there are a thousand of them being launched! Do you see Agamemnon, the King of Mycenae? He's standing on a purple carpet – or maybe it's scarlet. In any event, he's partial to having a royal rug under his feet.

- Is that a "royal rug" on his head, Papi? And why is he standing by an altar with a young girl?

- No, that's his real hair, Cruz. He hopes his dreadlocks will cause his enemies to "dread" him! And he is about to sacrifice his daughter Iphigeneia to secure the blessing of the gods for the Greek expedition against Troy. So far the winds have been unfavorable, and Agamemnon doesn't want to blow the departure! But his wife Clytemnestra is none too happy.

- Gosh! Killing his own daughter! I wouldn't want to be in his sandals when he gets home from Troy! The situation could turn tragic for Agamemnon!

- Precisely what Aeschylus thought!

- Say what?

- Tragedy, my boy, Greek tragedy! There is a rumor that he didn't actually kill his daughter. Think of the biblical story of Abraham and Isaac. The blood of a slain deer was used to fool the Greek army, while the "dead" Iphigeneia was shipped off to a place called Tauris - but not in one of the "thousand" ships! If truth be told, though, Agamemnon could have used the wise counsel of Athena to ensure the goodwill of all the gods. But alas, he was owl-less at Aulis!

- Gee, two stories about what happened to Iphigeneia!

- It worked for Euripides. Money in the bank, Cruz, money in the bank! Come on, we can board one of the ships as camp followers. Just think – in all those films about Troy, we would have been movie extras! You could have gotten Brad Pitt's autograph!

- What's that island, Papi?

- That's Cyprus. The ship we are on is stopping over at this island which is sacred to Aphrodite, so that a sacrifice may be offered to placate the goddess who – when you think about it – was responsible for starting the Trojan War! It's a favorite spot for newlyweds - like Niagara Falls was for your Manie and me! Let's walk around a bit, and visit the shops.

- There's one, Papi – Pygmalion's Pottery.

- Come on in. You can purchase an object from my fine collection of female figurines. They are my specialty! Or you can walk around and simply browse. I have some wonderful "Browser" figures – little monster bobbleheads I recently imported from Japan. The best one is called Browser's Fury. If you purchase it, you get a free wall plaque complete with inscription.

This one reads "Hades hath no fury like a woman scorned". The plaques were ordered from Marius' Mementos in *Magna Graecia*. But for cross-Mediterranean trade, Marius prefers to be called Mario. His brother, Lucius - Luigi for their international trade - is joint owner. They are doing so well, that their personal delivery service, "manned" entirely by females called Amazons, has been dubbed "Super Mario Brothers"! If this young boy is your slave, you probably have Master Card.

-        No, no! If anything, back home it's the other way round! Stavros here is my grandson. I am not his master, but rather his doting grandfather. Looking at all your statuettes and inscriptions and Amazon shipping, one would say that you are really into women, Pygmalion. By the way, do you have any larger objects in your shop?

-        Woe is me! Despite daily offerings at the shrine of Aphrodite, there is no woman in my life. That is why I am sculpting a life-size female statue in the back-shop in order to pretend she is the woman in my life. Alas, the only thing "life" about her is her size!

-        May we see her?

-        Yes, walk this way.

-        Papi, do we really have to walk his way, with our backs doubled over?

-        Direction, Cruz, not description! One of these days…

-        Behold Galatea! My woman, my life!

\-   Pygmalion, Stavros here was given a phial of magic liquid by Medea, and wants to know if you would like to pour some on Galatea's beautifully sculpted features.

\-   Actually, Medea had two phials, labeled B and G – well really *beta* and *gamma*. At first I thought the letters stood for black and gold, but when she insisted on keeping the "B" phial, saying she thought it would probably come in handy one day, I realized the letters stood for Good and Bad. So, unless you use it on your statue, I will have to class it under Phial G.

\-   I suppose it couldn't do any harm. Here goes…

\-   Pygmalion, the marble is becoming soft. Is she coming to life – or Mt. Olympus forbid – is she melting?

\-   There is no life. Her eyes remain shut.

\-   I've read a story where a princess choked on an apple, but when a prince kissed her, he dislodged the apple from her windpipe, and she awoke. As in your shop, there were also little figures nearby – seven of them!

\-   As a matter of fact, every day I place beside her an apple – the fruit sacred to Aphrodite! Do you think…

\-   Yes, Pygmalion, try "kissing her softly with your love".

\-   Is that a song, Papi?

\-   I am not asking you to take any "flak", Cruz, but don't spoil the moment!

\-   Galatea is opening her eyes? But that's impossible!

\-   No, Pygmalion, **I'm** possible! Can't you see what a difference an apostrophe makes!

\-   As my grandson just exclaimed, Pygmalion – Your woman, your wife!

\-   Thank you so much, you two! The next time you visit my shop, you will see in the place of honor, bobbleheads of a grandfather and his grandson!

\-   We have to head back to the ship which will join the others at Troy.

\-   Right, Papi, but now I'm thinking about that short story you wrote where Greek statues come to life.

\-   Just a story, Cruz! But people will be talking about Pygmalion and his transformational creativity for a long, long time. George Bernard Shaw wrote a play called *Pygmalion*. And based on that play, a musical and a film called *My Fair Lady* were produced. Even a little wooden boy comes to life with a growing nose. Pinocchio came to life through the power of dreams!

***

\-   We've been here, for what seems like years, Papi. Achilles has been on again, off again! He sure is no Brad Pitt! I get it, though. He lost his best friend on account of war. I remember the sadness on your face when you once told me how your best friend in high school was killed during the war in Vietnam. I did think, nevertheless, that Achilles was over the top in his treatment of Hector's body after he killed him to avenge the death of Patroclos. War sucks!

- Yes, Cruz, but I guess if you're a warrior, it's your war! Let's finish off our supper and prepare to turn in. But those fire beacons shining on our tent make it hard to sleep. Say, who is that elderly man making his way towards us?

- I'm looking for Achilles. I'm old and gray, and have come a long way!

- And a sometime poet, you forgot to say!

- Now's not the time to be clever, Cruz! Can we help you? Why do you wish to see Achilles? Wait a minute – you are King Priam! We have access to Achilles, since my grandson Stavros and I are responsible for cleaning his tent. He finds us quite efficient, and affectionately calls us his "Clean Machine"!

- I would like to recover the body of my son Hector in order to give him a proper burial. Will you help me?

- We'll do our best. Come along.

- Yes, King Priam – walk this way!

- Cut that out, Cruz! Forgive him, King Priam, he sometimes acts and speaks with mischievous mirth.

- Or mirthful mischief! No matter. You are fortunate to have such a grandson. Enjoy every moment spent with him! I have a grandson – Hector's little boy. But I have a troublesome premonition that a terrible end awaits young Astyanax – "lord of the city". Alas, soon there will be no city in need of a lord!

-        Here we are at the tent of Achilles. Let us enter.

-        Greetings, loyal cleaners! But who is this? I am puzzled by my Machine's machinations.

-        Not too puzzled to produce some fine alliteration, O Achilles. This is King Priam and he wishes to recover the corpse of his son Hector.

-        The gods are granting me the occasion to slay the father and have him join his son.

-        Lord Achilles, in the name of the father and of his son, and of the holy ghost his son has become, I mean his sacred soul, King Priam showed great courage in coming to the Greek camp alone and as a suppliant in order to honor his son and to give glory to the one who slew him.

-        Dionysios, you have pronounced the three words dear to my heart – courage, honor and glory. You may have your son, King Priam. May the gods be with you!

-        Papi, I thought he was going to repeat the three words that Don McLean sang in his song "American Pie" - words you just mentioned yourself!

-        Faithful cleaners, I fail to grasp the trinity of which you speak !

-        Different jokes for different folks, Cruz! And what a tragedy it will be for Greece the day the music dies!

- Cruz, there seems to be a great commotion in front of the walls of Troy, and most of the Greek ships are sailing away from the beaches of Troy.

- Papi, there's a huge horse in front of the Trojan gates. I think it's a gift to appease the gods, but it's too big to fit through the entrance to the city.

- Watch what the Trojans are doing. They are carefully detaching the head and the legs. The remaining bulk can be dragged into the city, and then each piece re-attached. The reconstructed horse – now all in one piece – will symbolize peace. But really too many pieces for my peace of mind!

- What are those holes underneath the horse's belly, Papi?

- Air-holes to allow the Greeks hidden inside the horse to breathe.

- Now I get it! So that's why Odysseus and his men piled wood beside their camp.

- And it explains why all that hammering kept us awake most nights. As if the beacons weren't enough! Well, Cruz, Troy is burning. The war is over.

- About time - it lasted ten years! There's a Trojan prince running out the back way and he's carrying an old man over his shoulders. He's also holding a young boy by the hand. The boy seems to be about my age.

- I have this strange feeling that we will meet them again one day.

***

\-   Nice of you to allow us to return with you to Greece on your ship, Odysseus.

\-   I must warn you, it won't be a walk in the park.

\-   Papi, why would he say that? Of course we won't be in a park, we'll be on the sea.

\-   Just a figure of speech, Cruz, to tell us it will be a perilous voyage. In fact, we saw many of those dangers when we were with Jason. Apparently, they shared the same map. So some *déjà vu*. But new challenges as well.

***

\-   All right, a few of us will search for food on that island. Are you and Stavros up for it, Dionysios?

\-   Sure, our trip is an all-inclusive.

\-   What's that you say?

\-   Wouldn't miss it for the world – ancient or modern!

\-   What nonsense are you muttering? Too much of the grand sun?

\-   I could never get too much of my grandson!

\-   Maybe you'll be helpful on land. You weren't much use on the ship. If I seemed angry with you, it was because you obviously don't suit oars.

\-   No doubt his spoiler alert for "suiters", Cruz.

-      Grandfather Dionysios, Odysseus, there is a huge one-eyed giant carrying milk and cheese in abundance out of that cave – enough to feed a shipload of men!

-      Are you thinking what I'm thinking, Odysseus?

-      I don't know – let me think!

-      Now who's muttering nonsense, eh Cruz? But how do we get into the cave without the giant seeing us? "What can you do if you're caught by a giant without pity?"

-      "The best thing you can do, the best thing you can do, is fall on your knees"!

-      Hey, you two, he won't show mercy, even if you do fall on your knees – and especially if you keep singing like that.

-      We still want to take back a rack of cheese. We can criss-cross the beach in front of the cave to avoid him.

-      No, he might become more deadly.

-      Or, if he runs backwards – "Dudley" - Dudley Moore!

-      This whole exchange is doing my head in.

-      That's because he hasn't seen the movie *Arthur*, Cruz.

-      Papi, pass me your watch. Ah, "here comes the sun". There – the sun is reflecting off the glass face of the watch into the giant Cyclops' eye, temporarily blinding him.

-        Brilliant!

-        Are you talking about the sun or me, Odysseus?

-        Both, I guess. But what's with the singing? I didn't expect to undergo that torture until we reached the Sirens! And how did you know the giant is a Cyclops?

-        Easy peasy! It's a Greek word meaning "one eye in the middle".

-        "One is the loneliest number"!

-        Papi, you'll never be Chuck Negron – maybe "Le Groan"!

-        And you, young man, concentrate on becoming "Le Grown-up"!

-        Enough chatter! The temporary blinding, and your name, Stavros – a "stake" – have given me the solution to the threatening Polyphemus. They don't call me "wily Odysseus" for nothing! Do you get my point?

-        Well, I'm sure Polyphemus will get it! And how do you know his name?

-        I'm on a ten-year journey to reach Ithaca. I've had time to read the script!

-        Papi, Polyphemus is shouting that he will catch us, even if he has to chase us to the ends of the earth!

-        He'd have a better chance of catching us if he pursued us to the end of time - especially if he had access to a time capsule. But he'll probably end up continuing to drink that wine that Odysseus gave him to get him drunk. So, "Time in a Bottle"!

***

-       Here we are at last in the land of the Phaeacians, Cruz. It's been quite the ride! It seems that Odysseus was found by Nausicaa, the daughter of the King, and taken to the palace to make arrangements for transportation to Ithaca. I was once in Ithaca – Ithaca, New York. It's no big deal. Nausicaa had entertained thoughts of marrying Odysseus, but changed her mind when she learned he was already spoken for. And speaking of entertained, Odysseus will tell the whole story of his adventures tonight to entertain the Phaeacians – a trade-off for free passage back home. His audience is sure to hear how he was truly *polytropos* – meaning "of many twists and turns". This could refer to the many tricks or the many travels of the hero Odysseus.

-       Will we be attending, Papi?

-       No, I'd rather read Homer's account in the *Odyssey*.

-       And I want to check on some details about the Trojan War in his *Iliad*. Before we leave Phaeacia, I'd like to ask you something, Papi. Nausicaa came to say good-by, kissed me on the cheek, and said she wished I was older. Why do girls keep telling me they wished I was older?

-       Don't be in a hurry to find out, Cruz!

Chapter Seven: Cruz and I Get Some Advice

-       Time to press the green button, Cruz. We are about to turn the pages of Ancient Greek history! Except that the "pages" will be people, places and pastimes. First stop – Delphi.

-       I'm so excited by our imaginary journey to the ancient world, Papi! I can't wait to tell my friends at school about it!

-       Maybe one day you could write a book describing our "adventures" in Ancient Greece and Rome. Maybe you could call it "Journey into Antiquity"!

-       You mean write a book like you did, Papi?

-       Cruz, Society needs writers like the night needs stars. Both shine bright and shed some light!

-       Gosh, Papi, you're a real poet, and you never cease to show it!

-       Point taken, little guy!

-       Delphi has to be the most majestic spot in all of Greece, nestled on the slopes of this mountain.

-       Mt. Parnassus, Cruz. Climbing Mt. Parnassus is like going off in search of knowledge. Just marvel at that huge bronze statue of the Charioteer. His eyes tell you he has been imbued with the wisdom of Apollo! And speaking of Apollo, games were held here in his honor and were known as the Pythian Games. Of course they couldn't match the fanfare of the Olympic

Games, which began in 776 BCE. A pity we didn't attend the opening ceremonies of those first games. And there was no ABG sports coverage!

-        Don't you mean ABC, Papi?

-        No, ABG – *Alpha, Beta, Gamma*!

-        Can we consult the Oracle?

-        Yes we can. Wouldn't you know it, I had just enough *drachmai* left after my payment to Charon to cover our admission to the Pythian precinct. Let me read my Apolline advice – "Nothing in life is free"! Say, he's good! What piece of advice has the Oracle given you, Cruz?

-        Whatever happened to "the best things in life are free"? I guess Apollo feels his fame came at a price! My advice from the Pythian priestess came with a barley biscuit. Maybe the god realized he could make a fortune with cookies! My Pythian pronouncement reads "Even if life doesn't always give you the gifts you desire, know that the real gift is life itself"!

-        True that! I was more impressed by the Delphic Oracle than the "Oracle" I saw in the film *The Matrix*. Come on, Cruz, we are off to Athens to tour the Acropolis.

***

-        Isn't the Parthenon wonderful, Papi? That statue of Athena is humungous! But what is that temple with the lady columns?

-        The Erechtheion - it was named after a king killed by Poseidon. Don't forget that the god of the sea received some worship up here, even though he lost the contest for naming the city to Athena. He's always had his faithful group of "horse whisperers"! By the way, do you know why the horse is considered the saddest animal, Cruz?

-        Probably not just because it caused Poseidon to lose the contest. So, why?

-        Because when you say "Woah", the horse says "is me"!

-        Woe is me too, Papi! Try to rein in your jokes!

-        Cruz, the female-figure columns are called caryatids, named after the pretty girls from the village of Karyes who posed for the sculptor. I guess they were the first "super models"!

-        One of them seems a bit loose, Papi – I mean the column, not the girl who posed for it!

-        Mind your mouth, young man! Be cautious, precocious boy! That caryatid will probably be replaced one day. In fact, not everything you see up here will remain as is.

-        Why is that, Papi?

-        The British are coming, Cruz, the British are coming! In our day you will be able to see some of these Greek marvels in the BMW.

-        They'll be carried off in a car, Papi?

-       No, I'm talking about **British Museum Wonders**! We don't have time to visit the whole Acropolis – which, as you know, means the "citadel, or summit, of the city". But over there is the Asklepeion, in honor of the god of medicine who worked under Apollo, the "head doctor". Off to the side is the Theater of Dionysos, where all Greeks could exclaim "the play's the thing"! Finally, I want to point out that small temple dedicated to Athena Nike, from the Greek word for "Victory".

-       No wonder my friend Nick always beats me at chess!

-       We are going to test your maturity a bit, Cruz, but I have secured for us two tickets to the Eleusinian Mysteries. However, we'll be in the cheap seats – reserved for initiates.

***

-       All those ceremonies and prayers were very strange, Papi. I couldn't understand most of it.

-       That's why they're called "Mysteries"! Life itself can be a mystery. But it's ours to live, Cruz, without making it one continuous problem to solve! The word "mystery" actually comes from the Greek word for an initiated individual – *mustes.* This word also gave us "mystic". When I was a graduate student, I had an assignment in an ancient Greek religion course to consult a mystic. He turned out to be a pseudo-mystic. That means he was a false mystic, Cruz. I'm being polite – he was, for all intents and purposes, a fake and a fraud. After every pronouncement, I found myself saying "that's a mistake, mystic"! I did play golf

80

one time at Mystic Pines, which is well-named, since I couldn't solve the mystery of how to avoid hitting all those pine trees! The name Eleusis itself may be connected to *Elysion*, the Greek "heaven". Thus, the secret ceremony here may be a ritual prelude meant as a preparation for a happy experience in the afterlife. A bit like yours truly singing "Stairway to Heaven".

Chapter Eight: Wars and Words

-       You see that man over there, Cruz? That's Herodotus, and he's reading to a captive audience from his history of the Persian Wars.

-       His Greek sounds a bit different from the Greek you taught me, Papi.

-       That's because he writes in the Ionian dialect, and you read Attic Greek. But if you listen closely, you'll realize there is not much difference between those two dialects. Herodotus is from Asia Minor, and since the seeds for a Persian invasion of Greece started there, it is fitting that he gives us an account of that war.

-       But why is he called the "father of lies" and the "lover of barbarians"?

-       Well, it is "his story" to tell, and some of his anecdotes are a little far-fetched.

-       Did you just play on the word "history", Papi?

-       Nothing gets by you, Cruz! After all, he and the tragedian Sophocles often touched on the same themes. One was writing fiction based on the "facts of life", and the other was writing "facts" based sometimes on "fictitious lives"! So "fact" or "fiction" – take your pick! But they were both literary "pros"!

-       And literary "bros", Papi!

-       Ah, who knew I would have a cross to bear named Cruz? Herodotus also believed that circumstances rule men, that men do not rule circumstances – a belief a little too fatalistic for my liking, Cruz.

-        Did Herodotus believe that the gods caused circumstances?

-        Actually, Herodotus believed that the gods were "setters", that is, they "set" everything in order, because he claimed that the Greek word for "god" - *theos* – came from the verb *tithemi*, meaning "to place" or " to set" – but that's just Herodotus. When you are older, Cruz, you'll often hear the word "thesis" – that signifies a position or opinion that is "put forward". On the other hand, the Greek word *kosmos* meant a world "set in order". So if we were travelling right now through a Greco-Roman world that was completely "well-ordered", we'd be cosmonauts! One day, Cruz, your sister and cousins will probably come across another word from *kosmos* – "cosmetics". But if they continue to grow up as pretty as they are now, that word shouldn't become part of their vocabulary! In fact, Herodotus was a writer of anthropological history. What I mean is that his account of the belligerents includes a description of the peoples involved, and of their customs and beliefs. Book Two of his history, for instance, is a fascinating study of the ancient Egyptians. He also informed us of the Persian system of communications along the "royal roads". The Persian King made use of a messenger system with horses placed at strategic intervals. Yes – the ancient version of the pony express! The Persian credo was "Neither snow nor rain nor heat nor night prevents the messenger from completing the course as quickly as possible". And people think that the U.S. Postal Service came up with that idea! But since we are in the middle of this war, let's head out to the action.

-        I've been checking my calendar faithfully, Papi. We are in 490 BCE. There's a massive number of Persian ships ready to wipe out the Athenian naval fleet here at Marathon.

-        That's right. The Athenians had sent Pheidippides to run all the way to Sparta for help, but the Spartans refused to come because of a religious festival. Funny how in later history, religion will constantly cause peoples to go to war, rather than to stay home peacefully practicing their religion! I suspect the Spartans' winning record in battle had partly to do with their knack of knowing when to pick a fight! Not to say they weren't tough as nails with all that training they did. Spartan youth had to undergo long periods without eating. In fact, competitions were held to determine which Spartan boys could endure the lack of food for the longest period. These contests might be referred to as the Hunger Games. The Spartans admired warriors who RUN fast – **towards** the enemy, not **from** the enemy! – and CAN fast – that is, go for long periods without food. Spartan youth who demonstrated these qualities would be fast-tracked into the Spartan army. In any event, the Athenian runner ran all the way back to give the Athenians the bad news. Before he collapsed and died, he said two things – "They're not coming, and my name is actually Philippides!"

-        Look, Papi, the Greeks are winning! The Great King Darius is not going to be happy!

-       Why don't you run to Athens and tell everybody the good news, Cruz. It's only fourteen miles. I'll catch you up later!

-       Okay! This will be my first marathon!

***

-       Ten years later, and the Persians are back, Papi – this time under King Xerxes. I can see him looking down on his troops, vastly outnumbering the Greeks, but he is forever complaining that his Persian paratroopers fight like women. Just think, Papi, in our modern world that wouldn't be a bad thing!

-       Cruz, three hundred Spartans are marching to Thermopylae under King Leonidas. This is the third time I've witnessed their heroics, since I saw the movies *The 300 Spartans* and *300*! So, sadly, I know they will all be killed. Their sacrifice will always be synonymous with unflinching bravery. Talk about removing the fear factor! The good news is that their sacrifice bought time for Athens and her allies to prepare battles at Salamis and Plataea. We're not far from Plataea in good old Boiotia, so let's go take in the action.

-       We got here just in time to see the allied forces under the Spartan commander Pausanias defeat the Persians. But will we get to travel through the Persian Empire, Papi?

-       Funny you should ask. That vast territory is actually on our itinerary. Following the Trojan War and the Persian Wars, it's now Greece: 2, Asia: 0! So for

85

now let's celebrate the Greek victory and Greek culture. The Greeks are probably "oozing" with pride, or maybe just with ouzo, but remember – no wine for you!

\-   But, Papi, I read in one of my catechism course books that wine is mentioned in the Bible 286 times, and in France even young boys are served wine.

\-   Cruz, there was a French film called *Les Diaboliques*. It involved a love triangle of adults, so that's not why I am bringinging up the film. The story is set in a boarding school where the boys are badly treated by a cruel headmaster. There is a scene where wine is mentioned in a Latin phrase – *Bonum vinum laetificat cor hominis*, meaning "good wine delights man's heart". But the adults, not the boys, are drinking the wine! The students are ill-fed and all-suffering. The film is considered a classic and was directed by Henri-Georges Clouzot.

\-   Papi, wasn't he the Inspector in those Pink Panther films we saw on TV?

\-   No, Cruz, that was Inspector **Clouseau**, played by the inimitable Peter Sellers.The Inspector never had a clue, though! Good reference, Cruz, though. Clouzot also directed the film *Wages of Fear*, the original French title being *Le Salaire de la Peur*, like the novel it was based on.

\-   Papi, Clouseau reminds me of Crusoe, as in *Robinson Crusoe*, the novel by Daniel Defoe.

\-   Cruz, if you are embarking on a word play contest, I'll have to consider **you** "de foe"!

- Papi, that "foe-ny" wordplay will cause you to lose by default.

- What - "de fault" of being too good? So no more "whining"! Cruz, I brought up that film about boys suffering at that school because I also want you to realize how lucky you are to be in a good school. Since I've brought up school, here's a little Biblical lesson. The full expression about wine comes from the Old Testament book *Ecclesiasticus – Vinum et musica delectant cor* – "Wine and music give pleasure to the heart". The real lesson is in the conclusion of that proverbial saying – "but love of wisdom surpasses both of them"! You'll get to appreciate what "love of wisdom" is all about when we meet a certain Socrates later on our journey.

- Thanks for the spoiler alert, Papi! But didn't that book of the Old Testament also inspire The Byrds for a song?

- That was *Ecclesiastes*, Cruz, and the words were "To every thing there is a season and a time to every purpose under heaven". The song was actually written by a singer-songwriter named Pete Seeger.

- Well, I still like the song "Turn, Turn, Turn".

- Whatever turns you on!

- Why are all the people gathering in the Theater of Dionysos, Papi?

- I read on some papyrus posters that there is a panhellenic conference on literature and science taking place, and all the important writers will be there. Most of them wrote plays, so the theater is a logical venue. Before they start, we can read the bios of the Seven Sages of Ancient Greece. That's "bios" in the sense of "biographies", and not the Greek word *bios*, meaning "life", but I think you get the connection. They are Thales, Bias, Pittacus, Solon, Cleobulus, Periander, Myson, Chilon, and Anacharsis.

-        Papi, you just named nine sages!

-        Just wanted to see if you were paying attention, Cruz! Actually, two of the last three I named are often interchanged to maintain the list at the canonical – you might say "magic" - number seven.The first hour will be devoted to a video presentation – don't ask! We get to see Homer and Hesiod reading from their works. Who would have guessed that they had been taped when they were alive! Next, Anaxagoras – he's a friend of Socrates, you know – will do a power-point presentation on the Presocratics – Thales, Anaximander, Parmenides, Democritus, Heracleitus, Xenophanes, Pythagoras and finally, Empedocles, who was considered to be the father of rhetoric. Speaking of "speaking", the Sophist Gorgias is in attendance. He boasted of being a clever speaker. Another Sophist – Protagoras – is also present. While he talks about Pythagoras, Anaxagoras has asked the spectators to refrain from eating beans. Actually, depending on which way the wind is blowing, that might be a good suggestion for the whole conference! Again, Pythagoras will become more important to you when you start learning geometry. If you're wondering why I keep referencing math, Plato, another friend of Socrates, stated no one could enter his Academy without a knowledge of mathematics! Xenophanes is famous for saying men made their gods to look like men, whereas horses would make their gods look like horses. As far as the orthodox religious beliefs of the day, you could say he was a "neigh-sayer". However, since anthropomorphism – from the Greek words for "man "and "form" or "shape" - was merely a convenient vehicle for thinking and talking about, as well as portraying, the gods, one can wonder whether Xenophanes was not putting the horse before the cart! A little-known anecdote about Heracleitus relates his vacation by a river in Boiotia. He enjoyed swimming the first day, but when invited to go swimming again the next day, he protested that it wouldn't be possible to go swimming twice in the same river! Protagoras famously said "man is the measure of all things". For him, not just beauty, but also truth, were "in the eye of the beholder"! Reality would be based on individual perception, as opposed to some form of "objective" truth. I suppose you could say "what you see is what you get"!

-	What is rhetoric, Papi?

-	The art of public speaking, Cruz.

-	Oh, you mean speaking good?

-	I think we'll have to get you reading Empedocles and followers sooner than later, Cruz!

-	Papi, just look at all that beautiful pottery on display, as well as those statues.

-	Yes, Cruz, the conference is part of culture week. You'll see fine examples of black-figure and red-figure vases, as well as archaic and classical sculpture. The most popular figure on those vases is our old friend Herakles. But look at all those vases featuring the women warriors known as Amazons. Although they are mentioned in many Greek myths, they were really - and here I mean historically – Scythians, who fought alongside men on horseback, using bows and arrows. Their exotic nature appealed to the Greeks, who otherwise were not into the women's liberation movement. That is why Greek heroes fell in love with Amazon queens – but with tragic consequences! Herakles, on a panty raid, unwittingly killed Hippolyte while wrestling her for her girdle. Achilles, after killing Penthesileia in battle, realized that he had fallen in love with her. He had probably been turned on by her prowess in fighting! Theseus kidnapped and married Antiope. After the escapade with Ariadne, and the asylum he gave Medea, you can probably guess that he was into foreign women! But he turned out to be a "love 'em and leave 'em" type of guy! Much like Odysseus with Circe and Calypso! You will notice that the Amazons are fully clothed, and not portrayed naked with one breast removed. That's why I am letting you look at those vases! The legend of cutting off a breast to better shoot arrows with their bows is fake news – simply not true! It was all part of a false etymology used by the sensational press to sell news parchments! In truth, the Amazon women fought with bows, but alongside their beaus! Cruz, when you're older, and, hopefully, get to study Greek art, you will discover that, for a long time, all female statues were fully clothed – only males were sculpted nude. That was because Greek women did not have the freedom to parade in public, and so sculptors had no "models" to use for their female representations.

- Papi, thanks for keeping me abreast of practices in early Greek art!

- Cruz, you are becoming very quick with your repartee. It's becoming a case of "same old, same old", or should I say, "*plus ça change*…". But, full disclosure, I'm quite proud of you! I would like to draw your attention to that large group of pots on an extended table. They are the unsigned work by the same artist. Because they were all made in a relatively short time, this artist, who was both craftsman and painter, is known as the "Hurry Painter". His work is mostly black-figure – notice the large male figure in black on his largest vase. The character is wearing a high, broad-rimmed hat. The other two characters are smaller, one male, the other female. The artist seems to have experimented with red-figure, since the smaller male figure is depicted with red hair. Next to that collection are sculpted figurines by the Hurry Painter's cousin. We know of their family ties, because he signed his work with "Hurry Potter"! This is a *hapax legomenon* – Greek for "single occurrence" – since it is the only example of that name. He used a technique called *cire-perdue*, meaning "lost wax". In this process a molten metal is poured into a mold that has been created by means of a wax model. After the mold is made, the wax model is drained away, or "lost". In any event, he became known as the "wizard of wax'! Many of his figurines are now in a museum.

- A wax museum, Papi?

-      Did anybody ever tell you, Cruz, that when you were born they took away the mold?

-      Or maybe they "lost" it! I guess the two cousins were on a mission.

-      More likely on "commission"! I can just imagine them "rolling in" the money!

-      Or, Papi, if they were rewarded in leafy garlands – "raking them in"! But now I see two very old men going to the podium.

-      The one being cheered by all the athletes in the audience is the Boiotian poet Pindar. He was the forerunner of today's sportswriters, since he wrote odes to celebrate the victors at the various athletic contests held at different festivals, such as the Olympic Games. Aeschylus will no doubt read from his trilogy, the *Oresteia*. I'm hoping he will also read from his play *Prometheus Bound*. That should stir some memories – right, Cruz? Now, the three keynote speakers will address the audience.

-      I hope, Athenians – and other members of the audience – that you will continue to produce and ponder my plays – all 120 of them – for many years to come. Never forget that it was I, Sophocles, who brought to the stage the tragic story of Oedipus and his dysfunctional family, where brothers killed each other, and a mother marries her son. A certain Freud is going to let slip that this will lead to complex consequences! My play *Antigone* will no doubt animate for centuries to come the contentious question of the separation of Church and State.

-       Greetings, all theater lovers. I, Euripides, have often been called a misogynist – perhaps because it is a catchy Greek word, and I am a Greek! Be that as it may, consider the evidence. My plays have presented a woman who kills her son in a fit of orgiastic stupor, a woman who yells rape when her step-son refuses her ill-conceived advances, a betrayed wife who murders her children in an act of vengeful retribution – true, she had form, having carved up her brother - a father who slaughters his daughter in sacrifice – and she in turn is saved so that she herself may kill innocent passers-by. I could go on, but I shall cease speaking because time is short, and now that I have read the evidence out loud, I implore you, on second thought, to forget what I just said! On a lighter note, the other day I took some tunics to a tailor for repairs. He couldn't believe it was me – perhaps he thought overly enthusiastic *maenads* from my play, in an orgiastic ecstasy of frenzy – ah, I can see many of you foaming in a horny sweat – had torn them. Euripides? he asked. Eumenides? I replied, wanting to ascertain his identity.

-       Peace, my fellow-citizens! Peace is in my heart – and in many of my plays. I mention by way of example that play where men must make peace if they want a piece! They call me Aristophanes, that brilliant poet of Old Comedy. But, friends, we all know that comedy never grows old! As this conference comes to an end, I would like to convey to you apologies from Thucydides, that noteworthy historian, who at this very moment is taking worthy notes on the terrible conflict that is pitting the great bastions of our culture, Athens and Sparta, one against the other.

-        Cruz, Aristophanes just alluded to the
Peloponnesian War. It is not going well for Athens.
She suffered great losses on a Sicilian expedition.
One of her up-and-coming stars – Alci "Bad Boy"
biades - has let her down. Fleeing the harbor of
Athens, he was dubbed the "pariah of the Piraeus"!
Thucydides talks a lot about the role of chance – *tuche*
in Greek. The cause of this war really goes back to the
situation in Greece at the end of the Persian Wars.
Athens had become the saviour of all *Hellas* when her
"wooden walls" – her ships – had defended the Greek
world against the Persian barbarians. The Greek city-
states felt they owed a debt of gratitude to the
Athenians, and a common treasury was set up on the
island of Delos. Using this money, Athens built up an
empire. Sparta still had the best land army in Greece,
and fearing a very unstable balance of power because
of Athenian expansion, formed counter-alliances. Just
as happened in World War I, a pretext was found to
launch hostilities. One of the dark moments in the war
occurred when Athens refused to acknowledge the
neutrality of the island of Melos, and bullied that state
into submission. The Athenians put forth the argument
that "might is right", and subsequent history has
proven that many nations in similar situations of power
think they might be right!

-        But how did Athens manage to build all those
magnificent temples while fighting the war?

-        As far as I am concerned, Cruz, the glory that
accrued to Athens was down to one man – Pericles.
He was the great statesman *par excellence*! He was
such a great orator, such a convincing leader, that the

majority of Athenians accepted both his war policy and his building program. Of course – as in any society – there were the naysayers who wished to remove Pericles from power - and even from the city. This could be done through a process known as ostracism. In this practice, citizens would write on pottery shards called *ostraka* the name of the person they would like banished from the city. The person with the most votes, if a minimum number of votes had been cast, was forced into exile for ten years. I suppose if someone today can be voted off an island, a man could be voted out of the city in Ancient Athens! An interesting anecdote on the history of ostracism involves a politician named Aristeides the Just. One day, an illiterate citizen, not recognizing Aristeides – so, ignorant as well! - asked him how one spelled "Aristeides". When Aristeides asked him why he wished to ostracize Aristeides, the man replied that he was tired of hearing him called Aristeides "the Just"! Aristeides wrote down his name for the man! He even added the alternate spelling of his name, "Aristides", thinking that one letter fewer would allow the poor soul to use a smaller *ostrakon*. How just is that! Pericles had quite the public image. He was always portrayed wearing a helmet – probably to hide an overly wide forehead, or a pimple! After all, they didn't have photoshop in those days! He also liked parading his "first lady", Aspasia, in public. As a foreigner, she was not obliged to remain out of view of the public eye. But tragedy struck Athens – no, this time not a Greek play – but a ravaging plague, which, as Thucydides describes it, was characterized by fever, swelling, dryness of the throat, vomiting, and violent convulsions. Many, like Thucydides himself, survived, but so many others died - including Pericles. But before he perished, he had spurred on the Athenians with a brilliant funeral oration for those who had been killed in the early battles of the war. In this speech he highlighted the place in history occupied by Athens, and her role in educating all of Greece – all of *Hellas* – in the lofty ideals and marvellous culture that were synonymous with Athens. A truly magnificent speech in defense of democracy! True, the Athenians did tend to snub their noses – even at other Greeks who did not speak the Attic dialect. That was not, though, the reason Socrates had a snub nose! Greek in the Hellenistic world was like English in the British Empire – to be "civilized" you had to speak English. That is why you have people from Hong Kong and India who speak beautiful English. At least Asian peoples were not told to "speak white", although that was probably the mentality in South Africa until the arrival on the scene of Nelson Mandella. He courageously played a part - "tide of change" was the new sign of the times!

-        Wow, Papi, the plague was even worse than Covid-19!

-        What's more, from everywhere in Attica the Athenians were crowding into the city. Social distancing and confinement were out of the question, as was a mandatory curfew. The Athenians were constantly gathering in assemblies to vote on war measures, so a vaccine passport would not have been effective. All the more so, since they didn't have vaccines! Masks were out of the question, because they were all reserved for actors on the stage. They did report numbers of casualties and deaths.

Thucydides could attest to them on site, but not on a web site! There was limited access to his news reports – no television, after all. Reading his book – which was not even complete when he died – was only of benefit to those wanting to read some really good Greek! I believe, Cruz, that the death of the charismatic Pericles spelled the beginning of the end for Athens in her conflict with Sparta. I believe the Athenians lost confidence and started second-guessing themselves when they no longer had their great leader who like no other justified and glorified their way of life when he said "The Empire you hold is a tyranny. It may have been wrong to acquire it, but it would be dangerous to let it go"! Yes, there were attempts at negotiating peace, but intervals, such as the "Peace of Nicias", were merely periods of a temporary truce until an ultimate victory by the Spartans at Aegospotami in 405 BCE finally ended the war. If it had been a 1950's Hollywood western, it would have been called "The Battle at Goat River". John Wayne would have had to play the role of a Spartan general! Naturally, as today, the victors set up a puppet government in the defeated state.

-       But, Papi we've visited Sparta – remember those awful spartan accommodations! Strange, though, my favorite variety of apple is Spartan!

-       Talk about an apple with appeal!

-       Papi, every apple has a peel.

-       I suppose you expect a peal of laughter for that slice of humour.

-       That would be peachy, Papi!

-       And to think you are one generation removed from the fruit of my loins!

-       When you tell me to stop making jokes, does that make me the forbidden fruit?

-       This conversation is turning out to be fruitless, Cruz! Besides, when we get to Rome, you will probably claim that your favorite variety of apple is Empire!

-       By the way, Papi, was their warning of not returning home without their shields like not leaving home without American Express? And just look at amazing Athens! How can we believe that Sparta won and Athens lost?

-       That's what Thucydides said! And no more "credit card" jokes. We could lose our visa! Sparta – unlike Athens after the heroics of the Persian Wars – was not bent on empire-building. They kept much more to themselves, and the tourism industry was definitely out of the question – having hordes of visitors like Athens was not on the table. Sparta had a large population of serfs called helots, who tilled the land of Sparta. So while the helots were out working, the Spartans were working out! While the frugal Spartans were working hard, the leisurely Athenians were hardly working! Indeed, although they had no California beaches, the Spartans did benefit from a "serf city"! The Spartan opinion of the Athenians can best be summed up in their reaction to Pindar's statement when he said "Athens is the mainstay of Greece". Sparta's retort was "Greece would likely fall if she relied on a mainstay like Athens"! The Athenians had always snubbed Spartan culture – or perhaps lack of. However, to the Athenian claim that the Spartans were unlearned, the Spartans replied that they were the only people who hadn't learned evil from the Athenians! So then - "see no evil, hear no evil" and "learn no evil"- "do no evil"! I've been reading some Spartan sayings collected by Plutarch. He's a writer whom I hope we'll meet on our journey. His Greek is pretty nondescript, but his works are varied and extremely interesting. I guess in his case, contrary to Marshall McLuhan's theory, Plutarch's "message" was the "medium"! Spartan wisdom – unlike Athenian wisdom, which is universal – was more folksy and home-grown. Here are some examples, Cruz. "Don't ask how many the enemy are, but where they are". That's vaguely similar to "ours is not to reason why, ours is but to do and die". To him who says "I did wrong unwillingly", the Spartan replies "then take your punishment unwillingly". Today we would say "you do the crime, you do the time"! When asked how many Spartans there were, the terse reply was "enough to keep all bad men away"! Not quite sure how that would look on a census report! Likewise, land surveyors could have trouble when, asking questions like "how much property do you own?" and " how much land do the Spartans control?", they received answers like "not more than enough" and "as much as they can reach with a spear"! To the query as to why their swords were so short, the Spartan answer was "so they could be close to the enemy"! The Spartans, men of few words at the best of times, still could believe that speech was the most important thing, and that if you were silent, you were useless. I admit to being a bit perplexed at that notion in Sparta, since their response in war was always brutally brief – with the end of their swords! I think Frontenac must have been reading up on the Spartans when he told the British he would reply to their request with the mouth of his canon!

-       Whatever happened to "silence is golden", Papi?

-       Well, it did very well as a song recorded by The Tremeloes. But the Spartans had no use for gold. They were not into bribes, and acquiring wealth was not in the cards.They firmly believed that keeping little wealth in their treasury would prevent their treasurers from becoming corrupt. Another example of Lacedaemonian logic! This last Spartan gem is very telling. A kind of battle-cry bravado can be summarized in the words "if you are frightened when you are victorious – imagine the losers"! Something about "you should see the other guy"!

-       But Papi, Athens did go on to become great again.

-       Maybe it was their DNA – the "**D**aring **N**ew **A**thenians"! Here's a little secret, Cruz. The "official" end to the Peloponnesian War only came in 1996, when Sparta and Athens signed a symbolic peace treaty – a pledge of friendship - to formally end hostilities between the two cities! That means the Peloponnesian War lasted 2,227 years! It kind of puts The Hundred Years' War to shame! And it's too hot in Greece to call it a "Cold War"!

-       That funny comment deserves a "cold shoulder", Papi!

- And the total of the numbers in 2227 is 13! So maybe old Thucydides was right about *tuche* - chance - good or bad luck! - playing a part in the Peloponnesian War!

Chapter Nine: Cruz Gets A Lesson About Life

-        Right now here in Athens the political situation is a little up in the air – just like Socrates riding in a basket in Aristophanes' play *The Clouds*! Cheer up, Cruz, all is not lost!

-        Tell me then, if it is not lost, where is it to be found?

-        Can it be, Papi? Is this Socrates?

-        Yes, Cruz. If the Socratic irony of his question wasn't a clue, that ugly kisser of his would be a dead giveaway. You know, Socrates, in some parts of the world, and in certain periods of history, your gentle teasing, not to mention your complete mesmerizing, of debating opponents would result in you ending up as the philosopher stoned!

-        I gather you did not use the word "stoned" in the sense of "intoxicated", since that could never happen. True, sticks and stones could hurt me, which is why I would prefer to leave this world by drinking poison. After all, one man's poison can be another man's meat – or substance - for writing an interesting dialogue narrative. My friend Plato pointed that out to me. I have also learned that names can ultimately hurt me!

-        Socrates, you have a demonic sense of humor? Is that the *daimon* that was always getting you in trouble with your fellow-citizens?

- Quite the contrary! The devil never made me do it! Often, while I was mulling things over, the opportunity passed, and so I ended up being prevented from doing things. I took up questioning my fellow Athenians without hesitation, though, knowing that future generations, following my example, would produce wealthy individuals who would develop more sophisticated ways of asking people questions, which they would call surveys. But I myself refused to charge for my services. Not having to declare fees on my tax declaration meant I was not obliged to make big contributions to the Athenian treasury.

- Socrates, can I ask you two questions?

- Certainly, young man, what is your second question?

- But what about my first question?

- Can we not agree that you have indeed already asked two questions?

- Socrates, you may not be corrupting my grandson here, but you certainly are confusing him!

- Well the Oracle at Delphi did mention that I was a wise guy!

- Indeed the very wisest, Socrates, since you never claim to know something you don't actually know.

- I don't know about that! I have often told my wife Xanthippe that I would be home for dinner, when, in fact, I had no clue when I would roll in. I'd like to say she was always understanding. I'd like to say that, but since a philosopher seeks and professes truth, I honestly can't say that. Some writers have said she was a shrew. Would that make me shrewd?

-        Socrates, what can you tell my grandson and me about the gossip in the *agora* that you don't worship the gods of the city, but that you invent new gods? Surely, you have heard of a possible trial for impiety?

-        Why should I reinvent the wheel, when I can catch my accusers arguing in circles! The accusations being bandied about by Anytus, Meletus and Lycon claim that I am corrupting the youth of Athens and that I am inventing new gods. Here is the plain truth of the matter. The youngsters around here are so intrigued by my open and free discussions that they worship me! If that makes me a god, and the sandal fits, well...

-        It seems to me, Socrates, that you are simply a good teacher, who doesn't give homework and written exams. Instead, you assign them projects – to find the meaning of life. This can hardly be considered corrupting the young. Moreover, in your discussions, you get your listeners, in turn, to contribute information to the lesson for the benefit of all. This is called cooperative learning, and these days it's all the rage in education where we come from!

-        Well, the Sophists are upset with me since I don't charge for my lessons, and they are worried they might have to lower their rates. My method – let's call it the Socratic Method for want of a better name – allows for trial and error. But let me tell you this. If

Athens brings me to trial, it's going to lead to one big error!

-       Socrates, what lessons for life can you teach my grandson? His name is Stavros. What is the secret to happiness?

-       So that he doesn't become cross, I'll avoid wordplay.

-       Socrates, "Stavros" means "cross"!

-       Doesn't count – I haven't started yet!

-       Socrates, my grandfather is teaching me Greek because he loves me. But what is this thing called love, and how can I practice it?

-       Well, first of all, when you are really good at it, you won't have to practice!

-       Socrates!

-       Sorry! My dear Stavros, "Love is a many-splendored thing"! You will want to sing about it from the roof-tops! And I've just given you a song title to get you started! But let me ask you, Stavros, do you love your grandfather because he is teaching you Greek, or are you learning Greek because you love your grandfather?

-       Both statements are true, Socrates!

-       Correct answer. Because love, after all, can be both subjective and objective. So, "All you need is love"! There's another song for you! My dear friends, happiness will be attained by following these principles: Love and be loved / Be kind and civil to others – treat them with humility and respect – yes, "R-E-S-P-E-C-T", Stavros, if you're looking for another song title! I hear you singing already – "find out what it means to me" – to me it means "judge not that you be not judged"!/ Stay healthy/ Waste not (and, therefore, "want not", as they say)/ and, finally, Enjoy your freedom – it's not a given! What a coincidence, I will be attending a symposium on Love. And *sumposion* – that's the Greek word, Stavros – means open bar! Pity, you two, it's by invitation only, and there's no BYOB – I can't "bring my own buddies"! But not to worry, my good friend Plato is going to write all about it.

-        Thanks for all your advice, Socrates. How can I repay you?

-        Weren't you listening. I'm not a Sophist – I don't charge a fee! And don't worry about me, I'll be around for a long time – in history books, that is! Just remember, young Stavros, a MEANingful life does not "mean" a life full of MEANness! Say, if you ever meet Aristotle, he'll tell you all about "the Golden Mean"! One more thing – the "meanies" of this world always think their ends are justified. The only ends that are justified are the ones that will put an **end** to the "meanies"!

-        Socrates is no sophist – just a little **sophist**icated for *Hoi Polloi* – you know, the run of the mill rabble. For my part, I'm not sure what he means! Surely, even noble ends or goals won't justify the actions of those meanies!

-        Papi, people always say "the" *hoi polloi.*

-       That's just wrong, Cruz, since *hoi* is the Greek article meaning "the". *Heureka*!

-       Papi, I only had one piece of garlic – no need to say I smell! I'm sure I don't reek!

-       No, no, Cruz. I've been trying to think of a gift for Socrates. And I know the perfect gift. *Heureka* is the Greek verb meaning "I've discovered" - like shouting "success"!

-       You mean like me saying "bingo" or "bazinga"?

-       Bulls-eye! When you're older, you'll find out that all the knowledge you've acquired through discovery will be referred to as "heuristic learning"! I'm going to buy a cock that Socrates can offer to Asclepios, the god of making sick people healthy.

-       But Socrates isn't ill, Papi.

-       Yes, but he has this notion that he'll soon be cured of the disease of life – you know – mortality. The "cock to Asclepios" would be his gift of thanks for being sent off to the eternal, to become "immortal", as it were! I can get some *drachmai* from an ATM machine. That's an "**A**ncient **T**ransactions **M**echanism" – apparently invented ages ago by Daedalus!

-       I've been thinking, Papi. Socrates is a bit like Jesus, isn't he? They are both great teachers who didn't write anything. Of course, Jesus had Matthew, Mark, Luke, and John to write about his teachings. And Jesus' message is a lot like that of Socrates – loving one another. And Socrates claims to love the gods. I think his hesitation about the "gods of the city"

107

may be due to a hunch he has that maybe there is only one true god to be loved – so like Jesus!

-       You impress me more and more, Cruz. I wonder if you have been benefiting from Greek knowledge since we've been in *Hellas*? Note to self: suggest this to travel agencies to make Greece an appealing tourist attraction. Socrates had Plato for preserving his preaching for posterity!

-       Great alliteration, Papi!

-       P's, Cruz!

-       Right back at you with "Papi"! We sure have fun together, don't we?

-       That we do! And be careful with your peace sign. Make sure you only show the two fingers, since waving the full hand is a gesture signifying the casting of the "evil eye"! If you want to greet someone here, wave the back of your hand.

-       Ouch! A grumpy-looking old man flashed two open hands to me this morning! What an eye-opener! Say, Papi, if I were to write a book one day about all the lessons you have taught me, would you help me work on it?

-       "Work", Cruz? It would be a labor of love! Speaking of love, Jesus died for us and Socrates I'm sure will one day choose death rather than betray the message he has for us. I'm reminded of four great Americans who died for the cause of humanity. Like the New Testament and the Socratic Dialogues, a song by Dion is testimony of their sacrifice – "Abraham, Martin and John…and Bobby"! Jesus had his disciples, and if we are lucky we'll get to meet two disciples of Socrates – Plato and Xenophon.

- Abraham Lincoln, Martin Luther King, John and Bobby Kennedy – great Americans – great human beings! There's a soldier over there taking care of his horse.

- That's Xenophon, Cruz. He wrote some accounts about Socrates, but also a history called the *Hellenica*, which continued Thucydides' account of the Peloponnesian War. You've been reading one of his books – the *Anabasis*. You like it because the Greek isn't too difficult. Maybe you can get him to autograph a copy for you.

- Hello you two – new in town?

- My grandson and I have been here for a few weeks.We got to talk to Socrates a little while back, and we know you're an admirer of his.

- It seems that you are not aware that Socrates was recently put on trial, found guilty and executed. I'm here for the funeral. Funny, he already had a cock to offer to Asclepios. Sad story – I blame the kangaroo court. Oh, don't be puzzled – we don't import animals from Australia! Since we haven't even heard of that place, that would be impossible! I'm just saying the majority - a small one at that! – of the 501 jurors declared Socrates guilty by "jumping" to conclusions. Apparently it was a sad scene indeed at the execution. The jailer applied hemlock, and Crito applied heimlich – you know the maneuver to save a choking victim. But Socrates wasn't choking – he was just choked up on seeing the loyalty of his friends! He did, however, tell Crito to get a grip. He meant, of course, for him to chill out – taking a chill pill was out of the question – not for him to grab Socrates by the waist!

-       Well, Xenophon, Socrates kind of predicted his peculiar predicament, from which he would perhaps perish.

-       Your particular penchant for p's is probably praiseworthy – one over which I could not possibly pass!

-       Papi, it seems alliteration is more contagious than the plague – which is understandable, I guess, since "plague" begins with a "p"!

-       And ends with an "e"! Back to my *Anabasis*. Get it - the prefix *ana-* means "back"! But full disclosure – *ana-* more often means "up" or "inland". So my book – the way we Greeks look at accounts, really seven books! – so impressive, isn't it – tells the story of my march up-country with ten thousand mercenaries, after our boss, Cyrus the Great, was killed. We made it back to the Black Sea. Because we knew that the sea meant being with Greeks again, we were elated, and cried out *thalatta, thalatta* – "the sea". Those not using the Attic dialect actually yelled *thalassa*. But that's all water under the bridge!

-       Why do men become "mercynaries", Xenophon? They don't seem to show much "mercy"!

-       That's merCENary, young fella! It's from a Latin word - *merces* – which means "pay". Don't confuse it with the word *merx*, which means "merchandise". There is a connection, though, since you always have to pay for merchandise. I know it may sound strange, but a certain Roman god didn't always pay for goods, even though he was the god of merchants and commerce. You see, he was also the god of thieves! With mercenaries, you don't only get the "goods" – you also get the "bads". Say, maybe your grandfather here can teach you Latin. He seems like he could be a polyglot – especially since that word starts with "p"! We mercenaries fight not only for money, but also for adventure or for a cause – or even just to get out of the house!

-        Thanks for the compliment, Xenophon! I don't like to brag, but I've taught Stavros here that the prefix *poly-* means "much" or "many". So if we combine that prefix with the word "elocution", meaning "discourse", a speech that is too long would be "word poll-ution"!

-        Are you trying to give me a hint? But just let me say, I have been called philosopher, soldier, writer, and historian. The truth is, I've been trying to figure out what I really am! I want to apply the advice that Socrates received from the Oracle and passed on to me – "Know thyself"!

-        Well, it has been nice knowing you, Xenophon – all of the different "you-s"! But we are off to meet Plato.

-        Take care! As you know, I have written a treatise on horse-breeding. I know you are expecting me to say "never look a gift horse in the mouth". But never say never! "Why?" you may ask. Two words – "Trojan Horse"! Well, see you around.

-        Not if we see him first – right, Papi?

-       Cruz, xenophobia is fear of or hatred towards strangers, but not hatred of Xenophon! – from the Greek words for stranger and fear – *xenos* and *phobos*. But I wouldn't want you to be thought of as a xenophobe merely because you want to avoid the strange Xenophon – even if his name literally means "speaking like a foreigner"! Yes, *phone* is "voice" – so hold the phone! There's Plato standing on the steps of his Academy. Aren't you lucky that your school is called an academy, Cruz? And don't you feel privileged to be able to attend school, since that word comes from the Greek *schole*, which meant "free time – leisure". Ungrateful students "kill time" in school, whereas the unfortunate child laborers have to work it to death!

-       Hello, you two. I recognize you. You were recently hanging out with Socrates before he died. We had tried to get him to escape from jail, but he protested that "Prison Break" didn't fit the times, and chose to drink the poison hemlock. Socrates no doubt appreciated the irony – his wife had always said that the drink would eventually kill him!

-       Greetings, Plato! We admire your Corpus!

-       I hope that's my body of writings you are talking about, and not my – you know – body! You, like so many others, have probably read my works in translation. Was it the Sumerian or Egyptian translation?

-       It was a struggle, but we read them in the original.

-       The Greek too hard to grasp?

\-   No - the meaning! Actually I'm a purist when it comes to language.

\-   So you don't swear. Neither do I – except by the gods!

\-   Not "pure", Plato, purist! When it comes to reading the "Great Books" – and a couple of yours are in that collection – I try to read them in their original language. That is one reason I am teaching my grandson Greek and Latin. I myself am fortunate in being able to read Dante in Italian, Molière in French, Cervantes in Spanish, Seferis in Modern Greek , and I've read *Steppenwolf* in German.

\-   Papi, I've heard you listening to Steppenwolf in English! Was it an audio-book?

\-   Cruz, like one of their songs, I sometimes think you were "Born to be Wild"! Like another one of their songs, let's just enjoy this "Magic Carpet Ride" in ancient Greece! That group is o-Kay – you remember the name of their lead singer? But I am referring to the novel written by Hermann Hesse. In that novel, a character says "He avoided him like the healthy avoid the sick"!

\-   Maybe I should be spending less time with you, Papi, because of your "sick" jokes!

\-   Fortunately, Cruz, you haven't turned into a "Wild Thing" described in the song by The Troggs! Nor are you the "Wild One" in Bobby Rydell's song!

\-   Rydell? Isn't that a school in Greece? Maybe in "sandy" Pylos?

-        No, no, Cruz! You're thinking of Rydell High in the movie *Grease*! Of course, Plato, translations can be useful, since they will "carry across" the story from one language to the other. That's what the Latin verb *transferre* means. Greeks will say *metapherein*, describing the process as a "metaphor", producing, as it were, a sort of comparison. Regrettably, I cannot read the novels of Dostoïevski in the original. For this "Crime" my "Punishment" is finding myself rushin' through them, and thereby looking like an "Idiot"!

-        Well, I understand you travelled through the land of myth, before arriving here in modern-day Greece. If you have been reading my books, you obviously enjoy Classics! I am known for some great myths of my own. Can you name one, young man?

-        Er...

-        That is correct! I thought you didn't know, and were about to cave in! Besides the myth of Er, I talk about an enchanting land of mystery called Atlantis. You may have heard of a cataclysmic tidal wave – a veritable *tsunami* - that destroyed an island, and swept its inhabitants into the sea.

-        Papi, is he referring to those people who arrived at Crete, while we were there with Theseus? They said they were from the island of Thera, and could never go back there, because the island's name would be changed to Santorini! Moreover, if they returned to their homeland, future generations would be deprived of all the books, films and television shows based on the incredible legend of the underwater kingdom of Atlantis.

-       Plato believes what he wants to believe, Cruz, but also rejects what many other people want to believe. Tell me, Plato, do you think you will find the ideal ruler described in the *Republic*?

-       I thought I had, while working with Dionysios in Syracuse. Before you get a swelled head, Dionysios, I don't mean you – even if you have been to Syracuse, New York! Besides, you're too much philosopher, not enough king.

-       Papi, do you think we should tell Plato about that Canadian singing group, The Philosopher-Kings?

-       Did you just mention Canadians? Aren't they the ones who took land away from the natives? Is that why they sing "our home AND native land" in their national song? Speaking of song, I hope future generations will acknowledge that I am the first male feminist. After all, I called Sappho the "tenth Muse"! I know - Hesiod had placed nine female Muses on Mt. Helikon – but who's counting? I do think it marvellous – "too marvellous for words" – and that's saying something – coming from me! – that in the distant future, a planet will be named after me!

-       You're thinking of Pluto, Plato! The good news is that Pluto is no longer considered the "ninth" planet from the sun, but now is a minor "dwarf planet". So you won't be around to suffer the embarrassment of being demoted. But you are deeply interested in government and law-making. You have even written a book called the *Laws*. I guess we can place you in the company of such great lawgivers as Solon and Draco in Athens and Lycurgus in Sparta, and Hammurabi in Mesopotamia.

\-   Yes, one might say the Great King's *Code of Law* cleared things up for the people living in a land that was up until then rather "Messy-potamia"! I'm thinking "Muddy Waters" after *potamos*, the Greek word for "river". But that just conjures up a gentle soul singing what he calls "the blues". And let me tell you how excited Xenophon was when he read about a so-called "river-horse" in Herodotus, which I will call a hippopotamus. The Greek word for "horse" is *hippos*, which brings to mind a little joke. What oath does a horse-doctor take? The HIPPOcratic oath! I guess when it comes to horse jokes, I'm hip! That's because when I get together with Xenophon, we always start horsing around! We do so much gleeful yelling, we end up being too hoarse to talk. Athens has seen a steady move towards democracy, with some bumps along the way, sometimes 400, sometimes 30. Oh, you call those bumps oligarchs. Occasionally, we've seen one big bump – yes, you call him a tyrant. As for Sparta, in that city laws are plain harsh – too DRACOnian for my liking! Not that I am SOLD ON all Athenian laws, but the helots claim "our Spartiate masters - LIKE…SCOURGE US! Well, it is what it is! Nevertheless, it is extremely important that laws be written down. In this way, laws can be known – and so people can break them. How many times have we heard in reply to "it's an unwritten law" – "I didn't know"? When people break the law, we can punish them – it's a win-win situation!

-        Plato, you just repeated the names of the lawgivers I mentioned, but with respect to government and the law, how do you stand?

-        On my, legs – like everyone else!

-        No, I mean how do you feel?

-        With my hands – like…

-        I can't stand this, Cruz! Plato, I just want to know how you see laws developing in the future. On second thought, don't answer – with your eyes, right?

-        Oh, I get where you're going with your question! The easy answer is the notwithstanding clause. Case closed! Of course, only outstanding governments will be able to pull it off! But FYI - my student Aristotle and his cronies are tracing the laws and constitutions of the Greek city-states on a large chart. He's thinking of giving this chart a Latin name, maybe like *Magna Carta*, since many of his works will be translated into Latin anyways.

-        You seem very preoccupied with the just society, Plato.

-        Yes – "just in time", "just in case", "just a gigolo" – shall I go on? I don't know if I am "just inside" or "just outside" your expectations, Dionysios.

-        I'm thinking more about justice among the different classes. In your hierarchical society, citizens are not all equal.

-        Indeed they are! But some citizens are more equal than others!

\-   Why do we have slavery, Plato?

\-   So that others may learn to appreciate freedom!

\-   Again, speaking about future generations, people will be concerned about social justice.

\-   Just like the Jesuits, right Papi?

\-   Yes, Cruz. As a matter of fact, the thought just occurred to me that S.J. – Society of Jesus – could just as well stand for "Social Justice"! Their founder, Ignatius of Loyola, believed very much in the importance of feelings, which could help us to fully understand the plight of the socially-downtrodden, and therefore seek to correct the injustice in this world. You might say, then, that the Jesuits have a "feel" for justice. Naturally, St. Ignatius would have appreciated "Feelings", a song by Albert Morris! I suppose the best way to be one with your feelings is to follow the suggestion of The Five Keys, when they sing "Close Your Eyes"! Plato, I took great pleasure in reading your *Symposium.* Of course, following your notice of mature subject matter, parental discretion is advised, my grandson was not permitted to read it. Your account of Eros, the child of Aphrodite, was quite erotic, even if a little erratic! I suppose you are aware that love will be the most popular theme in books, plays, films, etc. for all time. In fact, there will be a book and movie called *Love Story*. But it won't play out like your "story" about love.

\-   Dionysios, you often speak like a man ahead of his time! Yes,we can always count on three things – love, death and taxes! I do know that beautiful instrumental melody called "Love's Theme". Music is mathematically based, and since no one can enter my Academy without a knowledge of mathematics, he can also expect to be part of our school choir or orchestra. I'll have you know that I am not only interested in the things of the mind – I am quite fond of all aspects of culture. Just as Socrates was featured on stage as a character in a play by Aristophanes, I should very much like that comic playwright to portray my life on stage. No fancy or foreboding title would be necessary – it could simply be called "Play-to"!

- In truth, it is more a case of the present times being "ahead of me"! I've got to hand it to you, Plato. At times, I didn't know if you were pulling my leg, or actually sticking your neck out with your socio-political theories. Your body of knowledge has obviously given you a head start in political science. You cheerfully accepted me sticking my nose in your business, even leaving me with quite the belly-laughs! You obviously have your ear to the ground with respect to the life of the soul, so I will keep my eyes open for future writings on the subject. I'll always buy the book of someone who doesn't always go by the book!

- Right on, and I'll continue to write on! Lest you think you deftly gave me a biology lesson with your references to the human body, wait until you meet Aristotle.

- I suspect we will come across him in our travels. So long, Plato!

- You gotta love Plato, eh Papi!

- Yes, Cruz, I guess we'll call it Platonic love!

\-   Right now we're going to move along in time by using this remote and the fast forward button. I picked it up in one of the shops in the *agora*. It was invented back in the day by Daedalus. He had wanted to use it with the television set he invented.

\-   The Ancient Greeks watched television?

\-   Of course not – his invention didn't work, since electricity hadn't been discovered yet! Just to let you know, the years we skipped saw the rise of the city of Thebes. Thanks to the skill of two military commanders – Epaminondas and Pelopidas – Greece witnessed the Theban hegemony for about a dozen years. A *hegemon* was a leader in Ancient Greece. And if I hedge my bets correctly, we will be meeting other leaders in the Greek world.

Chapter Ten: Cruz Meets a Democratic Demagogue

- Papi, I'm enjoying our walk along the sea coast! Hey, there's a man picking up pebbles along the seashore, and he's stuffing them into his mouth! I've heard of rock candy – but this is too much! Why is he shouting? Didn't his mother teach him not to talk with his mouth full?

- According to the little guide-book they gave us at the Science Museum when we entered the time capsule, this scenario fits an anecdote about Demosthenes, the greatest orator in Greek history. He developed his powerful voice by shouting above the noise of the crashing waves, all the while keeping his mouth full of pebbles. He was determined to be able to capture the attention of a large audience – even with many of them speaking at the same time – think waves, Cruz – or...

- Die trying, Papi?

- Well, that, or be struck down with asphasia!

- This whole scene reminds me of a place I've seen on TV. Now I remember – the golf course at Pebble Beach! I wonder if Demosthenes will have as much success as Tiger Woods? But I'll bet he can whistle with soda crackers in his mouth!

- All I know is that Demosthenes is a member of the PGA – the **P**olitical **G**reeks **A**ssociation. He was an Athenian statesman, and believed it was his duty to make his fellow-citizens aware of any dangerous enemies who might threaten their liberty. His talent for persuasive speaking made him what was called a demagogue. Literally, from the words *demos* – "the people" – and *agein* –" to lead", he was a "leader of the people". Many demagogues in ancient Athens were bad men, bent on capturing the favor of the crowd through their rabble-rousing in order to pursue evil policies and plans. However, the demagogue who brought about the greatest destruction - indeed the greatest crime against humanity - was a certain Führer, who caused a furor in his own country, and unleashed a murderous fury on all of Europe. Not all rats were furry creatures! But Demosthenes believed in fighting for democracy – with words, of course – he would leave the *mano a mano* to soldiers. "Democracy" – there's that word *demos* again – means "power to the people", this time combined with *kratos* – "strength or power". Even his name begins with *demos* – third time lucky - or not! The second part of Demosthenes' name - from *sthenos* - means "strength, might, prowess". By this reckoning, Demosthenes would be the "strength" of Athens. Unfortunately for Demosthenes – and ultimately for Athens – he came up against a shrewd and powerful king – Philip of Macedon. At times, Demosthenes probably felt like referring to him as Philip the Mastodon! The Athenian statesman gave it his best shot – but he was no Herakles!

-       Is my voice carrying enough? All that practice in front of the mirror has helped my stammering at last. How do I look? Presentation is everything! Now that the hair I shaved off has grown back in, I can go before the assembly and rally the Athenians against Philip. I've prepared three speeches against him – the *First, Second*, and *Third Philippics*. I know, not so clever as titles, but the key word is "Philippics"!

- Notice, Cruz, how demonstrative Demosthenes is whenever he mentions Philip's name. Maybe he's not a horse-lover like Philip. Of course, Philip's name means "lover of horses" – from the Greek words for "to love" and "horse" – *philein* and *hippos*. But how did you become such a great orator – could you give us a demonstration, Demosthenes?

- You'll get a "demo" only if you pay me. But you will only have to pay half-price since a "demo" is only "half" a "Demosthenes". I wonder why no historian mentions my sense of humor? You see, it's like this. I've made my living by writing speeches as a *logographos.* That word is composed of *logos* - "word, speech" and *graphein* –"to write". That Greek word might be too complicated for the young boy here, so let's just say I'm a professional logographer. I also deliver speeches in court for clients who aren't capable of giving speeches themselves. Not everybody has my talent!

- I have read that you had access to quite a few talents, Demosthenes. You were accused of taking bribes. Some orators like Aeschines were providing demos of their own – a demolition, that is, of your reputation!

- Trumped up charges! I'm a democrat, so nothing trumps me! My patriotism will eventually prevail over all this fake news. I shall not be robbed of victory. There is definitely a conspiracy against me. I went into exile, but as I had promised – I returned!

-       So your successful career as a lawyer led to a position in politics. You do know that when slightly mispronounced, "lawyer" sounds like "liar"? And that "politics" is sometimes referred to as "po-**lie**-tics"?

-       To tell you the truth, I have never heard that. I am too pol-ite to say more!

-       You had to face many attacks in the law-courts, Demosthenes. Your name is a little complicated. Can my grandson here call you "Dem" for short?

-       All right – but not for long. I am up for a big prize, and I have a reputation to maintain.

-       What prize is that, Dem?

-       Ctesiphon is proposing a golden crown to be awarded to me for my services to Athens. But Aeschines is planning to prosecute Ctesiphon. So I will have to defend Ctesiphon in order to defend my reputation and my policies.

-       Damn, Dem! How do you think you'll do?

-       My speech – *Peri Tou Stephanou* – has to win – it represents my whole life's work!

-       Who is Stephen?

-       My dear lad – *stephanos* is the Greek word for "garland" or "crown". My speech will probably go down in the history books – at least in the English ones! – as "On the Crown".

-       Cruz, Demosthenes had success as a speaker the same way you can be a successful golfer - by applying my three principles.

-       I know, Papi – practice, practice, practice!

-       But your golf swing has to look good. What did Demosthenes tell you were the three most important elements in oratory?

-       Delivery, delivery, delivery! The last time I heard that was the interview we watched with a major league baseball pitcher!

-       Demosthenes, some of your detractors are saying that there has been some hanky panky going on with young boys who have stayed from time to time at your home - and we are not talking here about that innocent song - "(My Baby Does the) Hanky Panky" by Tommy James and the Shondells!

-       They were there strictly for tutorials. That's my story – and I'm sticking with it. Besides, one day you will be able to ask the great historian, George Grote, and he'll back me up! Right now, I have to prepare for some meetings with Philip – but first, I have some back-room politics to take care of with Thebes, Sparta and Corinth.

-       Good luck, Demo…sthenes! Papi, do you think he will win his case against Aeschines?

-       Cruz, I have read Aeschines 'speech – *Kata Ctesiphonten* – "Against Ctesiphon". It's interesting how *kata*, meaning "down" – remember those "katachthonic" gods, and our *katabasis* – our descent – into the underworld? – So I guess, "down with"

Ctesiphon! The Latin title is *Contra Ctesiphontem.* Aeschines presents a pretty good legal case on technical grounds, but I have a hunch Demosthenes will win. Maybe George Gote tells us why in his monumental nineteenth-century *History of Greece,* which, by coincidence, ends with the time of Alexander the Great, just like our journey into Ancient Greece!

-        By George, that is a curious coincidence, Papi!

-        What do you say we go on up to Macedonia and check out Philip for ourselves?

***

-        Papi, there's a soldier lying drunk over there. He looks like he's having a bad hair day – and he's missing an eye! Do all one-eyed creatures spend their time drinking wine?

-        That, my dear Cruz, is Philip II of Macedon. And although he looks like he couldn't make it from one chair to another – his son actually made that observation – he's planning to make it to Asia to lead his army against the Persian Empire. He has built up a professional army featuring the Macedonian phalanx, which has become a veritable weapon of mass destruction.

-        Your royal highness, my grandson and I would like to know if you are planning to over-run all of Greece?

-        Not RUN over, but RIDE over, dear man! We Macedonians love horses. In fact, my son Alexander is the best horse-whisperer around – he has to be, if he's going to name his horse Bucephalus!

-       But won't the Greeks mount a resistance against you?

-       Not at all - my dipsy-doodle diplomacy will have them eating out of my hand! Besides, the Greeks love me! Anyhow, they don't have enough horses to MOUNT much of anything! Get it?

-       Yes, congrats on your "Philipian funnies"! But what about Demosthenes?

-       What about him? He's merely the exception that proves the rule! He's royalty too – a royal pain! The Greeks would rather have me rule as head of a religious council - they're really into religion, you know – than rule them with an iron hand! Would you like to feel my iron hand, young man – of course I'm talking about my iron sword! This Amphictyonic Council the Greeks have formed will suit my purposes just fine!

-       Philip, you are a polygamist, and have many wives.

-       I might have felt insulted if I knew what "poli-game-ist" meant, but, yes, I have seven wives, and I don't share them with any brothers!

-       I think he's referring to the film *Seven Brides for Seven Brothers*, Cruz. And he probably got some of his wives in the rough and boorish ways that the "Brothers" did.

-       I married those women to form alliances with neighboring kingdoms. In our part of the world, you have to be clever at the Game of Thrones! Besides, a wedding is a good excuse to get drunk!

-        You must have a special relationship with the mother of your son Alexander?

-        Olympias? No special beauty! She's certainly no Angelina Jolie! I wouldn't trust her as far as I could throw her! And believe me, I have thrown her a few times! It always makes Alexander mad! That's him – Alexander, the great mother's boy! Anyways, I'm going to divorce her and marry Cleopatra – no not THE Cleopatra. I know that name can only mean trouble. I suspect people will expect her to produce a son who will be a more legitimate successor to the Macedonian throne. Alexander is sure to be cheesed off, and make a big stink, although I suppose that depends on the cheese – no matter how you cut it!

-        But, Philip, how will the conflict end with some of those Greek states – I'm thinking of Athens and Thebes among others ?

-        If you're a betting man, here's some inside information. It's all going to come down to a battle at Chaeronea in Boiotia. I can reserve spectator spots for you, if you'd like. You'd be sitting near this big lion statue, and you are welcome to take selfies!

-        Have you noticed, Papi? There's always something going on in Boiotia!

-        And Thebes is usually at the center of the action!

***

-       It's a sad day for Greece. It was all **Hell - as** Philip had predicted!

-       It was neat seeing Alexander leading the Macedonian cavalry as the Theban Sacred Band all perished, fighting heroically to the last man! They reminded me of Leonidas and the Spartans at Thermopylae.

-       But unlike that battle, Cruz, this one didn't save liberty, but rather marked the end of the independent Greek states.You have just witnessed a turning point in Greek history! You've got a demoralized Demosthenes licking his wounds – oh, not literally – he took off during the battle! And you have the rising star of Alexander. He too will conquer by his sword – a real "man of steel" – a "superman" of sorts! And yes, you have Philip organizing a big booze-up to celebrate his victory! Same old, same old…

-       Papi, there's a big commotion, and – I can't believe it – Philip has just been assassinated! The guards seem to have killed a suspect.

-       I had heard some talk about a lover's tiff in Philip's inner circle, involving four people.

-       Is that what they call a love triangle, Papi?

-       No, Cruz, a triangle involves THREE people! But since you haven't started learning geometry yet, I'll just apply the "let it slide" rule.

-       Papi, some pro-Macedonian Athenians have been telling Alexander that the Greek states, encouraged by Philip's death, are planning a revolt against Macedon. It's the old story of "when the cat's away, the mice will play"! But the lion statue at Chaeronea should remind them that they are not dealing with any old cat! They will be facing a young tiger and nobody masters this tiger!

- Are you thinking about golf tournaments again, Cruz? The word on the street is that Demosthenes has organized a coalition against the new King, referring to Alexander as "boy" and "*margites*" – meaning "fool". Well – more fool him!

***

- It's official, Papi. Alexander completely defeated the Greek states. Sadly, he destroyed the city of Thebes!

- Except for Pindar's house. They say it was out of respect for the poet, since he had praised one of Alexander's ancestors – also named Alexander. But probably not his great-grandfather, because that would be one "Alexander the Great" too many! But Alexander also spared Athens, and I rather think that he wanted to show himself a champion of Greek culture, and even spread it to eastern empires, since he had firmly decided to take up the expedition that his father had planned against Persia. Athens still symbolized – and was *de facto* – Greek culture. Alexander could not spread Greek culture if there was no longer any Greek culture to spread – so Athens remained relatively unscathed.

- What happened to Demosthenes, Papi?

-       Well, Cruz, since he couldn't beat Alexander, and he didn't want to join him, the great orator committed suicide.

-       Do you think we could meet the great Alexander, Papi?

-       That's Alexander the Great, and yes, we'll be able to join his expedition as secretaries to his secretary's secretary.

Chapter Eleven: In Alexander's Footsteps...Sort Of

-       So, Papi, we get to write down notes for the historical records of Alexander's exploits!

-       No, Cruz. We have been hired to carry the scrolls that the historians write their notes on. The head honcho is Callisthenes, the official historian for the expedition to the East. As far as keeping track of what is done, said, discussed, dismissed, argued, attempted, accomplished – I could go on, but I think you get my drift - well Mr. C is the Big Kahuna! Others who are writing accounts of Alexander's activities – his battles and so forth - are generals, admirals, and engineers like Ptolemy, Nearchus and Onesicritus. Since they have those other important functions, they have less time to collect anecdotes or keep extensive historical records. When I was a graduate student many, many moons ago, I read a Latin account of Alexander's campaigns called the *Histories of Alexander the Great – Historiae Magni Alexandri*. It was written by Quintus Curtius Rufus in the first century CE. We might be able to talk to Aristobulus, since he is only a junior officer, and is less likely to stick his nose in the air when we stroll by – unless of course we've been eating those beans that Pythagoras didn't like. And no, Cruz, not like the America song "BEEN through the desert... on a horse with no name"!

-       But Papi, I picked up one of the pairs of footwear that Alexander discarded. They are a little big for me, but if I walk a mile in his sandals, that's got to count for something! I'll be able to tell my friends I followed in Alexander's footsteps! I'll have a tiny grasp of what he's going through!

-       Those are mighty big shoes to fill! Alexander will be a pretty hard act to follow, especially since he's on horseback, and we're on foot!

-       Papi, who is that over there writing something on a card? And there is a drawing on the card. Could it be a postcard?

-       Possibly - Alexander had use of a postal relay service. It wasn't exactly the Pony Express, but it involved horses.

-       Isn't that dangerous, Papi? Out here they shoot horses, don't they?

-       Only those who have seen that movie! A real sad ending – the guy shoots his girl-friend to put her out of her misery, because, as he claims - "they shoot horses to put them out of their misery"! The movie did feature, though, a dance marathon, which I think your Manie and I could have won back in the day! Nowadays, I move one step at a time, like the Ice Man, Jerry Butler! Of course I never danced with the grace of Fred Astaire. Whenever I tried, people would just give me a stare or look at me with a funny face! But Astaire danced so gracefully in the movie *Funny Face*. The scene where he danced with an umbrella was something else! His golf swing with the umbrella was smoother than my swing with a real golf club. It seems like great dancers love to dance with umbrellas – like Gene Kelly in *Singing in the Rain*. I guess if you can't escape a sudden rainstorm you might as well dance! Another great dancer, Donald O'Connor, also starred in that film. His number, "Make 'Em Laugh", is also good advice when life throws you a curve-ball – unless, of course, you happen to be a .300 hitter in the Major Leagues! But that young man doesn't look much older than you, Cruz. Why don't you ask him what he's up to.

-        Writing to anyone special?

-        Why yes, as it happens. I'm writing to my teacher. I've taken time off from school to join Alexander's war of revenge against the Persians, and my teacher wants me to keep him posted. I have been hired to do menial tasks and clean up Alexander's tent after his banquets – and believe me that's a lot of work!

-        I hear you! My name is Stavros. My grandfather and I used to clean Achilles' tent.

-        Achilles – the Greek hero who inspired Alexander? I thought he was only a legend we could read about in Homer.

-        My grandson and I had connections to travel into the world of Homer, and join the Greeks at Troy, which, come to think of it, was the last panhellenic expedition into Asia Minor. True, this campaign is more than a "Minor" undertaking. However, Xenophon has also inspired Alexander with his *Anabasis* and his *Cyropaedia*, which outlined the military and political methods used by Cyrus the Great to conquer the Neo-Babylonian Empire. But why do you say this is a war of revenge? Isn't Alexander's goal to spread Greek culture to the East, and perhaps even merge eastern and western civilizations politically and culturally into a World State?

- My teacher taught us that barbarians were inferior. The Persians had invaded Greece in the past, and now it was pay-back time! He wants me to chronicle a blow-by-blow account of Alexander sticking it to the Persians.

- Allow me to jump in, boys. I don't want to tarnish your teacher's teachings, but it was the Alexander scholar W.W.Tarn who attributed such lofty ideals to Alexander.

- Darn that Tarn! My teacher convinced Alexander to keep a copy of the *Iliad* under his pillow, and thereby be inspired to lead the Greeks to victory over the Persians, just like Achilles had led the Greeks to victory over the Trojans. Now the Macedonians would be considered full-fledged Greeks. My teacher doesn't like non-Greek speaking foreigners, and predicted that in a distant time in the future Macedonia would again cause trouble for Greece.

- By the way, we didn't catch your name. And just who is your teacher?

- My name is Craptippus - but please don't call me "Crap" for short, like my fellow- students do when they want to tease me. Once, when my teacher had a dead bull brought into the science lab so that we could examine its anatomy, since he did extensive studies on animals, the student who bullied me the most yelled out in my direction "that's a lotta bull, Crap"! The other faculty members call my teacher "The

Philosopher", but I refer to him as "The Master". Some of the other students speak of him as " The Man Who Knows Everything".

- 		Cruz, that is, Stavros, the boy here is talking about Aristotle, the greatest philosopher in antiquity, and truly a "know-it-all" in a good sense. By the way, is your name pronounced Cr**A**ptippus, or Crapt**I**ppus?

- 		I've heard both. Actually, my uncle Theophrastus who got me into the school, since he'll probably take over from Aristotle one day, says that if I ever become a philosopher or a real historian, I should change my name to Cratippus. But I think if I did write a history on some *papyri*, I'd be too afraid of anyone reading them and probably bury them somewhere like at Oxyrhynchus in Egypt. That name is so hard to say and spell, it is unlikely that they would be found.

- 		Stranger things have happened! Gosh, Aristotle and Theophrastus – what great thinkers! Wouldn't you like to be a great stinker – I mean thinker – Crap…tippus? Sorry, I was still thinking about which syllable to stress.

- 		Never mind a syllable. Your slips of the tongue are stressing all of me! Some students think I'm just a "plant" to keep tabs on them. I mean, my uncle wrote a history of plants for our botany studies, but me a spy – that's a lot of… well I won't say the word, but I know you're both thinking it! I don't even like plants, and I have never bought any!

- 		Stavros, Craptippus here is evidently a student at the Lyceum, founded by Aristotle. It is known as the Peripatetic School because the Greek word for "walking around" is *peripatein,* and that's what he did when he lectured. I guess he didn't want to be accused of sitting down on the job! Yet, in the future, most jobs will require people to be sitting – and in front of a screen at that! Boys, when I was a professor, I was a peripatetic.

- You were a great philosopher?

- No – I walked around a lot! But Craptippus, I guess you know why Aristotle has such a great interest in Alexander's success. Did he ever talk to his students about the years he tutored Alexander? He had spent his early years in Macedonia since his father was a court physician. In later years he studied in Athens.

- Our teacher mentioned that he was well treated by the King, because Philip had read an account in Herodotus of a king who had the intention of killing a magician, because he didn't believe in magic. He wanted to test the knowledge of the magician by asking him when he - the magician –would die. The magician was aware of the king's plans, and said he would die three days before the king. Naturally, the king did everything in his power to ensure a long and comfortable life for the magician! Aristotle would tell us how keen a student Alexander was and of how the young Prince was always asking questions. Because of this, the proud mentor affectionately referred to his protégé as his "Little Prince", telling him he would one day reach the stars, and maybe even an asteroid!

- What do you know! My little guide-book says that Aristotle will die a year after Alexander, but will have fled Athens when Alexander died in order to prevent Athens from sinning twice against philosophy. That's a reference to the death of Socrates.

- Gee Papi, you're my tutor and you call me your "little Prince", or, when you talk to me in French, *"le petit prince"*! But why is philosophy so important? And what exactly is it?

- A twelve-year-old might have a hard time grasping the concept, but since we've been in ancient Greece, you have been demonstrating the maturity of a twenty-year-old! Well here goes! A philosopher is a "lover of wisdom". Careful – that's not the same as a "wise guy"! If that were the case, you'd be up there with Socrates, Plato and Aristotle – the "Big Three"! You remember when I told you about The Big Three – Larry Robinson, Guy Lapointe and Serge Savard – those great defencemen for the Montreal Canadiens? Well, the Philosophers are still around! The word philosophy comes from the Greek words *philein* - "to love" - and *sophia* – "wisdom". Basically, philosophers are interested in finding the meaning of life, and how to live life. This pursuit is so important that at the turn of the millenium UNESCO declared that the third Thursday of November would be celebrated as World Philosophy Day! People who want to use a witty quote, and don't know who uttered the witticism, usually end up saying "in the words of The Philosopher"! When your grandfather was studying at university, he was known as "The Latin Student". It just meant I was really into Latin – oh, and I guess I was at the top of my game! Not every philosopher "knows everything" or even the "secret to life", as perhaps Socrates and Aristotle did. However, realizing you don't know everything or that, in fact, you don't know anything, can be considered a philosophical approach to life. And how often do we hear of people, after a serious setback, attempting to deal with the situation "philosophically"? On the other hand, too much knowledge can possibly be a dangerous thing. An evil person who knows that bombs can destroy, and knows how to make bombs, can become a threat to humanity! The great film director, Alfred Hitchcock, made two versions of the same film to prove this point – both called *The Man Who Knew Too Much*.

-        There's my grandfather for you, Craptippus! Ask him a question, and he'll write a book! But what did you learn from Aristotle?

-        You mean what didn't I learn! He told us how to be happy, how it really comes down to the individual. He calls happiness *eudaimonia* – literally, "possessed by a good spirit". I guess it's what your grandfather meant when he said he was "in good spirits". The individual can achieve happiness by practicing personal excellence, which he calls *arete*. Aristotle investigated the nature of science in so many domains – medicine, botany, biology, physics, and something he wrote after his work on physics, called "after physics" – *Metaphysics*. Physics, of course, just means "natural things". The Greek word for nature is *physis*. He also wrote on the subjects of political science and psychology. In fact he invented that word by combining *psyche* – the "soul" – or perhaps more exactly – the "mind", and *logos* – the "study of something". He wrote on rhetoric and also on literary criticism in a work called the *Poetics*. One of his major principles was The Golden Mean. The basic idea was to avoid extremes. The Delphic Oracle had advised against excess, but Aristotle's "rule for life" looked as well at the opposite extreme. He explained The Golden Mean rule with this example - if a person is a spendthrift, he should try being a scrooge. He will most likely end up being somewhere in the middle – a modest spender. Maybe we could call him an informed consumer.

-        Aristotle also expounded on moral philosophy, boys. He wrote the *Nichomachean Ethics*, in honor of his son – or perhaps his father, since they shared the same name. And speaking of ethics, I can humbly say that I maintained a laudable work ethic that started when I was in high school, holding down two jobs in the summer. Cruz, do you remember your neighbour Billy, who got fired while working part-time?

-        Why did he get fired, Papi?

-        It was a full-time job!

-        Wouldn't working all the time make you boring, Papi?

-        Better dull than idle! All work – no play! But no work – no pay! I had a German professor who insisted on working seven days a week in order to be successful. He referred to this principle as Kohl's Law. But we called our professor the "Sour Kraut"!

-        I really enjoyed my time at the Lyceum. Do you two know that the word comes either from *lukos*, meaning "wolf", or *luke*, meaning "light". Both words

140

are connected with Apollo – the "wolf-slayer" and the "light-giver"!

-        Makes sense, doesn't it – the god of knowledge bringing the light of knowledge to students, and protecting them from the "big bad wolf", while they wolf down the food of knowledge! Stavros, the word for high school in France is *lycée*, after the Lyceum.

-        Like that song you sometimes sing, grandfather, "*champs et lycée*"?

-        No, the song is " *Les Champs Élysées*", recorded by the French singer Joe Dassin. Actually, he was the son of film director Jules Dassin, and was born in the United States. He moved to France with his parents, but returned to the U.S., and earned two degrees at the University of Michigan.The song was a French version of "Waterloo Road", named for a backwater street in London. The English song was never a commercial or popular success like the dainty ditty "Penny Lane" recorded by the Beatles. Nor was the street the elegant thoroughfare that was the *Avenue des Champs Élysées* in Paris. The song came out in 1968, and became the anthem of the massive protest movement known as *Mai 1968*, which paralyzed the economy of France. The song was resurrected in 2018 as the anthem of the *Gilets Jaunes,* a protest movement that has been rampaging in the *Champs Élysées.* It would be heartening to think of these yellow vests being worn in solidarity with war-torn Ukraine! Blue could be added for France and the Ukraine. However, a French leader could again "meet his Waterloo", if this movement of popular unrest were to materialize into a 21st century "French Revolution"!

Joe Dassin sang in the same six languages that I sang in for a Classics promo when I was a graduate student – English, French, Italian, Spanish, Greek and German. He acted in his father's film, *He Who Must Die*. It is sadly ironic that the singer passed away in his prime, but his song "*Et si tu n'existais pas*" is a reminder of how empty my life would be without my dear little guy – my cherished grandson! You have allowed me to embrace a second childhood, and to continue to feel young! And as they say, you are as young as you feel!

-        I think I'm going to cry, Papi – and so is Craptippus!

-        Just because the world is now "*sans* Dassin", please don't make me feel like a "*sans dessein*", boys, a rather complete idiot, for becoming overly emotional. But I didn't want you to be lacking plans for your future - to be "*sans dessin*"! Nor to be lacking a future altogether – "*sans destin*"! Indeed, I wouldn't want you to end up, in the words of William Shakespeare, "sans everything"! Allow me to explain. In his play *As You Like It*, the speech "All the world's a stage" presents seven stages in the life of a man, the last being oblivion. One can wonder why the Sphinx in mythical Thebes only came up with three!

-        Papi, I've got to hand it to you! It's amazing how you have all those facts at your fingertips!

-        You will also have them at your fingertips as you grow up, Cruz, thanks to computers and the Internet!

-       Papi, I think Craptippus and I have really bonded, because he has shown me a parchment labeled "For Your Eyes Only"! It appears a student had been writing down gossip and false rumors about Aristotle and the Lyceum. The documents are entitled "Ari's *Tattle*" and "*Lies*-ceum". I have sworn to become neither a tattletale nor a source of lie serum.

-       Great on you two for forming a **bond**! Live and let die! Maybe Aristotle is really a "Doctor No - it all"! But Alexander is getting ready for his first battle against Darius. Let's take in the action!

-       He certainly looks gallant, riding on Bucephalus, doesn't he, Papi?

-       Yes, and every bit as impressive as the "Alexander" in the two movies I saw – Richard Burton in *Alexander the Great* and Colin Farrell in *Alexander*. Alexander will definitely be aggressive in his march against the Persian Empire, taking advantage of pre-emptive strikes. He'll be as fast on the trigger as cowboy Roy Rogers was on his horse,Trigger. You won't find Alexander biting the bullet! How about that – Roy Rogers' dog was called Bullet! You know, boys, Paris, the Trojan prince, was sometimes called Alexander. But I don't think our Alexander would appreciate being associated with the Trojans, and he would be even less likely to look favorably on being linked to Helen.

-       Stavros, did you and your grandfather get to watch the ceremony at Troy, where Alexander placed a wreath on the tomb of his hero Achilles?

-       Yes, Craptippus, but who was that soldier with him? He placed a wreath on another tomb.

-       That's Hephaistion, Alexander's closest friend. He usually has a calming effect on Alex, who can sometimes become pretty feisty. Did you catch my wordplay – "feisty" – He-**phaisti**-on?

-       *Oy vey*! Very clever! You must have Jesuits teaching at the Lyceum! You can always count on the Jesuit teachers to tell their students jokes to get them into the spirit of the lesson, and in religion class – into the spirituality of the lesson, Ignatian Spirituality that is! The other tomb was that of Patroclus, best friend and bosom buddy of Achilles. Dirty-minded writers have put emphasis on the "bosom" part! The offerings at Troy - Alexander used the Greek name, *Ilion* - were very symbolic. Alexander is professing to invade the Persian Empire in the name of all of Greece, and, of course, expects to show the same daring bravery and enjoy the same glorious success as Achilles. By showing he is imbued with Greek culture, he is counting on the anti-Macedonian Greeks back home to finally acknowledge him with an accepting "He's Greek to me"!

-       Papi, I'm not sure Hephaistion will want to be a Patroclus-type stand-in for Alexander if things start to go south.

-       Actually, he will be heading south – to Egypt. But right now he is about to engage the Persians after he crosses the Granicus River. Fortunately, we are close enough to get a good view of the action, since there is no closed-circuit TV!

144

- Did you guys see how Alexander dodged a bullet? His life was saved by one of his Companions named Cleitus. Apparently, he's always been considered a bit of a dark horse among Alexander's inner circle, and so everyone calls him "Black" Cleitus. Some of Alexander's generals warned Alexander that they risk danger as they progress further into Persian territory, because the Great King will "set a trap" everywhere. However, Alexander's intelligence sources clarified original reports which had been erroneous due to the language barrier. In fact, the King had "satraps" everywhere! Moreover, to help advance across the tricky parts of the many Persian districts, Alexander will make use of GPS – **G**eography of **P**ersian **S**atrapies!

- So Alexander dodged a spear.You keep those wisecracks up, Craptippus, and you're going to be trouble. Stavros, if Alexander gets himself killed, the Persian Expedition will be over – and that will mean the end of our trip to Ancient Greece.

- Papi, that general Parmenion seems to be pretty important.

- He wields a lot of power, and some of it is shared by close family members. It seems they all graduated from the Macedonian version of West Point.

- Stavros, you told me your grandfather's name is Dionysios. But you prefer to call him "Papi". Is that a Greek dialect word for "grandfather"?

- Actually, it's a French word, Craptippus. I guess, since it's not Greek, French will sound a bit *bar-bar* to you. By the way, do you have a girlfriend?

-       That's another thing I get teased about. My girlfriend isn't Greek. She's from Sicily, so she speaks with an accent. My classmates claim they can never make out what she's saying. They call her "Barbie", as if she were a barbarian!

-       What's her real name?

-       Barbara.

-       You've definitely got a quirk, Craptippus – I just can't put a name to it! What does she call you?

-       Her pet name for me is "Platypus" – obviously she made that up. Barbara says she combined the name of Plato with my name. She says when I grow a beard, she'll be able to combine my teacher's name, Aristotle, with mine. But with her accent that tends to aspirate words, it will come out as "Hairypus"! When I'm in a bad mood, she calls me "sour-puss". She doesn't like to see anyone sad. Once, when her father's horse was out of sorts, she started stroking it, asking "what's with the long face?" But she's a great cook. Even my friends admit that, and since she's from Sicily where there are lots of Romans, they give her the Latin name *Quaesita*, which means "outstanding", whenever she is roasting lamb on a spit. Of course they shorten it to Barbie Q. They still manage to tease her though. Once, when she offered to cut a piece of lamb into four pieces for my classmate Perakes, he told her he wasn't hungry enough to eat four pieces, and so she should only cut it into two pieces! I nearly went to pieces. I had one piece for him – a piece of my mind! But Barbara intervened, and told me to keep the peace.

146

-       It's official, Craptippus, there's definitely no hope for you! But there is a lot of Bob Hope IN you! Years from now, when archaeologists dig up your skeleton, they'll only find funny bones! You definitely won't be cremated – with your jokes, you're already on fire! No, they will definitely "inhumorate" you! Cruz, I'm just glad he won't be around during our time to hear Patsy Cline singing "I Go To Pieces"! On the other hand, her song "Crazy" could be Craptippus' theme song!

-       Stavros, we've been following the Macedonian and Greek forces through Asia Minor. One of my older classmates joined this expedition as a scout. He says it will fulfill the "Studies Abroad" component and complete the necessary credits for his international studies program. He was selected to accompany Alexander to Gordium. He told me about a fellow international student from a very distant land near what is called Scotland.

-       Was he Scot?

-       -Ish. This Scot-ish student often bragged about his father, also named Alexander, who had the reputation of being a great musician – and a plumber. Apparently, he carried pipes around in a bag. The student refers to his father as Alexander, the great Scot! As I was saying, before I rudely interrupted myself, Alexander was at Gordium, and was brought this massive and complicated-looking knot. There was a legend that the one who successfully untied the knot would conquer Asia. Vowing not to be undone by a knot, Alexander summoned my classmate for advice. On seeing how young he was, Alexander is said to have exclaimed "Why you're just a boy, scout!" But since students from the Lyceum are on the cutting edge of science, my classmate, who had earned a laurel badge in tying and untying knots, advised Alexander to cut to the chase. Alexander correctly interpreted this as an invitation to cut the knot with his sword. I suppose he who lives by the sword unties by the sword. For weeks, Alexander joked that, while his fleet was advancing in nautical miles, he would have his land forces move forward in "knottycal" miles!

- Craptippus, are all the details of that legend true, or are you just being naughty?

- Guys, I'm always anxious to get a scoop for you, but as camp cleaner I have to deal with scoops you don't want to hear about! I'm wondering if my name had anything to do with my being hired for this job, or perhaps my "clean" record at school.

- Yes, Craptippus, I guess you do have to avoid telling "dirty" jokes! One day Stavros and I will get to look at Alexander verses.

- Alexander versus who, Papi?

- No, no, I'm talking about lines of poetry, which were most beautifully executed in French. The Alexandrine verses were inspired by works such as *The Alexander Romance.* Won't it be uplifting to read about Alexander versus the Persians in Alexandrine verses! *En route* to engage the Persians, Alexander attacked the Athenian colony of Soli in Cilicia, which is part of Asia Minor. The probable reason was that the inhabitants had neglected the proper use of Greek. From their name comes the word "solecism", which means a *faux pas* in language or etiquette. I realize I may be the sole person here who knows that!

- *O sole mio* - right, Papi?

- That phrase means "my sun", my little sunshine! However, sun or no sun – remember the Bill Withers song "Ain't No Sunshine"? - during his Persian campaign the Macedonian King regularly found himself under the weather.

- But Papi, since Zeus controls the skies from Mt. Olympus, aren't we all always "under the weather"?

- Very clever, Cruz, but it depends on **whether** you believe that or not! Hey, I just used one of your puns! However, on this occasion Alexander caught a fever which almost proved fatal, but his doctor's injections provided a shot in the arm, and Hephaistion, as usual, was a real booster. Alexander's physician had warned that his "chills were multiplying", and that he'd "better watch out".

- Even though we will soon be leaving Greece, Papi, you're still into *Grease*!

- Ah yes, the movie! Be that as it may, Alexander is not about to procrastinate.

- What does procrastinate mean, Papi?

- Later! Since it's a Latin-based word, I'll explain it when we get to Rome. Right now, Alexander is preparing his troops for the Battle of Issus.

- He's going to fight the Egyptian goddess Isis?

- No! The Battle of ISSUS, Cruz, not ISIS!

149

-        Oh – double *ka*!

-        If that's a reference to what I think it is, that universal word bearing a resemblance to your namesake, Craptippus, you are in deep doo-doo! But if you are indeed referring to the Egyptian soul, the notion of a person's "double" is inaccurate.

-        No, Dionysios, I'm just thinking about Alexander's plans to visit Egypt.

-        While we've been talking, Alexander has routed the Persian army. Darius may not have been a run of the mill king, but while his troops were milling about, he chose to go on the run, but not before he posed for that marvellous mosaic that we'll probably see in Pompeii, Cruz. I think Burton Cummings must have gazed on the Great King's panic-stricken eyes when he composed "These Eyes"! The King's royal bodyguard – The Immortals – all ten thousand of them - just think, for some countries that's a whole army – did not run away. They were no "band on the run", riding roughshod over beetles in the sand! One Persian commander, riding a donkey, approached too close to Alexander, who was astride Bucephalus. Alexander – or maybe it was his horse – ended up kicking the Persian's ass! As the King made haste to ride off, he most likely did not have a tape in his chariot of Del Shannon singing "Runaway"! The engraved letters CD actually stood for "**C**hariot of **D**arius". The King abandoned his wife and daughters. Alexander had them placed in a tent, and provided them with food and wine. One of the daughters was quite adept at whining! At one point Alexander found them choking on the rich eastern food. Upon which, he

150

remarked "Must be the spice, girls!" When Alexander asked the Persian Queen how she wished to be treated, she replied with R-E-S-P-E-C-T! I guess everybody wants to be the "Queen of Soul"! Darius sent a message to Alexander, asking what the governors of the Persian Empire could do for him to intercede with Alexander. Alexander's historic reply was "Ask not what your governors can do for you, but what you can do for your governors"!

- Gosh, Papi, we are so lucky to be here to witness Alexander's triumphs!

- As long as we don't become witnesses in the modern-day sense of the Greek word - "martyrs"! The next step in the conquest of the Persian Empire was the siege of Tyre. Alexander finally prevailed with a multi-tiered attack, leaving the inhabitants multi-teared! Cruz, we will press the fast-forward button, since the siege lasted seven months, and you might find it tiring.

- Stavros, tell your grandfather we are already in Egypt. Strange how time flies.

- No flies on you, Craptippus! Yes, the great conqueror was bent on using the oracles to his advantage, his own publicity agent, so to speak. He really was a master of marketing! When a bird of prey dropped a stone on Alexander's head, a soothsayer said Alexander would conquer the city of Gaza, but would have to be prudent. Alexander indicated that it wouldn't be the last time he'd end up stoned! Alexander felt a special affinity with Zeus Ammon, and visited his temple. He believed that Ammon might be his father. If his mother - a mortal woman – gave birth to him after being inseminated by a supreme god, that would place him alongside some biggies in the history books! Alexander's favorite seer was Aristander, which sounds a lot like "Alexander", especially if you say it after a few cups of wine! Alexander would call him "Stander" for short. It was kind of funny when, as they parted, Alexander would say "Bye, Stander". But I guess that was a "standard" joke! Presumably, he always had his seer on "stand-by"! It was he who had predicted that Alexander would become the Lion King. He did not however foresee the Disney movie *The Lion King*! Alexander had already visited Zeus Ammon's sanctuary at the Oasis of Siwah.

- Say what, Papi?

- That's **Siwah**, Cruz!

- So many altars and temples in Egypt! Holy, Crap, this land is holy!

- Shortened my name, eh Stav? Or would you prefer Ros? That would make you "Ross the Cross"!

- Boys, boys, we have a lot of territory to get across. We want to avoid the fierce and cruel Sassanids, who would taunt and tease their enemies so much they were sometimes called the **Sassy**nids! Have you noticed that Alexander has been naming many cities after himself, calling them Alexandria?

- Was that due to a lack of imagination?

- I don't think so, Cruz. The most famous Alexandria is the one here in Egypt, which will become the storehouse for the greatest works of Hellenistic Civilization. Unfortunately, the Library of Alexandria was burned on different occasions – by Julius Caesar, and in religious conflicts involving Christians and Muslims.

- Holy smokes, Papi! Religious fires!

- Yes, Cruz, burning religious zeal had a part in the destruction of most of the scrolls. But, on an interesting note, a great female philosopher and mathematician named Hypatia may have been the last Head Librarian at Alexandria. On a less interesting note for her, she was tortured and killed by Christians for her pagan Platonist teaching and beliefs. When you're older I'll show you the film on her life. It's called *Agora*, a title which identifies her connection to the glory days of ancient Athenian culture. It is interesting to note that Alexander had a tolerance towards different religious beliefs – perhaps because he believed himself descended from a god. He marched on Jerusalem, but was greeted as a saviour from the Medes and Persians. He allowed the Jews to practice their religion according to custom, and many enlisted in his army.

- Papi, I never realized there could be a library with a bigger collection of books on Ancient Greek culture than yours! When I get back home, I'm going to go on Google and scroll down all the information on those lost scrolls! And while we are here in Egypt, can I call you Papi-rus?

- Okay – what the **hell**-enic! Although it sounds a bit Franco-Russian to me. We are now at Gaugamela,

153

boys, where Darius has regrouped his Persian army along with allied forces.

\-   Look at those charging chariots, with their archers shooting fiery arrows at the Macedonians! Talk about chariots of fire, Papi! But once again, Darius and his troops will flee in fear, their undergarments surely full of...

\-   Crap! I know, Stavros, and I'm getting used to it – just like Alexander is getting used to defeating his adversaries.

\-   Right on, Craptippus. After the rout at Gaugamela, Alexander pursued Darius to Arbela, where the King disappeared and was soon assassinated by his own men – nobody likes a loser! As victor, Alexander was now in reality the Great King. He soon appointed a Persian satrap, and this was a step towards being recognized by the Persians as well as by the Macedonians and Greeks as ruler of the Persian Empire. We've been following him to Susa, where he is sure to recover all the treasures of Greek art carried off from Athens by Xerxes during the Persian invasion of Greece in 480 BCE.

\-   Stavros, look at all those Grecian urns!

\-   What's a Grecian urn?

\-   About 15 *drachmai* an hour.

\-   You boys have obviously not had the pleasure of reading Shelley's *Ode to a Grecian Urn*. But, Cratippus, a poet you are not. So less talk about urns, and get off the pot!

-       I can never earn praise! Let's get some rest before we all follow Alexander to the capital city of Persepolis. Rumor has it that Alexander will try to impress his Macedonian soldiers with a *tour de force* to ensure their loyalty.

-       I like time travel, Papi! We are able to move quickly to battle-grounds.

-       Right, Cruz – and since we have no problem with logistics in arriving at the next event, we get to bring everyone along with us!

-       Look, Dionysios! Look, Stavros! The Macedonian army has set fire to the great Palace.

-       And it is spreading to the tents that shelter the Persian army.

-       Hey, that's right – the fire really is in**tense**!

-       A burn, Papi! But I can just imagine you listening to Jim Morrison singing "Light My Fire"! Funny how we keep referring to that singer from The Doors. Is it because he was infatuated with your namesake – Dionysos? Or because his fans **ador**ed him?

-       Boys, have you formed a conspiracy to gang up on me with your wordplay?

-       Speaking of conspiracies, Alexander executed his generals Philotas and Parmenion on a charge of treason, and also his historian Callisthenes. The court pages were involved in a plot against Alexander, and were eliminated.

-       And that put an end to the "pages" of Callisthenes' history of Alexander's expedition! Right, Papi?

-       To put everything in context, you should know that Alexander was now becoming "part Persian". He had married a Persian princess named Roxane, and he obliged the Macedonian Greeks to prostrate themselves before him in the eastern custom of submission to their rulers. This was known by the Greek name of *proskynesis*. However, when the Macedonians refused to bend to Alexander's wishes – physically and mentally- he ultimately rescinded this obligation.

-       Papi, Craptippus is able to get us into a banquet, where Alexander will probably drink so much, he'll end up talking with us as if we were important Macedonians. Poor Craptippus has to spend this time washing everything, including Alexander's writing tablets, because Alexander is about to begin his campaign in India, and he wants to start with a clean slate! Say, Alexander is motioning us over.

-       I've seen you two carrying scrolls from time to time. I guess you've been pretty busy now that I'm on a roll!

-       Should we bow down, Papi?

-       No, Cruz, I think laughing will do the trick this time.

-       King Alexander, my name is Dionysios, and my extremely young colleague and I very much admire all that you have accomplished – especially for one so young.

-       That's Great!

-       We are humbled by your approval!

-       No – that's GREAT King Alexander!

-       Please excuse our shabby greatings – I mean greetings!

-       Indeed, I am Alexander the Great King, but to make it easier for posterity, I shall allow myself to be called Alexander the Great! It shall be known that I have seen six wonders of the world – the Great Pyramid of Giza, the Colossus of Rhodes, the Mausoleum at Halicarnassus, the Statue of Zeus in Athens, the Hanging Gardens of Babylon, and the Temple of Artemis at Ephesus. I believe that a huge lighthouse will be needed in the harbor of Alexandria, and therefore someday the Pharos of Alexandria will be added to the wonders of the world. Let all the other Pharaohs take note!

-       I don't have the powers of Aristander, O King, but I am willing to predict that one day only the Pyramid of Giza will be visible, and perhaps some fragments of the Temple of Artemis. The Colossus of Rhodes will come to life only in a film of the same name. As for the Gardens of Babylon, their exact location will leave archaeologists hanging! For the Great Lighthouse, it will be lights out! But another great lighthouse will eventually see the light of day in a distant land. As well, another mausoleum will eventually rival the original dedicated by Mausolus. The only statues of Zeus will be located in museums.

-        Will wonders never cease!

-        Cruz, the modern world will replace the Seven Wonders of the Ancient World with the Great Wall of China, Chichén Itzá – the Mayan Pyramid in Mexico, Christ the Redeemer Statue in Rio de Janeiro, Machu Picchu in Peru, Petra in Jordan, the Taj Mahal, which is a mausoleum in India, and the Colosseum, which we'll get to see when we move on to Ancient Rome. All those more recent wonders you'll be able to visit, Cruz, without leaving home, but by using metavision, a type of virtual reality which allows you to feel like you are actually in front of a location or natural wonder that is really a great distance away! Technological wizards have added a new dynamic to the D in 3-D! Today, one can find oneself in the middle of a whole new "universe" – beyond what one ever dreamed of – a metaverse! Likewise, you'll be able to visit virtually the Industrial Wonders of the World, featured in a British documentary. Namely, the 19th century SS Great Eastern, the first ship constructed entirely out of iron, the Brooklyn Bridge, which is a suspension bridge in New York City, the Bell Rock Lighthouse off the coast of Scotland, the London Sewage System – not a sinkhole, but perhaps a stink hole!, the Panama Canal, the Hoover Dam in Colorado, and the First Transcontinental Railway crossing the United States. This last engineering wonder reminds me of the railway tracks you used to configure in your basement, Cruz. It is also a sentimental reminder of the television show that you enjoyed so much – "Thomas and

Friends". Full disclosure – that we both enjoyed so much! Do you recall the names of those trains?

-       Yes, Papi. They are Thomas, Gordon, James, Edward, Percy, Douglas, Donald, Emily, Toby, Cranky, Duck, Oliver, Annie and Clarabel. Then there were his international train friends from such faraway places as India, Japan, and Australia. And there was, of course, the trainmaster, Mr. Topham Hatt.

-       Or, as I called him – Topham Fat, because of his rotund figure! A bit over the top you might say – and me being a ham! But my hat's off to the show's creators! As I reflect at this moment upon that show, I realize that Thomas was a bit of an Aristotelian with his "lessons on life", dealing with friendship, fair play - Aristotle would call this justice - good character, bravery, and so on! All this talk of trains and good feelings has me thinking of some wonderful messages in a couple of songs about trains. There's the O'Jays song "Love Train" and the Cat Stevens song "Peace Train". "Peace and Love" was an expression I heard a lot when I was a student at university, Cruz. Great King Alexander, I have been reading about world empires for many years.

-       For sure – you're no spring chicken!

-       Noted, O Great King! As I said, for quite some time I have been reading up on that rising power in the West – the Romans. No doubt you have heard of their armies and their victories. They could very well be bent on rivalling your Empire, possibly even contemplating a comprehensive confrontation.

- I "C"! You have obviously been around the block a few times! How else would you come up with such clever alliteration? You "C" my point!

- Point well taken – definitely! And the "C" comeback on the alliteration – well played!

- But where are you going with this?

- Where will YOU end up going with your army, Great King? That is the question! If I were Alexander, I would head back home, with the view to moving westward against the Romans.

- And if I were Dionysios, I would indeed entertain such an expedition. But I am Alexander, and I will do all my "entertaining" right here, thank you very much!

- Well, boys, after that sardonic reply, "Go West, young man" is obviously not in the cards for Alexander. Of course, having surreptitiously looked at the time guide once more, I know for a fact it's never going to happen.

- The alliteration you just used, Dionysios, smacks of a systematic seizure of the "s" sound!

- And the side-by-side sophisticated words to seriously stump you were a bonus! So we're off to accompany Alexander on his incursion into India.

- Don't forget the elephants!

- Well, if they are true to their nature, the elephants won't forget you! Of course, we can't ignore the elephant in the room – namely the desire of the

Macedonians to end the Persian expedition, and return home.

- Stavros, how do you get down off an elephant?

- I give up, Craptippus, how do you get down off an elephant?

- You don't get down off an elephant, you get down off a duck!

- A bit of a quack, eh Cratippus? If you were an elephant, I'd tell you to pack your trunk and leave!

- Tusk tusk, Dionysios. How much wine did Alexander serve you? Would you have me holed up alone in some ivory tower?

- While we have been trading pachyderm puns, Alexander has defeated the Indian rajah, Porus.

- What did Alexander say when he saw the elephants coming, Papi?

- "Here come the elephants!" The chants of the Indian natives – "Porus, Porus" soon changed to "Poor us, Poor us"! But Alexander's soldiers have mutinied. We are all going to be homeward bound.

- Shall we sing the Simon and Garfunkel song, Papi?

- No, I believe Alexander would prefer to be alone with his thoughts. The "Sounds of Silence" would be more appropriate! His megalomania took a hit. It seems fair – maybe even safe – to say that Alexander was a great conqueror of mighty Empires, but seemed intent on mixing the peoples of his conquests into some kind of unified and harmonious world society and culture. He tried to entwine different political ideologies and social practices of East and West into an all-encompassing philosophy of man. He introduced mixed marriages eons before they became fashionable. He remained faithful to the mission of expanding Hellenistic influence, but with a piercing – or "Persing" of what would become the Byzantine and Muslim world. We might say he died young, but given the lifespan of soldiers in a world of constantly threatening diseases, Alexander can be considered to have lived out an average life in terms of life expectancy.

-       Papi, your guide-book mentions several causes for Alexander's death – wounds, fever, disease, alcohol. Which one do you think it was?

-       All of the above, Cruz. Did I tell you that the name "Alexander" means "defender of men" . His name in Greek was *Alexandros*, from *alexein* - "to protect" and *aner* – "man". The "dr" is from the stem of the noun. While it is true that many men died because of his campaign, Alexander did defend the "honor" of the Greeks in avenging the previous Persian Wars, and he did preserve Persian customs. I suppose he was really a "defender of mankind"!

-       Craptippus, my grandfather and I are going to Italy soon. Sorry that I'll miss your graduation at the Lyceum.

-       Will you write to me, Stavros?

-     I think there will be a better chance of your letters reaching us, Craptippus, if the archaeologists do their job!

-     Not sure what you are talking about, Stavros, but I will miss you and your grandfather. May the gods be with you!

-     I'm going to miss his humor, Papi.

-     Like I would miss a tumor, Cruz!

-     Papi, what will happen to Alexander's Empire?

-     As often happens in these situations, there will be a lot of in-fighting. The so-called succession will feature wars between a number of generals and the end result will be the establishment of the Ptolemaic Dynasty in Egypt, the Seleucid Kingdom in Asia Minor, and the Antigonids in Greece, although a number of Greek states regained their independence, and formed various leagues to defend mutual interests. The Macedonian successors eventually lost their hold on territories east of the Euphrates, but Egypt became thoroughly Hellenized. Culturally, New Comedy will feature the plays of Menander, and new schools of philosophy will emerge like the Epicureans, who followed the teachings of Epicurus, the Cynics, like Diogenes, and the Stoics, named after the Stoa, or "Porch", where the founder of this movement, Zeno, did his teaching. More on these when we are in Rome! Hellenistic science flourished with mathematicians such as Euclid, Archimedes, Eratosthenes, and the astronomer Aristarchus. We'll have to take out your telescope when we get back home, Cruz! And

Craptippus' uncle, Theophrastus, did his bit in biology and botany.

-        Wow, Papi! So many names and ideas!

-        Just remember, Cruz, that those ideas all started with Aristotle, and, in a way, owe a debt to his famous pupil, Alexander the Great. The marriages between Macedonian soldiers and Persian women were just a microcosm of the marriage between western and eastern culture and the spread of ideas in both directions! Craptippus would have interjected that Persian rugs must have been hair pieces fabricated by young Persian brides for their balding Macedonian husbands! I hope that marching in Alexander's footsteps will leave an indelible footprint on you, Cruz, as you make your way on your journey in your own world. Actually, I'm hoping that our whole trip to the world of Ancient Greece will have a lasting effect on you, and that you'll never forget our thrills in those Greek hills! But before we return home, we're off to other hills in Ancient Rome!

Chapter Twelve: When in Rome…

-       Okay, Papi, I've pressed the red button for Ancient Rome, and the green button for Roman mythology. Will we get to meet all the Roman gods?

-       I doubt it, Cruz – there are over two thousand of them! You see, the Romans were a very religious people, at least in front of their neighbours. Religion really was a part of their social fabric. They found out about the Greek Olympians, and made them Roman. They had gods from the Etruscans, who greatly influenced the Romans, and even ruled them for a while. They would later import gods from Egypt, and all the other lands they conquered. For the Romans, who were very superstitious – and don't even think about singing the Stevie Wonder song! – all nature, like streams and forests were gods. All human activities, like tilling the soil, were divinely inspired and so associated with a divinity. Moreover, all ideas, such as liberty and courage, were represented by deities. I'm sure that we'll bump into some of them. The Romans were bilingual and bicultural. In other words, they loved all things Greek, including the Greek pantheon on Olympus. The Romans, like the Greeks, built temples for their gods. In fact, when Rome was about to become an empire, the top general for the future emperor Augustus, Marcus Agrippa, built a temple called the Pantheon, a Greek word meaning "all the gods". Hopefully, we'll get to visit it. But for now I've been able to get us these invites to a *lectisternium*, which is a banquet for the gods. It was as hard as getting tickets along the boards at the Bell

Center. But we will get to talk to the gods, who will look like statues, but…remember our experience with Pygmalion! So it will feel like being in the Habs dressing room! In fact, we are here early, and have the benefit of chatting with the gods during the warm-up sacrifice. By the way, don't forget that here in Rome I am Dionysius and you are Lucius Crux. And don't insult these Roman gods by asking who their Greek counterparts are. If you are paying attention, the connections will be obvious!

-       You're right, Papi, er…Dionysius. We're the first ones here. Except for those statues.

-       Gods, Lucius Crux, real gods! Looking up at all these Romanized Olympians reminds me of a poem I wrote in university called "*Sur l'étude des dieux romains*". It really was the translation of a poem I had written in high school called "On Studying the Greek Gods". Like the poem, the Greek gods were "translated" to their Roman equivalents, since that verb comes from the Latin *transferre* – "to carry across"!

-       Like a "transfer" - right, Papi?

-       Yes, indeed! Surely you remember the past participial form that I taught you – *translatum*? To get you into the right frame of mind to meet the Roman gods, a.k.a. the Greek gods, here are a couple of stories about Jupiter. The first one relates the story of the bee, who was so exacerbated by humans stealing her honey, that she asked Jupiter to give her a deadly weapon to solve the problem. To sweeten Jupiter up, she approached the god, and said "Try this, honey!".

166

"How sweet it is!", uttered the god. This exclamation would be recalled centuries later by Junior Walker when he recorded a song with that title! Jupiter gave her the sting, which would be fatal for mortals – but which would also be lost when used. I guess the moral of that story is "bee" careful about what you ask for! On the other hand, when Cassius Clay – or you might know him as Muhammed Ali, Cruz, - would "sting like a bee", he did it fight after fight! Your Manie often calls me "Honey Bee" – I guess because I'm so sweet on her!

-       Good way to avoid sticky situations - right, Papi?

-       Now, if you can mind your own beeswax for a moment, I'll tell you the other story. Jupiter happened to be sweet on a priestess named Io. He probably had eaten too much honey! To be near her, he changed himself into a black cloud. However, Juno recognized the cloud – like Carly Simon, she probably "had clouds in her coffee"! And she was aware that her husband was "so vain"! Since she was "having a cow", she turned Io into a white cow. Jupiter thought making it with a heifer would require too much effort, and so he opted for a heifer-less life. But Juno took the bull by the horns and sent the thousand-eyed Argus to guard Io. Jupiter, in turn, sent Mercury to tell Argus stories so that he would get – literally – "some shut eye". It worked – just like when I used to read to you at bedtime a few years ago, Cruz! Incidentally, I think Argus inspired Bobby Vee to record the song "The Night Has a Thousand Eyes"! Since that singer had five big hits – the others being "Devil or Angel",

167

"Rubber Ball", "Take Good Care of My Baby", and "Run to Him", it was appropriate to change his name from Velline to V - the Roman "5"! Of course he had to write it as "Vee" for reasons of pronunciation! On a tragic note – you'll notice, Cruz, that I am often tragically hip – on "The Night the Music Died", when Buddy Holly, Richie Valens, and The Big Bopper were killed in a plane crash – taking with them a slice of "American Pie" – Bobby Vee had to fill in at the planned show! The other headliner, Dion, had not taken the plane. Interesting that his name is a shortened form of the name Dionysius, that I adopted for our journey! When Juno sent a gadfly to sting Io, Jupiter decided to protect her. Approaching her, he whispered "Io, Io, it's off to Egypt you go". She fled there with seven little calves, and became the first priestess of Egypt, and was able to milk the situation for all it was worth! I guess every cloud does have a silver lining after all!

-       Welcome to our 'hood. Speaking of which, you two should be wearing a hood to sacrifice to us. You know – *capite velato* – with the head covered, *capiche*? One day you'll thank me for the fashion tip, since hoodies will become very popular – almost like a religious garb for young folks! Of course, if you sacrifice to Apollo and Ceres over there, you'll do so with heads bare like the Greeks. Something seems very Greek to the Romans about those two. Why, they couldn't even bring themselves to give Apollo a Roman name! In the beginning we gods were worshipped in triads – which is why people will one day worship the gods of their hockey team during three periods in a place called Montreal - a "royal

168

mountain" like Mount Olympus. More of a hill, though, like these seven hills of Rome. In the arenas of a very distant future time hockey heroes will be venerated with religious fervor, just as gladiators will be worshipped here in the arenas of Rome. In that place called Montreal, a religious man called Brother André will be called "the wonder man of Mount Royal". But the real "wonder man" will bear the name Rocket Richard. Please don't ask me to explain how a human rocket can exist. I am Jupiter, the DG of this group, that is the "Divine God"! Neptune over there can freeze water for our skating pleasure. If you desire refreshments, just beckon Bacchus, who is standing behind the altar of hot gods. Oh my, he has spelled god backwards. To be expected, I suppose, since he is forever sampling that beer imported from Egypt. The god with the anvil is fabricating special scepters in the shape of a seven in honor of seven kings who will one day rule this city in our name. He no longer uses wood, since the goddess Diana refuses to have any more trees cut down in the forests she loves so much. Therefore he makes use of special fibers he creates from glass. His name is Vulcan, and so he names the material he uses for the small round objects of worship he produces "vulcanized rubber" after himself. Minerva here will gladly knit you a sweater to keep you warm. The letters CH obviously stand for "Cosmic Heater". Don't mind the helmet she is wearing – it's for protection against those round hard objects that Vulcan is wont to throw around. They are all black from the soot in his workshop. Vulcan is the god of builders, but he has suffered from fallen arches ever since his mother Juno tossed him out of our Olympic home because he didn't have the matinee idol looks of his brother Apollo. That is why many of the Roman temples will eventually end up in ruin, suffering in turn from their "fallen arches" – even though the Romans took great pride in the arches, as well as in domes and vaults that they developed. Bottom line – the god of "construction" was not always "constructive" in his activities! Mars also wears a helmet since Vulcan sometimes attacks him with his anvil, because Mars gets too friendly with Vulcan's wife Venus. She's the pretty young lady in a swimsuit. Her apparel is very appropriate given the story about her being born from the foam of the sea. I guess if she had sought protection under a domed roof, she'd be a real "foam dome" – just a little joke I picked up visiting my Greek counterpart in Greece, but why the place was spelled "Grease", I don't know. Mars will often pick a fight with Vulcan, and so Vulcan has built a small box to which I confine Mars for various periods of time – even up to ten minutes! Venus is selling beauty products created by Mercury, who has always had a commercial bent. She is especially proud of her line of cosmetics, which she calls Cupid's Choice, after her son. You two look intelligent, and so will likely be able to follow as I explain that "cosmetics" is from the Greek word *kosmos*, meaning "order". Naturally, women buy these products to put their face in order! The Greeks used the word to describe the world order, or cosmos. We Romans prefer the word "universe" from the Latin *universus*, meaning "whole". There will one day be a church that will proclaim itself universal – so "wholly holy"! Just to make sure everybody understands, they will use the Greek term for "wholly - "catholic". The Greek version is *katholos*. In case you are wondering why I know so much Greek, it's because I know that we Roman gods worshipped in Roman temples were descended from the Greek gods who inhabit Mount Olympus. I mean I wasn't born yesterday. But I was born! In fact, the whole history of the birth of the gods makes fascinating reading, if you ever have the time and inclination. So we are not eternal – we were born! However, we will live forever - we are immortal! Rome will be known as the "Eternal City" – but only because it seems to have been around forever. I'm sure you will find out how the city got its start. I must tell you I really enjoy being King of the World! That reminds me that a young man will shout out that he is "king of the world". That's because he will be aboard this huge ship named the Titanic, after other members in our family tree. Of course it won't be true, but I can understand where he's coming from in that moment of sheer euphoria. If you travel long enough in the Roman world, you may meet someone who likewise will proclaim himself king – but of another world! It may sound kooky, but there will be something about him that will be very convincing. His god – or himself, if you know the whole story – is said to be eternal. His followers, called Christians, will prove to be quite the team on fire! Another group called the Jews – although there is apparently a connection between the two groups, something about old and new testaments – also believes their god to be eternal. Notice I said "god". Hard to believe, but these two groups are monotheists! They are obviously going to cause problems for the polytheistic Romans. The authorities certainly won't be greeting the followers of that Christ-King with a "Merry Christians to you"!

-        How about "Merry Christmas"?

-        'S no reason for that! Both groups claim that their god is all-knowing. Juno often calls me a "know-it-all", so I can relate to that – or not! There will come a singer – older than you, old man – but she will appear younger – ah, those cosmetics! – who will record a song called "I Believe". Many Romans, as well as many non-Romans, will take up the cry of "I believe" when they meet this man who claims to be the son of the Christian god, and proclaim faith in his resurrection. Incidentally, that song resurrected the singer's career. Strange coincidence! I am also reminded, by looking at you, that a male singer will record a song called "Old Man". He will be born in Toronto, a city that will rival the city of Montreal that I talked about. The two cities will be such fierce rivals, that they will even decide to speak different languages! Hockey will not be a religion in Toronto, but nevertheless will be "big business". Young man, I have not wished to insult your older companion by referring to his venerable age, and since I have a "heart of gold", I am going to give him a gift – made of gold! I noticed that you are wearing a Timex watch – obviously bought in a bargain store in the Roman Forum. I say "Roman" Forum, because the citizens of that city of Montreal will erect a Forum, where they will gather for many years to worship their gods of hockey. On the other hand, the citizens of Toronto will gather in a garden full of maple leaves. Don't ask me why they will misspell the word and call them Maple Leafs. Better to "leave" well enough alone! Vulcan produces watches that are purely Roman, combined with the old technology of the Timex brand. They are called Ro-lex watches, and I am glad to give you one. All Roman sentinels wear one so as to know when their "watch" is over! Their surveillance period is called a vigil. I prefer the Latin term – *vigilia*. You may be fortunate to meet the future writer Virgil. Try to remember to spell his name the Roman way – Vergil. There will come a time when Romans will gather for the *Vigilia Vergilii* - a vigil for Vergil! Notice the V's, young man. You can form them by sticking the two fingers next to the thumb in the open position. The V's that are formed will stand for "victory". Another well-known hill – Churchill – will make that symbol famous. My son Mars hates that sign, because apparently it will become a "peace greeting". There will be a queen in the land of Churchill who will be named after that symbol – Victoria. She will give awards called the Victoria Cross – I think because she was often very cross, and seldom amused! This just in – since V is our number 5, you will be able to use this sign for a "high five"! I had mentioned Mercury. He has patented special skates that allow him to skate the fastest. He seems to literally fly around the ice surface! And Vulcan has made him a customized little scepter. Apollo is always ready with a song when we decide to have a festive get-together on our rink, and sometimes sings a national ode before competitions. When he finishes his hymn – you know, his anthem – everyone will begin shouting "he shoots, he scores"! That is because Apollo shoots arrows and scores music! When we decide to engage in an Olympics-style contest on the ice, my wife Juno is our head coach. She can be tough – believe me, I know! – and masters strategies that can transform opponents to the point of not performing like their old selves! I think female coaches will one day become a trend. Which is why Ceres has been added to her staff as a nutritionist, and her daughter Proserpina assists her. However, the daughter is away scouting for six months during the year in a lower league, where players who can no longer perform on earth end up. Mercury actually brings these "deadbeats" to her. They have lost their scoring touch. In fact, they have lost their touch altogether - as well as all their other senses! She is provided with accommodations by my brother Pluto. He claims to be thriving, but reports are that down there business is dead! Proserpina says the temperature is quite hot, but she prefers Florida. Just as well, because while she is away, the weather up here is not so hot! Vesta handles warm-up practices. She is quiet and unassuming, yet she is able to motivate everyone, and seems to light a fire under them, so to speak! Juno has also brought my son Hercules on board as a physical trainer. Juno was at first reluctant to hire him, since he is my son from another relationship. But after doing a series of odd jobs for the organization - actually they were twelve in number, and he calls them "labors" - he eventually got full recognition from Juno. When we do have inter-divinity competitions – that is, when gods from other parts of the world take part, we reserve heaps of gold, silver, and bronze as prizes. The Greek Olympians play the same style as us. They also have a female coach – Hera – and she is every bit as tough as my Juno! Sometimes a fight will break out between my son Mars and the Greek Ares, with Mars always the winner. The crowd also always cheers for Mars. Sometimes, after the games some of the players let off steam with childish games. The Greek Poseidon and our Neptune, for example, will have water fights! The Greek Dionysos and our Bacchus are both usually too hammered to even suit up! I have to admit that their star player, Athena, is always at the top of her game. She also protects some of the less gifted players. Because of their experience with games, the two Apollos always organize our contests. The Greek Hephaistos and our Vulcan serve as goaltenders, because they have experience with nets. Someday, Aphrodite and Venus can tell you stories about those nets! Oh, in case you are wondering, we always win – when we play in Rome. When our games are in Greece, the Olympians win. Something to do with home temple advantage! The Egyptians are always led by their best players – Ice-is, Osir-ice and Nephth-ice. Anub-ice is a good player, but Thoth is lethargic – like he couldn't give a toth, oops, I mean toss! Seker is almost always thrown out of the game for throwing his illegal "seker" punch. They have a player listed as Ptah. I keep thinking his name must be Peter, but pronounced Peetah, because of his southern Memphis accent! Pharaoh is the team owner, but rarely watches the games, as he is usually off gallivanting with a pretty young thing he calls his "Pharaoh" – Mia Farrow. They tend to avoid the woods, because Mia is allergic to anything woody. The Assyro-Babylonian team – as the name suggests – was formed from two originally different teams. Their best player, their centreman Bel, is so conceited, he is convinced they will name their arena after him, calling it something like the Bell Center. But personally I think he is just confused! When Asshur is tending goal, they tend to play with assurance. Ishtar is a star…ish, and Sin spends so much time in the penalty box that many commentators refer to it as the "Sin-bin". They have a player who has invented a special tape for sticks.

Since his name is Marduk, they call it Marduk tape. The other team that usually competes is the Teutonic team. They favor a rough and tumble style, and so we call them the Teutonic Team Toughies! Why couldn't they play a less bullying style, as if they were from a city of "brotherly love"? I guess, to use the Greek name, that city would be Philadelphia. There is an Egyptian connection to that name, but nobody wants to play there. A certain W.C. Fields once said "not even over his dead body" – or something to that effect. Naturally, their toughest player is called Thor, because, believe me, when you finish a game against him, you are "thor" all over! You can't even say "sore" because he has probably knocked out your front teeth! Woden is a valuable player for their team, if only because he provides them with all their sticks – woden sticks, that is. Some of their fans get so drunk, they can't even pronounce his name. You hear them chanting "Odin, Odin"! Well, our Roman fans hate him, so they chant "*Odi* Odin"! You two have probably figured out that the chant is Latin for "I hate Odin"! The Teutons have one decent player, Loki, who is able to score goals from impossible angles. He does this so often that we have taken to calling them "Loki goals"!

-        Papi, I think Jupiter must have heard you talking about the Bell Center and hockey tickets.

-        We are always glad to have new worshippers. Are you aware that in the future some of us will be honored as planets?

-        Because you are out of this world?

- I like this little *puer*! I called you "boy" in Latin, but switch the letters around, lad, and you become "pure", which I'm sure describes the joy you bring to your elder companion. You're a good'un all right! Are you two Roman?

- Yes, my grandfather and I will be roamin' around the city for the next little while.

- You are lightning fast on the word play, young man, but I am the god of light and of lightning. I'm so brilliant it hurts! So don't make any plans to become a "lightning thief"! Besides, my son Mercury wrote the book on thieves, just not one called "The Lightning Thief ". I have so many names, I could be a divine roll call all by myself! However, my favorite epithets are Jupiter *Optimus Maximus* – the greatest and the best. If I took up boxing, I'd be made of clay, but that sport is not up my ali – oops – I meant to say alley! I can out-fight, out-throw, outsmart…

- Out-talk.

- Out-talk. Time out! You got me fair and square. But don't try to put another one over on J.J.!

- Who is J.J.?

- Why – Joking Jupiter or "Joe King" Jupiter or Jesting Jupiter or "Jest Jupiter" – make that "Just Jupiter"! Did you know I can order my favorite dessert and tell you how I order it with the same words?

- How's that?

- I scream! Say, do you know how I organize a party for the gods up here in the heavens?

177

- How, M.J. – **M**ighty Jupiter?

- I simply "planet"! Last week we all ate at a divine restaurant on the moon. The food was great, but there was no atmosphere! I came with a date for Bacchus, but he prefers grapes! As *per* her habit, Juno threw Vulcan off the moon – she felt he needed some space! Needless to say, he was not over the moon! When he was condemned to work in a blacksmith's shop, he was so poor, he couldn't even pay attention! He actually made an iron "E" to indicate the entrance to his workshop, but, ironically, all his customers bump into each other because they think it means exit as well! OMG – **o**nly **m**y **g**ossip! Aren't I too much! Juno says I tend to babble on all the time. But what, may I ask, are your names?

- Cruz, now do you believe these gods are the Roman equivalents of the Greek Olympians? Jupiter just used the same jokes we heard from Dionysos when we were on Mt. Olympus. Planet, space...honestly, divine humour must be universal! I am Dionysius and this is my grandson, Lucius Crux.

- Ah, Bacchus sometimes calls himself Dionysius.

- Shouldn't that be Dionysus?

- It should, but he always puts in the extra "i" when he has had too much wine. You'll discover sober authors who should know better that will confuse the two spellings. That is why we usually urge him to call himself Liber. That name is much easier to pronounce, and he can use it freely. And Lucius the light. You could be Lux Crux! I'm feeling a bit light-headed –

178

must be the nectar I've been drinking. I'm also feeling a bit light on my feet. This is a good time to sit down on my beautiful throne. Oh, oh, here comes trouble – I mean my wife.

- We read you, O Father of gods and men!

- Greetings, dear worshippers! Welcome to the sacrificial banquet. Move away from the sacred altar, as I will probably have to **alter** some of what my husband has been telling you. In fact, often that god needs a halter! Look at him gloating on his royal throne, when, in fact, he spends more time on the throne in the little boys' room! You know that I am Juno, and I overheard your names. A little bird told me that you used to sing, Dionysius. And no, that little bird was not the dead sparrow of Catullus' girlfriend Lesbia. I hope you get to meet Catullus some day. I know I wouldn't kick him out of bed! Oh, sorry, Lucius Crux – I shouldn't be dreaming out loud in the presence of such a sweet little boy! If only you were older!

- Papi, I'm still getting that "older" bit – even in Rome! Why don't you tell Juno you used to sing "Venus". Maybe the goddess Venus will give you free beauty products that you could pass on to Manie.

- The operative words, Cruz, are "used to sing"! Besides, I'm sure the goddess would prefer the song "Venus" by Shocking Blue. As I recall, the song starts off with "Goddess on the mountain top" – that would be Mt. Olympus. The lyrics continue with "the summit of beauty and love… and Venus was her name". But the real "shocking" news here is that the group is a shocking "blue", yet Venus' favorite color is red. The only thing keeping her from seeing red is respect for Apollo, since the song could be sung at his theater, and maybe in the future at the Apollo Theater in New York, and ever since the "beauty contest", Venus is partial to anything that happens in the "Big Apple"! I told you the story of the beauty contest won by Venus. She was awarded the apple "for the fairest" by Paris. He was "bribed" by Venus with the gift of Helen. That's what really started the Trojan War! As for beauty products for Manie, I think that ship has sailed. Besides, Manie never needed cosmetics. She was always prettiest with a natural look. Cruz, you'll probably understand better when you are older what I'm going to tell you about love and marriage. The secret of happiness for your Manie and me is having always put into practice what the Little Prince says in Antoine de Saint-Éxupéry's novel – "Love does not consist of gazing at each other, but in looking together in the same direction"! But since you have mentioned singing for Venus, I imagine she would love listening to the Lovin' Spoonful or the 1960's band called Love. They may have been the first racially diverse band. I guess love is what is needed to embrace diversity! She would surely appreciate the singer Darlene Wright, who changed her name to Darlene Love. It certainly proved to be the "right" choice!

-        I think I get it, Papi. Love is a powerful force. So I'm thinking that the "L" sign we make on our forehead could stand for "love" instead of "loser"!

-        Unless the "L" stood for *Love's Labor Lost*, in which case you would still be a "loser" – except for a very "winning" use of alliteration! Of course, since the "L" is the Roman numeral 50, one could think of the film and the song by Paul Simon – "50 Ways to Leave your Lover". The Latin version would be "L Ways to Leave your Lover" –which would be one "L" of an alliteration!

-    Not to mention a whole episode on "Sesame Street" brought to us by the letter L!

-    You have just **literally** amazed me, Cruz! But I would like to conclude our little conversation on love by mentioning Peter Abélard, a medieval philosopher and scholar, who adhered to the teachings of Aristotle, and like the polyvalent Greek, was deemed "a man who knew everything"! He tutored a young girl named Héloïse, and their love story went viral – like Erich Segal's *Love Story*! At first it was a Platonic relationship, but, in turn, they fell in love with each other. By that time, Abélard had turned from Aristotle to the poetry of Ovid. He had transitioned from the head to the heart, and wrote love poems, claiming "Love was my inspiring Apollo"! They could not marry, because, at that time, Oxford dons were not permitted to marry. However, they were married in secret, and Héloïse became pregnant. Her uncle had Peter castrated, and they decided to live out their lives in religious institutions – he in a monastery, and she in a convent. Their relationship again became Platonic! It was quite the romantic tale for the learned Abélard, who once said "A woman rejected is an outrageous creature"! He had based this statement on the line "Love hath no fury like a woman scorned", which was taken from William Congreve's play *The Mourning*

Bride, who perhaps was a less than pretty "morning bride"! Hence, the betrayal! That title reminds me of Eugene O'Neil's play *Mourning Becomes Electra.* But that's just me digressing!

-       Well, you two, if you have done whispering, let me just say that I appreciate singers so much I think that one day my name will be used to honor the best singers.

-       Who knows?

-       No – **Junos**! Will you look at brother and sister playing a game together!

-       A board-game, Queen Juno?

-       No, young man, they're not bored. They are playing with a deck of shards. Maybe your grandfather and you will be delighted to know that in a far distant time and in a far distant land an Empire will grow, borrowing much from our own Roman Empire, but less dependent on Latin than we are. They will be formed of states that do not remain divided, but rather united. That's how they will stand – united states. Well, a modern version of shards, called card games, and something called game shows will be very popular in that land, and a game show host, Wink Martindale, will record a story-song called "Deck of Cards". I'm not joking – but someone will see fit to add two jokers to the deck! Let's watch the twins playing their favorite game – "Go Hunt".

-       Apollo: Diana, do you have a X?

-       Diana: Yes, I have II of them. Apollo, do you have an VIII?

- Apollo: No, go hunt!

- Diana: Yippee! I love hunting!

- Do other gods play shards, Juno?

- Well, Bacchus never plays with a full deck, and Neptune, with his connections, has become a bit of a shard shark. Ares won't play because he's always a sad sack. Ceres enjoys playing a series of games. Mercury never finishes a game, because he only likes the red shards. Besides, he's always off on business trips, especially to Greece. You two should visit Greece – it's a beautiful place.

- Been there, done that, O Queen Juno!

- And my grandfather and I got the T-shirt. His says "Nothing in excess", but it doesn't fit because of his over-eating! Mine says "Know yourself", but I almost didn't get it, because it has somebody else's name on the label. I would like to know how the shards are organized into the 52-shard set.

- Well, young Lucius Crux, the shards come from red-figure and black-figure pottery we pick up in southern Italy. By the way, avoid invitations from Mercury to play "LII pick-up" – the little trickster! The shards represent four classes of society – clubs, like weapons, for soldiers, spades, you know – shovels – for farmers, diamonds for kings and emperors, and hearts – bless them – for women. Shards are numbered from II to X, and then there are shards with our pictures – Jupiter for Kings, Me - Juno, for Queens, and Mercury, because he is kind of a "jack of all trades". Finally, there are shards with the letter A for Apollo, since he is an ace at shard games. If you are wondering, Jupiter tends to play solitaire when he is on his little boys' room throne. He evidently cheats, because he always claims to have a royal flush.

-       I guess a "straight flush" would cause messy weather problems for inhabitants on Earth!

-       Let's just say too much Falernian wine in the offerings at the *lectisternium* always leave him a little flushed! The banquet is nearly finished. I hope you realize how privileged you have been to be the only two mortals in attendance. I have arranged for Minerva to accompany you as you pay a visit to other Roman gods. She is, after all, well-placed to act as your guide. She is the protector of artists and schools. You, Lucius, are no doubt a student, and your singing past, Dionysius, however nondescript it may have been, makes you an artist of sorts. I have given you a letter of introduction so that the deities will accept you most graciously. On behalf of all the gods here, I bid you *adieu* – I like that word – it is very godly! Jupiter is probably still playing with shards that are his, but not mine – I call them his "bastshards", since I'd love to give them a good basting!

-       Some of my family members have left little notes for you two. Venus says she loved meeting you and would love to meet you again sometime. She hopes you will love your trip around Rome. Well, easy to figure out what she's all about. And she has some advice – Do what you love, and love what you do! If she continues to overwork that word "love", it could become a four-letter word!

\-   But it is…

\-   Let it go, Cruz. Any more notes?

\-   Yes, Apollo says to always look at things on the bright side, and never be afraid to consult. And Vesta reminds you to always light her fire. "You know I would take Apollo's lyre if it would make the fire much higher, and may I sink in mire if you think I'm a liar"! I wonder where that came from? Oh, here's a little P.S. – a "personal statement". She saw these verses on Jim's doors at Venus Beach in a place called Los Angeles. She must mean "a gym's doors". I'll have to ask our Venus if she knows anything about this. Neptune hopes you will have a whale of a time in Italy, and hopes to sea you again one day. Aw, he misspelled "see". He did the same thing when he was copying lyrics for Apollo – Oh say can you "sea"! Ceres has sent a surreal message – "Seeyareal soon"! I believe she's off to eat her cereal soon. Even Pluto warns you that it is a dog eat dog world. Doggone that Pluto. Maybe he's taking the mick. EE…mouse over there!

\-   I'll take care of it, Minerva. It's only a very small one – a mini mouse!

\-   I guess you find me a little goofy – a goddess afraid of mice.

\-   You can overcome that fear. A fellow named Walt Disney did exactly that.

\-   It's like I'm in a world of my own. I rise at dawn, duck out of the house in a daze …EE…mouse again! True, I help the Romans produce olives, but not cheese!

185

- Disney also has his own World! And try working with a computer, Minerva. You'll get to handle a harmless mouse, and you won't be so nervous.

- Me - nerves? Me nervous? No way! Minerva is the epitome of courage! Mercury has a message by the way. He says to always be prepared, and never fly by the seat of your pants or try to wing it. If that were Neptune speaking, I would have said "right from the horse's mouth"! Mercury also says *Caveat emptor* – Latin for "let the buyer beware"! I would add "especially if Mercury is selling"! Vulcan advises you to always iron out your differences, but also, in threatening situations, to display nerves of steel. Diana wishes you happy hunting, and invites you to drop in if ever you're in her neck of the woods. Bacchus, almost sober, has written down a song title - "Keep on Dancing"! You know he makes fun of Juno, and calls her the "Dancing Queen". Then he tries to recite verses in an ABBA rhyming scheme. Mars reminds you to always fight the good fight, and, not to steal Jupiter's thunder, offers this little ditty – When life hits you with a jolt – don't just turn and bolt, but stand and face the fight – for everything you know to be right!

- Amen!

- Oh, have you two met the Christians on some street corner?

- No, Minerva, but Amen Corner does have an august appeal.

- Well different strokes for different folks!

- But it don't mean a thing if you if you don'have the swing!

- I'm afraid I'm stymied by what you're saying. What is this note that young Lucius has handed me? "Let's fore-get the whole thing"! But you've misspelled "forget". I think since we've gone from stone inscriptions to wax tablets in the schools, spelling has gone downhill. People rush their words, since they can easily erase their mistakes, and there is no longer the fear of the teacher casting an "evil spell" check!

- I will be sure that Lucius Crux gets extra tutoring, but in the big scheme of things, it will be a light cross for him to bear!

- Dionysius, you just translated his name, and I think you would be the ideal tutor for your grandson.

- I couldn't agree more, Minerva.

- And Jupiter agrees as well. Here is his note – "Even sitting on the can, I shall do the best I can – for if anyone can squeeze a message into a can, Jupiter is the one that can"! So here is his canned message. "My dear Dionysius, my delightful Lucius Crux, education is extremely important – just ask Minerva . I must truly say that to attain truth and to profit from the best lessons in life, one need only consult stories where the actions and words of animals – fanciful as they are – shed true light on the nature and workings of mortals. Back in the 6th century BCE – that is, "before censorship existed" - you may get the chance to ask Ovid and Augustus about censorship - a slave told stories through the mouths of animals. These stories were eventually written down and became known as fables. They are fabulous, but genuine, lessons about and for life! I urge both of you to read the Greek or Latin version of Aesop ASAP!

Jupiter Optimus Maximus, etc. etc.

\- Fortunately, Cruz, I kept my Greek text of Aesop from my student days. I always enjoyed reading tales about creatures with tails! You will notice on many Roman coins, a head on one side, and an animal on the other. This occurrence has led to the "heads or tails" choice when flipping a coin. I don't know, though, who first coined that expression! Perhaps it was first used in *Koine* Greek – you know the Greek of the New Testament.

\- Well, gentlemen, isn't it good to be out in the country, breathing all that fresh air? There's Faunus. He is always busy making predictions.

\- We wouldn't want to bother him if he is all tied up.

\- On the contrary! He can only make his predictions when he has been duly bound. And he is bound to utter a prophecy for you, if you call him Lupercus. But do it quickly. He won't tell you to hold your shirt on. Quite the opposite, since he likes to get naked.

\- Greetings, I am the god of fertility. I can safely say, old man, that your days of fertility are now ancient history, and you, young man, will continue to have a fertile imagination.

\- You're funny, Faunus!

188

- Let's go, you two. I can see the Faun becoming a little too fond of young Lucius.

- Say, Papi, maybe if there were two of them, the Fauns would see happier days!

- The young girl over there with a spring in her step is Flora.

- Even though we're not in San Francisco, Cruz, I feel somehow that we should be wearing flowers in our hair.

- So do you like flowers, kid?

- Well, there are two "Roses" in my family.

- Yipes! Only two? Look at my fields full of roses of all colors. What color are your two roses?

- The same color as me! I'm talking about my sister Everly Rose and my cousin Mandy Rose!

- With all that vegetation for names, you must have quite the family tree! What is your name?

- Cruz…er… Crux!

- So – Cross. And crosses are made from trees. I think I got my point across! You are definitely part of a tree – a family one at that! Well, I'm off to prepare a festival – mine! Glad we crossed paths!

- She's funny, Papi!

- Yes, Cruz, not a cross word at all. Although, at first, you probably had her thinking she was doing a crossword!

- We are now approaching the city.

- You can tell by those buildings - right, Minerva?

- No, Lucius. The city gods have come out to greet us.

- Welcome! I am Fortuna. You are very fortunate, since I'm having a good day today. I'm accompanied by some *lares, penates* and *genii*. They are from the public sphere, but so many more of them are in each house, protecting families and individuals. Did you know you had a *genius,* young man?

- Thanks for setting my grandson straight, Fortuna. Sometimes he thinks he IS a genius!

- We are not ready to enter the city yet, but I'm sure these two accept your blessing, Fortuna.

- I see that you are about to spirit them back into the countryside, Minerva. I guess they are off to seek their own "fortunes"! I hope they will be inspired by my play on words.

- Fortunately, we picked up on it. There is someone I want them to meet. I believe Saturn is approaching. Oops – it's Ops.

- Hello, Minerva. Have your friends brought me some offerings?

- Coming from you, that's rich, Ops! Dionysius, Lucius Crux, this is Ops, the god of wealth and riches. He is also in the running for "god of sick jokes"! You can see how I mistook him for Saturn, who is also the god of abundance. They have pretty well taken over from Mars, as the agricultural deities *par excellence.*

You two wouldn't know this, but Mars was originally an agricultural divinity. That was back in the day, when the Romans were just a group of farmers, busy tilling the soil. Mars was their chief god. Eventually, the Romans started to pick fights with neighboring tribes, and gradually became farmer-soldiers – or maybe soldier-farmers! In any event, the Romans began conquering other settlements. The "fights" gradually expanded into full-blown wars. Mars remained their favorite god, but now he was the god of war. He is the god you know and love, and whom you met at the *lectisternium*. Here comes Saturn now! He's wearing a few rings. For some reason, Saturn will always have this thing for rings.

-       Saturn, when you're around I feel so "opsolete"! It's like an "opsession"!

-       Hi Minerva and friends. Hello, Ops. When is the selection for "god of sick jokes"? I hope these two strangers will be attending the *Saturnalia*. It's the party where we can forget our inhibitions. By the way, you two would be overdressed. Shed those nice togas for simple tunics! Everybody who is somebody will be there.

-       And everybody who is nobody will also be there!

-       Thank you for that, Ops! He means that masters will serve slaves during that festival. It will be quite the party. All public activity will be suspended. Such scenarios will occur in the distant future. But people will refer to them as strikes.

- We are getting a little afield with these two agricultural jokers. We should put their pictures on shards! One more god to meet!

- Minerva, that god seems to be waving hello to us and good-by to Saturn and Ops.

- More like good riddance to those two! But you're right, Lucius. Janus has two faces, and so he can look ahead and look back. His name actually has a connection to your name, since Janus was most likely derived, like Diana, from the root *dius*, which evokes the idea of a bright sky – like your name which means light.

- Papi, Are you thinking of the song "Two Faces Have I"?

- Yes, recorded by Lou Christie. I know that Janus is the unofficial "god" of New Year's Eve, since he says good-by to the old year and welcomes in the new year. He is also the god of doorways, that is, of entrances and exits. Vulcan is thinking of hiring him as a consultant to help him with the "ins and outs" of his workshop. He is "two-faced" in a good way! By the way, I didn't want to mention that other hit song by "Lightning Lou" – "Lightning Strikes" to Jupiter, since the King of the gods was already full of his own thunder! And the song "Rhapsody in the Rain" would only lead to an outpouring of boasting on his part!

- Janus is the ideal god to meet now, as you are leaving the realm of the Roman gods, and about to begin your encounters with Roman heroes. Have fun!

Chapter Thirteen: Cruz and I Begin at the Beginning

-        Papi, doesn't the month of January get its name from Janus?

-        That's correct, Cruz. But in the beginning, the Roman calendar began with the month of March. This calendar had ten months – 1- *Martius* - March, 2- *Aprilis* – April – named for the Etruscan *Apru* , 3 - *Maius* – May – from the word *maius* – more, hence growth – or possibly for Maia, the mother of Mercury, 4 – *Iunius* – June – named for Juno, 5- *Quintilis* - Fifth, 6 – *Sextilis* – Sixth, 7 – *September* - Seventh, 8 – *October* – Eighth, 9- *November* – Ninth, 10- *December* – Tenth. Later *Januarius* and *Februarius* – from *Februa,* a purification festival, became the first and second months. The fifth and sixth months were renamed *Iulius* and *Augustus* in honor of Julius Caesar and Emperor Augustus. September, October, November, and December became the ninth, tenth, eleventh and twelfth months, but the names were not changed, which may suggest to future historians that somebody along the line forgot how to count! Most of the calendar reform was done by Julius Caesar, and a change in leap year under Pope Gregory XIII in 1582 finalized the calendar we use today. Three days in the months have names – *Kalends* – with a K, because it is a Greek word – is the first day of each month; *Nones* – nine days before the *Ides;* and *Ides* – thirteenth or fifteenth day of the month. The Roman Calendar is called the *Fasti.* The word *fastus* meant permissible. So *fasti* were days on which legal and religious activities were permitted, and *nefasti* were days on which those activities were not permitted. By the way, never agree to being paid on the "Greek calends", since that day doesn't exist – it's in the Roman calendar! In fact the word "calendar" itself comes from the name of the first day in each month of the Roman calendar! The Romans began their chronology with the founding of Rome in 753 BCE, which became their Year One. They eventually started naming their years for the two consuls in office. It's as if when JFK was elected President of the United States, instead of saying the year 1960 we said "in the year of Kennedy and Johnson". When Julius Caesar was consul, he so overshadowed the other consul Bibulus, that instead of saying "in the year of Caesar and Bibulus", that year was referred to - unofficially, of course – as "in the year of Julius and Caesar"! "In the year of Caesar and what's his face" would have lacked *dignitas!* Of course, by the time of Caesar, the Romans could be very precise in their dating. For example, they might say "beware the Ides of March" – which would be March 15 for us, Cruz. Since Julius Caesar was gung ho on having an accurate calendar, he may have had the Ides of March encircled in his personal agenda.

-       The Romans had agendas, Papi?

-       Since *agenda* is a Latin word meaning "things that had to be done" – like my "to do" list – that's entirely possible.

-       Listening to all that was exhausting, Papi!

-        Yes, Cruz, a little time-consuming! I wonder if Julius Caesar, like Neil Sedaka, loved his "Calendar Girl"! Well, as they say, where one sees a pretty girl, there also Julius Caesar! I don't know if there is any truth in the tale that on those occasions he would concoct the famous "Caesar's salad" – "lettuce alone"! So rather than a dressing, there would likely be some "undressing"! But no doubt too many trysts with young calendar girls in bikinis –as depicted on the mosaics at Pompeii – would lead to Julius' seizures.

-        Papi, there is a man over there carrying something – or someone - over his shoulder. There are a few people walking with him, including a boy who looks like he is about my age.

-        If you look closely, Cruz, that group should look familiar. Especially if I tell you that the group's leader is carrying his father over his shoulder.

-        You're right, Papi! We saw them leaving Troy, after the Greeks had set fire to the city. I think I'll go over and talk to the boy.

-        Why not, Cruz? Just like in school, everybody wants to be your friend!

-        Hi, I'm Lucius Crux, and that's my grandfather, Dionysius, over there. Where are you folks heading?

-        I wish I knew! Even my Dad doesn't know. And that's my grandfather Anchises being carried over his shoulder. My name's Ascanius, but my friends call me Iuli.

\-   Is that short for the wandering hero Ulysses? And if you don't mind me saying, there is something very familiar about your face.

\-   No, my son is not named for that Greek hero – whom the Greeks actually call Odysseus – but his mother Creusa and I felt that his nickname Iulus could one day become very popular if we lengthened it to Julius, and maybe even make him famous.

\-   I see.

\-   Iuli sees too! Say, did I just say "Ulysses"?

\-   Lucius Crux, you probably see a resemblance in me with my grandmother Venus. She was married to my grandfather – don't ask – and my Dad Aeneas is her son. But FYI – address him as "*pius* Aeneas". Maybe because he is "hopelessly devoted" to me – and to finding a new homeland.

\-   I've heard that phrase in a song in *Grease*!

\-   No, we are definitely not going to Greece!

\-   I was actually talking about a musical… no, forget it!

\-   You and your grandfather are welcome to come along with us.

\-   We'd love to, right, Papi?

\-   Sure, Lucius. You might point out to your new friend that your name "Crux" may also be associated with great events one day. I happen to know, boys, that the adventures we will share together won't be entirely new for my grandson and me. I have a feeling,

Crux, that you are going to be reminded of our adventures with the characters from Homer's epics. They will go much faster, though, because a writer named Vergil will describe a war and the heroic adventures of a man who also wandered before reaching his goal. Only he wasn't returning home, but was heading to a new home. But, whereas Homer's stories were spread over 48 books, Vergil's narrative is told in 12 books, with the result that Roman readers digest the story in much less time! Crux, hold on to your hat, because we are about to accompany the wandering Aeneas, as he makes his way to the shores of Italy.

- Two things, Papi. One – I'm not wearing a hat! I don't want people to think I'm an ex-slave. Two, will you be singing that song "I'm a Wanderer" by Dion, during our voyage?

- One, Cruz. It was just a figure of speech – like "keep your shirt on", or "don't get your shorts in a twist" – and something tells me, young man, that you may not be wearing those either! Two, the short answer is no. But, now that you have mentioned that name, there is a connection between "Dion" and my name Denys – as well as my "travelling name", Dionysius! We won't talk about Ricky Nelson's song "Travelling Man", but "Dion", from *dius* – "light", like the "god of light", since he obviously has some Apollo in him, being able to sing like he does, and *deus,* meaning "god", make him a "child of heaven and earth". And poor Dion just wanted to be a "Teenager in Love"! But that etymology may explain why Céline Dion is a diva, a "goddess of song"!

-       Iulus, tell your friends we'll be spending some time here in Carthage as the guests of Queen Dido. And young Crux may need a hat after all, because we are apparently in for a big rain-storm. Don't worry, son, Dido and I know where to take shelter. The Queen is always humming a song called "Gimme Shelter", all the while rolling stones along the ground. It's probably part of their religious ceremony to the Carthaginian god Baal, who followed them – or maybe led them – when they left Phoenicia. It isn't a coincidence that the Carthaginians under Dido are a maritime commercial force! But don't worry, son, I'm not about to cave in to her demands!

-       If I may interject, Aeneas, that song you just mentioned will one day signify two things – a war involving a great power, and an affair between a groupie named Anita Pallenberg with a certain Mick Jagger while she was living with his friend Keith Richards. As I recall, a lot of swearing of oaths – and swearing period - went on. Far be it from me to dictate your course of action, *pius* Aeneas, but I kind of see the same things happening here – a dubious affair and a mighty war. And by the way, Dido's nurse, Anna, has a name very similar to Anita! Just saying…

-       I appreciate your concern, Dionysius, but I will leave Dido here and sail on towards my destiny. So she can like it or lump it!

-       Well, history will record that she lumped it! When your Carthaginian caper is over, Vergil's readers will learn that the Queen died – oh what a tragedy!

-      Must you repeat her name? I won't bore you with the details of the monsters and dangers we will face, since I heard your Crux telling my Iulus about the fantastic perils you faced on a previous voyage in these parts. You are probably thinking of changing travel agents! Try to keep yourselves amused, since I've got to go into the underworld – we heroes have this thing about going down there!

-      Boys, when Aeneas gets back, we'll be making our way to the shores of Italy, to a "land called Latium" – let's call it LL. Eventually, a nearby land called Etruria will be powerful. So the gods may tell us to go to ELL – the **E**truscan **L**and of **L**atium!

-      What... the Ell?

-      Ascanius – er, Iulus – your father will marry the King's daughter Lavinia and call their city Lavinium. Did I mention the Romans don't have much of an imagination? One more thing - since Lavinia is engaged, your father will **engage** in combat – mortal combat to be more specific – with her betrothed, Turnus. At first the battle turns in favor of one, then the other. Each has the advantage in turn. Then Turnus will take a turn for the worse. I know, Cruz, that you are thinking, that I will break into "Turn, Turn, Turn" by the Byrds, but our two dueling rivals – should I say "dualing" since there are two of them? – will find that song to be for the birds – a complete turn off! After they each take turns calling on the gods by oath, Aeneas will call out to Turnus the words, "Turn Around, Look at Me". This seemed to be a battle-cry in vogue at the time! For some reason, Turnus will utter the famous words "the quality of mercy is not strained". Oh, he didn't make the words famous – somebody named William Shakespeare used that line in his play *The Merchant of Venice*. I thought it would be appropriate to mention that play, since Venice is in the land of Italy! Cruz, William Shakespeare was a bard, in a manner of speaking, since he was a masterful "teller of tales", and he studied Latin. He also knew a bit of Greek, but I'm sure he was never as good a student as you! Your father, Iulus, will be about to freely show mercy – no strings attached – when he will notice his friend's sword attached to Turnus. The same friend who had been slaughtered by Turnus. Thereupon, Turnus' life will turn upside down as Aeneas will mercilessly kill his foe. I doubt that, even if he had turned up, Marvin Gaye's plea "Mercy, Mercy, Mercy" would have saved him. It just goes to show how life's fortunes can turn on a dime! The good news, Iulus, is that the story will turn out well for you. A city, Alba Longa, will be ruled by you, and more good news is that a group called The Vogues – in case you missed the earlier reference I made to them – will record a song called "Magic Town", and that could point to the grandeur of a city that will be called Rome.

- Gosh, Papi, your description of events caused me to turn on to the story of Rome's beginnings and, of course, to tune in to those songs you mentioned. I'm glad my friend Iulus doesn't just drop out of the picture. But I'm still a little leery of what Carthage might do to avenge the deviously destructive Dido's disastrous disappointment! It won't be a hippy…I mean happy ending!

-        After your delightfully deft demonstration, the mighty confrontation between Rome and Carthage will ultimately come down to the "D" – "**d**o or **d**ie"! You can see that surely!

-        Yes, Papi, how the two cities will be able to "**d**efend" themselves against the other. But why did you call me Shirley?

-        More smart remarks like that, and I won't be calling you for dinner! But we will be hearing more about the foundation of Rome. As The Carpenters sang, "We've Only Just Begun"!

-        And as Chicago sang in their song "Beginnings" – "It's only the beginning…it's only the start"!

-        I'm back from the underworld. I hope Iulus has been behaving himself.

-        Compared to Lucius Crux, young Ascanius has been a pious saint!

-        Sounds like you've given him my title, perhaps slightly mispronouncing *pius.*

-        Related words, Aeneas, but a different context.

-        I know you two are moving on, and probably won't hear anymore from us.

-        But we'll hear a lot ABOUT you, won't we, Papi?

-        Definitely! We'll even be able to read about you and your famous descendants for centuries to come.

201

-       Lucius Crux, that word you use for your grandfather seems like it could be part of my Latin native tongue.

-       It's French, Iuli, one of the languages that will evolve from Latin.

-       Won't Latin live forever? Won't glorious Rome endure eternally?

-       Yes - *mutatis mutandis*! I mean with some necessary changes. Latin will always be dear to my heart as well as that of my grandson! So long, we're off to meet some of those famous descendants of yours.

-       I'll miss you truly, Iuli!

-       Me too, Crux!

-       Papi, they'll go down in history, won't they?

-       They will certainly be remembered, Cruz, but "history" is perhaps not the best word to describe how they will continue to live in our minds and hearts. They will not be "historical" characters *per se*, but will become part of the fabric of the story of Rome, thanks to a bit of "erratic embellishment" by historians such as Livy. On an interesting tangent, "erratic" means "wandering", like our friend Aeneas is doing. The stories of heroes, like those of the gods, are part of Roman mythology – although some heroes may have evolved from some legendary characters. Myths can be retold, revised, reinvented, removed, restructured, in short, "re-everything"! Discussing mythtakes and mythconceptions can be interesting, but dangerous. Oh, sorry, I meant to say **mis**takes and

misconceptions! However, the most dangerous "Miss" of all the universe is myth**information**! Make that **mis**information! History, on the other hand, should be "what you see is what you get"! "This or that happened" – no ifs, ands or buts! How history COULD have changed is a different kettle of fish – no, not "fishtakes, etc.! Investigating and discussing who did what, where and when as well as why can be a beneficial exercise. The age-old maxim is that we learn from our errors – another "wandering" word! But do we?

-       Papi, while "wandering" through these woods, I wonder if we'll run into the goddess Diana.

-       It's more likely that we'll have to run away from wolves. Be careful, for as the Hungarian proverb warns "while running away from the male wolf, you often run into the she-wolf"! The wolves in question may not be from Hungary – just hungry! And they certainly will not be wolves you see hanging around Aristotle's Lyceum!

-       Look, Papi – two boys my age are play fighting outside that hut.

-       They seem to be taking their "play fighting" pretty seriously, Cruz. If they used your karate moves, they could really hurt one another. Why don't you go over and introduce us?

-       Guys, I don't want to spoil your fun, but I'm Lucius Crux and over there is my grandfather Dionysius.

-       Welcome! I am Remus and this is my brother Romulus. We are into bird-watching, and we always get into arguments over who sees the biggest birds. We write down the names, times and places we see the birds. We have an on-going competition, and the winner will get the new room our father has added to our hut. Oh, he's not our real father, since the god Mars is our father. Our step-father is convinced of this since we are always fighting! Our real mother, Rhea Silvia, is dead. Her name - Silvia – is from the Latin word *silvae*, meaning "woods". I guess that's why we feel at home here, and even the wolves don't bother us. She was a Vestal Virgin for a while, but not for long, since she claimed that Mars raped her. Because of that accusation, Mars bars other Vestals from entering these woods. As is the punishment for violated Vestals, mother was put to death.

-       What Remus didn't tell you is that we are fighting now because he cheated. He claimed to have seen an eagle in these woods, and wrote it down with today's date – April 21. When I told him eagles are only found on the mountain summits, miles from here, he crossed out "seen in the woods" and wrote "seen on the Capitoline Hill" – even though he has never been there. He also hasn't admitted that I usually win the fights because my name comes from the Greek word *rhome*, which means "strength". In fact I'm going to build a city one day, and give it that name. I'll build it in those hills where the eagles fly, and my father Mars will be especially honored, because one day that city – Rome – will raise fighting legions who will win many wars for the city. Venus will also be honored, since the

Latin name for the city – *Roma* – spelled backwards is "Love" – *Amor*! I will be the first King of that city!

-        Over my dead body, Romulus!

-        Boys, boys! Remus, be careful what you wish for!

-        Papi, do you have a crystal ball that will tell us if all that Romulus is telling us will come true?

-        Better than that, Cruz – I can consult the Science Museum guide-book that we received when we entered the model time-machine. Yes, in fact, Romulus does become the first king of Rome. Sadly, he does also slay his brother Remus. Fratricide was all the rage! In Biblical accounts, Cain slew his brother Abel. At first he would only diss Abel, but eventually decided to kill him. He did it rather quickly, thus earning the nickname "Hurry Cain". Of course, when his parents got wind of the murder, they were not at all pleased, and kept their distance from their murderous son! In Greek mythology, Eteocles and Polydeuces committed reciprocal fratricide. You remember our time with their father, Oedipus, don't you?

-        Yes, Papi. He became the King of Thebes, after ridding the city of the scourge caused by the Sphinx. But a new plague struck, and the shoe was on the other foot!

-        Cruz, Oedipus didn't wear shoes, and if he had they would have been orthopedic shoes because of his swollen ankles! It's a pity all those brothers didn't get to hear the song by The Hollies called "He Ain't Heavy – He's My Brother"! We had better make

205

tracks, since ahead of us the road is long, with many a winding turn, that leads to who knows where. Pressing the remote will ironically bring us to a remote time in Roman history, where legends mingle with historical events. Think of sports heroes – people who actually lived – but whose feats became legendary to the point of exaggerating their actual accomplishments. Cruz, I have secured VIP tickets for a special ceremony called the Bravery Banquet. This event will honor Roman heroes who displayed exemplary courage in situations critical to Roman glory and renown. They paved the way for Rome to advance militarily, territorially, socially and politically.

-        Wow, Papi. VIP! I didn't know we were that important.

-        We're not, Cruz. VIP just means "visiting in person". We are hardly front row material! I know you are sometimes in the habit of virtual meetings, even with your teachers. You and your friends find your hearts all a-twitter, even enjoying an instant gram of satisfaction, unlike in my youth when I usually had my face in a book. I prefer those occasions when you and I discuss what's up in the world with a simple chat. As much as my generation can rightly be called "baby-boomers", I believe, Cruz, that we can justifiably label your generation "baby-zoomers"! But just look at all those Hall of Famers on the dais. A veritable Who's Who of Roman mythology!

-        Having said that, Papi, could you tell me who exactly is who up there?

\-   You must recognize the guest of honor sitting in the middle. He is the Greek Herakles 2.0.

\-   Sure, Papi, after watching all those Hercules films with you, I'd recognize him anywhere. Was he as special to the Romans as Herakles was to the Greeks?

\-   The Romans often added their own twists to the stories about the Greek gods and heroes they adopted. And of course they erected temples to Hercules. Mark Antony, for example, had a special devotion to Hercules. The story of the hero's birth is recounted with a comical touch by Plautus in the play *Amphitryon.* In his play *Hercules Furens*, Seneca explored the hero's struggle with madness. Hercules is especially venerated by the Romans for having defeated Cacus, the giant son of Vulcan, who was terrorizing the Roman countryside. His name is derived from the Greek word *kakos*, meaning "bad". As you would say, he was one bad dude! He was able to breathe fire, obviously a genetic trait on his father's side. So, fortunately, we are not guests at a celebrity roast!

\-   There is a screen up there showing a simultaneous translation from Greek to Latin.

\-   That's Evander talking, Cruz. He was the one who brought all things Greek to the Romans – the alphabet, the pantheon of gods, and laws. His name – in contrast to that of Cacus – means "good man". After all, he did bring the Greek goods to Italy! Unfortunately, some of the bads also came along. The hero next to him, eating with his left hand, is Gaius

Mucius Scaevola. When he was captured after failing to kill an Etruscan king, he thrust his right hand into a burning fire. The reaction of the king was to say with admiration "I have to hand it to you, Mucius, you are indeed the epitome of bravery!". From that moment, the courageous soldier was known as *Scaevola*. That means "Lefty", Cruz. You'll realize just how brave Mucius was when I tell you that the other word for left in Latin is *sinister*. The word had the same pejorative significance for the Romans as it has for us. When you consider the stigma of being left-handed that has marked individuals throughout history, imagine the shame it caused for a Roman no longer able to show any dexterity – from Latin *dexter*, meaning "right. I can't help thinking, though, that Scaevola might have succeeded in his assassination attempt had he been ambidextrous. You'll know what that word means, Cruz, when I tell you that *ambi* is a Latin word for "both". Next to Scaevola is Coriolanus – yes, the same guy in Shakespeare's play of that name. He performed some heroics during the siege at Corioli against the Volscians, who happened to be "public enemy number one" until the rise of the Carthaginians.

- The two heroes at the end of the table look so much alike, Papi, that they could be twins.

- They ARE twins, Cruz. In fact, they are often called the *Gemini*, which is Latin for "twins". We are talking about Castor and Pollux, known as the *Dioscuri*. This title means "sons of Zeus", but, in fact, only Pollux was the son of Zeus. The god, in the form of a swan, raped Leda. Yet, this was not to be Zeus' swan song – he had many more feathers in his cap!

Castor was the son of Leda and her husband Tyndareus, who was also the father of Helen and Clytemnestra. So Tyndareus was the brother-in-law of Zeus. All these relations and relationships – but, alas, not one big happy family! The Twins aided heroes on the battlefield, and were Romanized in yet one more example of cultural transfer. These half-brothers rescued their sister Helen from Theseus. Fortunately for us, they did not save her from Paris! Can you imagine, Cruz – no *Iliad,* and hence no *Odyssey*, and hence no *Aeneid*, and hence no *Divina Comedia,* and hence, no James Joyce's *Ulysses*, and on it would go! They sailed with Jason on the Argo, and were connected with healing and travelling. In a sense, they were the "Peter and Paul" of Ancient Rome!

-       I bet the two disciples couldn't sing like Peter, Paul and Mary!

-       Well, they did sing the praises of Jesus! As for the folk trio, they did their share of travelling, as suggested in their songs "Leaving on a Jet Plane" and "500 Miles", as well as healing with songs like "Puff the Magic Dragon", "If I Had A Hammer" and "Where Have All the Flowers Gone".

-       Papi, that girl sitting next to Coriolanus looks familiar.

-       She should, Cruz. That's Cloelia, and her story was brought to the big screen in the film *Hero of Rome*, which you once watched with me. The "hero" of the title is Scaevola, and Cloelia led an escape of some Roman girl hostages, who had been captured by the Etruscan king, Lars Porsenna. Impressed by her courage, the king allowed Cloelia to redeem half of the hostages. She chose to free the best soldiers, so that the war against the Etruscans could continue. The treatment of hostages was sometimes cruel, and involved torture. But you know what was worse than being a hostage, Cruz?

-        Being half a hostage! Papi, I actually like watching those films you have about ancient Greek and Roman heroes. The films you bought lately like *300, Clash of the Titans*, and *Wrath of the Titans*, as well as a series of films about Spartacus, are kind of gory, though. I remember that you referred to the older films as "sword and sandal" films. Are they like "cloak and dagger" films?

-        Yes and no, Cruz. Those Spartacus and Hercules films from the 1950's and 1960's – and many others – were called "sword and sandal" or "*peplum*" films because of what the hero was wearing and the weapon he was fighting with. As a matter of fact, "cloak and dagger" films had plots centering around suspense and spying, with characters "cloaked" in mystery. They were a genre introduced in the 20th century. But the Romans, including soldiers, often wore cloaks – called a *pallium* in Latin, and would fight with daggers instead of swords. So that description of the film genre could have applied to films based on legends from Greece and Rome as well. Julius Caesar sometimes wore a red cloak when going into battle, thus making him very conspicuous. This was not to make him a target for the enemy, but rather to enable his own soldiers to more easily spot him, and thus offer their protection. The original French and Spanish garment being referred to was a cape. The film was then always about the "capers" of a master spy or some other secret character.

- I believe we also watched a "*peplum*" film about Romulus.

- We did indeed. Roger Moore, who played "The Saint" on TV, starred in the role of Romulus. However, he was no "saint" in the film, since the plot recounts the abduction of the Sabine women. However, Romulus becomes a "dashing hero" in the Italian film *Romulus and Remus*.The English version of the film is called *Duel of the Titans*. But since the film stars Steve Reeves and Gordon Scott, it could have been called "Mr. Universe battles Mr. Universe"! Another woman in Roman lore was Lucretia, the lady sitting on the other side of Hercules. Rather than live in shame and dishonor, after she had been raped by the son of an Etruscan king, Lucretia committed suicide. This act catalyzed the downfall of the Etruscan kings, and her husband became the first consul of the Roman Republic. Next to her is Mettius Curtius, who offered himself to Hades, by riding into a chasm that had suddenly appeared. Lake Curtius then appeared over the chasm – named obviously for the hero. The Romans had no qualms about naming locations after heroes. Whereas today, finding a suitable location to honor a deceased hero is often problematic! Next we have Silvius Brabo, a soldier who killed a giant. When Romulus killed Remus, it was one small killing for a man, but Brabo accomplished one giant killing for mankind!

-       Papi, the man next to Brabo pales in comparison. He doesn't even look Roman.

-       That's because he is Etruscan. His name is Numa. He is said to be the successor to Romulus. He wasn't a war-monger like some of the other kings. His claim to fame is that the Romans "found" religion because of him. The remaining five kings were more historical than legendary. They were Tullus Hostilius, Ancus Marcius, Tarquinius Priscus, Servius Tullius, and Tarquinius *Superbus* – that is, Tarquin the Proud. Can't say that he did Rome proud, however! Next to Numa is Camillus, a 4th century dictator who did so many good deeds on behalf of Rome that he has been called "the second founder of Rome". Beside him is Horatius, known as "Horatius at the Bridge". Why? Because he performed a courageous act - you guessed it – at a bridge. He fought off the Etruscans long enough to allow the rest of the Roman army to escape after they destroyed the bridge.They destroyed the bridge over the river. Why? The Romans had built that bridge over troubled waters, but now the enemy could no longer cross that bridge when they came to it, since it was no longer there! If you are thinking of that film we saw called *Bridge over the River Kwai*, it's understandable. Sitting at the far end of the table is Cincinnatus, who was dictator before "dictator" became a bad word. It is no coincidence that he is sitting out of the limelight, ready to leave right away. He was twice appointed dictator, and both times returned immediately to his farm after saving Rome. He had to gather his cows, since they were always MOOving about!

-       Papi, Cincinnati is where you were born. Did you leave so the city would not get a bad name? Especially from your sad jokes!

-       One more crack like that, Cruz, and your name will be mud!

-       I'm going to try to remember the names of all those Roman gods and heroes, Papi.

-       We are sure to hear about some of them again when we meet the poets and historians of Ancient Rome. It's time to press the green button, Cruz. A whole bunch of fascinating people, places and events await us.

Chapter Fourteen: Back to the Future

-       The big advantage of being able to control time and space, Cruz, is that we'll get to see the whole Roman Empire, including monuments and cities without worrying about chronology and distance. Our visit will not be just a tour – it will be a *tour de force*! Once we have "checked the place out", as they say, we can meet the great people and witness the great events of Roman history. Right now these hills will be alive with the sound of music.

-       You are talking about the seven hills of Rome, aren't you, Papi? And you're feeling proud that your hometown of Cincinnati was built on seven hills! But what is it with the number seven – seven hills, seven kings, 7-Up?

-       I guess that last "7" was to let me know that you are "drinking in" all the wonders of Ancient Rome. Cincinnati is just one of the many cities around the world that claim to be built on seven hills, including Moscow and Kyiv – so go figure! Actually, there are presently more than seven hills surrounding the city of Cincinnati. I was fortunate, in a sense, to leave Cincy before I was "over the hill"! There is a festival in September – yes, the seventh month in the original Roman calendar – celebrating the seven hills of Rome. It is simply called "Seven Hills" – *Septimontium*. As I have often mentioned to you, Cruz, the Romans very much believed in luck – good and bad. They always considered 7 to be a lucky number, ever since the founding of the city by

Romulus on April 21 – a multiple of 7! Even the year of of the founding of Rome according to our calendar begins with a 7 – 753 BCE! The Romans were aware of the Seven Wonders of the Ancient World. They erected a monument to the seven planetary deities – Mars, Mercury, Jupiter, Saturn, Venus, Sun and Moon. This infatuation with the number seven has continued on through the ages to the present time. We have a week of seven days, which is compatible with the Biblical story of Creation. And Jesus himself makes a reference to seven times seventy. In Rome today there are seven principal Catholic basilicas. The combination 777 is considered lucky – is it because they add up to the "21" of Rome's birthday? Even James Bond felt the need for a 7. But at least "007" didn't overdo the sevens. The "total" is exactly 7! And did you know that the Arch of Titus, commemorating the capture of Jerusalem, is sometimes called the Arch of 7 Lamps, after the Jewish *menorah*?

-        I think Mom and Dad always try to have lottery tickets with the number 7.

-        Having you and your sister has already made them winners, Cruz! And I get to share in their good fortune! Right now we're on the Palatine where Romulus is said to have laid the foundations of Rome. There's the Temple of Apollo and a temple dedicated to the eastern goddess Cybele – the *Magna Mater.* You see those huge houses over there? They belonged to various emperors. The Palace of Augustus could be the original "Caesar's Palace", since the first Emperor was Caesar Augustus. And I'm sure a lot of entertainment went on in that house! The other palaces are those of Tiberius and of Domitian. This is the wealthy part of Rome, where the well-to-do citizens live.

-        Is this like Westmount, Papi?

-        Yes, all things considered, you could make that comparison. After all, many houses in Westmount are up steep hills! The next of the seven hills is the Aventine, where we can see the Temple of Diana and a temple consecrated to the Triad of Ceres, Liber and Libera – the patron deities of the common people. Close by are the private houses of Emperors Trajan and Hadrian. Next up is the Caelian Hill. I wonder if that name could refer to the "heavens", perhaps derived from the Latin word *caelum.* There's the Temple of Emperor Claudius.

-        Papi, that hill over there looks important. It has so many temples built on it.

-        It's the Capitoline, Cruz. And it is important – like the Capitol in Washington. You remember Jupiter bragging about his titles? That temple over there is dedicated to *Jupiter Optimus Maximus Capitolinus.* Not to be outdone by her husband, Juno is honored by the Temple of *Juno Moneta*. Then there are the Temple of *Virtus*, the Temple of Saturn, and the Temple honoring the Capitoline Triad of Jupiter, Juno and Minerva. If a university were to be built up here, they would have to name it Temple University! Maybe the Romans would appreciate the diversity, and since the American university of that name has an owl as a mascot, Rome would benefit from a bit of Athenian wisdom!

-       Papi, that palace over on the next hill is amazing!

-       Cruz, that's the *Domus Aurea*, Nero's Golden House. You're looking at the Esquiline Hill, where you will spot beautiful gardens commissioned by Maecenas, who was cultural adviser to Augustus. We can also see the Temple of Minerva and the Baths of Trajan.

-       That next hill seems important, Papi.

-       It is, Cruz. That's the Quirinal, named after Quirinus, a Sabine god of war. As you can imagine, his role was taken over by Mars. That's the Temple of Mars over there. You will sometimes hear the Romans called *Quirites.* You can see the sanctuary of Flora, the gardens of the historian Sallust, and the last imperial baths to be built – those of Constantine.

-       Not much to see on that hill over there, Papi.

-       That's right. The Viminal is the smallest hill. Even its name meaning "twig" is insignificant!

-       Golly, Papi – I bet Sisyphus would rather be hanging out in these hills!

Chapter Fifteen: King of the Hill(s)

- Long live the Roman Republic!

- Papi, what is all the commotion over there?

- Cruz, we are in the middle of the beginning of a new government in Rome. Saying that out loud now sounds like a strange ending to my sentence! It appears that the last king of Ancient Rome has been overthrown. He was the last of three Etruscan kings in Rome, as his name Tarquinius suggests. He was known as Lucius Tarquinius *Superbus*. This last word means he was haughty!

- He was a hotty, Papi?

- No, Cruz "h-a-u-g-h-t-y", as in proud – not "h-o-t-t-y", as in your Papi! But, now that I think about it, the use of violence and intimidation, as well as disrespecting Roman custom and the Roman Senate, was tantamount to "playing with fire"! Say, why don't you ask those two boys what's going on? They look to be about your age, and you seem to have a knack for making friends with people from the Ancient World!

- Hi, guys. My name's Crux. What's going on?

- I'm Remulus, and this is my brother Troysarus. I was named for the founders of Rome – Romulus and Remus. Troysarus was named for the ancient city of Troy, the home of Prince Aeneas, who came to the shores of Italy and whose son Iulus founded the race that would become the Romans. Tarquin the Proud has been chased into exile for a crime committed against Lucretia – we don't know all the details. Our uncles, Brutus and Collatinus, said we were too young to hear the whole story.

- My brother should also have mentioned that Tarquin was basically a creepy King! So, Crux, do you know that old man standing over there?

- That's my grandfather Dionysius. We're both interested in learning as much as we can about what's going on in Rome. Would you like to meet him?

- Sure! He looks like he could be one of the *patres conscripti,* who will oversee the new government. It's going to involve a lot of old men!

- Wise old men, brother! They will be known as senators. But we have to tell Crux and old Dionysius that our uncles, Brutus and Collatinus, will be the big cheeses of this new Republic. They will be called consuls. But we will remain the little hams that we are!

- I guess, boys, that there could be worse combinations for the new political regime than "ham and cheese"! You know, Crux, this situation reminds me of a song I've always liked. It's a French song by Renée Claude, who, alas, recently passed away. It is called "*C'est le Début d'un Temps Nouveau*", and is quite an apt anthem for this new episode in Roman history.

- Say, Crux, you and Grandpa don't look like you are from around here. Where do you come from?

- Well, Remulus, my Papi – that's what I call him – says we are to answer that question with a song title

– "So Far Away"! It was written and sung by Carole – oh, you won't like her family name – it's King!

-        What's with all the *carmina* – all those songs? Yes, *rex* is no longer an acceptable word in Rome – and you've added a "four-letter" version to boot!

-        I know, guys, that there were seven kings of Rome – just like there are seven hills. Each hill could have had its own king!

-        Hill- no! Crux, would you like my brother and I to tell you about the six kings who preceded Tarquin the Proud?

-        Well, Troysarus, I know a little bit about Romulus. He carried off the Sabine women. Not because he was a feminist, but because these women would be the future wives and mothers of his new city. After all, having only men in Rome would be like having a dance at a boys' school without inviting any girls! Interestingly enough, the King of the Sabines, Titus Tatius, was co-regent with Romulus for a while. Maybe that gave the Romans the idea of having two consuls when they started organizing the Republic! Of course there was also the two-faced god Janus to inspire them. Janus was not "two-faced" in the sense of having a good and a bad face, but rather one that looked forward, and one that looked back. By the way, did I tell you that Papi and I actually met Remus and Romulus before they founded Rome?

-        Say what? Well you probably didn't meet "pious" Numa, the second king. He was responsible for the Romans finding religion. There was certainly no separation of church and state under his rule. In fact, public - or state - religion got a boost from Numa when he introduced the role of *Pontifex Maximus* and the cult of the Vestal Virgins.

- We didn't know "pious" Numa, but we got to meet "*pius*" Aeneas. Papi and I noticed that the non-desirables that were killed during the overthrow of the monarchy were dragged with long hooks to the Tiber River and thrown in.

- That's right! In fact, you could probably get a job dragging those polluted corpses. That way, they would be sure to be dragged by hook or by Crux!

- You're a riot, Remulus! So you would fit right in during the end of the Roman Republic, when they had all those street riots! Too bad, Cruz, they haven't invented rockets yet – so I can't tell them about the Rocket Richard riot that I once told you all about.

- Remulus and I wonder if you could MUSter up the courage to face the rats while burying those criminals, Crux.

- Cruz, Troysarus is "toying" with you, since *mus* is the Latin word for "mouse"!

- Fellas, if I were a *MaxiMUS,* would that make me the strongest mouse – a sort of "Mighty *Mus*"!

- Good comeback, Cruz!

- Instead of playing cat and mouse, Crux, we'll go on with our lesson on the "Royal Romans"! The third king was Tullus Hostilius, who was responsible for Rome's first great military expansion. He came up with the slogan to enlist Roman boys into the militia –

"Uncle Tullus wants you!". The next king, Ancus Marcius, who was the grandson of Numa, combined peace and defensive wars into the young state's fabric. He was peaceful and religious.

-        Just like you and me, Cruz!

-        Papi, Remulus just flashed the peace sign!

-        No, Cruz, I believe he is telling us he is up to king number 5. You remember that the Roman numeral 5 is V.

-        Thank you, *avus*! You don't mind me calling you by the Latin word for grandfather?

-        Of course not! After all, we have all been speaking Latin since we met. By the way, Cruz, as my grandson you are a *nepos.*

-        The fifth king was Lucius Tarquinius Priscus, who was instrumental in Roman expansion. During his reign, the Temple of *Jupiter Optimus Maximus* and the *Circus Maximus* were built.

-        My grandfather and I actually met Jupiter O.M. – and many other deities!

-        In your dreams, maybe! The sixth king was Servius Tullius, who built the *pomerium* walls around the seven hills. He instituted a new constitution and introduced citizen classes. During his reign, the Senate became important.

-        Cruz, the Senate was the original – and literal – "Old Boys Club".

-       Ah, another Latin word – *senex* – meaning "old man".

-       You are not going to sing that Neil Young song, Papi, that you break into whenever my sister Everly teasingly calls you "old man"!

-       When we get to walk along the Tiber, maybe I'll sing "Old Man River"! Cruz, I don't have to look for the conventional signs of aging with the constant reference to songs like "Old Man"!

-       Again, what's with all the *carmina*? Well, not *carmina*, but "Karma" best describes the reign of the seventh and last king – Tarquin the Proud.

-       Papi, how does he know about Karma?

-       Well, Cruz, these brothers are obviously smarter than they look! I am glad there was no King number 8. Then we would probably have had a song like "I'm Tarquin the Eighth, I am, I am"!

-       Grandfather and grandson, there is really nothing "grand" about your *carmina*!

-       Remulus and Troysarus, please don't take this the wrong way, but through no fault of your uncle, he will have a descendant of the same name who will live through the ultimate end of the Republic that is starting off right now. His end will be "brutal". On the upside, he will have the starring role in a play called *Julius Caesar* to be written by one William Shakespeare.

-       Shaking a spear! He is destined to be a great warrior!

- Not really, boys. Well, maybe a "warrior of words"!

- Julius? Any relation to our legendary Iulus?

- As a matter of fact... yes!

- Since Venus was Iulus' grandmother, I guess this Julius *Kaiser* will be a great lover.

- He will think he is! By the way, you used a future German name for him. His name will be Julius CAESAR.

- Okay, don't get your toga in a twist, Grandpa Dionysius, over someone who will probably never become important or anything. And who are these men who are "germs"?

- Well, Troysarus, a little bird – or maybe an eagle – tells me that this Julius Caesar will become a household – or at least a "schoolhouse-hold" - name for centuries to come. His books will help young Crux here to learn Latin properly. The Germans are a people whom the future Romans will battle as Rome rises to become the greatest power in the world.

- Rome is already great!

- Baby steps, Remulus! Baby steps!

- Papi, I thought you were the one who is teaching me proper Latin.

- Yes, but with a little help from my friends – Caesar, Livy, Tacitus, Lucretius, Catullus, Vergil, Cicero, Horace, Martial, Ovid, and Juvenal!

- You don't have very many friends, Dionysius.

- Oh, but I do, Troysarus. We just don't have time for me to name them all. As a matter of fact, Crux and I will have to make tracks. We have places to go and people to meet!

- Okay! Remulus and I are going to go back to the celebrations. I hope there will be a lot of fun festivals like this one!

- You won't need to worry about that, Troysarus. Maybe you two will one day complete the *cursus honorum.*

- Are you saying it's an honorable thing to curse?

- Not at all. It means a "race for honors". Any swearing you do will be by the gods! I'm talking about rising through the different magistracies, and becoming heads of the Republican government. Wouldn't you boys like to become consuls one day like your uncle Brutus?

- You mean keeping it all in the family?

- Strangely enough, that phrase "all in the family" will be commonplace throughout history, including the distant future days of television – something too complicated to explain. So, yes, nepotism will be rampant.

- Papi, did you just refer to me? You know – *nepos!*

- Sort of, Cruz. That word is at the origin of all that family favoritism in society. Let's say our good-byes – which is actually short for "God be with you"!

-       Too bad you're leaving, Crux. You told us you were a fast runner, and it would have been fun racing you for honors!

-       It's time to press the fast forward on the remote, Cruz. We are about to travel through the history of the Roman Rebublic!

-       Were you just anxious to get away from Remulus and Troysarus because they were getting on your nerves, Papi?

-       Those two brothers may not have been the brightest fires on the altar, but at least they weren't killing each other!

Chapter Sixteen: This Means War!

-       Papi, the Roman Republic seems pretty organized. I mean it's not just the city of Rome, is it? It seems that the Roman government has organized all of Italy under its power, including the southern part which has a lot of Greeks. You told me it was called *Magna Graecia.*

-       Very astute observation, Cruz! Early in their history, the Romans developed a knack for two things – fighting wars and administration. After defeating nearby tribes and towns, Rome went on to complete the conquest of all of Italy. She could then set her sights on territories outside of Italy, like the islands of Sicily and Sardinia. The conquered states would become known as *provinciae*, which I personally believe is a reference to the conquest of these states, since *vincere* is the Latin verb for "to conquer".

-       But that's the word "province", which doesn't have anything to do with conquest. The provinces are peaceful, and so is Canada.

-       Actually, Cruz, as you'll no doubt learn when you study Canadian history, "conquest" is part of the story of Canada and of her provinces. You'll realize that more when you study the histories of France and England. But the Roman provinces were also peaceful during a large part of Roman history. The Romans were able to conquer all these territories through the strength and efficiency of their armies. However, Rome did not automatically make the conquered peoples slaves. Besides, there was already a fairly big slave population due to other circumstances. Rome was successful in securing the loyalty of the conquered peoples by offering them privileges, such as protection and trade benefits. These peoples could sign treaties to become allies. But the biggest incentive for the defeated peoples was the chance to become Roman citizens. In fact, the Romans were quite liberal in granting the right of citizenship. And one did not have to give up his language, religion or customs. Politicians of today, take note! As long as you paid your taxes, and swore loyalty to Rome, everybody was happy! But you can't please all of the people all of the time! Some states didn't want to become part of the Roman dominion. Some states went to war against Rome in order to break Rome's monopoly over the Mediterranean world. Some states outside of Italy resisted, and were conquered in war. When you think about it, the Romans had a simple mindset - be our friends or be our enemies!

- 	Maybe those people didn't want to learn Latin, Papi.

- 	Perhaps that was part of it, Cruz. But your Latin lessons are going to continue, young man!

- 	So the Romans fought wars in order to establish peace!

- 	That's right, Cruz. In fact, a Roman piece of practical wisdom goes like this - *Si vis pacem, para bellum!*

- 	I think I can translate that, Papi. "If you want peace, prepare for war"!

- Excellent, Cruz. The Romans did, in fact, obtain peace – a "piece" of Europe, of Asia and of Africa!

- That's so lame, Papi, I should call you Vulcan!

- Well, any vul can tell a joke!

- Say, Papi, there's a large army over there, and it doesn't look Roman.

- That's the Carthaginian army, Cruz, and it's being led by one of the greatest generals in history – Hannibal. Rumors are that he inspired his troops by inventing the WOKE movement.

- What's that, Papi?

- **W**arriors **O**f **K**arthage, **E**ngage! Even the Romans spelled Carthage with a "K" since it was a foreign, Greek-like word that had a "k", but no "c" in the alphabet. In the wake of the WOKE regiment, Hannibal certainly wasn't weak! Are you ready for a little history lesson?

- Even if I'm not, I know you are going to give me one, Papi!

- So, Cruz, you remember the story of Aeneas leaving behind Dido, the Queen of Carthage, to pursue his destiny. She cursed his "destiny", which was ultimately the city of Rome, and swore that the two cities would become bitter enemies. Even if you don't believe the mythology behind that story, the two Mediterranean powers did become rivals. The Carthaginians, like the Phoenicians, who had founded their city on the northern shores of Africa, were a commercial empire, with a strong maritime presence.

The Romans wanted to expand in the Mediterranean, and so clashed with Carthage, doing Carthage sufficient damage, and securing the province formed of the two islands of Sardinia and Corsica. Rome also secured her dominion over northern Italy up to the Alps, and in *Illyria,* which today is Albania and Montenegro, countries across the Adriatic from Italy. True, when you are old enough to study World Geography, Cruz, the world map may look different, as it does from the days when I studied World Geography. All these conquests were won through wars. In my lesson, we are now approaching the last twenty years of the third century BCE.

-        But what is Hannibal doing in Italy, Papi, and how did he get here?

-        That's an interesting story! When Hannibal was about your age, Cruz, he was told stories about the first war with Rome. By the way, these wars with Carthage were called Punic Wars, not because they were small or "puny", but after the word *Poeni*, which was the Roman name for the Phoenicians. Hannibal was so upset by Rome's treatment of Carthage, that he vowed to be Rome's enemy forever! "This means war" was essentially his mantra until he was old enough to lead a Carthaginian army against Rome. You remember how Alexander faced elephants – they were Indian elephants. Hannibal led African elephants across the Alps into Italy. Needless to say, it was not an easy journey. Nor was it as pleasant as our "journey" into antiquity! But despite the hardships, Hannibal's troops did not mutiny. So here we are, witnesses to some of the greatest defeats that will be inflicted on the Roman armies.

- Papi, there is a Roman soldier lying over there. Maybe he's dead!

- Let's go over and have a look. That Carthaginian army is moving in the other direction.

- Papi, this knapsack has some letters scrawled on it. I can make out the Latin letters. Q.P. DOL.

- Sounds kind of like your little cousin Mandy's favorite doll! He seems to be breathing, but he is losing blood. I'm going to wrap a piece of my toga around his leg wound. You give him some water from your water-pouch.

- Papi, his eyes are opening. I think he wants to say something.

- I am *legatus* Quintus Publius Dolabella, soldier of the legions of Rome, and I refuse to surrender to the Carthaginian enemy!

- Well that explains those letters, Cruz. They are the abbreviation of his name. Roman officers – even subordinate ones like legates – don't surrender. Elvis Presley's record "Surrender" would definitely not be popular with the Roman army, even though he himself served in the American army. But then, he was posted in Germany – yes, Cruz, *Germania* – which would make him even less popular!

- We are not Carthaginians, Sir legate. But with your injury you obviously could not "leg it"! I know that the knight the Roman military hates the most is "Sir Ender".

-       You have just made me laugh, young man! And you two have saved my life. Since you are not with Hannibal, you must be allies.

-       I am Dionysius, and this is my grandson, Lucius Crux. I have actually had a little experience saving lives in my youth. Rome is up against a formidable foe in Hannibal. I have heard that he can rouse his troops with inspiring speeches. He stands up on a little wooden podium to address his army. They call it Hannibal's lectern! But for all that, for some reason, he doesn't have the support of his government back in Carthage. Perhaps it is the longstanding fear of Rome, or lack of confidence in Hannibal's ability, or maybe even jealousy of their general's popularity.

-       You are too old, and your grandson is too young to serve. So you two can be my *aides-de-camp*. I picked up that expression while serving in Gaul. Someday we will have a general great enough to conquer Gaul! I managed to escape from the slaughter that Hannibal inflicted on us at Lake Trasimene. Now his army is headed for Cannae. We have a larger army, yet he finds a way to defeat us.

-       It's all about tactics, legate. If you like, we can help you make your way there.

***

-       We're too late. The battle is over. It looks like Hannibal has just inflicted the worst defeat on Rome in Roman history. He will probably move against Rome herself.

-        Somehow, I don't think so, legate. You see, he hasn't brought any siege weapons with him. I suspect he is counting on Rome's allies to abandon her, and maybe cut off Rome's supply lines.

-        Papi, I was just talking to some survivors of the Cannae disaster. There is word that a Roman general named Scipio has regained *Hispania* from Carthage and is planning to invade Africa. Hannibal is being recalled to Carthage to defend against Scipio and his army.

-        We are witnessing the course of history, Cruz! Rome has not been conquered. Otherwise I would have been teaching you Carthaginian instead of Latin!

-        Although I am injured, I can still fight in Scipio's army. You two are welcome to join me in his camp.

-        Can we, Papi?

-        Of course! Everybody is saying this war is down to the African Queen. I'm sure they are referring to Dido, and not the film with Humphrey Bogart!

-        What's that, Dionysius? I understand the Dido reference, but who is Hum-free Beau-gart? The last name sounds like he's from Gaul.

-        Not important, legate. It seems like there is going to be a showdown at a place called Zama.

-        Then let's get going. There is a boat leaving for Africa tomorrow. It's called The African Queen.

- What are the odds, Papi?

- That's Hollywood for you!

- Are you saying there will be a battle in the forest, Dionysius?

- No, legate! There are no forests in North Africa. But there are details I won't **skip - I owe** you an explanation. Crux and I have come from the future, and I know that Scipio will defeat Hannibal.

- Did you just play on the name "Scip - i – o"?

- My Papi does that all the time.

- I don't know where you come from. Your polished Latin made me a little suspicious. No – make that **very** suspicious! I wonder – are you a soothsayer?

- No, legate – a "truthsayer".

- My Papi just did it again!

***

- You were right, Dionysius! Scipio was victorious. He is now called "*Africanus*". Apparently, Hannibal has gone off to Bithynia, where he is still considered Public Enemy Number One by Rome. Because of my injury, I can benefit from an honorable discharge, and receive free land that they are giving to veterans. They call it *latifundia.* So where are you two headed?

-        We are going to move on to the future in Rome's history.

-        Oh yes, that "future" thing. Well, thanks for everything – especially for saving my life!

-        So long, Sir Legate! Papi, what's going to happen to Hannibal?

-        He's going to commit suicide, Cruz. But he will be remembered in a few films – and by Roman history buffs like me!

Chapter Seventeen: As the World Turns – Roman Revolutions

- Time to move the fast forward button, Cruz. Or as the Romans would call it – the *"fasti"* forward button. The *fasti* refer to days in the Roman calendar. Just another example of a "fast" joke, Cruz! Although I know that when it comes to my sense of humour, you can be very FASTidious – even without knowing what that word means! Once Rome had defeated Carthage, she went on to conquer other states and oriental kingdoms around the eastern shores of the Mediterranean. You might say it had become "their sea"! The states of Asia Minor – although for now remaining independent – had to pay "protection money" to Rome. I believe that was the start of a practice that continues to this day. In fact, the King of the Asian kingdom of Pergamum willed his kingdom to Rome. Eventually, Rome established the Province of Asia.

- How did the Romans treat the Greeks, Papi?

- The Greeks, forever in love with freedom, revolted against the Romans, and the city of Corinth was destroyed in 146 BCE. Rather ironically, Carthage was also destroyed in the same year in a third Punic War. A famous Roman, Marcus Porcius Cato, reportedly ended every one of his speeches in the Senate with *Karthago delenda est* – Carthage must be destroyed! I guess the Romans grew tired of him nagging all the time, so they carried out the destruction!

-       But didn't the Greeks capture the Romans, Papi?

-       Only their hearts, Cruz, but not their heads, and certainly not their "arms", if you know what I mean! The Romans also conquered most of Spain. Just as today, there remained a few pockets of "resistance". But the Romans, for the most part, could "bask" in their conquests! Just another old historian's attempt at humour, Cruz, which anyone from the Basque region of Spain would appreciate!

-       So Rome was really expanding, Papi!

-       That's right, Cruz. Here we are in 133 BCE, and Rome has acquired the provinces of Sicily, Sardinia and Corsica, Hither and Farther Spain, Cisalpine Gaul, *Illyria*, Macedonia, Africa and Asia. Of course, I don't mean the continents of Africa and Asia! Rome sent governors to these provinces, and provincial taxes enriched her coffers. *Plus ça change...*! Latin literature was beginning at this time.The poet Ennius was considered the father of Latin literature, as he developed the genre known as satire. Although early and even later Roman writers often imitated Greek writers – remember the "hearts", Cruz! – *satura est Romana*! But when you continue your Latin studies, you will be able to enjoy the comedies of Plautus and Terence. I had major roles in Latin versions of a couple of their plays in university! You might remember your parents saying how much they enjoyed the movie *A Funny Thing Happened on the*

Way to the Forum. It was originally a play, based on Plautine comedy. "Comedy forever!". But I digress. And we have to pay attention to Roman worship of the gods. You remember our friend Dionysus, who you sometimes called Bacchus? Well he ended up in Rome's bad books, and his worship was outlawed in 186 BCE. But Bacchus is back – just not so wild! However, not everything was hunky dory – as we are about to find out!

- Papi, what's that awful smell?

- That's the onerous odor from the overflowing sewers, Cruz. The gutters overflow with the debris thrown unceremoniously from the windows of the poor suburbanites. In ancient Rome the crowded inhabitants of the *Subura* were not as well-off as today's suburb-dwellers. And they were actually called *suburbani*. The resulting foul stench invades the streets of Rome during the March thaw. I believe it is the origin of the expression "beware the tides of March"!

- I never read that in my books on Rome. But you opened up with nice "O's" for the nose, Papi!

- I see you're trying to be funny, Cruz. Usually, you're just trying! But I wonder who that young man is over there. Now he's heading towards us.

- Greetings, old man and young man. You seem to be new in town – I say town, but I really mean city – *urbs,* and not town – *oppidum.* Allow me to introduce myself. I am Quintus Ennius Dentatus, but most people refer to me as Q.E.D.

-       Ah, *quod erat demonstrandum!*

-       What are you saying?

-       It's a well-known Latin expression.

-       I know it's Latin! I'm descended from a distinguished Roman plebeian family! But what were you trying to prove? My noble ancestor was named Curius, so call me curious!

-       It means "that which was to be proved".

-       What was to be proved?

-       That you are a noble and distinguished Roman.

-       Papi, from where I'm standing, he has only proven that he is a Roman.

-       Sh, Cruz! My good man, I am Dionysius, and this is my grandson Crux.

-       How fitting. I've approached you for a reason, and I am anxious to get to the crux of the matter! Did you pick up on that touch of humour?

-       Papi, he's barely touching humour!

-       Again - sh, Cruz! And just why have you approached us, Q.E.D.?

-       I am one of nine certified guides who offer their services to visitors to our fair city. We call ourselves the *decemviri.*

-       But that means **ten** men.

-       I know, but "novemviri" doesn't exist. And besides, *decemviri* has a nice ring to it.

\- Why don't you hire one more guide?

\- You know, young Crux, I never thought of that! You are an inspiration. Young man, YMCA: **Y**oung **M**an – **C**lever **A**dolescent! But why are you moving your arms in a strange way?

\- So how is the Roman Republic doing these days?

\- Well, Dionysius, to tell the truth, there is a lot of in-fighting going on. It's like this – there are two major factions. There are the senatorial aristocrats – you can call them oligarchs – who want to preserve their acquired privileges. They are known as the *Optimates*, the "best men". Another group is pushing for social and economic reforms. They are called the *Populares*, but they are not really a "People's Party", since they are also led by oligarchs interested in obtaining their own privileged status. Their spokesmen are two brothers, Tiberius and Gaius Gracchus. You two are in luck. Tiberius, the tribune, is about to deliver a speech in favour of land reform, and is seeking re-election as tribune.

\- It seems, Q.E.D., that 133 BCE is a year that will go down in history.

\- Judging from that mob that is gathering, Papi, the year may not be all that is going down!

\- Oh my gods! Tiberius has just been murdered.

\- Better make ourselves scarce, Cruz. Especially since I happen to know that his younger brother Gaius will also be murdered in a few years. Unfortunately, some of the supporters working for the Gracchi brothers didn't help the cause of the agrarian reforms. Some of the farmers were a bit clumsy and very naive. There is the story of one farmer who obviously didn't have his ear to the ground. He was to deliver a wagon-load of corn to the city, not realizing he would be attacked by enemy thugs. He happened to get drunk, and fell off the wagon. Consequently many ears ended up on the ground – ears of corn that is!

- Papi, I think that's not the only corn in that story!

- Those murders will indeed mark the beginning of mob violence in the streets of Rome, since senatorial lackeys bumped off both Gracchus brothers. But you two are safe with me, since I have friends in both factions. I always go with the flow.

- I hope it's not that smelly flow we've already experienced in the *Subura*, Papi!

- Cruz, when is the "ship of state" in trouble? Answer: when the ship is a DICTATORship! Of course, back home the ship that carries us into troubled waters is CENSORship. Simon and Garfunkel singing about a certain bridge doesn't help!

- I'll have to let that sink in, Papi!

- Rules are now being broken left and right, and measures established in the Republican constitution were now being ignored or completely changed.

- We are going to have to part with your services, Q.E.D.

- Why?

- Q.U.O.D. – "Because"! We are headed for the future.

- Aren't we all?

- Yes, but some of us will get there faster! Come along, Crux!

- Where to, Papi? Oh, and I understood the "*quod*" joke, since that word actually does mean "because" in Latin!

- We are headed for the 80's, Cruz.

- If we are talking age, you certainly are, Papi!

- Very funny, my little whippersnapper! But we are about to watch Marius and Sulla lead violent mobs against one another as they pursue their ambitions to become the top dog in Rome – you know – the head honcho! Cruz, I've activated the remote to 88 BCE. We will just mingle among Sulla's followers.

- Let's talk to that young couple, Papi. They might be able to explain all this violence.

- Oh good sir! You are surely one of the priests of Rome. My girlfriend and I wish to wed. Could you marry us?

- Papi, those hooligans are grabbing the young couple.

- Unfortunately, Cruz, to this pro-Sulla crowd, the young man seemed to be saying "Marius", and not "marry us"! But I think I see the young man's father coming to the rescue. I believe he has convinced the crowd that his son would never sully Sulla's name!

-       But you almost did with your silly Sulla reference!

-       We need a sullen countenance, Cruz, as we sally forth through this rough mob. I have gathered that Marius has been named consul for a seventh time. No one had ever achieved that before. Sulla, on the other hand, is seeking the consulship as well. In fact he will settle for no less than the dictatorship. His supporters feel he can keep the boat afloat. The "boat", of course, is Rome!

-       Important people are being killed, Papi.

-       Yes, many of them Roman senators. This revolution is becoming much too ugly. I am going to exercise parental discretion and move to the end of this chapter in Roman history. Marius dies in 86 BCE, and Sulla relinquishes the dictatorship before his death in 78 BCE.

-       Will this put an end to the power struggles in Rome, Papi?

-       Do you recall that song by The Carpenters, Cruz – "We've Only Just Begun"?

Chapter Eighteen: Hail Caesar!

- You two must be freedmen.

- Of course we are free men!

- I didn't say "free", but "freed"! You most certainly benefitted from Sulla's general manumission. As for me, I am a man on a mission!

- Am I mishin' something, Papi?

- *Et tu*? Cruz! Good sir, who are you, and what is your mission?

- The name's Tiro – private secretary to Marcus Tullius Cicero. Perhaps you have heard of him. I happen to be *incognito*.

- I certainly have heard of Cicero, the *novus homo* – the "new man". I have also heard of you, Tiro.

- I sometimes call my Papi the "old man" – *senex homo*!

- Please forgive the "young man" – *parvus homo*. His attempts at humour often miss the mark. My name is Dionysius, and this is my grandson Lucius Crux.

- Why are you *incognito*, Mr. Tiro?

- Because it's a Latin word! For someone named Lucius – "man of light" – you are not too bright! I'm *incognito* so as not to be recognized.

- Says the man who just told us his name!

-        Don't be impertinent, Crux, even though that word also comes from a Latin word. Are you on a mission for Cicero?

-        I most certainly am. He wants me to be his "eyes and ears" for what's going on in Rome and indeed, in the Roman world.

-        Eyes and ears – he would have made a great Persian satrap, right, Papi?

-        Interesting snippet of history from one so young. Actually, the Great King's "eyes and ears" spied on his satraps. Where are you two from, Dionysius?

-        We are from around – all around!

-        Excuse me for thinking you had been slaves. We are still a little uneasy since the slave revolt led by Spartacus. Such a pity! He had put on great gladiator shows with his friend Flixus, a *retiarius* – you know, the one who fights with a net. I can still hear Spartacus urging his companion on with "Catch him with your net, Flix!" I guess you heard about the 6000 crosses set up along the Appian Way by Marcus Licinius Crassus. The crucified slaves all claimed to be Spartacus. Isn't history fascinating – from 300 **Spar**tans to 6000 **Spar**tacuses!

-        Yes, for sure, but they all ended up in the movies anyhow, "**spar**ring" with enemies!

-        What's that?

-	Oh, that's just my grandson trying to make light of the mass crucifixion. He finds any event bearing his name Crux extremely excruciating.

-	Well, we all have our crosses to bear. I, for one, find Cicero's tirades tiresome. You see, when I'm away from my overly serious master – even if he is the "father of his country" – I can be quite funny. But I must warn you, *in joco veritas* – there is always some truth in my jokes!

-	Papi, I've already heard Cicero called *pater patriae.* Sounds better in Latin, doesn't it?

-	Say, why don't you two accompany me on my mission? I can fill you in on recent developments.

-	How about that, Papi, Tiro just became a trio!

-	That would have happened anyways, since apparently he is dyslexic.

-	In case you haven't heard, my super patriotic Cicero succesfully prosecuted the Roman governor Verres for corruption, and almost single-handedly saved the Republic from a conspiracy led by the traitor Catiline. Cicero is definitely single-minded. In fact, he is so distinguished, one can easily single him out in a crowd. But he is so wrapped up in his writing and in his single purpose to preserve harmony among the three classes of citizens – what he calls the *concordia ordinum* - that I thought he was going to end up single. But he married into money, and he worships his daughter Tullia. Well not really "worships" – after all, he is a bit of an expert on Roman religion. You should read his *De natura deorum.*

-       My Papi is an expert on Roman…

-       Now is not the time, Cruz. What my grandson was about to say, Tiro, is that I have read Cicero's treatise on the nature of the gods. And I am aware that he hopes to maintain a certain balance among the patricians, equestrians, and plebeians. But what is the precise goal of your mission?

-       Cicero is anxious to have the great general, *Pompeius Magnus*, defend the senatorial interests against rising opposition from populist factions. And I realize I just said "great" twice. But Pompey has accomplished much. He put Spain under Roman control, and rid the Mediterranean of those nasty pirates. Cicero had successfully defended a proposed law to give Pompey command in the East. The general was so successful that he returned to Rome in triumph – and for a triumph! Pompey is very wealthy, and built a theater for Romans to enjoy Greek and Roman productions. His chariots are perennial victors.

-       But Tiro, as I understand it, powerful men are emerging here in Rome.

-       Indeed, there is talk of a deal involving Pompey, the extremely rich Crassus and the new consul, Julius Caesar. Pompey has married Caesar's daughter Julia. This arrangement would be called a "Tirumvriate".

-       He means "Triumvirate", Cruz. I told you he was dyslexic. Is it not true, Tiro, that Caesar has received a five-year proconsulship in Cisalpine Gaul?

-       That is correct. Rome also holds the province of *Gallia Narbonensis*, which runs along the Mediterranean coast.

-       When we get back home, Cruz, you can look up the French Riviera. But most of Gaul is still non-Roman, is it not?

-       That is true. *Gallia comata,* or "long-haired" Gaul, which Caesar names among the "three parts" of Gaul, seems to be his target of conquest – his future claim to fame. As proconsul, he is permitted to raise his own army. This doesn't bode well for the senatorial supporters back in Rome. And I wouldn't put it past Caesar to find a way to maintain his popularity and his influence in Rome during his absence in Gaul.

-       Papi, I would really love to join Caesar on his military campaigns in Gaul! You have told me so much about him, and also about modern Gaul – France.

-       Well, tighten your toga, Cruz, because that's the next step on our journey. Tiro, we wish you all the success on your mission, and I know you are going to be very busy editing Cicero's speeches, letters and philosophical treatises. Be proud that you will be doing posterity a great service.

-       Thank you. Happy travels. I think I'll travel myself – to Tyre!

                               ***

-       That was a long journey we just completed along the longest road in Italy.

-       Yes, Papi. I was famished, and thought we could grab a bite to eat when I saw the AW sign.

-       That sign was just indicating the name of the road – the Appian Way. Although when we did stop into a roadside eatery, I was anxious to order that huge salad on the counter. I was disappointed to be told that it was Caesar's salad. Apparently, he had a reservation, and would be arriving shortly.

-       Lucky for us, Papi , that Greek traveller shared his pie with us. He said he was a mathematician, and insisted on talking about pie! He even wrote the word down on a napkin, but left out the "e"! Yet, when he was leaving and said "Bye-bye", I started to miss American pie, like we used to eat when we visited Cincinnati! And I even miss that song you used to sing… "Bye bye, Miss American Pie". Maybe we could have saved time if we had hitch-hiked.

-       No way, Cruz – Appian or other! I wanted our journey along this road to be completed without a hitch! There could have been brigands along the way, as along the other Roman ways, that is, roads, but nothing ventured, nothing gained.

-       Papi, you just made me think of all those Venture albums you have in your basement. You once told me The Ventures were instrumental in your decision to learn how to play the guitar.

-       That instrumental band is also the reason I said "Walk, don't run", when we started out on the *Via Appia*.

-	That's the Latin name, isn't it, Papi? That must be the reason for the VApp signs.I thought they had to do with 5 applications for travelling along this route, since "V" is the Roman numeral five.

-	Believe it or not, Cruz, you are not completely wrong. The single "V" at the start of this road really does stand for "five". The smaller VA sign stood for **V**eteran **A**uxiliaries. The Roman legions used this road, and the five units were signified by single V. They were Legion, Cohort, Century, *Contubernium*, and Maniple. This last division, which meant "a handful" of soldiers, was eventually done away with.

-	Was that because some of the soldiers were "quite a handful", Papi?

-	You know, Cruzie, those periodic L signs, which were probably 50-mile markers since L is the Roman numeral for 50, could have been temporary signs to indicate a "loser" was now travelling along this road!

-	If you mean me, Papi, then the C signs, must stand for Cruz - or Crux, and not 100-mile markers!

-	You are off the mark…er, Cruz! Nor do the D signs stand for Dionysius, but are rather 500-mile markers. I am aware that you know that C stands for 100 and D stands for 500 in Latin.

-	So M is not for "Marcus", the name you sometimes use for me at home.

-	*Oy* way, I mean *vey!* You know that M is the Roman numeral 1000. Not to lead you amiss, but here we are, Cruz, in 58 BCE, and camp attendants once again to another great man - Julius Caesar. You remember our service with Alexander the Great. What a coincidence that the two conquerors were compared by Plutarch in his *Parallel Lives*. He quotes Caesar as complaining that Alexander had accomplished so much at a young age compared to himself. However, Caesar was confident in his star. There is the story of his capture by pirates, in which he had them raise his ransom price! Would have made sense if he had been receiving a commission! In any event, he returned and killed all the pirates, as he had boasted. I guess Caesar knew how to put his mouth where the money was!

-        At least with the Romans we obtained a promotion, Papi. We get to take care of the legionary weapons. These swords look and feel like the replica you have back home.

-        Good thing we have them ready, Cruz. Caesar is about to lead the troops against the Helvetians. This Celtic tribe was leaving their home in what is modern Switzerland, in hopes of settling in Gaul. Caesar probably plans to "neutralize" them.

-        Is that a joke about neutral Switzerland, Papi? Does he plan to do it with gifts of chocolate?

-        Since we don't yet have Swiss clocks, we don't have time for frivolous banter. And for sure their weapons are more formidable than Swiss knives!

-        Guess what, Papi! Caesar has defeated the Helvetians and sent them packing back to their own territory.

- Good thing it wasn't Caesar who had been defeated, because the "packing" would have been our job! The word in the camp is that Caesar intends to subdue the Belgian tribes, and force all of northern Gaul into submission.

**

- Aren't we lucky, Cruz! We were chosen among the attendants to accompany Caesar as he invades Britain. It seems that one of the commanders discovered that I spoke the language of the tribes there, and I could be deployed in communications. You are coming along to carry documents – and you've done that before. It seems that Caesar is writing a commentary on his campaigns in Gaul. He is writing in the third person to appear modest. On the other hand, he is constantly pointing out his successes and how great a general he is.

- And he is writing in the present tense, so that the Romans feel his presence.

- Was that a deliberate play on words, Cruz? If so, I'll be sure to reward you with presents when we return home! I am also grateful to Caesar for using this verb tense, which has allowed us to read parts of his Latin text together. I hope you had the presence of mind to jot down the year – 55 BCE.

- Papi, the weather is so bad here – constant rain. The Britons are not proving an interesting enough challenge for his military tactics.

- Would you say they are not his cup of tea, Cruz? I think he was discouraged when a group of

252

savages armed with bent sticks did not attack his soldiers, but started batting this tiny ball around. And there was another group with straight sticks batting a ball right back at each other.

-       Papi, I saw some Britons in two groups fighting and grabbing each other to get possession of an oval ball.

-       And there were others in two groups, running and kicking a rather huge ball. To think that in our time the descendants of these barbaric Britons will be playing civilized sports like golf and cricket and rugby and soccer!

-       Come hither, translator. What are their chiefs saying?

-       O mighty Caesar, something about blood, sweat and tears – and I don't think they are referring to a future musical group, since you are definitely not making them "so very happy"! Their wagon has stopped advancing because of the mud, and is just spinning wheel!

-       Now I need an interpreter to figure out what YOU are trying to say! If you are going to babble a lot of bull, why don't you stick to bird-watching and inspection of animal innards. But tell me before we leave this gods-forsaken land, is that a religious shrine up on that mound? We should name it to certify our conquest of this land. What name do you suggest?

-       How about "Church-hill", O Caesar?

-       I had thought of "Mount-battered". But you win! I think that in future invasions, it will be more profitable to ford the channel with cables.

-        Yes, O Caesar, cable channels are the way to go!

***

-        Papi, now that we are back in Gaul, there seems to be a movement to unite all the Gallic tribes into a single force to combat Caesar.

-        Yes, Cruz, and they will be gathering in a fortress at a place called Alesia under a single leader.

-        Is his name Asterix?

-        No!

-        Obelix?

-        Of course not!

-        Idefix?

-        I'm glad you like those books, Cruz, but seriously! His name is Vercingetorix. We will again be accompanying Caesar. I have a feeling something historic is about to take place.

-        You're right, Papi, it's happening. Caesar has starved them into submission, and

Vercingetorix has surrendered to Caesar. I know that means he will be the prize trophy in Caesar's triumph in Rome.

- Cruz, a little fun fact – Alesia is situated close to the modern Dijon.

- That makes sense. It was obvious that the Gauls couldn't cut the mustard!

- Not the time for mustard jokes, Cruz!

- But when you're hot, you're hot!

- Again, no mustard jokes! Besides, we are heading back to Rome. Crassus has been killed in a disastrous Roman defeat at the hands of the Parthians. First he had to swallow his pride after being captured, and then he had to swallow molten gold, as an insult to his attachment to money.

- Papi, since there has never been a "duovirate", what is going to happen between Caesar and Pompey?

- That is the 64,000 *sesterces* question! Caesar has to decide if he wants to cross the Rubicon River and risk civil war. He has invited a few followers, including us, to play a game of dice with him so that he can relax.

- You roll first as you are the youngest, Lucius Crux.

- Darn, I rolled too fast. Oh well, *alea iacta est,* as they say, too late to roll again.

-       Brilliant, young man! The die is definitely cast –
my mind is made up.

-       But I lost the game, O Caesar.

-       Yes, but I shall win the war! It is decided - we
cross the Rubicon to face Pompey. I will bring the
Gaul general with me for my triumph.

-       Cruz, Caesar doesn't know that General the
Gaul will one day ride in triumph through the streets of
Paris!

                              ***

-       Papi, Caesar has been doing really well so far
in the war. His second in command, Mark Antony, is
quite the soldier. He sort of reminds me of Alcibiades,
whom we met during that war in Athens. He seems
like he could switch sides or allegiance to suit his own
interests. I wouldn't be too quick to say "I fear him
not"! Pompey's advisers are proving to be a farce,
alas!

-       If you are humorously implying the final victory
at Pharsalus, remember – Caesar crossed the
Rubicon, not the Comicon!

-       Doesn't Pompey flee to Egypt?

-       Yes – where he is murdered, and his head
brought to Caesar. At the sight of the slain general's
head, Caesar bursts into tears. In tribute to his foe,
marking Pompey's contributions to the culture of
Rome, he had a memorial inscription erected, part of
which has been erased due to some ancient practice

of cancel culture. It reads: "POMP… AND CIRCUS DANCES". But intrigue is awaiting Caesar in Egypt, which is still free of Roman rule.

-        Thanks for the gruesome heads up, Papi. But isn't this when Caesar meets Cleopatra?

-        Yes. When Julius sees her, he is advised by Mark Antony with the words "Julius, seize her"!

-        Didn't Cleopatra arrive before Caesar rolled up in a carpet?

-        That's true, and from that moment, Caesar could no longer sweep his infatuation under the rug. In fact, he intended to prove to Cleopatra that he was a RUGged lover! Whenever he was with her, his inner demon urged him with "Julius, squeeze her"!

***

-        Isn't it great that we've been welcomed into Caesar's inner circle, Papi?

-        It has enabled us to be privy to all the maneuvering for complete power. He has been named to all the important offices, including Consul and *Pontifex Maximus*. He had originally been appointed Dictator for a ten-year period, and now he has been appointed Dictator for life. He also continued to assert himself in military battles. Do you recall, Cruz, what Caesar said after his victory over Pharnaces in Pontus?

-        I won?

257

- Actually, he took us step by step – "I came, I saw, I conquered"!

- Now I remember –*Veni, vidi, vici*!

- Julius Caesar is now master of Rome and of the whole Roman world! He's off in a few minutes to a meeting of the Senate. Obviously, we won't be able to enter the Senate House, but we can mingle with the crowd outside. We'll be with the curious outside the Curia! One of Caesar's great contributions to posterity was the reform of the calendar. Maybe that's why that old beggar keeps saying "beware the Ides of March". It's today's date! It's a bit weird, but I can't help thinking of a modern singing group called Ides of March, who had a hit song called ""Vehicle". Of course Caesar's "vehicle" would be a chariot!

- Papi, what's all the commotion about?

- Cruz, our beloved Caesar has just been assassinated! It was apparently the work of a group of conspirators led by Brutus and Cassius.

- You mean the ones in Shakespeare's play?

- The very same. They were muttering something about down with tyranny and long live the free Republic.

- Should we attend his funeral service, Papi?

- Considering we got close to him, and he treated us well, it's the least we can do. Normally, I wouldn't drag you along to this sad occasion, but Mark Antony is going to speak, and I know you are intrigued by him. He had convinced the conspirators to let him have

Caesar's body to honor as a god. They had allowed him to have Caesar's body with the fateful words *"Carpe deum"*!

- Wow! "Grab the god"! That's cool!

- And they didn't realize that Mark Antony was about to *carpe diem* as well. What did you think of his funeral oration, Cruz?

- Well, he certainly did "seize the moment", didn't he, Papi? When he asked everyone to lend them their ears, he wasn't referring to all that corn imported from Egypt, was he?

- Still the same corny Cruz, I see! Things are about to get dicey, and I'm not referring to the dice games back at the Rubicon. There's going to be a new sheriff in town.

- But Brutus and Cassius are still attempting to marshal resistance.This is exciting!

- All the more so since we are about to witness the end of the revolutions – but also the end of the Roman Republic! And don't think I didn't notice your sheriff - marshal "gunplay"! That was your notion of "Western" Civilization before I started teaching you the rudiments of the Greco-Roman legacy!

Chapter Nineteen: The Emperor's New Clothes

-      Cruz, we never got to meet the poet Catullus. Let me tell you about him. He was a love poet, who was infatuated with a lady – and I use the term loosely! – whom he called Lesbia. She was a Roman socialite who had friends with benefits. Today, she would be an influencer. I'll explain to you what all that means when you're older! Catullus also wrote some nasty poems about Caesar, so it is just as well that he died young – all the more so because the object of his affection for him had no predilection!

-      Papi, you're a poet too! Unless I'm mistaken and merit a correction! Sounds like Catullus was a man of verses and curses!

-      You also have a way with words, Cruz. I'm so proud of you! Catullus wrote poems suggesting that he and Lesbia spend all their time kissing, and sympathizing with Lesbia over the death of her pet sparrow. But he was saddened by the hard time Lesbia was giving him. One of his well-known poems starts off with *Odi et amo* – I hate her and I love her! There were other love poets like Propertius and Tibullus. Maybe we'll get to meet a special love poet named Ovid.

-      Papi, how could a state like Rome, winning wars and conquering peoples, produce so many love poets?

\-   Rome could also be about love, Cruz. After all, as we heard earlier on our trip, her name *Roma*, spelled backwards, is *Amor* – love! Not all Latin writers were love poets, of course. Lucretius was a follower of Epicurean philosophy, and wrote a long poem about the theory of atoms called *De rerum natura* – "On the nature of things". So David Suzuki did not invent that expression!

\-   Is he related to Nick Suzuki?

\-   No, Cruz, but they are both "experts" in their fields! Of course, Nick Suzuki is captain of a team that plays on ice and not in a field, but we are getting too far afield in our discussion. I can't field any more questions at this time. Right now we have to make preparations to be spectators at the war pitting the armies of the self-proclaimed "Liberators" – Brutus and Cassius – against the forces of Mark Antony and the young nephew of Julius Caesar named Octavian. In his will, Caesar adopted him as his son and named him as his heir. Although only 18 years old, Octavian was a pretty smart strategist. He pretended to support the Senate, and so put himself in Cicero's good books. To disguise the appearance of wanting to be sole ruler, he formed the Second Triumvirate with Mark Antony - now his main rival - and the general Marcus Lepidus. They needed him since, although it takes two to tango, it takes three to form a triumvirate! They have killed off many rich Romans to get hold of the money they needed. Cicero had ticked off Antony with his speeches against him called *Philippics* – you remember Demosthenes' speeches against Philip of Macedon – so Antony ticked off Cicero's name! Thus ended the life of the great statesman, orator, lawyer, and philosopher. And by a strange coincidence, Cruz, we are heading off to a place in Greece called Philippi!

***

-       Papi, the forces of Octavian and Mark Antony were victorious, and Brutus and Cassius both committed suicide. I guess it will be smooth sailing for Rome now, and her leaders.

-       Actually, Cruz, the only sailing in the immediate future will be Mark Antony heading to Egypt to be with Cleopatra – but it won't be all that smooth! Mark Antony and the Queen of the Nile will lead the forces of the East against Octavian and the Roman forces of the West, and Caesar's young heir will emerge triumphant.

-       Is it true, Papi, that Cleopatra and Mark Antony will commit suicide? Still, they must have made a remarkable couple!

-       If they had been more aware of each other's potential success in opposing Octavian's forces, they may have been victorious in that war, and so avoided a premature death. As it were, Richard Burton and Elizabeth Taylor as the two lovers – on and off the screen! – became more famous!

-       So Octavian becomes the new Dictator of Rome?

-       No, Cruz. He cleverly professes to protect the institutions of the Republic, but dresses up his one-man rule as *Princeps,* or "first citizen" – first among equals as he would have the Roman Senate believe! But whatever "clothes" he decides to wear, he is, as posterity will call him and his successors, "Emperor". His Principate will forever be known as the Roman Empire, not least of all because he took the title *Imperator*, requiring a slight change leading to its derivative "Emperor". He will be granted the title "*Augustus*", a word implying religious dignity, and that is how moderns prefer to call him. Religion will remain – officially – a powerful force in Roman politics and society. The *Princeps* will strive to portray himself as the epitome of moral rectitude. I can't help, though, seeing the irony in the fact that the Master's Tournament in golf is played at Augusta, Georgia, named after the "master" of the Roman world! On the next leg of our journey, Cruz, we will get to know the Augustan Age a little better.

Chapter Twenty: Pax Augusta

-     Wow! Papi, the imperial palace of Augustus is amazing! But how did we get here? And what are we doing here?

-     Cruz, I've managed to get myself hired as one of the Emperor's wine-tasters. Fortunately, I'm more adept at drinking wine now than in my university days. By the way, you are now one of Augustus' official food-tasters. But just as a heads up, be careful when tasting figs! On the other hand, I think an eventual food poisoner would not want to waste good poison on a mere boy like you.

-     Thanks, Papi. I wouldn't want to go down in the history books as the *Princeps*' poisoned *puer*!

-     Another "fig"-ment of your imagination, lad!

-     Not history book material, Papi, but your jokes kill me!

-     You two stop dilly-dallying, and bring wine and food for my guests Agrippa and Maecenas.

-     Immediately, Sire!

-     Dionysius you say your name is. That should make you an excellent wine-taster! And you, young lad – not an ounce of fat on you. You will be able to taste all of the banquet's delicacies without any harmful effects to your physique. Welcome, Marcus Agrippa! Greetings, Maecenas! The table has been set while I awaited your arrival with great anticipation.

-       Are you sure, Octavian, that we can discuss State business in the presence of these two foreign-looking, albeit handsome, domestics? And while they are present, should you and I even address ourselves by the personal names we've used since our boyhood friendship?

-       They represent no danger, Marcus. *Au contraire* – do you like that phrase uncle Julius taught me when he came back from Gaul? I've gotten to know them a little while they were preparing our feast. It is amazing what Dionysius – he's the older one – knows about Roman religion. It's almost as if he had written books on the subject! Do you know that he has suggested that I introduce the cult of the Emperor? I have always wanted the people to like me. Now they will worship me – literally! He has also proposed that a temple be built in honour of all the gods. As such, it will be called the Pantheon – the man is fluent in Greek as well as Latin. He also speaks the language of the Gauls and of the inhabitants of *Hispania,* and even the tongue of those exasperating Germanic tribes. He is a rare find indeed.

-       Still, we can't be too cautious.

-       Marcus, he has convinced me that your name be placed above the temple of all the gods! I heartily agree, since you were instrumental in my victory over Antony and Cleopatra at Actium. You have been such a king-maker.

-       As I was saying, it would be a cautious move on our part to take advantage of this rare find! And don't you mean "Emperor-maker"? Remember what happened to Uncle Julius!

-        You're so right! The word *Rex* wrecks havoc on a man's life and career! Did you pick up on that clever word play with the Latin word for " king"?

-        I suppose so – other than the fact that all the words we are using are in Latin!

-        Oh – where is your imagination, Agrippa?

-        The same place it has been for most Romans throughout time – nowhere!

-        The young lad is his grandson. There is indeed something very touching about the mutual admiration of a grandfather and grandson! And that Lucius Crux – that's the boy's name – has quite the sense of humour. He cleverly advised me to turn Rome into a "marbleous" city. When I countered that he surely meant to say "marvellous", he replied no – a "city of marble"! And that's what I'll do. Down with brick and mortar. Up with the golden gables, the silver spires, the bronze bastions...

-        Lord Augustus, don't hurt yourself!

-        I'm all right, Maecenas. But those two also have an uncanny knowledge of our Latin literature, and inspire me to wax poetic. However, I do realize I am a *Princeps* first, and a poet second. A poet in **verse,** and not a *Princeps* in **re**verse! Do you find that to be said cleverly, Maecenas?

-        Most certainly, Sire!

-       Funny, my two learned domestics disagree. Something about *in vino veritas* - truth from the wine-taster – and *ex ore parvulorum veritas* – kids always get it right! Crux said it "sucks" – a word I had only heard once before – my daughter Julia used it to describe her life in exile. They say no man is an island, but her island of exile is so small that maybe it does make **her** an island! Now, that is clever! I should think no *Princeps* of Rome would consider being known as a poet first, a *Princeps* second. Especially when *Princeps* suggests "first"! When I broached the subject of the possibility of a future successor getting it backwards with the erudite Dionysius, he offered only this reply – "Oren" . I take this to mean "backwards… **or**… **en**…igmatic". I must say, it remains an enigma to me . Oren…backwards… I must continue to ponder that!

-       What of your grand scheme for peace in the Empire, Lord Augustus?

-       My dear Maecenas, my dear Agrippa, I do want peace. I want a piece of *Hispania, Lusitania, Noricum, Raetia, Illyricum, Pannonia, Africa, Judaea, Galatea…*

-       Again, Lord Augustus, don't hurt yourself!

-       Oh, Maecenas, I find the young boy's wit rubbing off on me. Did you catch that play on words – "peace" and "piece"?

-       Papi, why are they laughing?

-       Well, it wasn't because they had recently seen *"A Funny Thing Happened on the Way to the Forum"*! Augustus has just listed the territories that will be added to the Roman Empire – basically, Spain, Portugal, Switzerland, Bavaria, Austria, Slovenia, Albania, Croatia, Hungary, Serbia, Africa, Palestine and Turkey.

- Gosh! I guess Roman pupils having to memorize Roman Empire maps in Geography class may have mixed feelings about all those conquests.

- Not to mention those who will be called to a "foreign" posting as a legionary! Well, time to bring more goodies to the titillated trio so they can continue to wine and dine.

- Ah, Dionysius! I was just telling Maecenas about your suggestion to have my account of my exploits – my *Res Gestae Divi Augusti* – inscribed in Latin and Greek on pillars throughout the Empire. You said that in this way it would become what you referred to as a "best seller" – read by many! At first, I was insulted when I thought you were saying it should be relegated to the storage rooms. But I had confused that with what you were saying about the wine you were serving, which was the "best in the cellar"! Have you ever had the feeling that the wine was getting the better of you, Dionysius?

- Sadly - yes, Sire.

- Well, we've been talking about establishing peace throughout the Roman World. We'll call it *Pax Romana.* I'm hoping it will last for at least two hundred years. Do you think it will, young Crux?

- I think, *Domine*, that your accomplishments ought to put Rome in good stead for at least five hundred years. And that your achievements of expansion in the East should buy the Empire an additional thousand years.

- Why, that would bring us to about the year 2200 A.U.C. That's *Ab Urbe Condita,* young man of the nice physique, "from the founding of the city of Rome". Oh, not to worry about your grandson, Dionysius, that's the wine talking. And Agrippa is heterosexual. As for Maecenas...he wouldn't dare without my permission! Even though he considers himself the ultimate influencer!

- Notice, Cruz,how 2200 and our year back home – 2020 – have the same numbers if you move them around. And we have been doing a lot of moving around! How does 1453 CE sound, Sire?

- Dionysius, those numbers add up to unlucky 13. And does CE stand for **C**aesar's **E**mpire? Does that signify the unfortunate end of the Roman Empire?

- In a strangely roundabout way, you are exactly right, Sire! But if I may, would it not be more fitting to call this far-reaching peace to be established during your reign *Pax Augusta*? Even the fact that you were the first to establish all of *Italia* as a single unified peninsula is quite an accomplishment, since – and please don't ask me how I know – many centuries from now, that unification process of Italy will have to start all over! So you are indeed the *Princeps* of *Pax,* the Prince of Peace!

- Nice alliteration with the letter P. Here's another – Patron of Poets! Maecenas here, my Purveyor of Propaganda – gosh, I'm good – am I being wasted being a *Princeps*? – will be organizing a conference featuring some of our best writers. Dionysius, I want you and Lucius Crux to be there. It's BYOB! Just kidding – you two will be serving! Be that as it may, "**B**est **Y**ou're **O**n **B**oard"! But as a token of my gratitude for your services, here's an emoji.

-       Papi, how does an emoji show up in Ancient Rome?

-       Let's see. Ah, a golden yellow coin with the letters E.M.O.J.I. On the reverse side is the inscription in full – *Egregia Maxima Octaviani Julii Imperatores*. Cruz, that means "the very great and outstanding actions of Octavian and Julius, Commanders". It's a tribute coin to commemorate the victories of Augustus and his uncle Julius Caesar as military generals. I see it's changed the frown on your face to a smile.

-       Yes, Papi, I'm a human "emoji"!

***

-       Hey, Papi, there's a serving-girl helping out at this writers' conference.

-       No, Cruz, that's Sulpicia, who wrote epigrams. She's the only Roman poetess we know about. Some other important men of letters are here. I recognize the writer of *De Architectura*, Vitruvius. Augustus himself can't be here. Apparently, he has taken ill after having eaten some figs. Don't feel guilty about not having been there to taste them.They were from his wife Livia's personal garden, and so, as usual, she fed them directly to her husband. There's Maecenas fawning over the two love elegists, Tibullus and Propertius. But the historian Livy and the poet Vergil are deep in conversation. We can eavesdrop as we serve them wine and tasty tidbits.

-        My dear Vergilius, I hear you have nearly completed the *Aeneid*. You must be truly proud of your work. It was clever of you to link the Trojan hero Aeneas to Rome's glorious foundation. You know I bought into that theme when I recounted the story of Romulus and Remus, the descendants of Iulus, the son of Aeneas.

-        To tell you the truth, Livy, I am not completely satisfied with my epic. I'm glad I wrote other poetry. Right now I've got the *Georgics* on my mind. You know I'm supposed to be the Roman Homer. Well in that great poet's works, the Trojans were the bad guys. But I couldn't very well say the Romans are descended from the Greeks. I mean those foppish Hellene-bent know-it-alls already have their noses up in the air whenever we challenge them on cultural or language issues. Don't you think the world would be a better place if we embraced each other's language and culture, rather than looking upon them as a menacing threat. All languages and cultures should feel safe within society. Bottom line, I think I'll burn my manuscript of the *Aeneid*, which I left in the reception hall.

-        Well, if truth be told, I only put in some of those heroic episodes to please the Big Boss and so protect my ass.

-       You're only getting paid an *as* for your 142-volume history of Rome?

-       No, I'm well-paid. That's "a", "double-s" – it's about saving my butt! My mandate is to glorify Rome and the *Princeps.* My learned work is basically a PHD thesis – a story-line that is "piled higher and deeper", if you know what I mean!

-       Hi guys! Why the long faces? I'm the one called Horace! Get it? Long faces – Horses – Horace. Gee, you fellas do have it bad.

-       Listen, Horace. Like you, we have to kowtow to Maecanas and his mighty Master for our fame, and yes, for our fortune. Sure, we have both written a major work, but we feel our creativity has been stifled by the imposed theme of the grandeur of Rome and her rulers.

-       I genuinely feel for you, but take comfort in the fact that your works will be read by generations of Romans. I also had the same constraints when I composed my *Odes.* But the *Carmen Saeculare* sort of paid my debt to my benefactors. The secret is to write other major works. In my case, I had the freedom to write *Epistles, Epodes*, and *Satires.* The powers that be owed me that much. Get it? "Owed" – "*Ode*"! Writing satires is a lot of fun – no real Greek influence – entirely Latin stuff!

-       You know where you can stuff your "stuff"? And we're not being satirical!

-       You guys think you have it bad, but the word on the street is that something terrible is going down for poor old Ovid. Maecenas is talking to him now.

-       Did you hear, Cruz?

-       You mean that Ovid is poor and old? That must be satire!

-       No, no! About Vergil planning to destroy his manuscript. I'll bring everybody more wine, while you sneak into the empty reception room, grab the manuscript, and hide it on the salad tray. If anybody asks, just say it's Caesar's salad tray. Nobody will dare touch the Emperor's personal plate. Stay cool! Don't betray our secret.

-       I'll tray, Papi – er, I'll try. I wouldn't want to go down in the history books as a "traytor"!

-       More sick humour like that, and I'll feed you some figs! Then your sense of humour won't be the only thing that's sick! When you get the manuscript, bring some food over to Maecenas and Ovid.

-       No, tell me it's not true. The *Princeps* is not banishing me to the Black Sea. It's in the middle of nowhere. It's beyond civilization. The weather is bad, the scenery is bad, the people are bad, the…

-       You are bad, Ovid! Did you think you could get away with corrupting the morals of gullible citizens by writing filthy books about love? Besides, you didn't put in any pictures!

-       But, Maecenas, love is not bad. Love makes the world go round!

-       Only a square would believe that! Oh, the *Princeps'* daughter Julia did "go round" with her love! All around, so it seems. I think you were involved in covering up her rounds of "uncovering". So as with her, so with you. The path of love leads to exile.

-       I plead poetic permission.

-       Said like a true poet – with admirable alliteration. But don't you mean poetic licence? However, what you are portraying is poetic licentiousness!

-       But what of my great calendar poem, the *Fasti*?

-       Better cherish it while you can, Ovid. Your days in the *Fasti* lane are over!

-       Maecenas, you can get Augustus to change his mind.

-       Two things. At last word, the *Princeps* barely has a mind that he can change. And he is no longer physically capable of changing even his clothes.

-       But Maecenas, I can metamorphize.

-       Say what?

-       I can change! Banishment is such a cruel punishment, and will only lead to the detriment of a great poet. Surely you share that sentiment?

-       One more word ending in "-ment", Publius Ovidius Naso, and you will have a bruised nose. Ah – "Naso no longer has us, because he had to leave with a sore *nasus*!" How's that for poetry? I'm off to make arrangements for the ship that will carry you to the

274

town of Tomis on the Black Sea. Town of Tomis – TT. I bet you're really teed off now! Especially since it will be a long drive - "litter"-ally!

-        Greetings, Ovid. My name is Dionysius. And this is my grandson Crux. He has just rescued Vergil's manuscript before the poet could destroy it.

-        I should have destroyed my manuscript of the *Ars Amatoria* before it had a chance to destroy me.

-        We're sorry to hear that your ship is sailing so soon.

-        Oh, my ship has already sailed. What can life be like on the Black Sea other than dark and stormy nights?

-        "A dark and stormy night" could work in a new literary piece!

-        Too soon, Cruz!

-        Not everything in black is sad and gloomy, Mr. Ovid. The cover of my Papi's novel is black!

-        That is supposed to cheer me up, young man?

-        You will be remembered as a great poet. Your poem *Metamorphoses* will be read and studied down through the ages. Your recounting of the myth of Narcissus will introduce the world to the original "me, myself and I" guy. Your story about Pygmalion and his statue coming to life will inspire future artists to write plays on that theme.

-        And will inspire my Papi to write a short story about Greek statues of gods coming to life!

- Again – and no offence, er…Papi – but that is meant to cheer me up?

- Actually, my favorite story is "Cupid and Psyche". Yes, Ovid, I'm with you – love is a good thing! But here is Agrippa. He is going to announce something to the crowd.

- "Friends, Romans, country…" Sorry – I got carried away.

- Cruz, that's how Mark Antony began his speech before the assassinated Julius Caesar got carried away!

- But now that I have your attention, it is my sad duty to inform you that our dearly beloved Augustus has joined the other deities. He parted with these words, seeming to liken the world to a stage, "Have I played my part well? Then applaud as I exit!" The new *Princeps* is Tiberius.

- Wow, Papi! If Augustus knew Shakespeare's "All the world's a stage", he really must be a god!

- One thing is certain, Cruz - that Emperor won't be needing new clothes!

- Yes, Papi. May Augustus rest in peace! *Pax Augusta*!

Chapter Twenty-one: Love Is All Around Us

-       We'd better get a good night's sleep, Cruz. We will have to serve the refreshments at tomorrow's funeral. I'll tell you Ovid's story of "Cupid and Psyche". That should get both of us to sleep.

-       Dionysius, awake!

-       What the… hey I think I've seen you before. But you weren't wearing tight blue pants – and you didn't have arms. Are you Venus di Milo?

-       No, Dionysius, I'm Venus in Blue Jeans! And I do have arms. I've merely crossed them behind my back to appear sexy! In fact I'm dressed this way in order to appear thoroughly modern, and not in the traditional dress (or undress!) of the goddess of Ancient Rome.

-       Am I dreaming? After all, I'm in Rome, not on Mt. Olympus.

-       The Romans believe in their gods, Dionysius – or at least pretend to - offering prayers and sacrifices, and building temples and statues. That's good enough for me! So when in Rome…

-       But why are you here?

-       You recently said some nice things about love. I want to find out if you really know about love, and truly believe in it. Of course I know that you and your grandson have travelled to antiquity from the year

2020, and from a place called Montreal. So, in your mind, you will travel back to your time and place. You will be tested in this way: I will name numerous songs about love, and you must name the artist who recorded that song. If you really believe in love, you will know the answers. Naturally, I know you were once quite adept at responding to similar challenges involving songs! Obviously, I won't mention "Venus in Blue Jeans" by Jimmy Clanton, nor "Venus" by Frankie Avalon, which you might claim was also recorded by yourself. You see, I know about your demo during your university student days! In fact, all the songs will have the word "love" in their titles. You have recently spent time with some Roman poets – ancient song-writers, so to speak. You should feel inspired!

-        I'm afraid Cruz will wake up.

-        No, he shall sleep through your "love experience". Do you think it was your reading of the story of Cupid and Psyche that sent the lad to the land of dreams? Nay – it was I, a major player in the story, who induced sleep. Look at his angelic face. I have trouble with the word "angelic", since angels don't really exist. The Christians borrowed the notion of winged creatures after observing my little Cupid. Nor does he shoot love into people with tiny arrows! He causes people to fall in love through his boyish charm. We shall now begin the love litany. The first song is "Love Me Do".

-        That's easy! The Beatles.

-        "Love Will Keep Us Together".

- Captain &Tennille.

- "Can't Help Falling in Love".

- That's by the King!

- Are you saying that song is by Romulus, the first king of Rome?

- No – the "King" – Elvis Presley!

- Ah yes, the singer who moves his hips almost as well as I do! Next song is "I Will Always Love You".

- Whitney Houston.

- "My Love".

- There was a version sung by Petula Clark, and a different song with the same title by Paul McCartney.

- That's **Sir** Paul McCartney! How about "You Can't Hurry Love"?

- The Supremes.

- "I Just Called To Say I Love You".

- Stevie Wonder.

- "Can't Get Enough of Your Love".

- Barry White.

- "Whole Lotta Love".

- Led Zeppelin.

- "Love Me Tender".

- The K... er, Elvis Presley.

- "The Power of Love".

- Jennifer Rush.

- "Can You Feel the Love Tonight".

- Elton John… oops…**Sir** Elton John.

- "Baby Love".

- The Supremes – I almost said the **Sir**premes!

- Concentrate, Dionysius! Who sang "Bye Bye Love"?

- The Everly Brothers – Don and Phil!

- I don't want family history – just the artist's name! "What's Love Got To Do With It".

- Isn't that the point of this quiz?

- I just named a song title!

- Oh, that's right. That's a song by Tina Turner.

- "And I Love Her".

- The Beatles.

- "Can't Buy Me Love".

- Again – the Beatles!

- "Sunshine of Your Love".

- Cream.

- "To Know Him Is To Love Him".

- The Teddy Bears.

- "As Long As You Love Me".

-       The Backstreet Boys. My daughters and I saw them in the flesh!

-       You took your daughters to a show with naked men?

-       No, No, Venus. We went to a live concert!

-       Oh – you had gotten me excited for a moment! "Young Love".

-       Are we still talking about my daughters? No, I guess not. Ah yes, that's a song by Sonny James.

-       "Your Love Keeps Lifting Me Higher and Higher".

-       Jackie Wilson. His son Bobby also sings the song in tribute to his father!

-       Dionysius, if you insist on commenting on every song, your grandson will wake up – and he'll be a year older! "Love Hurts".

-       Nazareth.

-       "Chapel of Love".

-       The Dixie Cups.

-       "You Don't Have To Say You Love Me".

-       Dusty Springfield. She was…

-       Your favorite female singer. I know! "Silly Love Songs".

-       I don't agree, Venus. Love is not silly.

-       A song title, Dionysius, a song title!

-      Oh, yes… that was a song by Wings (with Sir Paul!).

-      "Love to Love You Baby".

-      Donna Summer.

-      "For Your Love".

-      The Yardbirds. But then, an earlier song with that title was written and sung by Ed Townsend.

-      Nobody loves a show-off! "Only Love Can Break Your Heart".

-      Neil Young.

-      "Only Love Can Break a Heart".

-      You can't fool me - this is a different song, and it's by Gene Pitney!

-      "Love is Strange".

-      Mickey & Sylvia.

-      "Crazy Little Thing Called Love".

-      Queen.

-      "I'm Still in Love With You".

-      Al Green.

-      "Will You Love Me Tomorrow".

-      The Shirelles. That group was named after their original lead singer, Shirley Alston.

-      Again, Dionysius, no musical history! How about "I Was Made To Love Her"?

-	Easy peasy! That was a Stevie Wonder song.

-	"All Out of Love".

-	Air Supply.

-	"What Is Love".

-	Haddaway.

-	"I Think I Love You".

-	The Partridge Family.

-	"Words of Love".

-	The Mamas & the Papas. But other songs with that title were written by Buddy Holly and the Beatles.

-	Now you are just showing off again, Dionysius. I remind you we haven't got all day. Just all night! A little humour to lighten the moment. Get it – "lighten" – it's night time – it's dark? Let's carry on. "Put A Little Love In Your Heart" and "What the World Needs Now is Love".

-	Both songs by Jackie De Shannon.

-	"Standing in the Shadow of Love".

-	The Four Tops. I also saw them in the fl…in concert!

-	"Stoned Love".

-	The Supremes.

-	"Love on a Two-Way Street".

-	The Moments. They didn't make the first recording of the song, but they made it a hit.

-       If you don't stop commenting, Dionysius, the next "hit" you hear will be my hand on your head! Who sang "Never Knew Love Like This Before"?

-       Stephanie Mills.

-       "Love Is Like An Itching in My Heart".

-       The Supremes.

-       "Love Is Here And Now You're Gone".

-       Diana Ross and The Supremes. Yes, she was there in the other songs, but… okay, I know – next song.

-       "The Look of Love".

-       Dusty Springfield, my fav…next song!

-       "How Deep Is Your Love".

-       Bee Gees.

-       "I'll Never Fall in Love Again".

-       Dionne Warwick. She was Whitney Houston's aunt.

-       Dionysius, how many times?

-       Sorry, Venus! Next song.

-       "Hello, I Love You".

-       *Ianuae*. That's Latin for The Doors!

-    I appreciate that you love Latin, Dionysius, but that is not what this love quiz is about! And don't let me get started on Latin Lovers!

-    "I'll Have To Say I Love You in a Song".

-    Jim Croce.

-    "This Guy's in Love With You".

-    Herb Alpert. I don't want to blow my own horn, but I know he was primarily a trumpet player.

-    I would say your attempt at humour struck a false note. Now back to business. "Crazy Love".

-    Poco.

-    "Love Child".

-    Diana Ross and The Supremes. Mary Wilson is still one of the Supremes.

-    You are getting obnoxious with your add-ons. What about "The Game of Love"?

-    I am still in the game, Venus!

-    No, no. That was a song title!

-    Oh, The Mindbenders – with lead singer Wayne Fontana.

-    You're incurable, Dionysius! You are a real DJ.

-    A disc jockey! Wow, thanks for the compliment, Venus!

-    That's no compliment! The "DJ" stands for divine jerk! But I do see a real P in the A.

\- Oh, sorry to be a pain in...

\- No, Dionysius, not pain. I see passion in your answers! The "p" in your "a"! Who sang "For Your Precious Love"?

\- Jerry Butler. And can I say – with The Impressions?

\- You've obviously learned how to ask for forgiveness rather than permission! Next song is "Dance Me To the End of Love".

\- Leonard Cohen.

\- "Never My Love".

\- The Association.

\- "Best of My Love".

\- The Emotions. That group was formed with three sisters.

\- Dionysius – stop! So, how about "Stop in the Name of Love"?

\- The Supremes – they were just "soul sisters"!

\- "Nothing's Gonna Change My Love For You".

\- George Benson.

\- "A Groovy Kind of Love"

\- The Mindbenders with...

\- I know – with Wayne Fontana. Who sings "I'm not in Love"?

\- 10cc.

\-   Strange name, but I'm not going to ask.

\-   Thank you, Venus. I don't really want to go there!

\-   Here's one – "So Much in Love".

\-   That's by The Tymes.

\-   This is an odd song for a so-called pagan goddess of love to bring up, but here goes – "I Don't Know How to Love Him".

\-   That was sung by Yvonne Elliman, as Mary Magdalene, in the rock-opera film *Jesus Christ Superstar*, composed by Andrew Lloyd Webber. I guess you know I saw that movie version in a drive-in.

\-   Of course! The drive-in – so many little love-nests! Another song for you – "Love Can Move Mountains".

\-   Céline Dion.

\-   "What Is This Thing Called Love".

\-   Good question! So many singers have asked, but I'll go with Billie Holliday.

\-   "Love Is A Many-Splendored Thing".

\-   Good answer to the question. That's by The Four Aces.

\-   "Let Your Love Grow"

\-   The Bellamy Brothers.

\-   "Love the One You're With".

- Crosby, Stills & Nash – along with James Taylor.

- "I've Got My Love To Keep Me Warm"

- Again, many singers, but I like Dean Martin's version.

- "Where Did Our Love Go".

- Once more – The Supremes.

- "Love Grows Where My Rosemary Goes".

- Edison Lighthouse.

- "If You Love Me".

- Olivia Newton-John.

- "Burning Love".

- Elvis Presley.

- "What Now My Love".

- A classic, but I'll go with Frank Sinatra.

- "Love and Marriage".

- Again - Frank Sinatra.

- "Somewhere My Love".

- One more time – as they say in so many songs – Frank Sinatra!

- "To Sir With Love".

- Lulu.

- "Somebody to Love".

-     Jefferson Airplane.

-     "Theme From Love Story".

-     I like the version sung by Andy Williams.

-     "I Can't Give You Anything But Love, Baby".

-     Once more – Billie Holliday.

-     "Goodnight My Love".

-     So many artists sang this song, but I'll name Paul Anka.

-     "Ruby, Don't Take Your Love To Town".

-     Kenny Rogers.

-     "My Mistake Was To Love You".

-     Marvin Gaye and Diana Ross.

-     "I'm in the Mood for Love".

-     Nat King Cole.

-     "It's Almost Like Being in Love".

-     Again, among others, Nat King Cole.

-     "Love on the Rocks".

-     Neil Diamond.

-     "Do You Love Me".

-     The Contours.

-     "Love Letters in the Sand".

-     Pat Boone.

- "Sea of Love".

- Phil Phillips & The Twilights.

- "Just Another Love".

- Tanya Tucker.

- "You know I Love You".

- That's the English part of a song by Shake.

- "When I Fall in Love".

- Nat King Cole.

- "I'd Love to Change the World".

- Ten Years After.

- "To Love Somebody".

- Bee Gees.

- "Just Another Love Song".

- Haley & Michaels.

- "An Old-Fashioned Love Song".

- Three Dog Night.

- "Everlasting Love".

- Carl Carlton.

- "You Don't Love Me Anymore".

- Eddie Rabbitt.

- "Dedicated to the One I Love".

-       The Shirelles sang that song – and so did The Mamas & the Papas.

-       Dionysius, "Love" is all around us!

-       The Troggs.

-       Oh, I wasn't referring to the song, but good on you for spotting that song title. So then, Dionysius "All You Need Is Love".

-       I know, Venus. Oh, we are still doing the quiz. That song is by the Beatles.

-        Right! I'll give the final word to that singer you named a couple of times – Dean Martin. "That's Amore", Dionysius, that's *amore*!

***

-       Papi, I slept so well. Ovid's story does wonders. I always love to hear it!

-       That word, Cruz!

-       What word, Papi?

-       Love! I've just had the strangest dream. Venus appeared to me to test my commitment to love by quizzing me on a bunch of songs containing the word "love". I had to name the singers who sang all those songs. I guess because it was a dream, I was successful. I named every singer.

-       Papi, could your experience last night be merely anxiety over the imperial succession to Augustus? You do have a replica of a Venus statue at home, and you did write a story about divine beings

291

"coming to life". Chances are the songs named in your "dream" are all in that vast record collection you own.

-        You're probably right, Cruz.

Chapter Twenty-two: Cruz Gets His Own Message of Love

-	Cruz, we won't be spending time in the imperial residence on Capri. That wouldn't be a healthy environment for you – nor for me! We'll let Tiberius and Caligula fill the roles of old man and young boy, as they lead each other down the path of debauchery and corruption. No, we are off to Judaea. After all, we can't take a journey into Antiquity without visiting the Holy Land.

***

-	Here we are in Jerusalem, Cruz. The reason the Roman soldiers seem so uptight is that the Jewish people have never accepted Roman rule, including Roman rules of worship. There are frequent popular uprisings, and the Roman authorities are afraid a strong leader will lead a full-scale rebellion against Rome.They are especially concerned about the one the Jews refer to as the Messiah.

-	Do you mean Jesus, Papi?

-	Yes, Cruz. In fact, I've timed our arrival to coincide with His triumphant entrance into the city. Maybe we can get more information from one of the locals.

-	Did I just hear that you were looking for a friendly guide here in Jerusalem? Allow me to be of service for a few *shekels*. My name is Brianus, and I am a Roman bastard.

- Don't put yourself down, my fine fellow!

- No, no, what I mean to say is that my father was a Roman legionary, and I was born out of wedlock. My mother had read a lot of Roman mythology, and had tried to convince her father that she had conceived me with a god. He didn't believe her, and banished her to a leper colony – the bastard!

- Your grandfather was born out of wedlock too?

- No, he was a real bas... Oh never mind! I'll probably never meet my mother. And my father died by the sword.

- He was killed in battle?

- No, he accidentally fell on his sword while he was trying to clean it.

- Well, Brianus, I am Dionysius. My grandson Lucius Crux and I would be delighted if you would accompany us on our visit here in Jerusalem. I think I can spare a few coins if you agree to be our guide.

- Over there is the official residence of the Roman governor, Pontius Pilate. Let me show you some graffiti I wrote. On the pedestal I scribbled "Pilate's Problematic Palate" – you know, because of his speech impediment! I think he'll "pee" when he sees it!

- I see, Brianus, that you've combined comic relief with alliteration.

- As well as another form of "relief", Papi!

-       And the level field over yonder I have dubbed "Pilate's Plain". Do you think that joke will take off, Dionysius?

-       *In joco veritas*! There may be truth in your humour, Brianus, but it seems to me that you're just winging it! Cruz, all this is reminding me of a funny scene in the Monty Python film *Life of Brian* where Brian has used incorrect Latin to say "Romans go home". He had written "Romanes eunt domus", which would mean something like "A people called 'Romanes' are going to the house". A Roman centurion forces him to write one hundred times the phrase in correct Latin – *Romani, ite domum*! Come to think of it, our Brianus bears the Latin name for "Brian". And they both loathe Pontius Pilate!

-       Look! The Master is riding into the city on a donkey, as the crowd is waving palm branches. Funny, when I tried to come through the city gates last week on a donkey, the Roman sentries kicked my ass!

-       Gosh, Brianus, such cruel treatment of your donkey!

-       No, young Crux, they kicked **my ass**! So I fell off my donkey onto my ass!

-       And so made an ass of yourself!

-       Leave it, Cruz. We don't want to make our guide the butt of your jokes! Why don't you try to get a closer look at the festivities?

***

-       Papi, He looked right at me, and smiled! I felt this weird sensation. And He gave me this little palm branch in the form of a cross!

-       Better tuck that back into your toga, Cruz. You know, now that I have said that out loud, I realize it could sound grossly offensive to a modern ear! I believe the sensation you experienced was love! Not the Venus type of love that I dreamt about the other night, but a life-changing type of love! A love that will transcend all time and all journeys you may take in the future! He smiled – do you remember the song "Smile a Little Smile For Me"?

-       Yes, Papi. Do you think Jesus would like the Bobby Darin song "If I Were a Carpenter"? He no doubt was an apprentice carpenter under His father Joseph.

-       Most certainly, and songs by The Carpenters! After all, He is "Close To You"! And because of His devotion to His Mother Mary, I think He would appreciate The Association song "Along Comes Mary".

-       By the way, have you two seen THIS?

-       Seen what, Brianus?

-       Not what – who! Titus Historicus Ignotus Secundus, that's who!

-       An unknown historian! But you say he is the second one. What happenened to the first?

-       I don't know. He was also unknown! So no one will ever read their historical accounts. But THIS

296

promised to take me to meet somebody important. Ah, here he comes. THIS, this is Dionysius, and this is his grandson Crux.

-        This is indeed a pleasure, folks!

-        This is confusing, Papi!

-        At this point, Cruz, better to be "thissed" than dissed!

-        Brianus, I want to take you to a special place. Your friends are welcome to come along. My unknown history has chronicled the lives of ordinary people – like you, Brianus.

***

-        But, THIS, we're at a leper colony! I'm no leper.

-        This encounter will require a "leaper" of faith. Do you see that woman full of scars and spots from beatings? Well, this is one leper who is about to change her spots!

-        My dear Brianus, at last I can gaze on you.

-        Mother?

-        Yes, Brianus, the One who entered Jerusalem recently passed by here, and said I would be reunited with my son. He said the meeting would be arranged by an obscure historian. Then I heard a strange singing in the air – "Reunited, and it feels so good"! Suddenly, there were peaches and a herb lying at my feet.

-        Excuse me! Not "obscure"! Unknown – yes. But not "obscure"!

-       Whatever! I'm just so happy at this moment, THIS! Thank you for this encounter with my mother. I want to be with her from now on.

-       And if the script plays out, Brianus' mother will be completely cured of leprosy. Although the song "Reunited" by Peaches and Herb was not in the script!

-       What are you saying, Papi?

-       Just a hunch, Cruz. One day, I'll let you watch my DVD of *Ben Hur*.

-       Are you and your mother coming along, Brianus?

-       No, THIS. Mother and I want to make up for lost time. You can talk to Dionysius and Crux about your "unknown history".

-       Take care, Brianus. And take care of your mother.

-       Will do. I'm sure THIS will fill you two in on developments with Our Lord and His mission. Ultimately, the Roman authorities will decide His fate. The Jewish leaders wish to have Him silenced. They realize His message of love is pretty powerful. But it is Pilate's licence to pass judgment and order execution that can prove to be the death blow.

-       Cruz, we both know that Jesus will be crucified, and we share the belief with many of our own time that He rose from the dead. His was not a "virtual" journey like ours. But the whole scenario of the Passion and death on the cross would be too painful to witness. It is interesting that Pilate washed his hands to indicate that he technically was not to blame for the carrying out of the wishes of the Jewish leaders and those that followed them. You know from your catechism lessons, Cruz, that the priest washes his hands during Mass at the consecration as a symbol of cleansing and purification, but also as a sign of humility in the Sacred Presence. I find this ironic in light of Pilate's gesture, and I don't really know why, but I've always considered Pilate's gesture to be likewise a recognition of something sacred in the Person he had condemned to death. But more to the point, it's really Pilate passing the buck. One could argue that he was emphasizing that the buck stops here. Or more precisely, the *sesterce*!

-       What are you two talking about?

-       THIS, we've decided not to stick around for the execution of Jesus.

-       As you wish. Have I shown you the gold-letter inscription which reads S.S.P.P.P.? I am probably the only historian who knows its meaning. Wait for it! **S**upreme **S**enate and **P**ontius **P**ilate's **P**rerogative. Be sure to tell all your friends that you met Titus Historicus Ignotus Secundus. Who knows, maybe you will get to read my book.

-       As we are all aware, THIS, the future remains unknown.

-       Probably like his history – right, Papi?

-       Definitely! He'll forever be the "unknown historian". The future may even decipher that inscription to mean **S**ecret of **S**urvival: **P**rivilege

People and Planet! It's time to use the remote to project us a little forward in the history of the Roman Empire. Get ready to meet an interesting character named Claudius!

Chapter Twenty-three: Presenting the B.B.C.

- Hey, you two! Want to make a few *denarii*?

- Good day, good sir! What service do you require of us?

- And how many *denarii* are we talking about?

- Cruz, don't be so mercantile. Maybe this gentleman, be he free-born or slave, can help us meet Claudius. My name is Dionysius, and this is my grandson Lucius Crux.

- Despite his name – Crux, that is "the cross" – I can't be cross with the young man! I guess you are feeling the weight of my wit already! My name is Tarquinius Historicus Ambiguus Tertius. But you don't have to call me all that. Just address me as THAT.

- Geez, Papi, demonstrative pronouns seem to be the "in thing" during the Roman Empire.

- Well, THAT, allow me to point out to my grandson that your name Tarquinius – strangely and archaically Etruscan – is followed by the notation of "uncertain historian". But why the "third"?

- Oh, don't be afraid to tell young Crux that "*Ambiguus*" can also mean "untrustworthy". In fact, my own father and grandfather were just that – not THAT! – more humour. I'm so funny, my full calling card is THAT.ca – "*comicus* also"! I, on the other hand, would not lead you astray. And you're right. My family tree has branches of Etruscan, as well as Oscan and Umbrian, with a little Carthaginian on my mother's side. Long story short, I'm actually an historical linguist. That's why I sometimes have to be a little "uncertain".

- Well, Papi, if ever we find ourselves with nothing to do, we can spend time talking about THIS and THAT!

- THIS? I don't think I know him.

- That's because he is the "unknown historian"!

- There was an unknown historian? Who knew?! But I heard you mention the name Claudius, Dionysius. If you mean Caligula's uncle, I can certainly arrange for you to meet him. After all, we are colleagues.

- You work with Claudius?

- It's more a case of work for him. I keep all his writings in order. He's so clumsy sometimes. I affectionately call him "Clod".

- Shouldn't that be "Claud" for Claudius?

- Well, young Crux, as an historian of language, I can justify the "Clodius-Claudius" connection. Anyways, he drinks too much. It makes him tipsy when he walks. He tries to cover up by claiming to have a serious pain in his leg. But that is just a lame excuse! His drinking also causes him grief with the ladies. He can never figure out when they are toying with him.

-       Your account of Claudius is a little ambiguous, THAT.

-       Precisely! I remind you that I am "Historicus Ambiguus"!

-       But he does have a hearing problem, does he not?

-       You'll have to speak louder, Dionysius – I can't hear you. Got you! No, Claudius is no more deaf than I am dumb!

-       Bite your tongue, Cruz! I know what you're thinking, so just play dumb! So, THAT, you assisted Claudius with his great works on the Etruscan language and the history of the Carthaginians?

-       Assisted? Were you not listening when I outlined my pedigree? I did the major part of the research on my ancestral peoples. You will see my name alongside that of Claudius on those monumental works. Here are my copies of the title pages. Read for yourselves – "Claudius and That Great History of the Carthaginians", and "Claudius and That Great Study of the Etruscans".

-       Did you notice, THAT – your name is not fully capitalized?

-       Yes, Crux. It's a scribal error that Claudius said he would have corrected. But he's always lost in thought. He's not too practical. Can you imagine him becoming *Princeps* one day?

-       Stranger things have happened,THAT. Rumour has it that he can't find his copies of those books for publication. They could end up being lost forever.

-        Don't tell me I'll go down in history as another unknown historian!

-        Papi, doesn't THAT realize he's not even going to go down in history?

-        OMG!

-        Papi, why do these modern phrases keep showing up in Imperial Rome?

-        Young man, I'm merely pointing out that if the written records are lost, only my gossip will survive as the historical account of our research – OMG!

-        THAT, is it true that Claudius has a great interest in law?

-        Yes, "law of the jungle" perhaps, Dionysius.

-        They have jungles in Rome?

-        A figure of speech, Cruz. Tell me, THAT, what's with Claudius and Seneca?

-        Well, to tell you the truth, Claudius is a little jealous of Seneca, who is a fine orator with a great philosophical mind. He is already starting to make a small fortune, and he is popular with the ladies. However, I don't believe he is messing around with a certain member of the imperial family, as some people are suggesting. Claudius and his cronies know that if you can't beat them, exile them. That will undoubtedly be Seneca's fate. But why the interest in Seneca, Dionysius? Thinking of writing a book about him?

-         Maybe one day, THAT. But I presume that Seneca will return to prominence in Rome when Claudius kicks the bucket.

-         Clumsy Claudius has kicked many a bucket, but I understand what you're saying. And I wouldn't put it past Seneca to write some satirical piece about Claudius. Do you know the word *Apocolocyntosis*?

-         As a matter of fact, I do, THAT. It's a Greek word meaning roughly "to turn into a pumpkin". Kind of reminds me of the word *apotheosis* – "being carried into the heavens as a god". I'm sure Claudius expects deification at the end of his days.

-         Or, as you say, it may end up being a kind of "pumpkinification"! But I did say I can arrange to have you meet him. He's probably in his study right now. Just follow me and walk this way.

-         Papi, he's limping like they say Claudius does.

-         I guess from working with Claudius he unconsciously imitates him.

-         Here we are. Go on in and introduce yourselves. I've got to go and spread some juicy gossip.

-         Excuse us, Sir. My name is Dionysius, and this is my grandson Lucius Crux. We were told by THAT that you would receive us.

-         Oh, are you friends of his?

-         Not really!

- Good! Then come on in. Just saying his name makes our speech so repetitive and clumsy. THAT is a brat on whose name I've often spat, and that is that! He's so fat he leaves broken chairs wherever he's sat! If I were a cat, I'd chase that rat! Did he tell you how good a poet I was? Probably not. Just what do you do for a living, Dionysius?

- I have taught and I have written books. Recently, Crux and I have been travelling.

- Have you ever been to *Gallia, Hispania* and *Britannia?*

- As a matter of fact, I have. To *Germania* as well.

- *Germania*! And you lived to tell about it? Tell me, how were the Germanic women?

- Where I was studying, Claudius, there were no women.

- Ah, I knew those *Germani* were barbarians. No women to make one's studies more pleasurable. Really! But how did you find *Britannia*?

- Well, I crossed this huge body of water which the locals call a channel, and there it was.

- Very funny, that! Again, not my pseudo-colleague THAT! I think one day I should like bragging rights with respect to the conquest of *Britannia*. That would make me more famous than Julius Caesar. He didn't even stay long enough on that island to catch a cold. Rather a strange inscription he left though – **CO VID** XIX. It was his neat little way of saying *Caius*

*Optimus **Vid**it* – "Gaius the Best has seen it"! The number 19 apparently represents the nineteen village communities he visited. He made the notation that he never stayed long among the tribes because they were always coughing, and he felt feverish when he was among them. You seem like a learned man, and the boy has a look of intelligence. So you both know that in a proper name "C" stands for "G" in our Latin language. I'd like to show you my notes. I'm writing my memoirs. But I'm having trouble coming up with a title. What do you think of "Me, Claudius", or "Claudius the Deity"?

-        They definitely have possibilities, Sir.

-        Papi, you could dazzle him with a description of those lands as they were when you saw them as a student! And what is a "look of intelligence"?

-        I'm guessing a look different from THAT's. Obviously, there's no point telling him about the author Robert Graves, and his books *I, Claudius* and *Claudius the God.*

-        Hail *Princeps*!

-        Why does the Praetorian Guard deem it necessary to enter my study?

-        Sire, Caligula is dead and we declare you *Princeps*! May we call you Emperor?

-        Call me what you wish, as long as you don't call me late for dinner!

-        Cruz, methinks Claudius could have been a stand-up comic in our time.

-     Shall we celebrate with wine, Sire?

-     Fill your boots! After all, you have removed your military boots as some sort of sign of respect, and so you might as well make them useful.

-     Sire, we are serious. And who are these two *paparazzi*?

-     Dionysius is my freedman, and naturally, his grandson also. Caligula is dead? But it is the Senate that must declare a new Emperor.

-     We are breaking with tradition, Sire.

-     Good grief, my reign starts off rated PG!

-     PG, Papi?

-     **P**raetorian **G**uard, Cruz.

-     Well then, officers, I wish to rid myself of my wife Messylina.

-     You mean Messalina, Sire.

-     You haven't seen her housekeeping!

-     Maybe even Las Vegas material, Cruz!

-     But, Sire, the Emperor needs a wife.

-     Get a grip, Officer! I have - A-grip-pina!

-     A Las Vegas headliner, Cruz!

-     Sire, you shall be presented to the people on the morrow.

-     Where's the morrow?

-      That's tomorrow, Sire.

-      Not surprising Shakespeare never wrote about Claudius, Cruz!

-      Papi, no wonder Claudius is astonished to be named Emperor. He's lucky to be alive!

-      As are we, I suppose. I guess you can say he's lucky to be Emperor, but his reign will last for thirteen years.

-      "Lucky 13" – right Papi! But that will be a long stretch for us.

-      As they say, Cruz, *tempus fugit* – time flies!

-      Because we'll be having fun, Papi?

-      No – because I still have the remote to skip over periods of time. In fact, our next stop is with Claudius' invading army in Britain. His commanding general is Vespasian – remember that name.

***

-      Dionysius, I want you and your grandson to chronicle the invasion of *Britannia*. Talk to the native peoples. I understand that you speak their anglo-celtic tongue. But why does young Crux call it "English"? Well, no matter. I want you to spread Roman PR.

-      Public relations, Papi?

-      No, Cruz, I believe he means **Pax Romana**.

-      Here comes one of the tribal chieftains, and a younger man who could be his son.

-      Are you a chieftain, Sir?

- Indeed! I am Gladuaskt. You are spokesmen for the Roman invaders. William, tell your brother to bring some apples for our guests.

- Father, all the apples have been stolen. And my brother has disappeared.

- Well, how do you like them apples? Your brother might have helped us find the apples.

- No doubt! Father, I've always said he's rotten to the core. He often feeds a bitter apple drink to his wife. There's no telling what ends up inside her. Oh, and Mother says my sister Nessie has been acting like a monster again, and so has had to lock Ness in her room. That's probably why few people claim to have seen her!

- Too much information in front of these strangers! Perhaps later on you can demonstrate for our visitors your prowess with a bow. We invite you both to share a cup of tea with us. Since you wish to conquer our world, we can refer to it as the "World Cup"!

- Everybody's a wannabe comedian, Papi!

- True, we are here as representatives of CTV – **C**laudius **T**riumphant and **V**ictorious. And to commemorate our advances beyond those of Julius Caesar, our slogan is CBC – **C**laudius **B**ests **C**aesar!

- Strange, you two speak our language without the slightest trace of an accent. My son William had started the study of Latin, but he became so frustrated with all those Latin abbreviations that he abbreviated his Latin studies. No will power, I guess. Now he often

310

roams willy nilly across our lands. Sometimes with his undisciplined brother Nelson – so Willy and Nelly! Ah, Willy, Nelson! Those two sons remind me of all the girls I've known before. Different mothers, you know. Will is fond of MM and CD, though.

-       Rap music?

-       No, young man, the Latin expressions *Memento mori* and *Carpe diem*.

-       Cruz, those expressions mean "Remember that you have to die" and "Seize the day". You have to admit, they do have a logical connection. Does Nelson also have a favorite expression, Sir?

-       Yes, *mens sana in corpore sano*. Why, I don't know. He doesn't have a body healthy enough to pump iron, and a mind sane enough to iron out differences with his brother. Lord, Nelson will be the death of me!

-       So, Cruz, obviously an ironic choice of expressions!

-       Well, the motto we bear reflects our lands and traditions. We stand for the BBC – **B**est **B**efore **C**laudius! Kindly broadcast that message to your Emperor in Rome. And tell your general Vespasian he can construct a huge stadium – a Colosseum if he likes – we shall never play ball with the Romans. Even if they foot the ball.

-       You mean foot the **bill.**

-       No such game as footbill! And nobody better put his foot to my son Bill! Furthermore, a mighty snake shall come slithering down from the mountain tops and make Roman rule a laughing stock. It will become known as the "Monty Python".

-        Papi, weren't they a British group of comics?

-        Yes, Cruz, but the name fits their "python from the peaks".

-        We also hate the Gauls, since Claudius was born in Gaul at *Lugdunum*.

-        He's referring to the city of Lyon, Cruz, where one of my university professors was born. I believe his first name was Claude.

-        Awesome, Papi!

-        Our chieftains know of a prediction that the people of Gaul will engage us in a war lasting one hundred years, and that Gaul will be saved by a warrior woman who will lead her troops with an arc, that is, a bow, or perhaps cross the Channel in a huge boat, or ark. That part is a little foggy – I suppose because of the weather in *Londinium*, where our chieftains often hang out. You can sometimes spot ten downing fine ale. But the Gauls will betray their saviour woman. You can't trust a Gaul as far as you can throw him, and our rather wild neighbours to the north do have competitions in which they toss Gallic prisoners of war. Although now, with fewer prisoners, they have begun tossing huge poles. But we've seen you talking to some Gallic prisoners. You both seem to speak their tongue with ease, but why the young lad refers to the language as "French" is beyond my knowledge. However, we Brits – I guess you never

312

heard anyone call us that since it's a local term - will have two tribal queens lead us against you Roman invaders.They shall bear the names Boudicca and Boadicea.

-       Cruz, he's referring to the same queen, known under the two names. Tossing the poles is the modern Scottish competition known as the caber toss. And I guess he was referring to Joan of Arc, who used a sword to rally the French, not a bow. And "Noah way" did she cross the English Channel in an ark! Don't you love it when I constantly open up the floodgates with the "Noah" pun?Jeanne d'Arc - to use her actual name - was more interested in celestial-inspired reigns, not in celestial rains!

-       When you return to your Roman leaders, give them this message of resistance written by our grand chief.

-       Papi, he signed it LOL. Do you have lots of love for your enemies?

-       Don't make me laugh out loud! That is the standard signature used by Lewellyn of Leeds! He happens to be very good with a sword. Any Roman who dares to challenge our chief will discover that he is a cut above the others!

-       Sire, I'm sure any such challenge would be chronicled on the front page of every historical account.

-       A sort of "Front Page Challenge", right?

-        Yes, Sire. Whether it happens in the East or in the West, whether it is a local or a national bout, whether it is a war gesture or a matter of sport.

-        Papi, we are LOL, too! We are "Lovers **of** Life"!

-        And while travelling in the Roman Empire, "Lovers **of** Latin"!

-        Hey, you two, Claudius has been murdered. Many are claiming it was the work of Agrippina. She often served her imperial husband mushrooms, but at a recent banquet she served Claudius a delicacy of mushrooms garnished with meat crumbs from so-called sacred cows imported from the Far East. Apparently, they are known as "mooshrooms".

-        So, Cruz, it would appear that the main suspect provided the main ingredient in the poisoned meal served to Claudius.

-        I guess that puts an end to our Mission Impossible, Papi.

-        On our particular journey, certainly an improbable mission!

-        Papi, listen to that song William is singing – "Na Na Na Na Hey Hey Hey Good-Bye". It sounds really modern.

-        I guess he's a "thoroughly modern Willy"!

-        Hey you two, you are summoned to the imperial court of the new Emperor.

Chapter Twenty-four: Oh Fiddlesticks!

-        Gosh Papi, I wonder what the Emperor wants with us. From what you've been telling me about the conflicts between Agrippina and other relatives of Claudius in order to ensure that her son Nero be proclaimed Emperor, there is enough material to produce a super edition of "Family Feud"!

-        Yes, Cruz, with a possible story-line for "Murder She Wrote"!

-        Greetings! My name is Seneca, and I am to be Nero's tutor. I believe your relationship as mentor to your grandson can offer me an inspirational model. My informers have assured me, good sir, that you epitomize the basic tenets of Stoicism, namely moral principles and peace of mind. Would you agree, young man?

-        Yes. My grandfather has taught me about the five L's – life, love, liberty, laughter and Latin!

-        Oh, the youngster has a sense of purpose and a sense of humour! Not altogether stoical traits, but I can dig it. We all of us seek the good life, do we not? Would you both not agree that knowledge can lead us to this life? Knowledge is therefore, as Stoics maintain, not an end in itself, but a means to an end.

-        Did you hear Seneca use one of our present-day expressions, Papi?

-        Not surprising, Cruz, since his writings will prove to be timeless. In my university studies, I "got along" quite well with Seneca, in a manner of speaking. I hope this will be the case with the actual Seneca!

-       You have mentioned my writings. Here is a collection I have not shared with many. I present it to you as an SOS – "**S**eneca **o**n **S**eneca". It is a justification of my words and actions. You may now accompany me to meet Nero and his mother Agrippina.

-       Greetings, Dionysius. Oh, don't be surprised that I know your name. My informers have briefed me on your many talents and past service to Claudius. And this is your charming grandson Lucius Crux. Ah, Seneca. So good to see you. I wasn't sure you would be welcomed by my mother here.

-       Nonsense, my son. What went on in the imperial palace now seems ages ago, all just BCE - **B**efore **C**laudius the **E**mperor. Then time passed to CE – **C**laudius as **E**mperor. All that was said about our imperial affairs was nothing but BS – **B**efore **S**eneca. I have asked our philosopher friend to serve as your guide and adviser.

-       Oh goody! Now, Dionysius, I know of your talent as a singer. You have established many singing records.

-       Actually, Your Majesty, my grandfather has a collection of records of songs. True, perhaps his collection is some kind of record.

-       All that you're saying, young man, don't make no never mind! Your grandfather will be my coach, as I audition for "*Illa Vox*" and "Rome's Got Talent". It was Petronius, my "*elegantiae arbiter*", who recommended me to the judges.

-        Cruz, I think he's alluding to the show "The Voice". But I wonder how a so-called "judge of elegance" can think that Nero has talent. In fact, his only talents are the coins he uses to bribe judges!

-        Right now gentlemen, you will all have to retire from my presence, since it is time for my lyre lessons. What do you think of this little ditty: "Lyre, lyre, Rome's on fire"?

-        Dionysios and Crux, I know my praise of his music on the lyre makes me a liar, but what can I do? I am trying to protect Rome and her citizens from a potential monster. Besides, I don't want my life to become a funeral pyre, and have Nero show me the doors! I use the plural because there are many doors in Nero's palace, including one to his personal gym. Young Cruz, I shall say no more. At least when asked, I can confirm I have never heard a voice like his, without being a liar! Say, there's a small gathering of writers taking place at my home tomorrow, and you are both welcome to come along.

-        Thank you, Seneca. We shall be delighted to attend.

***

-        Welcome all to this assembly of authors – our own little book club.

- Who is this stranger, Seneca? I thought our club was FYI – for your interests. Only published writers are to be in attendance.

- Lucan, meet Dionysius, who assures me he is a soon to be published author – if, as he says, time is relative. And since you are my nephew, we can allow his young grandson to attend on a family pass. Let's just say Lucius Crux is his grandfather's agent. After all, they've had a bond for... how long... oh...oh...7 years. But let's get started. Life, as we know, is short.

- Uncle Seneca, why must you plug your own works at these meetings. We've all read your *De brevitate vitae.*

- Merely for my own peace of mind, Lucan.

- Uncle...! We all know your treatise *De Tranquilitate animi.* But you don't see me making a farce of us by constantly referring to Pharsalus, the highlight of my history of the civil war between Caesar and Pompey. Come to think of it, that must be why some people refer to my account as *Pharsalia.* Hey, Petronius it's your turn to introduce today's book.

- Of course. Fellow members, honored guests – probably the only time you two will be honored – ha ha! – as the magistrate of manners, the referee of refinement, the critic of culture, the arbiter of attire, the sentinel of suavity...

- Please, Petronius! If you insist on ennumerating your self-acclaimed titles, we won't have time to finish the meeting!

-       Or even start it, Lucan. Dear Dionysius. I hope your grandson and yourself will realize that no offense was intended by Petronius in his heartfelt hint of humour.

-       None taken, Seneca. But we do appreciate and admire his allegiance to audacious alliteration! But what the "h"! Hallowed be your alliteration as well!

-       Alliteration with "h" and "a". Ha! Ha! Your mirthful wit is much more welcome than Petronius' comic-strip humour, which thankfully is always soon forgotten.

-       I shall now introduce today's book. It is the *De Medecina* by Celsus. Rumours are that this book will soon no longer be available. Ah, his labour of love will be lost.

-       Papi, it sounds like he's naming one of Shakespeare's plays. Do we get Celsius from Celsus' name? After all, we often use a thermometer when we are sick.

-       Cruz, my boy, kudos for recognizing William Shakespeare's *Love's Labour Lost*. However, the false association of Celsius with Celsus makes my temperature rise. In fact, the Celsius scale is in reality a centigrade scale based on 100 degrees from Latin words meaning "one hundred" and "steps". I taught you those words – *centum* and *gradus*. Apparently, the Swedish astronomer Anders Högen was given the Latin name *Celsius* – go figure! It kind of makes my blood boil when you consider that his scale had 100 degrees for freezing and 0 degrees for boiling. So he got it backwards!

-      I think I will use up my remaining time to talk about my work called *Satyricon* – you know, after the word "satyr". But I prefer to describe it as "satire". A chapter I am especially proud of is the description of the banquet given by one Trimalchio. I may be the "Toast of Taste", but poor Trimalchio's taste is all in his mouth. I mean, fifty ways to treat meat! There may be fifty ways to meet a lover, but fifty ways to be a meat-lover – too much! I don't know if future generations will appreciate it as a novel idea and call it a "novel" for short.

-      Hopefully, not for long, Petronius! Although your spicy scenarios - I'm not only referring to food - might inspire a different kind of presentation, just as the plays of your most probable inspiration, Plautus, will undoubtedly be the source of new ways of presenting "funny things happening on the way to the Forum". Dionysius, I have this premonition that something will bind Lucan, Petronius and myself other than books. I swear, these premonitions will be the death of me! Fortunately, young Cruz has not heard me talking about *mors voluntaria*, especially since suicide is not necessarily a "voluntary death"! The military credo of "kill or be killed" can be cruelly twisted by cruel Emperors to "kill yourself or be killed by us"!

-      Sadly, that will be the rule of thumb with some Emperors, Seneca. The fickle finger of fate will hand over to vilified victims the order to *sibi mortem consciscere* – "to commit suicide".

-      Papi, did Seneca just make a play on the words "book binding"?

- I'm afraid that those three will become part of another club - the SC.

- Isn't that the *senatus consultum*, Papi – the decree of the senate?

- I'm afraid they will be subject to the orders of a higher authority – the Emperor himself, and I am talking about a "**S**uicide **C**lub"! But let's change this gruesome subject. Seneca, I've heard that your brother Gallio is a chief magistrate in Greece.

- That is correct. In fact, he has been sending me correspondence about his meetings with a certain Paul of Tarsus, who seems to be a front man for a fervent religious group known as Christians. He's been writing numerous letters to the Greeks. Say, young Crux, your name meaning "cross", doesn't mean you are a member of that group does it, since their crucified leader died on the cross?

- We are Christians, Seneca. But *Quo vadis*? Where are you going, Seneca? To report us?

- Heaven no! Notice I used the singular! I know quite a bit about your religion, heaven and all that. I know you feel slavery is a bad thing. So do I as a matter of fact. Haven't you noticed that we've drunk quite a bit of wine? I'm going to the bathroom! But for the record, I'm too much a man of the mind to be grounded in faith. Besides, there is something fishy about their behaviour. Just joking! I know that the fish is one of their important symbols. So, *carpe diem*, young Crux! And that doesn't mean "fish of the day"! Actually, Dionysius, *carpe diem* and that other expression you have undoubtedly heard often in your travels – *mens sana in corpore sano* – would make good subtitles for a book!

-        I couldn't agree more, Seneca!

-        All this talk of Christians. But I would be "lion" if I didn't admit that life can be dangerous for them. You realize that lions believe that the arena is a good place to "meat" people!

-        Oh, piss off, Petronius!

-        Wasn't that what you were heading out to do?

-        I think we can adjourn this meeting of writers. But in defence of uncle Seneca, he writes for the ages. I think you two Christians will agree that his legacy will be what he wrote, not who he was. The books, not the man. Even Uncle Seneca will one day be forgotten, but his writings will live on. Wouldn't you agree, Dionysius?

-        Definitely, Lucan, but by the same token, Christ did not write anything, so He will be remembered, and followed for who He was – or rather, who He **is**! Let's go, Cruz. Seneca has given us a day pass to visit the Golden House – Nero's *Domus aurea*.

***

-        That was quite a sight, Papi! I especially liked having all that perfume and those flowers falling on us from the ceiling. But what do you think of those slaves whispering about how Nero is trying to have his own mother killed?

-        Knowing Nero from the time I've spent giving him singing lessons, I wouldn't put it past him. It seems he rigged a boat to have his mother drowned, but she managed to swim to safety. Poor Nero only succeeds in "drowning" his sorrows! Of course, if he sang for his mother, she would probably die of fright! When I inadvertently mentioned that I had some experience on the stage, Nero obliged me to give him acting lessons. Believe me, Cruz, the best acting I have ever done was to tell the Emperor he was a good actor. I played in many a Greek tragedy as a student, but Nero's horrific acting has brought "tragedy" to a new level! Some people call him the "Monster Emperor". I don't know about that, but his acting is definitely "monstrous! I don't know if the Bee Gees ever studied the Roman Empire, but their song "Tragedy" could certainly describe Nero's artistic career!

-        Papi, the slaves were also talking about a conspiracy and executions.

-        A series of suicides directly ordered by Nero, or caused by his actions. Seneca and his wife Paulina, his brothers Mela and Gallio, his nephew Lucan, and a petrified Petronius. And many others, involved or presumed to be involved in a treasonous plot to murder Nero, under the leadership of a certain Piso.

-        Oh yes, Papi, they named a tower after him.

-        That's **Pisa**, Cruz, but I'm glad to see you leaning towards the study of history and culture! Say, do you smell something burning?

-        Well, it's not pizza.

- I think you can drop that play on words. We're all dressed, so let's go! Look, lots of smoke out yonder.

- Papi, it seems like half of Rome is burning.

- Sadly, in the tradition of Troy and Paris. Ironic, isn't it, that the greatest French city, in its turn attacked by German forces during World War II, is named for the Trojan who was ultimately responsible for the burning of Troy!

- Cruz, there's someone on his knees, with flames fast approaching. It's Nero.

- Papi, he seems to be fiddling around for something on the ground.

- Nice rhyme, Cruz! Oh, he's trying to grab his lyre. I once saved a baby from a burning fire. Duty calls again.

- You are going to try to save a mad Emperor who today would be called the last madman of rock and roll?

- Consider it saving a sort of "boss baby"! I can hear him crying.

- Oh fiddlesticks! My lyre is extremely hot, but to this artist the words come not!

- My lord Nero, come to shelter. If you remain here, you will be the object of a roast — but it it won't be funny.

- Papi, are you thinking of those "Dean Martin Comedy Roasts" on the DVDs you watch?

-        Even stranger, Cruz, I'm thinking of some songs from my record collection – "Fire" by Arthur Brown, "Burning Love" by Elvis Presley, "Light My Fire" by The Doors, and, yes, "Disco Inferno" by The Trammps.

-        Papi, you didn't mention "Ring of Fire" by Johnny Cash. Wasn't he the singer always dressed in black?

-        With this bright blaze all around us, Cruz, I'm tempted to say that orange might be the new black! Nero, you're safe now.

-        Oh, my daring Dionysius, you have saved your star pupil for his public!

-        Yet will you be safe **from** the public if they think you started the fire?

-        But I was merely trying to put on a grand performance with that spectacular background of a magnificent blaze! I did not start the fire. In fact I wish to help the poor citizens who have been left homeless by the conflagration.

-        Nevertheless, there will be some who will pour oil on the fire, so to speak and attribute the cause to you.

-        Oh, fiddle faddle, am I to bear the heavy blame for the great flame. Remark how even when my thoughts are twisted and tortured, nonetheless I am able to wax poetic!

-        Papi, doesn't Nero realize that wax will melt when close to fire?

-       Now is not the time to be funny, Cruz!

-       Finally, my Praetorian Guards, are here to tend to their master. Guards, what shall I do? The people won't believe that I will now be able to implement a plan for urban renewal. Heck, they won't even know what "urban renewal" means!

-       Sire, why not blame the Christians for the fire. After all, they are often accused of incendiary remarks against Roman rule. You can claim they started the fire as payback for their many members who have been burned to death in the arena.

-       Brilliant. Not in the sense of a burning blaze, but in the sense of an ingenious idea. Am I not so clever with words and their meanings?

-       You're on fire, Sire!

-       Well, I am still alive – no thanks to you and your cohorts. Yet I shall spare you all for your slight attempt at rhyme. Now be off to carry out your duty. Dionysius and Crux, come with me to the Palace.

-       Sire, you spoke of duty. We have decided to rid Rome of her ruthless ruler. Now that's alliteration!

-       I shall leave the stage of life in a bath of glory. Now that's entertainment! You there, my faithful attendant. You will perform a "suicide" upon me by thrusting your sword into my side.

-       Won't that be assisted dying, Sire?

-       Whatever. Dionysius, as my blood pours out, so does my artist's soul. Write down these words – "What an artist dies in me!".

-       His famous last words, Papi?

-       Not quite, Cruz. Listen up.

-       Too late, this is fidelity!

-       Those are Nero's last words. I can't figure out if he is saying it's too late to change his mind, because the faithful attendant has carried out his task, or that he has been rather late in finally serving Rome faithfully by his death. In any event, perhaps we can consider Nero an honorary member of the Suicide Club.

-       Reminds me of your record by Carole King called "It's Too Late"!

-       Did you hear the words of the attendant as he struck Nero with his sword – "one small stroke for a man, one huge stroke for mankind". History will no doubt consider Nero the "Caligula 2.0". Which would make Tiberius the "1.0". But I guess without computer correlations, there's no point in trying to measure "the evil" among the evil Emperors. There's going to be trouble, Cruz, so let's get out of here before it's too late for us!

Chapter Twenty-five: Passing the Torch (sort of!)

-       How many years have we travelled on our journey through the Roman Empire, Cruz?

-       Let me do a quick calculation. Hmm. Carry the four. I think about 95 years, Papi.

-       And how many Emperors did we meet?

-       That's easy – five.

-       Funny, that just reminded me of the movie *Five Easy Pieces*. The film has good and bad characters – just as we've met good and bad Emperors. But since the film's title refers to musical exercises, I suppose we could say that there is a distant – make that very distant – connection with Emperor Number Five – Nero! Well, tie your toga on, because we are about to see four Emperors in one year! And they don't remind me of the old television show called "Four Just Men"!

-       The year of the Four Emperors.

-       No flies on you, Cruz! You know how scoring leaders in the National Hockey League change when a star emerges on a strong team. Well, the armies – the "teams" that count here in the Roman Empire – set up their "stars" – their generals – as Emperor. The general of the stongest team "wins the scoring title" and gets to be Emperor. Four teams were in the "play-offs", and Vespasian's "team" won. If you recall, he was the general that led the invasion of Britain under Claudius. Nero's death ended the Julio-Claudian dynasty. Titus Flavius Vespasianus founded the Flavian dynasty. And that name has nothing to do with Vespasian emerging as victor in the contest for "**flav**or of the month"!

-       And he will be instrumental in the construction of the Flavian Amphitheater and the Colosseum, right, Papi?

-       The two names designate the same building, Cruz. The name Colosseum was given to the amphitheater because of its colossal size. So the Lego model of the Colosseum that you built could just as well be called the Flavian Amphitheater. As Emperor, Vespasian will take the title *Imperator*.

-       I guess to remain connected with the army that put him in power.

-       Right on, Cruz. And it was clear from the outset that Vespasian intended to have his son Titus succeed him. The torch of imperial rule will be passed on in a family succession. No spoiler alert was necessary to figure that out!

-       And not for Rome to be "torched" as it was under Nero, right Papi?

-       For sure! That is why Vespasian sent Titus to put down a rebellion in Judaea. Titus was successful, and ended up destroying the Temple in Jerusalem. For his efforts, the Arch of Titus was built to commemorate his victory. I actually saw it when I was a student in Rome. Although we've zapped the remote and are in the reign of "the delight and darling of mankind" as the historian Suetonius called the benevolent Titus – but he was probably no "darling" to the Jews – we are going to visit Pompeii, where I also spent some time as a student. The year is 79 CE, Cruz. As I have observed you throughout our journey, I suppose I could refer to CE as "**C**ruz **E**xcited"!

***

\-   This place is great, Papi! The beach is even nicer than the beach at Fort Lauderdale that I visited last year with Mommy, Daddy and Everly. And the villa we are staying at is also more luxurious than the fancy hotel we stayed at. And did you see the welcome mat with a fierce dog pictured in the form of a mosaic and the warning to beware? Of course that could never be my dog Skye . She's only a Morki, hardly *cave canem* material! Ah, Pompeii – this is the life! But what's that noise, Papi?

\-   Well, Cruz, based on the sound and that foul odor in the air, but especially on my knowledge of Roman history, I would say that Mt.Vesuvius is about to erupt.

\-   But, Papi, none of the inhabitants are leaving.

\-   It's the shark denial syndrome. People will refuse to believe shark warnings until they get bit in the butt by one! But we're not waiting for them to play the theme from the film *Jaws*. We're getting out of here! Look someone's got a boat down there.

\-   Good sir, are you evacuating the inhabitants?

\-   Not really. My name is Pliny. I'm called The Elder because I have a nephew also called Pliny. So he's called The Younger. I'm here to inspect plans for

330

a museum. But to tell the truth, I can't think of what they are going to put in it. Nevertheless, a few people have decided to sail off in my boat, and you are wecome to join them. If you run into my nephew back in Rome, ask him to write. He loves writing letters!

-        Thanks for the use of the boat. Cruz, again relying on my knowledge of Roman history, this is the last we'll see of Pliny the Elder. Such a shame, since his study of natural history is fascinating. And as for those museum pieces he was wondering about, they will be the charred remains of the trapped inhabitants, preserved for eternity by the volcanic ash.

-        Papi, there it is. Vesuvius is blowing up.

-        A real cataclysm, Cruz.

-        Did you say catechism, Papi?

-        No, Cruz, cataclysm. But your catechism session could likewise be a disaster if you don't take it seriously!

-        Like the inhabitants of Pompeii and the eruption of Mt. Vesuvius!

-        Next year a fire will destroy much of Rome, and Titus will die of a fever.

-         Imagine, Papi, Rome and her Emperor suffering from being too hot!

-        Another sick joke, Cruz – literally! You're on fire – just like Rome! Unfortunately, the torch was passed on to the younger brother of Titus, Domitian. He began his reign by increasing military pay and providing the people with lavish entertainment. Not a bad start, but

Domitian became very tyrannical. He had Christians persecuted, and philosophers banned from Rome. He himself must have had a persecution complex, since the Stoics advocated rule by "the best men"!

- I guess, Papi, the shoe didn't fit!

- You mean sandal, Cruz! In 96, Domitian was murdered by order of his wife Domitia. His name was stricken from all monuments. This *damnatio memoriae* was the Roman version of cancel culture. He suffered this fate in part for what he did, and in part for what he didn't do, that is, take preventive measures against his wife.

- Papi, it's a clear case of damned if you do, and damned if you don't!

- That's what I said - **damn**atio! But cheer up, Cruz. We are again going to meet five Emperors – but five good Emperors! So here we are in the year 96, and the Senate has just named as Emperor Nerva, who will unite monarchy and liberty. That means he will respect the Imperial Constitution.

- Papi, there's the Emperor standing in front of the Senate House. He looks like a wise old man, just like you!

- Are you calling me old, Cruz?

- No, Papi – wise!

- Nerva is wise all right. He is aware that nice guys finish last, and that his humanitarianism will be no match for the powerful Praetorians.

- Were the Praetorians really powerful, Papi, or did you describe them that way in order to use a word beginning with the letter "p", and so introduce another example of your signature alliteration?

- It's called killing two birds with one stone. Be that as it may, Nerva adopted as his son Marcus Ulpius Traianus. But you and I – and most everybody else – will call him Trajan.

- Was he an historical journalist, Papi? I mean, I've heard of Trajan's Column.

- That's so sad, it's almost funny, Cruz. But guess what, that monument can actually be "read" as an historical account, a kind of sophisticated illustrated history. Heck, maybe we can consider it to be the first graphic novel! Like his adoptive father, he will respect senatorial rights and privileges. But you and I are about to find out what Trajan's claim to fame is.

- Excuse me, strangers. I say, strangers, but in fact I am the stranger. My name is Sanex, and I am from *Hispania*, just like Traianus. Or would you prefer that I call him Trajan? Full disclosure, my name is Hispandex. But since I've arrived in Rome, I have tried not to overplay my Spanish heritage. I thought abbreviating my name might do the trick. But "Spandex" makes me feel uncomfortable, so I chose "Sanex" – a combination of *sanus* - "healthy" – and *senex* – "old man". I strive to be a healthy old man in mind and body. Maybe you two have heard that new catch phrase – *mens sana in corpore sano*. You certainly seem to fit that description…er…

- Dionysius. And this is my grandson Lucius Crux. Do you know Trajan personally? Like most people, I realize that Trajan will become the next Emperor, even though he is from a province – your province as it seems. Rumour has it that he will go on a military expedition against the Dacians. That's modern Romania, Cruz. The Romanian language of today is derived from Latin. That name is proof of his future success, since it obviously suggests that the culture of the Dacians was Romanized and the language latinized.

- Ah, you wish to accompany the future Emperor on his upcoming military campaign to Dacia. You are in luck. I happen to be Trajan's Column writer.

- Are you being funny? My grandfather has already explained that Trajan's Column will be a monument, not a written history.

- Young man, let me enlighten you – even though your name Lucius already means "enlightened". The column will be an illustration of Trajan's campaign in Dacia. The events will be sculpted onto the column in accordance with my narration.

- Now I understand! The people of Rome, many of whom can't read, will be able to learn about Trajan's campaign through the pictorial history illustrated on the column.

- That's correct. I can see that the "*lux* bulb" inside your head is burning bright. And never cease to sing the praises of the old man here, your grandfather.

-     Are you listening, Cruz? Does all this remind you of the song "Old Man"? Kind of ironic that the singer is named Young – Neil Young!

-     Papi,we've referred to that song so often, it's old news!

-     Trajan is setting out to make war on Dacia. As official columnist, I will be riding under the protection of a legionary cohort. You two will ride with me as my assistants.

***

-     Papi, Sanex, that campaign was exciting! It was quite an experience to witness up close the battles, the sieges, the building of camps, the victory marches. I was shocked, though, when prisoners were slaughtered and towns burnt.

-     Young Crux, you were also privileged to see the barbarian costumes and weapons. When I have dictated all of this to the imperial sculptors, all the citizens of Rome will eventually be able to see played out everything in Trajan's triumph that you just mentioned.

-     Papi, is it true that Trajan protected Christians?

-     More that he did not actively pursue and persecute them. That was the policy he advised Pliny to follow when that epistolarian was governor of Bithynia.

-     I'll have to look up "epistolarian" in the dictionary.

- Don't bother, Cruz. I just made up that word. However, the word "epistolary" exists, and refers to the style of letter-writing. In fact, that word is related to the word "epistle", meaning "letter", or basically, something sent off, like "apostle" is some**one** sent off.

- I see you are an expert on Latin root words, Dionysius.

- Actually, Sanex, they are from Greek words.

- Papi, couldn't you just say letter-writer?

- I could. But, Cruz, what do we call a man of letters in our time?

- A professor? An author? A scrabble champion?

- A mailman, Cruz!

- Okay, Papi, what word beginning and ending with "e" has only one letter?

- I give up.

- The answer is "**e**nvelope".

- Before you two envelop me completely with your witty words, let me tell you about the great writers conference held in Rome a few years ago - in the year 100 to be exact.

- Was it a centennial celebration, Sanex?

- No, Lucius Crux. Just a *centum* festival. As a matter of fact, our motto was "Catch the Momentum – Come to the *Centum!*"

- Did you come up with that motto, Sanex?

-       Why, yes, Dionysius. I organized the event.We wanted to have seven star writers to echo the importance of the number seven in Roman history. I was especially excited to have as participants my Hispanic countrymen the satirist Martial and even the orator Quintilian, although he was quite old and hardly able to walk. So we had to be content with him "talking the talk". One thing is certain, Martial's art has a lot of kick in it!

-       I guess we could call it Martial Arts, eh Papi?

-       More wisecracks, Cruz, and you'll get a swift karate kick up your backside! Unlike the Beach Boys, you won't be feeling "good vibrations".

-       Papi, I remember you telling me they wrote that song when they learned that dogs can hear bad vibrations. I sure hope my dog Skye never hears bad vibrations.

-       Gentlemen, the field of history was represented by the one and only Cornelius Tacitus, as well as by Suetonius, who was finishing off the last of the *Twelve Caesars*. I mean the book of course, not the actual Emperors. His twelfth Caesar, Domitian, was finished off by that Emperor's wife, Domitia! As you probably know, what can be called the Silver Age of Latin Literature is best represented by Tacitus and Seneca. Tacitus read from his remarkable works – the *Annals*, the *Histories,* and the *Germania*. The satirist Juvenal was there. He complained that we served too much bread and that the service was a circus.

-       Yes, it seems I read the phrase *panem et circenses* in one of his satires.

\-   And Pliny the Younger read from his letters. He also paid tribute to his uncle Pliny the Elder, who died during the eruption of Vesuvius in 79.

\-   That's only six writers, Sanex.

\-   True that, young Crux. Our seventh writer was Plutarch. Yes, he is a Greek writer, but in his treatise called *Roman Questions*, he explained Roman customs to the Greek-speaking world. And in his work *Parallel Lives*, Plutarch compared great Greeks with famous Roman counterparts. As an honorary participant, he was the last to read from his works.

\-   Did he read from the lives of Julius Caesar and Alexander the Great?

\-   I don't know, Dionysius. It was Greek to me! I once knew a little Greek - but he moved away! However, I did manage to write some juicy gossip about those writers on a column.

\-   Are you saying there is another monumental column in Rome?

\-   No, Crux! I wrote those titillating tidbits on a parchment column!

\-   Sorry to love you and leave you, Sanex, but my grandson and I must continue our journey. Did you notice, Cruz, he described "news" the way we described food we were serving once at a banquet?

\-   Oh yes... tidbits!

\-   Well, good luck, you two. Do you mind if I mention your names in my next column?

-    No problem!

-    Papi, did he mean immortalizing our names on another marble column?

-    No, Cruz. He means one of those parchment tabloids.

-    But Trajan has adopted as his son Hadrian, who will become the next Emperor.

-    It seems that adoption of a successor is going to be the rule of thumb for a while. There is a reason why that strategy works, but I can't quite put my finger on it. I know you enjoyed Athens, so we are off to that city. Where did I put the remote?

Chapter Twenty-six: Greeklings

- Papi, it's so good to be back in Athens. And it doesn't seem to have changed, even though it's now part of the Roman Empire.

- Actually, the city has become even more beautiful, and the literary and philosophical activities more flourishing thanks to the new Emperor we are about to meet. It was very nice of Sanex to furnish us with VIP documents. He also wished to provide us with the necessary funds for our expenses. Unfortunately, when I showed the treasury magistrate the NIP he had provided, that bureaucrat understood it to mean "**N**ot **I**mportant **P**eople", and at first refused to splash the cash. Luckily, the Emperor Hadrian's private secretary happened to be in the neighbourhood, and he had seen us with Sanex, when they were both working for Trajan. That's why he has come to our rescue.

- Are you the Emperor?

- Heavens no, young man. Although I bear a physical likeness to Hadrian, I am his private secretary Adrian. But you will get to meet the Emperor soon enough. In fact, here he comes now. Looks just like a Greek, doesn't he?

- Greetings, Adrian.

\-   Hello, Hadrian.

\-   Must you insist on eating garlic? If you don't do something about your bad breath, it will be *Hasta la Vista*! I'm beginning to regret having a name that begins with an aspirate. Isn't it funny, though, how when we are in Gaul, the inhabitants pronounce your name with "H", and mine without it! And these must be the two philhellenes Sanex mentioned in his letter. Greetings, Greeklings!

\-   Greetings, Emperor Hadrian. Having travelled in *Hispania* in my younger years, I understood the Spanish expression you just used. Strange as it may seem, a certain actor from the region of *Germania* will one day make that expression famous on stage, which future peoples will call the "screen". In speaking with Adrian, I was informed that you are called *Graeculus*, to mock your fondness for all things Greek. Although being "a little Greek" makes you a "Greekling", it certainly does not make you a "weakling".

\-   Nor a "weak link"! Well spoken, Dionysius. The documents Sanex provided indicate that you and your grandson, Crux, isn't it, have travelled extensively. What places have you visited, young man?

\-   We've been to Athens before, and to Delphi and Crete, and to Macedonia. We crossed the Aegean and went to Troy and Egypt and across Persia and right up to India.

\-   My, my, that sounds a bit like the itinerary Alexander the Great followed on his famous campaign of conquest against the Persian Empire.

341

\-   It was exactly his itinerary, Sir.

\-   You seem very sure of yourself for one so young. Of course, you have read the historian Arrian's account of Alexander's expedition! And Dionysius, I believe you are both familiar with Rome's illustrious history.

\-   Yes, we visited Pharsalus and Philippi and Actium.

\-   So, you probably read Appian's account of Rome's Civil Wars. I often have those two Greek historians in my company for my regular *symposia* – you know, Greek banquets.

\-   Your "A" Team, I guess.

\-   Why yes, Dionysius. How clever – their names both start with "A"! And I would like to benefit from your wit at the *symposion* I am hosting tomorrow evening. Maybe for Crux here, I should use the Latin word – *symposium*. You two can be my "B" Team! That is, my "**B**anquet Team"! Such words of wit we shall share tomorrow! Perhaps, Dionysius, you can be our Socrates, and share words of wisdom as well.

\-   Genuine BS!

\-   What's that, Crux?

\-   **B**anquet **S**ymposium, Sir.

\-   I see you enjoy witty wordplay like your grandfather. Regrettably, my family members are not into wit.

- Crux was not always into it, but picked it up by being in my company so often.

- Not into what?

- Into wit.

- Yes, but what is "it"?

- Wit.

- So he's into wit.Then you shall come to the ball as well, young man!

- What does that even mean, Papi?

- I think he meant to say banquet **hall,** but spoke too quickly. Just drop it.

- Drop the ball, Papi?

- Cruz! Save the funny lines for tomorrow night.

- Smell you later, Hadrian!

- Rather, vice versa, Adrian! You and your ghastly garlic! Did you like my "alliterative arsenic"?

- Papi, they're seriously sick!

***

- Oh, Dionysios you spoke so cleverly as Socrates. I mean, you've probably read Plato's *Dialogues*, but you spoke as if you had actually met the man!

- Sire, the temples and buildings you have erected in Rome have that city rivalling Athens in beauty.

-        We all know how the Greeks admired beauty. But as they say, beauty is in the eyes of the beholder. For the Romans, an arch, a dome, a vault are beautiful. However, for me beauty is in the Greek-like temples, statues and monuments that I have had erected in Rome and throughout the Roman provinces. You have obviously gazed upon them in your travels. Have you seen the Great Wall I had built in Britain? Adrian, would you tell our much-travelled guests about the Wall.

-        Much-travelled! You could be speaking about Odysseus, Hadrian! We are still trying to think of a name for Hadrian's Wall.

-        Why not call it just that?

-        Splendid suggestion, young lad! You are sure to go far.

-        Well, I've already gone pretty far while travelling with my grandfather across the Roman Empire.

-        Always the quintessential quip! Notice I was right on cue with that alliteration!

-        Adrian, we shan't be lining up in a queue to hear more questionable quotes like that!

-        Message received, Hadrian. I won't quibble! Let me say that legionaries consider duty on the British frontier the last outpost. They are definitely not having the "wall of a time" they had imagined! They consider it the "outer limits", and that's probably why they find it so spooky.

- Keep that up, Adrian, and you will be sent out to the frontier to deal with Wallace, King of the Picts! Take one of two picks – Picts or *Pax*!

- Definitely Roman peace, Hadrian! But I must tell you of the ruses used by legionaries to avoid being sent to that distant outpost. One recruit tried subtly to have himself declared insane by feigning an exaggerated eagerness to serve. He claimed that such a posting would be for him a "flight of fancy", an answer to his "flair for fantasy", that he had no "fear of folly". He was willing, he said, to serve at F Fort, since it would require no effort! The "F Fort" is what the soldiers call the Flavian Fort. However, his free-flowing "F"-ervescence soon fizzled and his erstwhile enthusiasm eventually evaporated when his faked lunacy was revealed after he asked the question "Where's the Wall though?"!

- Sire, I must congratulate you on all that you have done to promote Greek culture in the Roman Empire – philosophy, literature, art, *etc*.

- What was the last word you uttered? I have glanced at the notes you are reading, and what you said doesn't sound like what is written.

- Two words, Sire, *et* and *cetera*, meaning, as you know, "and all the rest". I merely used an abbreviation.

- Adrian, inform the imperial scribe of that abbreviation. I think it could eventually come into regular use. And, Dionysius, thanks for the compliment. It's a complement to my many other accolades. Where is my slave Cari, who is to organize the random speeches by volunteer guests? We should be starting. Cari, okay?

-       All set, Sire.

-       Who's on first?

-       Adrian, you're up.

-       With me as lead-off, fellow imbibers, you're sure to have a big hit!

-       If you're going to speak for a long time, Adrian, make a short stop.

-       Yes, and for the sake of our young attendee, I'll strike out the nasty bits. I'll be sure not to have a single foul line in my speech. I wouldn't want to run afoul of the Umpire.

-       Say what, Adrian?

-       Oh, sorry! Must be the wine. I meant to say Empire.

-       Adrian, get thee off to home! Run! And Cari, take his dishes to his home – plate and utensils. If you find yourself in a pinch, hit Adrian.

-       Papi, everybody has been drinking except me, yet why do I have this crazy idea that I've been at a baseball game?

-       Could be the bats we saw flying near the sacred grove last night!

-       Or the DH we saw earlier in the imperial palace. You remember, Papi, the statue of **Divine Hadrian**!

- Thank you for inviting us to your banquet, Sire. The evening program was neatly divided into two parts, but I think most of the guests were a little too inebriated to enjoy Part B.

- That was deliberate, my dear Dionysius. After all what comes before Part B?

- Part A.

- Precisely! We will party on, but I presume you would like to get your grandson home.

- Yes, Sire. Thanks for your hospitality.

- Are we going to meet more Emperors, Papi?

- For sure. We are going to meet the first Emperor from Gaul. But while we are in Athens, I want to take the opportunity of meeting two interesting writers.

- Why interesting, Papi?

- Well for one thing, like us, they both went on incredible journeys.

- Back into Antiquity, Papi?

- No, Cruz, they already **live** in Antiquity!

Chapter Twenty-seven: Journeys **in** Antiquity!

\-   Cruz, that man over there rubbing the blisters on his feet is Pausanias. I would like to strike up a conversation with him.

\-   You two look like visitors. I suppose you wish to purchase one of my travel guides.

\-   It is an honor to meet you, Pausanias! My name is Dionysius, and this is my grandson Crux. I have actually read your *Guide to Greece*. I especially like all the information on religion that you include in your book. It is truly a handbook of consummate research and interesting anecdotes.

\-   Do you think people will cherish my book?

\-   Most likely they will place it alongside their Graves.

\-   What do you mean by that, Papi? Wouldn't they place it **inside** their graves? Although, it would hardly be the Greek treasure that archaeologists dig up.

-        What I'm saying, Cruz, is that future readers are likely to place Pausanias' book on their bookshelf' next to Robert Graves' *Greek Mythology*, which likewise contains scores of hypothetical conjectures and explanatory notes. But if it is encouraging for Pausanias to think future generations will be buried with his book, so be it!

-        Mr. Pausanias, you must have a very good knowledge of the geography of Greece, and a great deal of confidence in moving about in full security.

-        Well, young man, for my itinerary I relied on my GPS.

-        GPS?!

-        Yes, my **Greek Places Survey**. As well, it doubles as my protection packet – **Going Places Safely**. Unfortunately, I forgot to pack foot powder, and that's why I have all these blisters.

-        Your book seems to be popular with the community leaders and the most powerful merchants of the various city-states.

-        That's because I honored them with the title and subtitle of the book.

-        How so, Pausanias?

-        The title of my travel guide - *Description of Greece* – is often simply called DG. And the subtitle is CEO – "Cults *et* Oracles".

-        Cruz, what does *ET* suggest to you?

-        That we should be calling home?

-      Young man, *et* is the Latin word for "and". I wanted to attract Latin readers. So I replaced the Greek word *kai*.

-      And thereby avoid any confusion with the Ninjas of Ninjago, right, Papi?

-      Because they are a modern-day group of heroes with their own noble goals and their own version of special powers like the heroes of Ancient Greece, I will not make another reference to a possible threat to your backside. And especially because you resisted calling me "Papi Wu", as you are wont to do back home!

-      Have you two ever considered embarking on a long journey of discovery and interesting encounters?

-      As a matter of fact, Pausanias, we have.

-      It's very time-consuming. I suggest you get started. Especially, and please forgive me, Dionysius, since you probably don't have so many years ahead of you. Crux, on the other hand, might even consider travelling across the entire Roman Empire.

-      We shall take your advice into consideration, Pausanias. Maybe, like you, we shall write a book describing our journey.

-      Happy trails!

-      Why are you laughing, Papi?

-      "Happy Trails" – that was a song sung by cowboy Roy Rogers on a television show I used to watch when I was your age!

-       Roy Rogers again! Papi, there's a man over there talking to a group of tourists. But he's not speaking Greek.

-       Yes, Cruz, I noticed him as Pausanias was leaving. He's the other writer I wanted

to meet. He's from Samosata, so he's probably speaking in his native Syriac dialect to fellow Easterners that he has brought on a tour of Athens. But he speaks Greek, since all his writings are in Greek. He seems free now, since the group is moving on.

-       Good sir, are you Lucian, the writer of tall tales?

-       I am he. If you are seeking a tour, I'm fully booked today, but here is my card.

-       Hmm... lucianwrites@lottabull. My name is Dionysius, and this is is my grandson Lucius Crux, Lucian.

-       Ah, Lucius! Nice name that! And, Dionysius, just because your name sounds like Dionysos, don't go putting on airs, because those Greek gods don't exist. Call me an atheist, but that's the way it is. I originally had that on my business card, but a spacing problem caused me a lot of grief. The card read Lucian – a **theist**! Everybody started asking me to lecture on the gods! I eventually discarded them, and so now those cards are no big deal.

-       I know your opinion on myths and legends in Homer, Lucian, and even those in Plato,Thucydides and Herodotus.

\-   I think I've proved with my writings that anyone can write "Dialogues" like Plato, and don't get me started on Herodotus, the father of lies!

\-   But, Lucian, you will be credited with the invention of science fiction!

\-   Fiction, yes, but my stories have nothing to do with science. That's the domain of folks like the Presocratics and Aristotle. Writing can never be an exact science.

\-   Tell me about it! But I admire your *Dialogues* and your book entitled *OnThe Syrian Goddess*.

\-   The account of the Syrian goddess was merely a satirical way of looking at the cultural differences between Greeks and Syrians. Dialogues are an amusing way to make fun of stories that many people think are true.Those accounts by poets and historians are by no means the gospel truth. Moreover, there isn't any truth in gospels either.

\-   Being an atheist, Lucian, obviously you don't believe anything written by Christians, be they gospels, epistles or whatever. But I have to say, I thoroughly enjoyed reading *A True Story*.

\-   Not the greatest story ever told, but I warn readers at the outset that the account of my adventures on the moon - the battles, the encounters, the travels are all a lie. Other writers of incredible tales are not as honest with their readers. I might write about what happened to the adventurers on the moon, but I wouldn't hold your breath! And how about you, young man, would you like to write someday about a trek among the stars where no man has gone? A story like that would beam quite a message. In fact, readers would possibly have their faces lit up with pleasure. You could, as it were, "beam them up"!

-      That would be quite an enterprise! But a fantastic journey might be in the cards for my grandfather and me.

-      I have to leave you, as another tour group is waiting for me. They do appreciate my lectures on Greek and Roman antiquity. I wonder if such an interest will one day die out. Young Lucius Crux, your journey sounds exciting – real SF.

-      **S**cience **F**iction, Lucian?

-      Give it a rest. I'm merely saying "**s**urely **f**un"!

-      Lucian, my gut feeling is that studies and lectures on the Greeks and Romans, including the Greek and Latin languages, will be around for a long time. I myself will try to write books on those subjects, both fiction and non-fiction.

-      Is that even possible? Well, Happy Trails!

-      Papi, why do all ancient travellers use that expression?

-      Cruz, I really don't know what has triggered that common saying.

-      Papi, wasn't Roy Rogers' horse called Trigger?

-      Let's just bite the bullet and accept that it was a popular saying that will never bite the dust.

-        Papi, your biting wit never stops. Bullet was the name of Roy Rogers' dog! Like the expression "Happy Trails", references to Roy Rogers keep popping up! It will be fun to read the continuation of *A True Story*.

-        Not going to happen, Cruz. Lucian's promise turned out to be his "biggest lie"! But he has inspired other writers. I studied many of them when I was a university student. There was Jules Verne's *From the Earth to the Moon*, Thomas More's *Utopia*, H. G. Wells' *The War of the Worlds*. Come to think of it, that author's novel - *The Time Machine* - is sort of an inspiration for our virtual journey, isn't it, Cruz? You have heard of Jonathan Swift's *Gulliver's Travels* – which Lucian would probably have called "Gullible's Travels"! I also studied the series of five novels written by François Rabelais called *Gargantua et Pantagruel*. Then there was Skakespeare's *Timon of Athens*. Near the end of the 18th century, a German writer produced Lucian-like tales called *Baron Munchausen's Narrative of his Marvellous travels and Campaigns in Russia*. I haven't read it, Cruz, but I did see the film *The Adventures of Baron Munchausen,* which starred a host of zany actors like Robin Williams.

-        Wow! Lucian was an amazing source of inspiration!

-        That's not all. His story of a magician's apprentice probably inspired Walt Disney to make Mickey Mouse a "sorcerer's apprentice" in that well-known cartoon that featured opera symphonies. If I were to ask you who was "the face that launched a thousand ships", what would you answer?

-       My guess would be Helen of Troy.

-       Correct. It's from the first line of *The Tragical History of Doctor Faustus*, written by a contemporary of William Shakespeare named Christopher Marlowe. However, I was really surprised to hear Lucian, while he was reading to his tour group from his *Dialogue of the Dead*, quote a character who, while referring to the skull of Helen, says "for this a thousand ships carried warriors from every part of Greece"!

-       Papi, in the pictures of you as a young man, you were quite handsome. Maybe your face could have launched a thousand ships!

-       That ship has sailed, Cruz. I doubt I could even launch a raft! Do you know that a unit of beauty was invented to measure beauty. It was called the "millihelen", and corresponded to the amount of beauty required to launch one ship!

-       I know that instrument doesn't exist, Papi, but I can say for sure, that if we could measure beauty, my sister Everly and my cousins Mandy and Melody would launch a whole naval fleet!

-       What a beautiful thought! And your mother Nancy and your Aunt Cindy would have favoured flotillas as well!

-       But before we meet our next Emperor, there is one more "travelling" author I want us to meet. This one wrote in Latin, and I think we can locate him in Rome. Fortunately, we're only one zap away.

-      Funny, isn't it, Papi, that we call that instrument a "remote", when it brings us up close to where we want to be and what we want to see.

-      I haven't the remotest idea why that is so, Cruz!

***

-      Over there, Cruz, that's Apuleius trying to entertain a group of spectators with his magic tricks, but making an ass of himself by continually messing up. Nobody seems to be giving him any coins as they leave laughing.

-      Good sir, why is a writer of your calibre panhandling on the street?

-      Very hard to make a living if you're a writer. I am known for my novel about a donkey, but there is no gold in ass-stories.

-      My name is Dionysius and this is my grandson Lucius Crux. I recognize you as Apuleius, that writer from Numidia.

-      What a coincidence. And they say "what's in a name"! I happen to be an initiate in the Dionysian Mysteries, and the main character in my novel is named Lucius. You may have heard about a collection of speeches I delivered in Carthage. For these I'm known as "Mr. C". But I'm especially famous for my novel *Metamorphoses*. It starts off with my "magic moments".

-      Papi, that's the title of a song by Perry Como, but you call **him** Mr. C.

356

-       As Apuleius says, what's in a name?

-       The title *Metamorphoses* may remind you of a work of the same name by Ovid. And it is true that the frame-story involves the transformation of a human named Lucius into a donkey, but there is a digression on the tale of Cupid and Psyche, probably Ovid's best transformation story, or "*metamorphosis*". Some people call my novel *The Golden Ass*, but they're just being a pain you know where. I wanted to call my novel "Donkey O.T." – "Donkey **on T**our", since he is travelling on a journey - one that is filled with mystery and hardships. One might say he was following "an impossible dream".

-       The way he tells it, Cruz, he seems to be describing a well-known Cervantes novel that I read in Spanish about a windmill-fighting knight errant.

-       You mean like the knights of King Arthur, Papi?

-       Not exactly. King Arthur's knights sat around a table, talking of maidens and dragons, but Cervantes' knight spent his time in the village square before setting out on adventure.

-       How could a round table be surrounded by knights who were so square? Was the table in a den? Was it a Dragon's Den?

-       If you are trying to be cute, I'll be draggin' you home soon!

-       Papi, did you know that King Arthur's most cheerful knight was Sir Laughsalot?

-	No, but did you know that the most daring of the knights was Sir Goahead, and the most resourceful knight was Sir Vivor? And, of course, his knight with the most imagination was Sir Real. I guess you had to think a little outside the box if, as he did, you rented space in the kingdom to visiting emirates from Arabia, where they could leave their camels to be tended to. People started referring to it as Camelot. So, Apuleius, what happens to the donkey?

-	He hears many strange comments, some of them asinine.

-	Which he could understand quite well!

-	Oh yes, he is an ass.

-	And hearing all the news as a donkey - or an ass – he wouldn't have to be a fly on the wall!

-	What's that about flies? I know the donkey had to continuously bat them away with its tail.

-	Sir, then what happens to the donkey?

-	He returns to his human form with the words "I feel like such a mule, or rather, fool"! He becomes again your namesake, Lucius Crux.

-	So what are your plans, Apuleius?

-	If I were a little bird – which is what I had been hoping to become – I would tell you! Well, I'm in a pickle over an affair with a woman. But I'll get that straightened out, since I've already written up my *Apology.* That fancy name for a defence speech made Socrates famous.

-       Apuleius, Socrates was condemned to death after his speech!

-       What an ass I am! But I think my speech will have plenty of kick. I plan on becoming a priest of the cults of Osiris and Isis in Rome. There were even some travellers who, spotting me beside an Egyptian priest, believed me to be a sacred donkey, and asked the priest if they could kiss his ass! Truth be told, this ass was no ace! But I guess all that would be foreign to you, Dionysius. You can hardly expect to know the ins and outs of Roman religion. Like why sacred cows brought to Rome once refused to advance towards the sacrificial altar – they weren't in the MOOd! Or they may have been completely "cowed" by the ceremony!

-       I do know that Osiris and Isis were also foreign to the Romans.

-       Papi, tell him about your teaching and books on Roman religion.

-       No point, Cruz. How could Apuleius react kindly to being a footnote in a book dealing with his field of expertise? We have to continue our own journey, Apuleius. We'll be sure to keep our ear to the ground for any developments.

-       Are you making fun of my donkey ears?

-       No, just reflecting on your donkey years.

-       As long as you don't confuse my tale with my tail! *Adios*!

-       Cruz – that Spanish word! Again, shades of Cervantes' *Don Quixote.*

Chapter Twenty-Eight: A Man Called *Pius*, But He Wasn't Aeneas

- Cruz, we are now at the palace of the Emperor Antoninus. He had been adopted by Hadrian, but unlike the Greekling, he chose to pretty much remain in Rome. Since he's from Gaul, maybe we can speak French to him. We have Hadrian's seal to facilitate our meeting with him.

- Like having his ring - right, Papi?

- Heavens no, Cruz. Hadrian had us accompanied by one of his exotic animals that was captured off the northern coast of Britain. It entertained him to no end, bouncing a ball – and sometimes a Greek slave-boy – on its nose. Hadrian's approval of seals was evident. Fortunately, the acrobatic animal is now with the imperial keeper of seals.

- Enter, my dear friends. I know you must be weary from your many travels.

- *Merci*, Majesty!

\-   How clever! You are either practicing the language of my native Gaul or attempting, rather weakly I might add, to impress me with alliteration. But I hear you are a man of letters, Dionysius.

\-   Yes, sire. So I am wondering if you have been given the title *Pius* because of a special devotion to Aeneas, the Trojan prince who remained faithful to his duty, and sailed to the shores of Italy, and whose descendants would be the eventual founders of Rome.

\-   My dear Dionysius, dedicated to Rome's divine discourse, that is not the reason. I do hope however, that you were impressed by my alliteration. Just an Emperor's example of embarking on an enigmatic enunciation. As you can appreciate, I am very "a-lliterate"! But I did read with great pleasure Vergil's magnificent memorial to Rome.

\-   Papi, the only thing I understood was that Antoninus has read the *Aeneid*!

\-   Likewise, Cruz! Oh, I don't know how successful an "a-lliterate" he is, but at least he's not i-lliterate! So what is the reason, Antoninus?

\-   The reason? You want to know the reason? The reason?

\-   Yes, Sire! Cruz, he's sounding just like Jackie Gleason as Ralph Kramden in the television show "The Honeymooners" that I used to love watching many moons ago. Oh sorry! I guess you're not over the moon with my choice of time expression. But if you moon me, you will suffer where the sun don't shine!

-        Gentlemen, why all this talk of astronomy? And if you are putting forth the notion of the sun and the moon as gods, Hadrian is the new god on the block, since I persisted in having my predecessor deified. That is why I am called *Pius*.

-        I must say, you have everything under control, Sire.

-        The peace you see, does not stretch to the sea. I've had to order that walls be built in *Caledonia* near the firth of Clyde and his bonnie bride – Great Scott, how I love to burst into verse - and the Firth of Forth, this last meant to be the first of four.

-        Papi, I think it more likely that the only thing that will burst is his bubble!

-        Hush, Cruz. Surely, Sire, you are proud of your human rights legislation?

-        I am indeed. So much so that I am going to start my own little dynasty, and call it the Antonines. And just as I was adopted by Hadrian, I shall adopt Lucius Verus and Marcus Aurelius. You must meet Marcus, who I know will make a great Emperor one day. Why, he spends hours in his room meditating on just such a position. My M.A. is destined to become a Ph.D. **M**arcus **A**urelius will definitely bring **P**hilosophy to a **H**igher and **D**eeper level. He will be the stone upon which future philosophers will build. He might even become the truest of Emperors!

-        A kind of "philosopher's stone", Sire. A veritable *Verissimus,* so to speak!

-        Precisely!

- You are the longest-serving Emperor since Augustus. To what do you owe your longevity, Sire?

- Not dying. But when I do sell the farm – actually, I own many that I could sell – Marcus will become the fifth good Emperor. Quite a streak isn't it, given Rome's track record? But I fear he will be alas the last.

***

- My father has died, and I am to be Emperor. But my brother Lucius Verus will be co-regent with me. You two had been friends of my father. Therefore you are my friends. *Mi casa e su casa*, and all that!

- Sire, may we accompany you on your campaign against the Germans?

- You may, young man. We are actually in the middle of the Marcomanic Wars against the Germans.

- Will we get to meet Maximus?

- Who, pray tell, is Maximus?

- Cruz, not everything you saw in the movie *Gladiator* was accurate. There was no historical Maximus.

- I must tell you two that the Germanic tribes are giving us a particularly hard time. But we shall prevail, especially if we strengthen our borders along the Danube.

- What is that little book you keep glancing at, Sire?

-      This, my good man, is my diary, that doubles as a philosophical guide to the Stoic principles of duty. I meditate on it daily.

-      What is it called?

-      *Meditations*. It is written for my personal contemplation, but I shall share it with you, if you can read Greek.

-      As a matter of fact, we can, my Lord.

-      Doing my duty to the Empire was why I accepted the role as Emperor. But my son Commodus will succeed me. I refuse to adopt another son. Just as I refuse to adopt the practice of adoption favored by my predecessors. I am hopeful that his love of gladiatorial combats will present a strong military image for a future Emperor. My time on this earth is drawing to a close. Fortunately, I am able to face death stoically. Dionysius, have you heard of Seneca? Have you read his writings?

-      Yes and yes, Sire.

-      He would have been an interesting man to meet.

-      Indeed, Sire!

-      Will you two be around to meet Commodus? He will be joining me out here on campaign.

-      If he will accommodate us! I'll be sure to read your *Meditations* one day, Sire. My grandfather told me they are written in *Koine* Greek, and so not too difficult.

-       Nice play on my son's name! Let's hope, Lucius Crux, that you will never have to read about the fall of the Roman Empire.

-       If I may interject, Sire, the last five emperors – all good – have stablized the Empire. May you enjoy your twilight years.

-       *Bon voyage*! I just hope the reign of Commodus doesn't turn out to be a reign of Comedy. If so, may my son be damned! *Auf wiedersehen*! That's a little expression I picked up fighting the Germans. They also kept shouting *Gesundheit* when I reminded them that the Roman legions were nothing to sneeze at.

-       Take care, Sire! *Salve*! And *Dankeschön* for your autographed copy of the *Meditations*!

-       Papi, why were you so anxious to say good-bye before Commodus arrived?

-       You're lucky to have a copy of that book, since the Greek title – *Ta eis heauton* - means "things to himself". It was a kind of to-do list – but on a rather noble scale. It was not a bucket list to complete before he kicked the bucket! Cruz, I didn't want to be around to pick up the pieces when somebody broke his heart.

-       Papi, that sounds like a song you used to sing to entertain my Mommy and Aunt Cindy.

-       Fortunately, your mother and her sister never had their hearts broken.

-       How about you, Papi?

-       Cruz, with your grandmother around, I've never had to pick up any pieces – just clothes I would leave lying on the floor! And you won't have to read about the fall of Rome. You can watch my DVD of the film *The Fall of the Roman Empire*. Besides, Edward Gibbon's book *The Decline and Fall of the Roman Empire* is much too long! And for the record, Commodus will be damned. His memory will be removed from all Roman records. It's another example of the *damnatio memoriae* I once told you about.

- Will Commodus die in the arena fighting as a gladiator?

- Again, that's the film *Gladiator*. In actual fact, he will be strangled by a slave in his bath.

- Is that what you call a clean kill, Papi?

- Your jokes will be the death of me, Cruz! And speaking of death, many Emperors will follow in succession and meet with untimely deaths. But a new dynasty will emerge under Septimius Severus from Africa, called, not surprisingly, the Severans. There were several Severans, some very severe!

- How many Severans served as Emperor, Papi?

- There were seven Severans, if you include two who were not family members. The last was Alexander Severus, and some Severans were severely censored with *damnatio memoriae*. So no "severance pay" for them!

- Papi, there were seven Emperors during that dynasty, and Septimius means "seventh"! What are the odds?

-       Ironically, some of them were indeed odd. Caracalla – not his real name – made all free men of the Empire Roman citizens. The catch, of course, being that they now had to pay taxes. Part of those taxes went towards paying for the lavish Baths of Caracalla, which were much appreciated. Unfortunately for him, though, as an Emperor he was all washed up! Another Severan, Elagabalus – not his real name either – imported to Rome the Syrian Sun god. This Sun worshiper was ultimately dismissed as a son of the Empire. But the most influential religion imported from the East was Mithraism. Roman legionaries had a special devotion to the god Mithra.

-       Was it a "Mithry" religion, Papi?

-       The only "mystery" here is how you came up with that puerile play on words! There followed for the next sixty or so years a slew of Emperors, many of whom were indeed slain! So many aspiring candidates, hoping to become Emperor! There was the "Year of the Five Emperors", proving the saying "be careful what you wish for"! One can just imagine the prospective Emperors being asked "where do you see yourself in five years?", and answering "Dead"! The next long-serving Emperor was Diocletian, but we don't want to be around during his reign, since it was marked by the severest persecution of Christians in Roman history. Perhaps if he had been able to watch a movie like *Androcles and the Lion*, he would have mellowed, and been more chill towards Christians! One can imagine those Christians huddled in the Catacombs, chanting *Ora pro nobis* – "pray for us". Or the heavy scent of incense, as the congregation entreats the celebrant to "spray for us"! Even with our VIP credentials, as Christians our stay would be very unpleasant!

\-		Especially if Diocletian read our documents as Victims for Imperial Persecutions!

\-		Perhaps "virtual" persecution and execution are less painful, but I would rather not test that theory. You only live once, but imagine dying twice!

\-		Is our journey coming to an end, Papi?

\-		Yes. It's probably nearing closing time at the Science Museum, so we will end our stay in the Roman Empire, and our journey to the Ancient World of Greece and Rome by meeting the great Emperor Constantine, aptly known as Constantine the Great. He not only protected Christianity, but actually put that religion on the map.

Chapter Twenty-nine: Cruz Crosses Paths with Constantine

- Cruz, I've zapped us to the year 307. Diocletian had tried to fight inflation – that's right, it's not a modern phenomenon – with an economic edict, which failed. He also introduced the biggest bureaucracy in Roman history, creating a Tetrarchy, which is a Greek word meaning "rule of four". In theory there were two senior members – *Augusti* – and two junior rulers who would eventually succeed as co-emperors. They were called Caesars. But things got messy, to say the least!

- Who goes there?

- Dionysius and his grandson Lucius Crux.

- Grandson, eh? True, you do look like an old goat. In Ancient Greece, goats were associated with the god Dionysos and the theater, and your name is close enough.Tragedy was a goat-song.

- And a song by the Bee Gees, right, Papi?

- BGs? You mean the **B**est **G**oats?

- No, good sir, a group of singers.

- How interesting. I am called the GOAT, but obviously not because of my age. Nor because of my name – Hircus Caper.

-       Those are two Latin words meaning "goat", Cruz.

-       I am the **Greatest Of All Time!**

-       The greatest what, sir?

-       The greatest imperial envoy. So, in official circles I am known as the GOATEE –

Greatest Of All Time Emperor's Envoy! I have even grown a slight beard under my chin as a sign of distinction, by which all people will recognize me. I am so skilled, I can fill many roles for my Emperor, such as that of Imperial barber. Perhaps this is all over your head, young Lucius Crux, since you are ony a little shaver. I'll have you know that as the Emperor's chief informer, I have had many a close shave! As for your group of singers, I sometimes sing a duet with my wife Capella, but often she cannot accompany me, so I sing without her – "*a Capella*", so to speak.

-       Cruz, *capella* is the Latin word for "female goat"!

-       I am also Constantine's enforcer of morality. Why just the other day a group was presenting a performance of the story of Romulus and Remus. A "she-wolf" named Lupa Romula was supposedly protecting the two offspring when her husband Lupus tried to place the babies near the stage exit. "Nobody puts my babies in a corner", she growls, and embarks on dirty prancing around the stage. This lascivious dance was not an acceptable spectacle for God-fearing Christians. Imagine the shock that your grandson would have experienced, Dionysius.

-       I suspect I would be shocked as well, GOAT, er...GOATEE. Which do you prefer?

-       Oh, just call me by my entertainer's name, that is my real name, Hircus. Or if you like, **C**ircus **H**ircus!

-       Would the CH be a reference to Christianity? Are you a Christian? Is Constantine really a Christian? Is he aiming at becoming sole Emperor? Is he looking to establish himself in the Eastern Empire as well?

-       Hold on, young man! Is this "Twenty Questions"?

-       Papi, how does he know about that quiz game?

-       He doesn't, Cruz. Hircus probably just picked a random number to describe your inquisitiveness. Surely you are privy to Constantine's plans, Hircus?

-       I am indeed his closest adviser. Call me Caper if you wish to know about Constantine's capers.

-       The GOAT's lucky I don't call him "billy"! Hircus, tell us about the *Chi Rho* connection.

-       Well the soldiers are suffering from back pains because of the heavy shields they constantly have to carry in their service to the Emperor. Did you pick up on the "constantly – Constantine" connection? Well, no matter! The soldiers would often entreat me to soothe their backs. I would hear "Hircus, poke us!" all day long. So I finally hired a chiro – you know, a chiropractor – to treat them. He insisted on the free publicity by having those two letters for his profession engraved on their shields. That is why you see the

371

Chi Rho. In fact, whenever you say the letters, you pronounce the abbreviated word for his profession – "chiro"!

-        Hircus, may I be frank?

-        Aren't you happy being Dionysius?

-        Such a sense of humour. As when you told Crux and me about the soldier who always twittered with one eye. When fair maidens passed by, they thought he was winking at them. Once, when he was very weary, he twittered his eye forty times at the same maiden, and they both ended up catching forty winks! The same soldier became very inebriated one day while on outside guard duty. Since it was cold and windy, he tried to cover himself with three sheets of bedding. However, the wind was so strong it blew the sheets away. He had to explain to his superior about the missing bedding, and simply confessed to being three sheets to the wind! But, seriously...

-        Now you're calling me "Seriously"!

-        Hircus, I believe the Greek letters *Chi Rho* on the shields are there because they are the first two letters of the name Christ. I say name, but that word actually means "the Annointed One". Constantine is really playing up the Christian card!

-        Well I wouldn't want chiropractors to get their backs up, so we'll just make that our little secret, Dionysius. Another little secret is that I am planning a surprise for Constantine – to phrase a coin.

-        Don't you mean "coin a phrase"?

-       Not at all! The Emperor's mother Helena is financing a commemorative coin for her son with the phrase *Tempus fugit* to be stamped on the coin to remind Constantine that even an Emperor's time on earth is fleeting.

-       I've heard the Emperor's mother is a devout Christian.

-       Yes, she is, and very popular. Above all, Helen is generous.

-       Strange, what you just said somehow reminded me of the name of another popular woman. Well, no matter, but while we've been chatting, my grandson has taken the liberty of strolling through the imperial gardens. Perhaps we can join him.

***

-       Young man, are you looking for someone?

-       Actually, I'm hoping to meet the Emperor Constantine. Do you know if he ever takes walks in these gardens? I imagine he is accompanied by scores of soldiers and nobles wherever he goes.

-       Are you a Christian, lad? And what are you doing alone in the imperial gardens?

-       Is this "Twenty Questions"?

-       Excuse me!

-       Oh, it's just something Hircus said.

-       You know Hircus, the imperial envoy?

-       Yes, the greatest of all time!

- So **he** says. But Hircus is conceited.

- He seems very convinced.

- More likely, he's confused! But here comes the GOAT with another man.

- Sire, I see you've met Crux. Gentlemen, I give you the Emperor Constantine.

- Greetings, Hircus. It seems the young lad and I were strolling independently in the gardens, and our paths just sort of crossed. Interesting that the boy's name means "cross". Who is this gentleman, Hircus?

- This is Dionysius, Sire, the boy's grandfather. He's apparently well-versed in the Latin language.

- How fortunate! I am looking for a Latin slogan for my campaign against Maxentius.

- Gosh, Papi, I've been talking to Emperor Constantine!

- Young man, what is that object that just fell from your toga?

- It looks like a Christian cross, Sire. could this be the sign you've been looking for to ensure victory against Maxentius?

- Where did you get this little cross, Crux?

- Someone very nice gave it to me.

- He must have been very nice indeed.

- The nicest! In fact, this cross symbolizes victory over death.

-       How interesting! Dionysius, if I promise to return it, would you and Crux agree to

lend me this cross to inspire my troops against Maxentius. I'll have it attached to a giant staff with a bright background so that it appears to be shining in the sky. And, in gratitude, I'll let you two accompany me to the battle. It will probably take place at the Milvian Bridge. If I am victorious, I'll become the sole Emperor of the Roman Empire. By the way, Dionysius, any luck in coming up with a slogan? Hircus suggested *Constantinus carpit diem.* But for some reason, "Constantine seizes the day" doesn't sound too original.

-       Well, Sire, if you are planning to carry Crux's cross aloft when going into battle, you can attach this slogan to it, claiming it to be a divine message : *In hoc signo vinces.* Cruz, that means "In this sign you will conquer". Sire, I hope your troops will be inspired by the cross. How will you ensure that they see it as you approach the Milvian Bridge?

-       Dionysius, we'll cross that bridge when we get to it!

***

-       Sire, that was a great victory you won back in 312. Crux and I appreciated having a front row seat at the battle. My grandson is happy to have his cherished cross back in his possession. What are your plans for the Empire?

-       Well, Dionysius, I am anxious to recognize the importance of both the Eastern Empire and the

Western Empire, but with increased importance given to the East. In fact, I am going to establish the imperial capital at that great city Byzantium. But I shall name it the "City of Constantine" – Constantinople! Has anyone in history had the idea of uniting East and West, while recognizing the great cultural achievements of the East? And naming a great Eastern city after himself is a stroke of genius, is it not?

- Sire, a certain Alexander did just that. And he founded the great center of eastern culture, and named the city Alexandria after himself.

- Ah, yes! Alexander the Great. And I am Constantine the Great! Just goes to show you that **great** minds think alike!

- I'm sure they do, Sire. I realize you have given Hircus the Herculean task of organizing your new bureaucracy. I am honored by your offer to stay on as your personal adviser in all things to do with the Latin language and Roman religious matters. However, I am afraid my grandson and I must pursue our journey. I do promise, though, that the study of the Latin language and Roman religion will remain dear to my heart, as will the Greek language and culture that you will be promoting in the Empire.

- I understand your *Wanderlust*. That's a word meaning a strong urge to travel that I learned in *Germania*.They've become quite cultured there. You should visit it someday. I don't know why there is all this talk of eventual barbarian invasions. I mean, sure, the Greeks considered anyone who didn't speak

Greek barbaric, and Greek is becoming again the language of importance in the Empire, and I'm sure will remain so for a very long time. But the languages of the provinces throughout the Empire bring such a cultural richness that must not be ignored.

- I'm sure I will visit *Germania* one day in the future. My grandson Crux will definitely study the Latin and Greek languages thoroughly, but he is only twelve years old.

- Twelve years **gold**, Dionysius! You must profit from all the precious moments you spend with him. Happy trails!

- That expression again, Papi!

- A nice wish for sending off travellers. Our travels are coming to an end. Constantine's Constantinople is now called Istanbul, and is the largest city in Turkey. I have an old record at home by The Four Lads called "Istanbul (Not Constantinople)". And since I am about to press the RETURN button on our remote to leave Rome and return to the Science Museum, I'll try a few bars of "*Arrivederci Roma*".

Chapter Thirty: Journey's End – Happy, he who like Ulysses...

-       Were there other great Emperors, Papi?

-       Well, Constantine was succeeded by Constantine II, Constans, and Constantius II. So I guess that name was a claim to fame! Then came Julian, called the Apostate, because he attempted to revive the pagan Roman gods, and have them worshipped as before.

-       You mean the ones we met, Papi?

-       Yeah, kind of. However, in 395 the Roman Empire was officially split into the Western Empire and the Eastern Empire. The last Emperor in the West was Romulus Augustulus, who disappears in 476 – unless you believe that legend that he turns up in a Roman legion in Britain and becomes King Arthur, all this under the protection of a certain Merlin! The last Emperor in the East was the renowned Justinian, who reigned for 38 years until 565. Kind of ironic, isn't it, that the first Emperor, Augustus, and the last Emperor were the two who ruled the longest!

-       I'm a little sad to leave the ancient world of Greece and Rome, Papi, but I have to admit my feet are a little sore.

-       As are mine, Cruz. Which is quite strange, since we haven't left the Museum, and we only had to press buttons to move about in time and space. But the flashing lights in the Museum to announce closing time did make me think of the bright light surrounding the cross that Constantine carried into battle.

-      And, Papi, your amazing commentary made me think we were actually there in Greece and Rome, talking to gods and heroes and historical characters. But we met so many characters who are not mentioned in history books.

-      Be that as it may, it's been a long day. We made a journey of 5000 years, and probably as many miles. It's rather appropriate that we ended our journey into antiquity with the reign of Constantine, since his era marks, in a sense, the end of Classical Antiquity, which will lead to a transition into what will be called the Middle Ages. You know, one day we could make a journey into that period of history and visit the Holy Roman Empire, or even a virtual voyage to the Renaissance period, where the Latin and Greek you will continue to study will come in handy.

-      Sounds like a plan, Papi! Right now, though, I am anxious to go home and tell everybody about our visit to the Science Museum, and our fantastic experience in the time machine replica. I also want to hug my dog Skye.

-      Too bad Skye couldn't hook up to the Museum. You two could have communicated by Skype! Actually, most animals in captivity probably communicate by ZOOm! Skye is a great family pet, though. Do you know what the worst pet to have is?

-      Do I want to know?

- A pet peeve! Of course the animal with the most negative attitude is the horse.

- And why is that, pray tail – er…pray tell? At least give the "mane" reason.

- The horse is always a "neigh-sayer"!

- Papi, take me home – **please**!

***

- Hi Mom, we're home!

- How was your "trip"?

- Now I know why Papi spent almost his whole life studying and teaching about the ancient Greeks and Romans. I really enjoyed that amazing virtual voyage. But I made up a little poem, Mom. Here goes…

> In the Roman Empire we travelled to the East,
>
> Then we travelled to the West.
>
> But of all sentiments this is not the least –
>
> Being back home is truly the best!

- So cute, Cruz! One whole day with your Papi and you seem so clever, and in a funny way, more mature. I hope you learned a few things.

- You mean besides the fact that the favorite food of animals in captivity is ZOOchini?

- Very funny! Don't be alarmed, but we had to rush Skye to the vet's when she swallowed a bunch of Scrabble letters.

- Gosh, Mom, is she going to be all right?

- No word yet!

- Aw, Mom, you and Papi are too much for me! Actually, I learned how important the number seven was in Roman history – seven hills, seven Kings. And, of course, there were Seven Wonders of the Ancient World. Any others, Papi?

- You do have to place seven up there with the symbolic numbers. You remember the seven gifts of the Holy Spirit that you studied in your catechism group? Personally, the seven gifts I cherish are you, Cruz, as well as your Manie - you know she doesn't like to be called Granny, your Mommy Nancy, your Auntie Cindy, your sister Everly Rose, and your cousins Mandy Rose and Melody! Notice you are the only male, Cruz, which made you the ideal "travelling companion" on our virtual journey, since only males would have been allowed to travel alone in the Ancient World. So that's me – Holden Hainsworth - H H - "healthy and happy"!

- Mom, we "met" many virtual merchants. They would have been right at home today with all that on-line shopping. Papi, do you remember that Egyptian trader who wanted to sell you a so-called sarcophagus, and you told him a coffin was the last thing you needed. To his credit, he laughed when you explained that it was the last thing everybody needed! I also heard about SPQR.

-       Isn't that something to do with Roman Senate decrees, like the official seal of the People and Senate of Rome?

-       Mom, it can also mean "**S**weet **P**api, **Q**uestions and **R**esponses"!

-       I see you are picking up more of your grandfather's humour. But I guess your exploration of the Greek and Roman worlds was all about men.

-       Not entirely, Mom. During our virtual journey Papi told me about an Egyptian woman in Alexandria whose name was Hypatia. Her name actually means the "highest" or "brightest", as in "supreme"! She lived later than the time period of our virtual journey, so we didn't get to meet her in our virtual travels, but Papi told me how she was an extraordinary philosopher and mathematician, who fostered science even more than Christianity. That is probably the reason she was tortured and murdered. Papi described her as **B**old, **B**eautiful and **B**rilliant!

-       Way to "**B**", Hypatia! Sounds like her stats left no room for *ersatz*!

-       That's very clever rhyme, but I was never bored, Mom, because while there were pauses in our virtual trip, Papi would talk to me about different aspects of life in the Ancient World. For example he told me about bee-keeping. Did you know that the actual word is apiculture, from *apis*, the Latin word for bee? He explained that while serving the Queen Bee, all the bees have to be on their best "BEEHIVE-ior"!

-        Cruz, since you're an A student, and not a B student, I'll let that pass. As long as you don't argue that they are one and the same. That is to say, an "Apis" student or a "Bee" student! Say, why do bees avoid libraries? Because of all the "Bee Quiet" signs! Where do bees like to eat? At the "Beestro"! If a cow swallowed a bee, would that produce "BEEf? Why do bees read the "Sermon on the Mount" in the New Testament? They like reading the BEEatitudes!

-        Gee, Papi, I knew you had been a singer, but I didn't know you were a stinger!

-        Cruz, showing attitude is not a Beatitude! By the way, my favorite bee is Honey Bee – that's what I call your grandmother.

-        Is this your best "Bee-haviour"?

-        *Et tu,* Mom, *Et tu*?

-        It's okay. BEEn there, done that, got the Bee-shirt! "Bee" proud of your son! We transcended chronology, making distant time and space a reality – even if only in our imagination! So he will probably want to listen more often to John Lennon's song "Imagine".

-        And you will be listening to the Beatles' song "Paperback Writer", since you might write a book about our imaginary voyage, Papi.

-        What is that sticking out of your pocket, Cruz?

-        Just a little palm-branch in the form of a cross, Mom.

\-   Palm Sunday was last week! Has that cross been in your pocket for a whole week?

\-   I guess so.

The End